# Praise for *Sojourn*
## Time Rovers – Book 1

**Winner 2006 ForeWord Magazine's Book of the Year Award~Editor's Choice for Fiction**

**Winner Independent Publisher Book Award 2006~Gold Medal Science Fiction & Fantasy**

**Winner 2006 Golden Quill Award Paranormal Category**

**Winner 2006 Bookseller's Best Award Paranormal Category**

**Winner 2006 Daphne du Maurier Award Paranormal Catagory**

**Winner 2006 Prism Award Time Travel Category**

**Compton Crook Award Finalist**

**National Readers' Choice Award Finalist**

**Pluto Award Nominee**

‡

"A rousing mystery-adventure..." ~ Baryon Magazine

‡

"Sojourn is a rare, well-researched and entertaining tale of time travel set against the backdrop of Victorian England and the Whitechapel Murders." ~ Casebook: Jack the Ripper

‡

"This is a brilliant novel... Put this one on your list of absolute must-reads." ~ Coffee Time Romance (5 Coffee Cups)

# VIRTUAL EVIL

Time Rovers ~ Book 2

## JANA G. OLIVER

WWW.DRAGONMOONPRESS.COM

Virtual Evil: Time Rovers ~ Book 2

Copyright © 2007 Jana G. Oliver
Cover Art © 2007 L.W. Perkins
Cover Design © 2007 Christina Yoder (Dragon Graphics)
Time Rovers™ is a trademark of Jana G. Oliver

ISBN 13: 978-1-896944-76-0 Print Edition
ISBN 10: 1-896944-78-7 Electronic Edition

Library and Archives Canada Cataloguing in Publication

Oliver, Jana G., 1953-
    Virtual evil / Jana G. Oliver.

(Time rovers ; 2)
ISBN 978-1-896944-76-0


    I. Title.  II. Series: Oliver, Jana G., 1953-  .  Time rovers.

PS3615.L482V57 2007        813'.6        C2007-905176-6

The Alberta Foundation for the Arts
COMMITTED TO THE DEVELOPMENT OF CULTURE AND THE ARTS

Alberta
COMMUNITY DEVELOPMENT

Canada Council for the Arts        Conseil des Art du Canada

Dragon Moon Press is an Imprint of Hades Publications Inc.
P.O. Box 1714, Calgary, Alberta, T2P 2L7, Canada

www.dragonmoonpress.com

Dragon Moon Press and Hades Publications, Inc. acknowledges the ongoing support of the Canada Council for the Arts and the Alberta Foundation for the Arts for our publishing programme.

# Virtual Evil

Time Rovers ~ Book 2

## JANA G. OLIVER

WWW.DRAGONMOONPRESS.COM

WWW.TIMEROVERS.COM

To
**Adrienne deNoyelles**
**&**
**Ally Reineke**

Who refused to let this author take the easy way out.

## *Acknowledgements*

Below are some of the many wonderful people who helped birth this novel. I've probably left someone out, which means I'll owe them an apology and the first round at the pub.

My immense gratitude to Gwen Gades, my publisher, and Adrienne deNoyelles, my incredible editor. The reason the Time Rovers Series exists and has been so well received is because of these two extraordinary women.

My cover artists (L.W. "Lynn" Perkins and Christina Yoder) came through yet again. *Virtual Evil's* artwork is a testament to their abundant talent and their ability to work together as a team. When I joked that there should be rats in a Victorian alley, lo! there were rodents. Lynn and Christina spoil me. For those who like to know such things, the time traveler on the cover is based on Sir Lawrence Olivier.

Beta readers are the folks who tell you what you got right and where you fell short. Or in some cases, how bad the initial manuscript sucked. I have some great ones: Ally Reineke, who pulls no punches, Tina Rak who is always generous with her input no matter how crazed her life is at that moment, and my husband, Harold, who knows he can say just about anything and I won't put poison in his coffee.

Once all the changes have been made, Nanette Littlestone eyeballed the final copy so the typos don't make it into print. Thank goodness she's really good at this.

A special thanks to Heidi B. who helped this author sort out *Virtual Evil's* opening lines.

A nod to Dan Norder, editor of *Ripper Notes*, who gently took me to task on my lack of detail about the Transitives in the first book. He even suggested my shifters should wear buttons that read, "Thank you for not asking about our mysterious, unexplained origins." This one's for you, Dan.

A tip of the hat to J.R. Fisher who continues to play a plum role in *Virtual Evil*. Every novel should have a chief inspector like J.R.

An author needs a brass band and Two Sisters Promotions are mine. Between Sherry Rowland and Kristen McClish, the world is finding out about my books one press release at a time. Thanks ladies!

And finally, as the Beatles would say, "I get by with a little help from my friends." You know who you are. Thanks folks.

## Author's Notes

Just like a feral kitten, *Virtual Evil* fought and clawed me all the way from first draft to final manuscript. Whenever I thought I'd gotten the thing settled down, it'd bare its teeth and hiss. After countless hours of work and a lot of help from family and friends, the story finally tamed down and started purring. I'm hoping my readers find it worthy of their time and their praise. After *Sojourn's* success, it has big shoes to fill.

As with *Sojourn*, the book is a mix of fact and fiction. With luck, the blend came out just right. When I found out there was a London "pea-souper" (fog) on October 17th, 1888, I couldn't resist the temptation to put it in the story, both as a metaphor for Cynda's current assignment and to illustrate what life was like in Victorian London. Alastair's newfound interest in forensics is a mixture of fact with a bit of fiction. Most suspicious deaths would have gone to the local or to the Home Office Coroner, not a pair of freelancers such as Reuben Bishop and Alastair Montrose. Still, they make a dashing combo. Who was I to tell them no?

There was a lull in the Ripper murders between the Double Event (September 30th) and Mary Kelly's horrific death on November 9th. What Jack was up to during those five and a half weeks is anyone's guess.

"An invisible man can rule the world" – R.C. Sherriff

1

*Thursday, 11 October, 1888*
*London*

Firearms always add that certain something to a party.

Tonight had been no exception. Head spinning, Jacynda Lassiter pulled herself upright and hastily reassembled the last few seconds of memory. She'd heard a woman cry out, turned to see a man wielding a pistol, and reflexively leapt upon the gun's owner. They'd then tumbled to the floor in a tangled heap. She had always been that way—moving on split-second decisions that came back to bite her on the butt.

From the look of things, this one wouldn't be any different.

A few yards ahead of her, red-faced men in full evening dress wrestled with the assailant, their coattails fluttering like agitated gulls. It took five of them to hold him in place as they bound his arms with a drapery cord hastily snatched from one of the windows.

"My God, look at the Queen!" a voice cried.

Cynda stared up at the royal portrait above the marble mantelpiece. Queen Victoria's ample bosom sprouted a bullet hole where her left nipple should be.

"Oh, great," she muttered. Her time interface vibrated furiously inside a pocket, signaling that someone else from the twenty-first century was in the room. She gave it a surreptitious tap. It promptly started up again. A second tap silenced it.

A solicitous young fellow bent down to offer Cynda his hand.

"By heavens, miss," he exclaimed, eyes wide, "you could have been badly injured!"

He was cute...for a Victorian. A bit too much macassar oil, but handsome nonetheless. Cynda forced a polite smile. That always seemed to reassure these folks. Using his hand as leverage, she rose from the floor with difficulty, attempting to straighten her gown in the process. Fortunately, nothing had torn—a miracle in itself.

"I just need to sit down," she replied as smoothly as she could under the circumstances. Adjusting her bustle as delicately as possible, she settled into a chair. "Thank you, sir."

The young man nodded and moved away, his task complete.

Lady Sephora Wescomb knelt next to her now, her face alabaster. "My God, are you all right? Should I call for a doctor?"

Cynda gingerly maneuvered her left shoulder. She chose to fib: to do otherwise would invite too much fuss. "I'll be fine."

With a quaking hand, the silver-haired matron brushed back a strand of hair that had fallen free from Cynda's bun. "I've never seen such a thing," she exclaimed. "He...he could have killed the prince!"

*Or anyone else, for that matter.*

Though Cynda was the first to admit her job as a Senior Time Rover was anything but boring, keeping history on track did not usually involve tackling a murderously inclined guest in the middle of a posh Victorian dinner party.

*But who was he after?* That was hard to say; it was a target-rich environment. He could have chosen from the future king of England, the prime minister, his nephew Balfour, a slew of members of Parliament, a couple judges, and some very rich merchants.

The failed assassin was hauled roughly to his feet. As he turned to face her, Cynda gasped. She blinked in case her eyes were tricking her. The face didn't change. Every Time Rover knew this man like he was family. They called him the *Father of Time.*

"Fool!" he shouted at her. "Do you realize what you've done?"

It was *his* voice. She'd never met him before, but she'd heard him dozens of times in the Vid-Net interviews.

"You fool!" he shouted again.

With that, Harter Defoe, greatest of all time travelers, was frog-marched out of the room, his glower deepening with each step.

A chill crept through her. What had she just done?

"Miss?" a timid voice inquired. A maid offered her a dampened cloth.

"Thank you," Cynda murmured, pressing the linen to her throbbing forehead. Foreheads had a way of doing that after they'd impacted the floor. *I'm getting too old for this.*

"On your way, girl!"

The sharp command sent the domestic scurrying. Cynda raised her eyes to meet the irate face of Hugo Effington. Her host's jaw was set, eyes narrowed, spoiling for a fight. Given his sizeable build, he wasn't a man to cross.

*Why are you pissed at me?*

"Excuse me, sir," the butler interjected, "I've sent for a constable."

"What?" Then Effington was gone, dressing down the unfortunate person who'd made the report.

*Oh, this is just peachy.*

She surveyed the scene. It'd been pretty pleasant until the gun appeared. There'd been ample food and delectable gossip. The main topics had swirled around Sir Charles Warren's bloodhound tracking experiments in Hyde Park and the inquests of the latest Whitechapel victims. To hear the upper crust talk, you'd think that the West End was next on Jack the Ripper's itinerary.

Unaware that Cynda was not a contemporary, Lady Sephora had patiently coached her in the niceties of London society as a courtesy to someone supposedly from New York. Although she'd done her best, Cynda found Victorian high society too stilted for her comfort. Despite the bluebloods, the promise of a multi-course meal, and the sumptuous surroundings, she'd been truly bored. At least until she'd nailed Defoe.

*Subtle, Lassiter. Really subtle.*

She took in the scene again, taking mental notes for the report she'd inevitably file with her boss in 2057. T.E. Morrisey would want all the gory details, along with an explanation as to why she felt the need to be so "bold," as the Victorians would put it.

*How do I explain this? Gee boss, your business partner, your best friend, just tried to kill someone and bugger history in the process.*

She groaned at the thought. This was off the rails.

At the far end of the long room, near the fireplace and below the now-flawed portrait of his dour and sizeable mother, was the Prince of Wales, the future Edward the Seventh. He was surrounded by a group of grave men in evening garb. Known for his appreciation of the fairer sex, the prince's thickly lidded eyes were situated not on the men around him, but on a cluster of ladies nearby, each resplendent in a gown of unimaginable opulence. Then his gaze moved in her direction, followed by a faint nod. She returned it out of courtesy.

*He thinks I saved his life.*

Which didn't make sense. According to the Victorian timeline, there had never been an attempted assassination of His Royal Highness at a dinner party in Mayfair.

On the other side of the room, a pair of women busily fanned an elderly woman of immense girth who had sunk onto a couch, lolling back in a faint. She was clad in a rather unfortunate shade of orange, like a prize Halloween pumpkin.

Sephora held out a glass of sherry. Cynda shook her head. "Can I have some tea?" She noted that no one but her friend came close, as if her behavior were somehow communicable.

"Certainly. I'll see what I can do." Sephora downed the liquor and went for another, evidence the event had rattled even her usually unshakable composure.

At the door was a queue of couples keen to depart after the *entertainment*. As they waited, they shot nervous glances in her direction. One young woman was weeping on her escort's shoulder. Others just stared.

"Miss?"

She looked up into the eyes of a young man with a pinched face and small wire-rimmed glasses.

"Yes?"

"The prime minister offers his gratitude."

"I appreciate that. Thank you." *First the Prince, now the PM. Next it'll be the Pope.*

A curt nod and the fellow retreated.

By the time the tea appeared, the prince had departed, as had the prime minister and his entourage. The remaining gentlemen were joking nervously and tugging at their collars. Every once in a while they would look over at her, shake their heads disapprovingly and return to their conversation. The only one to genuinely acknowledge her was Lord Wescomb, Lady Sephora's husband. He gave her a quick wink. That made her smile.

"Miss?" A nondescript gentleman in a black suit approached, his face intense with concentration. He looked like a cop.

Cynda's nerves ignited as she prepared to bluff her way through this mess.

"Good evening," she said through a fake smile. "Great party, isn't it?"

He crooked a brown eyebrow. "I'm Inspector Hulme. I need to ask you some questions, miss."

"I thought the little sandwiches were too salty."

The eyebrow rose a little higher. "Miss?"

"The punch was really nice, though."

"Miss..."

*Best get it over with.* "I'm sorry. Go on, Inspector."

"Please tell me what happened, from your point of view."

*Somebody just tried to rewrite history?* "We were about to go in for supper."

"What happened then?" he asked, penciling lines into a

notebook. The sight made her wince. Rovers were not supposed to be part of history, and yet Home, or Holm, or whatever he was called, was busily putting her words on that piece of paper. Paper that might end up in a file for eternity.

*The boss is going to blow a gasket over this.*

She took a deep breath. "I saw a gent with a gun."

"Then what happened?"

"I threw myself at him."

Hulme frowned. "Why didn't you just raise the alarm?"

"I did," Cynda replied, irritated. "There was no...male nearby, so I thought I could slow him down until someone could...ah...secure him."

"I see. Do you usually act in such a rash manner?"

*You betcha.* "I'm an American. We're...forthright," she replied, hoping that would serve as a suitable explanation. Behind the inspector, she saw Sephora's anxious face. It had more color now. Apparently, the sherry had helped.

Inspector Hulme issued a quick nod. Cynda felt sorry for the poor sod. He'd been brought into the middle of a dicey situation, as the Brits would say—one that could easily make or break his career.

"The assassin spoke to you. What did he say?"

"He called me a fool."

"Do you know him?"

No choice but to lie. "No, I don't." Defoe had pioneered time travel; he knew the dangers of messing with history, and laid the ground rules for all Rovers. The man who'd pulled the gun was not the Defoe she knew.

Suddenly, another hideous thought reared its head. "I would prefer my name not be in the newspapers, Inspector," she added.

His eyebrow crooked up again. "You don't wish to take credit for saving the prince's life?"

She shook her head emphatically. "No, I don't. I *really* don't."

"I think it's only prudent, Inspector," Sephora chimed in. "It is possible that the assassin was not alone in his plot. If Miss Lassiter's name becomes emblazoned in the headlines, that might endanger her."

Cynda mentally thanked her friend, though it was entirely unlikely that Defoe had any accomplices. Rovers were loners by nature.

The inspector nodded thoughtfully. "I shall do what I can to see you are left unnamed."

"Thank you, Inspector," Cynda replied, and meant it. That might cut Morrisey's displeasure a notch or two.

*Just a Visitor, Never a Participant.* Or at least that's what they taught you in Rover School. In her experience, that was pure bull.

As the cop headed toward the group of men to hear their version of the incident, Sephora sat next to Cynda. "Don't worry, dear. It'll get straightened out."

"Hope so. How's our hostess?"

"Taken to her bed, from what I hear. They've called for a doctor."

Cynda let out a stream of air through pursed lips. "So much for a quiet evening."

It took some time before Inspector Hulme was satisfied. Once that moment had been reached, Cynda was allowed to leave with the admonition that she shouldn't travel beyond London until the investigation was concluded.

"We will need you for the trial," Hulme said, handing over one of his cards.

"Trial?" Cynda managed to squeak out.

"Of course. We will need your testimony to convict this anarchist."

*Harter Defoe in the dock?*

It couldn't happen.

There were hushed murmurs as she exited the house with the Wescombs. Near the front door she encountered the stone-faced butler, the fellow who'd taken the brunt of their host's displeasure.

"Good evening, Miss," he said. The dull sadness in his eyes told her that there was going to be hell to pay once the guests cleared out.

"Good evening," she returned.

"Thank you for what you did," he added in a lowered voice.

Behind them, Effington's voice rose in angry protest, followed by the inspector's equally vehement response.

Lord Wescomb glanced over his shoulder at the arguing pair and chuffed. "Quite a dramatic scene. It'll be the talk of the town by morning."

"I suspect we will be *persona non grata* for a time," Sephora remarked once they were seated inside the Wescombs' coach. She turned toward Cynda. "Is that how things are done in New York, then?"

Cynda groaned. "Not usually. I am so sorry. I just saw the gun and reacted."

"I must caution you against such rash behavior in future," Lord Wescomb said with a deep frown. "You could have been mortally injured. You should have left it to the men."

Wescomb was right, though not for the reason he believed. If she'd been mortally injured, her interface would have triggered the *Dead Man Switch*, as they called it, and she would have transferred to 2057 in front of forty-plus highbrow Victorians. That would require a "fix" of epic proportions.

Sephora's next question brought her back to the present. "How did he get into the party in the first place? Is he a friend of the Effingtons?"

Her husband shook his head. "Our host didn't know him, and he wasn't on the guest list. The butler had no notion how he got inside."

*Not a problem for a Rover. Transfer in, give yourself a few minutes to adjust and you're at the party. All you need is an empty room.*

"Do you really think he was after the prince?" Sephora asked, smoothing her gown and then tucking her hands under the mantelet for warmth.

"Don't know," Lord Wescomb replied. "There was a fine selection of notables there, any one of them worth a bullet."

"John!"

"I'm serious, Sephora. However, I did find it amusing where the missile lodged," he added with a grin. "I bet HRH thought the same. Probably wanted to do that for years. Can you imagine waiting around for your mum to die so you have a job?"

"John!"

For a hereditary peer, Lord Wescomb was remarkably republican in sentiment. Cynda sniggered, appreciating the comic relief.

Wescomb adjusted his waistcoat over a slight paunch. "I suspect that keeping *your* name out of the papers won't prove too difficult."

Sephora turned toward him. "I would have thought it would have been just the opposite."

Wescomb huffed and tugged on the waistcoat again, frowning in his wife's direction. "What man wants to admit that a young slip of a girl prevented an assassination while he was busy eyeing the ladies and snorting his host's liquor? It does nothing for our reputation as gentlemen."

Sephora adopted a quizzical look. "Where were you when it happened, then?"

He cleared his throat. "A call of nature," he muttered. Lady Wescomb tittered, causing her husband to glower at her.

Cynda looked out the window. *Pity I wasn't off powdering my nose.*

2

His medical professors would have found the situation amusing: Alastair Montrose, dedicated young physician, shirtsleeves rolled to the elbow, hammering a nail into a crude bench. This was his tenth, and he was getting rather good at it. His first three would have sent any carpenter into hysterics. Now he was a dab hand. By his estimation, he had another week's worth of work until the clinic was ready to reopen.

"Blast The Conclave," he grumbled yet again. Just because he chose not to exercise his Transitive ability like the others, his superiors had deemed him a threat, hiring thugs to harass him and to destroy his medical clinic. It had not changed his mind: a person was not supposed to be able to change forms at will, no matter what The Conclave believed.

Standing to ease a searing cramp in his back, Alastair took in his surroundings. The clinic had never been opulent, but the thugs' work had made it worse. He'd salvaged what he could of the supplies and dismantled the broken furniture in an attempt to reuse what pieces were still intact. Most of it was only fit for kindling.

He and Daniel Cohen had established the site just this last summer as a ramshackle attempt to help the poor find some decent medical care. They'd always been busy, sometimes seeing to thirty or more patients an evening. When Daniel and his wife left for America a week ago, Alastair struggled on. Until he rebuilt the benches and examining tables, and found another physician to help carry the load, his work among the East End poor would be severely limited.

Whenever someone passed by the open door, Alastair looked up, hopeful that his advertisement in the newspaper had yielded

results. He'd slaved over the wording.
*Caring Physician Sought to Aid the Poor in Whitechapel.*

In his heart, he knew that few would seek a chance to work for nothing.

He resumed his bench-building efforts. As the last nail drove home, the sound of shuffling boots caught his attention. A man eased inside, warily looking around. He clearly wasn't a doctor— more likely a dockworker from his build. His clothes were stained and hands dirty. Red hair jutted out from under a worn cap.

"Lookin' for the doc," he said in a thick Irish brogue.

"I'm Dr. Montrose. I'm sorry, but the clinic isn't open at present, unless it's a genuine emergency."

The fellow moved inside a few steps and then closed the newly rebuilt door behind him. Alastair rose, testing the weight of the hammer in his hand. Not everyone in the East End thought well of him.

"How can I help you?"

"I've come ta tell ya ta be careful, doc. Ya've made some enemies, helpin' the rozzers t'other night. Some might want ta bring ya harm."

"Flaherty, you mean." The man didn't reply. "If I hadn't intervened, he would have killed a police officer." As it was, the anarchist had still escaped, but with one less wagonload of explosives.

The dockworker eyed him intently. "There's nothin' ta stop someone from lobbin' a bit o' dynamite in here when it's full up."

Alastair's mouth fell slack. "Does he not realize that a goodly number of my patients are Irish?"

"They don't care."

Glaring, Alastair gestured upward. "There are families living above this clinic," he responded heatedly. "Would he harm them just to seek petty revenge?"

A solemn nod.

"I see." Alastair dropped the hammer to the floor with a loud thump. "I'll weigh your warning."

"Ya should know, Flaherty's put out the werd. He wants the sergeant ta pay the price for his interferin'. Ya'd best tell Keats, ya bein' his friend and all."

"Dear God." Alastair channeled his fury into the nearest bench, sending it skidding across the wooden floor to impact the far wall.

The new door hinges made no sound as the Irishman exited to the street, his message delivered.

✠

Once the scone- and tea-laden tray was in place on the table in her Charing Cross Hotel room, Cynda shooed the maid out and locked the door. When she turned around, she wasn't surprised to find something already nibbling on the scones.

"Leave some for me," she joked.

Her personal hallucination waved a blue leg in acknowledgement. It didn't slow the spider's ability to dismantle the scone—he had seven other legs to assist him with that task.

Hallucinations came with the territory for a Senior Time Rover; constant travel did unpleasant things to brain composition. Those who'd been in the business the longest, or who traveled the furthest without adequate rest between journeys, began to see things. Time Immersion Corporation, her now-bankrupt former employer, had pushed the envelope, reducing "down time" to increase the profits. The end result was delusions like the one noshing on her scones.

Accepting that some of her brain was now beyond repair, she'd dubbed her delusion Mr. Spider, though she admitted that wasn't very clever. The first time she'd seen him, he'd been the size of an omnibus. Now that the arachnid was down to about the size of an overfed mouse, they were on better terms. On the plus side, he'd proven to have a sixth sense about things, making him a hallucinatory canary in the mine—albeit one with eight legs.

"Defoe's been missing for nine months or so, and now he turns up in '88?" Cynda mused aloud. "Why here?"

"Maybe he's starting a second career as an assassin," the arachnid postulated, scooping up a hunk of scone between two legs. He acted like he was eating, but never seemed to notice the food didn't disappear.

She shook her head. "Doesn't make any sense. If you're going kill someone, why do it at a dinner party? Defoe isn't stupid."

"Unless he's off his nut," the spider replied, circling a leg around where his temple would be if he were human.

He had a point there. Rover scuttlebutt said that Defoe often suffered from killer time lag and serious hallucinations, the downside of leaping centuries. Could those delusions finally have gotten the best of him?

"God, I don't know!" Cynda plopped into the chair, bashing her bustle against the back. She'd never adjusted to the silly thing. Grumbling, she rose and stripped off the offending garment, pulling it over her feet and tossing it on the bed.

"Nice legs," he remarked. "Not enough of them to suit me, though."

Cynda ignored him. You could do that with delusions. She poured herself a cup of hot tea, mixed in some milk and two lumps of sugar. A sip proved the mix just right.

"Ah, that's better."

Placing the time interface on the table, she performed the required series of stem windings until the pocket watch chirped. A red holographic keyboard projected itself onto the table's wooden surface while a holo-screen hovered in the air above the watch. She keyed in her password and then took a bite of scone while she waited for 2057 to sync up. The time interface was her lifeline to home. Lose it, and she would stay a Victorian for considerably longer than was prudent.

The interface chirped again. *Log On Complete* appeared on the screen.

"Here we go," she murmured. This wasn't going to be pretty. *Ralph?* she typed.

*Hey! How's it going?*

Cynda stared incredulously at the screen. She'd expected lots of official frenzy.

*Didn't you get a Time Incursion Warning for '88?* she queried.

*No. A little ripple, but nothing to worry about.*

She typed in a fury of letters. *There was an attempted assassination at a dinner party. Target may have been Prince of Wales, PM. Name your favorite blueblood.*

*Whoa. Anyone hurt?*

*Only Victoria's boob.*

*What?*

*Never mind.*

While she waited for an answer, she could imagine the scene on the other end. Ralph Hamilton, her best buddy and chron-op for TEM Enterprises, sitting on a pillow in front of his holo-screen, with his oval glasses and silver-streaked ponytail. He'd be relaying the news to her boss, software genius T.E. Morrisey, a lean gentleman with salt-and-pepper hair and an I.Q. that defied understanding.

"Odd meets odder," she remarked aloud. She picked up her stuffed black-footed ferret from his position near the inkstand. Courtesy of Ralph, Ferret Fred looked quite dapper in his gray Victorian cutaway coat, waistcoat, top hat, gloves and cane. Her buddy had a bizarre sense of humor.

*What was the exact time spec and location?* Ralph typed back.

She set Fred on the table. *11 October, '88. Party at Hugo Effington's residence in Mayfair.*

More waiting. She stole a piece of scone away from Mr. Spider, who gave her a disgruntled look. As she munched, the screen lit up.

*Who was the assassin?*

Did she dare rat out the hero of her age? No choice.

Reluctantly, she typed, *Harter Defoe.*

*WHAT?*

*He walked into the party and pulled a gun. I stopped him. I didn't know who it was until after the fact.*

A long silence ensued. She began to wonder if they'd lost contact.

*You're sure it was Defoe?* Ralph typed.

Her buddy didn't know about the shape-shifters, and she had no way of talking directly to Morrisey, who did. She'd just have to tell it straight and hope that her boss could put the pieces together.

*It looked like him.* Maybe Morrisey would pick up that subtlety.

*Event didn't trigger a Time Incursion Warning. Something's very wrong.*

"You got it, buddy," she said.

Morrisey's *Fast Forward* software was supposed to alert them to events that could screw up history, so a Rover could intervene or fix the problem after the fact. It provided the foundation for the whole time immersion industry, allowing people from Cynda's time to romp through the centuries like kids on a field trip. After what happened tonight, Morrisey's software should have lit up like a Christmas tree.

*Interface read two ESR Chips at party. Both were invalid,* she reported. Essential Record Chips were supposed to be readable no matter what. It was how you know who was who. *Couldn't follow up as I was in PV.*

Rover shorthand for *public venue.* Rovers who failed to pay attention to their surroundings while accessing records from the future often found themselves bound to stakes with flames licking at their toes, accused of witchcraft. When they were pulled out at the last minute, those brilliant halos of light that accompanied a time leap were often confused with miracles...or more witchcraft.

More silence. Cynda sipped her tea to counter her desire to fidget. Mr. Spider had settled onto the linen napkin, dozing peacefully.

Her screen lit up. *Where is Defoe now?*

*In police custody in Mayfair.* She'd overheard that tidbit when Hulme was talking to Lord Wescomb.

She could hear the swear words without Ralph typing them. *Find him. We'll take it from there. Do it now!*

*Okay.* She bit her lip and typed, *No luck finding Chris' interface.*

Ralph answered instantly this time. *TEM says to forget everything but Defoe.*

For the last week she'd heard nothing but how vital it was to find Chris' time interface, no matter how difficult that might prove. Now it'd fallen off his uncle's radar completely.

Cynda pulled a small box toward her and opened the hinged lid. Inside was Chris' funeral portrait. She removed it, kissed his face reverently and returned it to the box, closing the top to the makeshift shrine.

Christopher Stone had been intelligent, witty, one of the good guys. Their love affair had held the promise of something more permanent. Morrisey might have teamed them up, let them work this time period together. That was all gone now, destroyed by a crazy "tourist" bent on creating his own Jack the Ripper.

The screen lit up again.

*Gotta go. Stay safe,* Ralph typed back. *Log Off.*

That was an abrupt farewell by her buddy's standards.

She logged off and leaned back in the chair, scratching the ferret's head in thought.

*What if they can't get Defoe out of here before the trial?*

‡

*2057 A.D.*

*TEM Enterprises*

"This does not make sense," T.E. Morrisey repeated in his clipped British accent. "The software would have told us if Harter had tried such a stunt."

As was customary, Morrisey was seated on a thick pillow in the chronsole room, clad in his signature black. He didn't like chairs, which was why Ralph was parked on a cushion as well. At least his back had finally adjusted.

His boss continued without waiting for a response. "Harter and I might not have always agreed on how to interact with a variable time line, but he would not do such a thing. It would be anathema to him!"

Ralph pulled off his oval glasses and polished them with the bottom of his tee shirt. "What if the lag's finally gotten to him?"

Morrisey's face saddened. "I'd hate to think that."

"Either way, something's up. You can bet the Time Protocol Board will use it to their advantage. They're always pushing the envelope to gain more power."

"I do find it highly suspicious that the assassination was attempted in front of Miss Lassiter, of all people."

"A setup?"

"Possibly. She would be the most likely to jump into the middle of a fray. Maybe they counted on that."

Ralph replaced his glasses and turned back to the chronsole. His fingers posed a question. The computer delivered the response. Another attempt with a change of wording. Same response.

"According to the records," he informed Morrisey, "the Prince of Wales was at his London club on the 11th of October, not some party in Mayfair."

"Victorian records are not always accurate."

"I ran a check of his mother's diary," Ralph persisted. "Queen Victoria makes no mention that someone took a potshot at her son. You'd think that might get a line or two."

Morrisey uncharacteristically drummed his fingers on the low table that served as his desk. "When was the last full realignment?"

"Thirty-one days ago."

More finger drumming. "How many Rovers in the time stream at present?"

Ralph accessed the in-stream report. "Twenty-seven, not counting tourists."

"That's an incredible load."

"Time In Motion's been shoveling tourists into the stream like mad. ETC to a lesser extent."

"Too many to do a realignment."

"You think this is just a Chron Alignment issue?" Ralph asked.

"I'm not sure. There's more to this than Harter supposedly going on a rampage. Verify all In and Outbound travel for the twenty-four hours surrounding 11 October 1888."

"No problem," Ralph said, addressing the keyboard.

Morrisey rose and took his cushion to sit in front of one of the pieces of artwork that lined the wall. Like all the artwork in the chronsole room, it was positioned about a meter off the floor. Too low to appreciate if you were standing. Perfect if you were sitting on a cushion.

When troubled, TEM, as he was known, would meditate on a painting of black holes and red dwarf stars, a rare Perkins original. This time it was the M.C. Escher, the one with reptiles trudging into a puzzle and out again in an endless circle.

Ralph turned back to his chronsole. If Morrisey was boring holes into the Escher, things were going south in a hurry.

3

*Thursday, 11 October, 1888*
*London*

Concerned for his friend's safety, Alastair waved down a hansom cab near Aldgate Station for the journey to Bloomsbury. As the jarvey negotiated the evening streets past St. Botolph's Church and then west toward St. Paul's, Alastair's worry grew. Jonathon Keats, an excellent copper, had made enemies during his time at Scotland Yard's Special Branch—most of them Irish anarchists, Desmond Flaherty ranking high among them. From what Keats had told him, Flaherty intended to make his mark in a spectacular fashion, the more destructive the better. With a wagonload of gunpowder and one of dynamite in his arsenal, he didn't lack the resources to make good his boast. If it hadn't been for Keats' heroic efforts a week earlier, the anarchist would have had even more destructive power in his grasp.

The cab turned onto Great Russell Street, drawing closer to the British Museum. Alastair's sense of caution weighed in. He'd openly visited his friend numerous times in the week after Keats' injury, assuming that the Fenians would not dare strike down a Scotland Yard detective. Now he was not so sure. To that end, he asked the driver to stop short of his ultimate destination.

After counting out the coins and paying the jarvey, Alastair walked a short distance and then halted to purchase a paper. Pretending to study the headlines, he studied the streets instead. In all honesty, it was too crowded to decipher friend from foe. There were a quite a few men about, but most were of the upper class, not Fenian rowdies keen to do Flaherty's bidding.

Folding the newspaper and tucking it under his arm, Alastair threaded his way through the carriage and foot traffic to Museum Street and then cut left into Little Russell. To his relief, he noted no suspicious characters loitering across from Keats' second-floor lodgings.

After a brisk knock, the door to Keats' rooms promptly opened to reveal his friend's superior, Chief Inspector J.R. Fisher.

"Your timing is excellent, Doctor," Fisher said, waving him in. "He's growing tired of my presence, so perhaps you will enliven the conversation."

Detective-Sergeant Jonathon Keats sat in a chair near the fireplace, a lap robe tucked around the lower half of his body. It made him look older than his thirty-two years. His face was covered by a nascent beard, and his moustache was untidy, at least by his standards. A thick bandage edged into his right hairline. A stack of newspapers at least two feet tall sat near the chair, threatening to topple over at the slightest provocation.

Keats greeted him with a slight frown. "Ah, there you are. I wondered if you ever intended to visit me again."

The rebuke stung. "I saw you just yesterday morning," Alastair retorted, dropping the newspaper into the injured man's lap. "Given your improvement, I didn't think I needed to check on you hourly."

A huff, and then a conciliatory nod. "It's just this sitting about. I don't like it one bit."

Fisher returned to his chair. "After his brawl with the anarchist, the sergeant is feeling useless."

"As he should be," Alastair responded, already leaning back into the remaining chair. "He's supposed to be healing."

"It's just that—" Keats began.

"How have you been, Doctor?" Fisher asked, deftly cutting across what promised to be another complaint by their host.

"I was doing quite well until tonight."

Fisher cocked an eyebrow. "What has changed?"

Alastair grimly related the threat he received.

"What did this fellow look like?" Keats asked, leaning forward.

"Red hair, dockworker's build, thick accent."

"Did he have a slight limp, as if one limb were shorter than the other?"

Alastair gave his friend a nod.

"Johnny Ahearn," Keats confirmed. "He's slipped me bits of information off and on over the past year, though never about Flaherty. He's one of the few who know what I actually look like."

"I'm surprised you allowed that," Fisher replied.

"For the most part, I go *en mirage* when I'm in the East End," Keats replied. "It is not that difficult to change forms in some back alley."

"For *you*," Alastair pointed out.

"It would be easier if you practiced. Your aversion to our capability compromises your form."

Fisher furrowed his brow. "I am still struggling to understand this strange ability of yours. Do others of your kind refuse to shift?"

Keats shook his head. "Almost all Transitives accept their gift. Alastair is one of the rare exceptions."

"It's an invitation to evil," the doctor replied curtly.

"Or good," Keats countered. "It depends on how you use it."

"We will never agree on this."

"Not while you're being so stubborn."

"I'm *not* being stubborn, I'm being sensible. Men will always abuse power. Being able to look like anyone we choose is an—"

"If the person is of a moral nature," Keats cut in, "there is no issue."

"Ah, but that is the crux of the matter, isn't it?" Fisher said, deftly interjecting himself between the disputants. "Ever since I've learned of this strange phenomenon, my gut tells me it only increases the threat to our country, despite your assurances to the contrary."

"The majority of us are decent folk, sir," Keats declared. "There are a few bad ones, I admit."

"Is Flaherty one of yours?" Fisher asked.

"Not that I am aware of."

"Well, that's one bit of good news. However, given that this anarchist now seems bent upon your destruction, I recommend that you consider visiting your family in Canterbury until he is caught, since you refuse to stay in your rooms."

Alastair frowned at his friend. "You've not been resting as I ordered?"

"Well, I did go out for a brief time the other day," Keats confessed, face reddening.

Fisher rose and collected his coat and hat near the door. "In future, I will not visit you until we have captured Flaherty and located the remaining explosives. I have no desire to bring that viper to your doorstep."

"Yes, sir."

Turning his attention to Alastair, Fisher asked, "Would it do any good to suggest you go on holiday somewhere out of London to deny Flaherty another target?"

"No. I have patients to tend to in hospital."

"As I thought. Good evening to you both."

The moment the door closed, Alastair rose and bolted it.

"You can't be serious about closing the clinic," Keats protested.

"I have little choice. I can't take the risk. This Ahearn fellow was quite adamant that Flaherty would kill anyone to get to me...and you. Besides, the way gossip travels in Whitechapel, there won't be patients anyway. No one will want to cross an anarchist."

"What do you intend to do?" Keats asked, puzzled.

Alastair sank into the chair recently vacated by Fisher. "I shall try to shore up my reputation at the hospital. My superiors are displeased with my intervention on your behalf the other night. They're quite adamant about that sort of thing. I was told that proper physicians do not get involved in street brawls."

Keats gingerly touched the bandage on his head. "It wasn't a brawl; it was a slaughter. If you and Jacynda hadn't come to my aid, Flaherty would have killed me. It was that simple."

"Not to those who work at London Hospital." Alastair popped open his Gladstone. "I should change your bandage while I'm here and I want to check how your rib is healing."

"Still broken from what I can tell." Keats added the newspaper to the pile. "If Flaherty hasn't been caught by the time I am well, we must go after him, you and I. Only then can we ensure your clinic will reopen. God knows the poor in Whitechapel need it."

"I do believe that is precisely what my superiors at the hospital would *not* want me to do."

A genuine smile emerged through Keats' beard. "Good. Then we shall get up all of their noses."

Alastair returned the smile, but with less enthusiasm. "Sometimes I wonder if that's what that old fox Flaherty wants."

✠

"Why was I not called earlier?" Fisher growled with authoritative menace. "The witnesses are now scattered all over London, rapidly acquiring faulty memories."

To his credit, Inspector Hulme did not cower. "I tried to send word, Chief Inspector," he replied, his words clipped. "However, my efforts were thwarted by Mr. Effington here."

Effington raised his eyes from the fire. He was leaning on the mantel, a drink in his hand. Given the furtive movements of the domestic staff, it appeared everyone in the household had been lashed with their master's tongue at least once.

"I did not want the Yard involved," he said.

"Interfering with a police investigation is a chargeable act, sir."

Effington huffed. "I was vehemently against this person contacting any of *your* sort. This is a personal matter, and I shall deal with it."

Fisher scrutinized the bullet hole gracing Her Majesty's bosom. "Who tried to kill you?"

Effington stared at him. "What do you mean?"

"You stated it was a personal matter. That means the assailant was intent on killing you or some member of your household, though they appear to have appallingly bad aim." Fisher gestured upward at the mutilated monarch.

"I meant..." Their host took a gulp of whiskey. "I meant that the incident occurred in my home. *That* is why it was personal."

"If it had just been you or your family involved, then Hulme would not have needed to contact me. However, since you had no less than..." Fisher reached out his hand and the inspector relinquished the guest list, "five Members of Parliament present, besides His Royal Highness and the Prime Minister, it becomes *my* issue, Mr. Effington."

"This is not a matter for Special Branch," Effington protested. "There are no anarchists involved." His eyes were less angry now. To the chief inspector, they resembled a hare with a pack of hounds on his tail. "It was just some crazy person. An American, I heard."

"America breeds anarchists as well as any country, Mr. Effington."

"I don't need your insolence, Inspector."

"*Chief* Inspector, Mr. Effington. If it proves to be a private matter, then I shall step aside and Inspector Hulme will continue his work without oversight. If it is not, then I am here until it is resolved. Whether or not you are pleased with this situation is not my concern."

Effington's face flushed with rage. "I shall take this matter to Police Commissioner Warren. I shall see you disciplined!"

"Possibly, though I doubt it. Once he hears that His Royal Highness was at this party, your umbrage is a moot point."

"Then to hell with you, sir!"

"Good evening, Mr. Effington. Please don't go too far lest we have more questions, which I'm sure we will."

Fisher's attention had already returned to the guest list before their host cleared the door. The chief inspector lowered his voice. "In what manner did he interfere with your investigation?"

Hulme looked dejected. "I asked one of the maids to have a constable dispatched to the Yard so that you might be notified, sir.

Over an hour later, I learned that my request was vetoed by Effington. The butler was livid when he found out his master had ignored my request. They got into quite a shouting match. The fellow got the sack on the spot."

"Interesting. Did you question the assassin?"

"He would not talk to me."

"Then why does Effington think he's an American?"

"Some of the witnesses said he had an American accent, sir."

"I see. Is his name on the guest list?"

"No, sir. The butler claims he did not admit him to the party, and the cook says he did not come through below stairs."

"Then how did he get in?"

"We do not know. Mrs. Effington is missing, as well. She was gone when her doctor arrived about an hour and a half after the incident. According to her maid, she took no clothes with her, nor any jewels."

"Extraordinary. You've searched the house?"

Hulme nodded. "I've put out word that we need to speak to her as soon as possible."

Fisher skimmed down the names. "Lots of toffs here," he said. That earned him a nervous chuckle from the inspector. "Lord and Lady Wescomb and a guest. Who was that person?"

"Miss Jacynda Lassiter," Hulme replied. "She is the lady who...stopped the assassination."

The chief inspector looked up abruptly. "Perhaps I've not heard the full story, Inspector."

"I'm sorry, sir. I would have if we hadn't been interrupted," Hulme replied, shooting a venomous look toward the door.

Fisher settled into the nearest chair, perching like a hawk eyeing a mouse.

"Then gather your wits and give me your report."

"You'll find it a most improbable one, Chief Inspector," Hulme replied, flipping open his notebook.

*Not if Miss Lassiter is involved.*

⸸

*Friday, 12 October, 1888*

Having managed to avoid one until tonight, Cynda had never really appreciated how a Victorian police station worked. For two hours or so, she looked on with morbid curiosity at the stream of humanity flowing by. There'd been a couple of drunken prostitutes, a visitor from France who claimed, in highly agitated and accented English, that he'd been robbed most viciously, and a man arrested for trying to steal a pair of trousers from a tailor. Every time the sergeant returned to his desk after one of these episodes, he'd note her presence and shake his head. Cynda refused to budge. It was now a matter of principle.

"Sorry, miss, I can't do that," the sergeant replied to her repeated request. He had a cup of steaming tea and half a bun near his elbow. It was plain he didn't appreciate these interruptions.

"All I want to do is take a look," Cynda said, leaning across his desk. "I'll be a couple minutes at most."

His eyes drifted to the tea and then back again. "Not until the inspector gives me the word."

"So please ask him."

"He's not here." The cop pulled the bun closer, a hint that this latest round was over.

Cynda took a seat on the hard bench near the door. "Then I will wait until Inspector Hulme shows up."

"Suit yourself, miss." The sergeant went back to his bun-munching.

It was nearing one in the morning when Hulme arrived, along with his foul mood. Cynda heard the words "Scotland Yard" and "Effington" growled at one of the other sergeants. A few minutes later, she was summoned to his office.

The inspector sagged into his chair. His tie was askew and dark circles resided under his eyes. "What are you doing here at this unholy hour, Miss Lassiter?"

"I wanted to have another look at the assassin."

"Why?" Hulme asked, his voice dulled by weariness.

"I might have seen him someplace before," she said. *Like in a ton of Vid-Net interviews.* "I just wanted to be sure, that's all."

"Where might that have been?" he asked.

"I can't remember."

The copper yawned, barely covering his mouth in time. Once he recovered, he called out, "Sergeant?"

The bun-eater poked his head in the door. "Sir?"

"Tea with lots of sugar. And keep an eye out for a toff named Fisher from the Yard. He'll be here once he gets done apple-polishing with the Police Commissioner."

"Yes, sir."

"What are these?" Hulme asked, gesturing at the pile on his desk.

"New prisoner's effects, sir. Thought you might like a look at them. I locked up the pistol for safekeeping, sir." The sergeant's head disappeared.

Cynda bent over to study the items on the desktop: a pocket watch, some money, a handkerchief.

She picked up the watch and gave the stem a couple of specific twists. Nothing happened. It wasn't a time interface. The other objects were appropriate to the period, but then you'd expect that of a seasoned Rover.

As she replaced the watch on the desk, she realized that Hulme was now watching her like she was the one who'd pulled the trigger.

"The chief inspector told me about you. Said you're an overly curious sort." Before Cynda could react, he asked, "How well do you know Mr. Effington?"

That she hadn't expected. "Just met him last evening," Cynda said. "Wasn't impressed."

"What about his wife?"

"Just met her as well. She's a friend of Lady Wescomb's. Why do you want to know?"

He screwed up his face. "Mind you, if it was just me, I'd not be talking to you, but Fisher says you have a way of finding out about things. By morning, there's going to be ten kinds of...there's going to an uproar about what happened last night unless we can dampen this down. If you know anything, I need to hear it."

"Such as?"

"There's more to this than just a botched assassination. Mrs. Effington fled the house a short time after the incident. We've since received word from Rotherhithe that her clothes were found near Church Stairs. She left a note, indicating her intention to end her life. We believe she drowned herself in the Thames."

"Church Stairs?" Cynda asked. "Why would she go there to kill herself?"

"The note did not specify. It only stated that life was too much of a burden at present, and that she sought the peace death would offer. It is my guess that the events at the party may have caused her mind to weaken."

Cynda frowned. Women and their weakened minds. That was so Victorian. "Do you have any notion why she would do such a thing?" Hulme asked.

"No," she said, her mind whirring with possibilities. Something didn't track. "You're saying she marched up to the Thames, stripped to her knickers and hurled herself in?"

The cop's mouth twitched noticeably at the mention of women's undergarments. "That is my belief."

Cynda shook her head. "That doesn't make much sense."

"I know it might be hard for you to accept that Mrs. Effington would commit such an act—"

"I'm not talking about her. Rotherhithe is a rough patch. A posh lady's clothes would have been gone in a—" she hesitated, sorting through centuries of appropriate slang. "Gone in a flash, probably ripped off her before she took two steps. To think they'd be sitting there long enough for a cop to find them just doesn't seem right."

A frown creased the inspector's forehead. "How did you know that a constable found the clothes?"

Cynda sighed. Keats was Mensa material compared to this guy. "Anyone else would have taken the clothes to the closest pawn shop and drunk the proceeds."

Hulme had the decency to look chagrined. "Yes, well, I see."

"You said that Mrs. Effington *apparently* committed suicide," Cynda observed. "That means you haven't recovered the body."

"No. It could be about anywhere. They get snagged on the rocks and such." His cheeks colored. "I apologize."

"No need." She tried one last time. "May I see your prisoner now?"

A reluctant nod. "Just don't talk to him. I haven't interrogated him yet, and the nob from the Yard wants to be here when I do. As if I can't run my own investigations," he grumbled.

"I just need a look, that's all," Cynda said. "I promise not to talk to him."

Cynda trudged alongside the sergeant into the heart of the jail, wrinkling her nose at the smell. Soap and water appeared to be highly rationed here.

"Has he said anything?" she asked.

"Not a word."

Once she determined Defoe's location, it was Morrisey's job to get him out of there. How they'd do that, she hadn't quite figured out. That was her boss' dilemma. Besides, confronting Defoe would be awkward.

They stopped in front of a thick door. "I'll have a look first to make sure he's decent," the sergeant said. He slid back the portal, then jammed his nose tight up against the grating.

"Bloody hell!" He fumbled with his thick ring of keys and fought with the lock. The door swung open with a screech. "Where is he?" the sergeant demanded, charging into the room and whirling in a circle. He bent and stared at the space under the cot, which was clearly devoid of a human being.

A haunted expression filled the man's face. Clearly, he was the one who'd take the blame. After another blistering oath, the sergeant stomped down the hall, keys clanking in his hand.

Cynda slipped into the cell and stared at the open space. A single candle sat on the window ledge, creating undulating shadows. *Nice trick. How'd you do it without a time interface?* Or had he managed to hide it from the cops?

On impulse, she lightly clapped her hands. "Well done."

A shimmer of movement near the door caught her notice. Cynda stared at it and sighed. Had to be time lag. Digging in her pocket, she munched her way through more chocolate: the subsequent endorphin rise usually helped mitigate the lag. Not this time. The shimmer didn't diminish.

The sound of tromping boots echoed in the hall a short time before Inspector Hulme stormed into the cell, hurling questions at the sergeant who huffed behind him.

"When did you last see him?"

"An hour ago. He was walking around the cell, talking to himself."

"So where'd he go? Prisoners don't just disappear."

*Unless they're a Rover.*

"I swear I saw him, sir!"

"Has anyone else entered his cell?" Hulme demanded.

"No, sir, not since he arrived. We let him be."

"Have you been drinking again?"

"No, sir!"

Hulme turned, his face florid. As he opened his mouth to dress down the sergeant, he spied Cynda and barely bit back the oath forming on his lips.

She was hastily chucked out of the building, along with an earnest request from the inspector not to mention the matter to anyone, especially those who worked for the press.

*Like they'd believe me.*

Cynda stepped out of the police station. It was colder now and she shivered. A hansom cab sat at the kerb. She blessed her luck, knowing how difficult it would be to find transport at this hour of the night. When she finished retying her bootlace, she saw someone hop inside the hansom. No one had exited the police station and she hadn't seen anyone on the street.

"Where'd you come from?" she grumbled.

As the hansom passed under a gaslight, she glowered at the passenger.

No one was there.

4

Cynda barely made it back to her hotel room before her interface began vibrating. She hurried to unfold it and then sank into the chair. The moment the keyboard illuminated, she typed her password.

A reassuring beep returned.

*Log On.*

*Ralph?*

*TEM.*

Morrisey was working the chronsole? That was a surprise. He always had one of the chron-ops do it. Her stomach did that knotting thing again.

The screen blinked.

She typed. *Defoe is gone. Well done.*

The screen blinked and then went black, like someone had just tripped over a decades-long extension cord. That had never happened before. She tried to reconnect without success. Three more attempts met with the same result.

She folded down the watch and tucked it away in her skirts. *Nothing to worry about. Maybe they're going through realignment. Yeah, that had to be it.*

After finishing her tea, Cynda heard the familiar rush of an Outbound transfer and clamped her eyes shut until the sound and light show subsided. When she opened them, she found T.E. Morrisey hunched on the floor in the *penitent posture*. By her count, this was his second trip through time. At least this trip he'd remembered to keep his head down until the effects of the transfer passed. The man was a quick study.

"Good morning, boss."

A mumbled "Good morning" came back to her as her guest took

deep inhalations, his forehead touching the carpet.

"I have some hot tea. Like some?"

A nod. Within a few minutes he was sitting on the couch, teacup in hand. His ability to recover was phenomenal...and supremely annoying. She had to admit he looked quite dashing in his Victorian duds, though his sock-footed Lotus posture took away from the effect. You couldn't have everything.

Morrisey didn't make social calls, so she cut to the chase. "So what did Defoe have to say for himself?"

"I have no idea. He's not in 2057."

"He's gotta be! The jail cell was empty."

"No transfer to '057, but there was a side-hop here in '88 at approximately half past twelve this morning. We think it might have been him."

"Didn't his ESR Chip register during the transfer?"

"No, and the interface wasn't registered, either."

"A non-reg interface? Would Defoe have one?"

Her guest shrugged.

"Twelve-thirty, huh? I just missed him," she said, shaking her head. "Damn."

Morrisey took a long sip and then set the cup aside. "Are you sure it was Harter?" he quizzed.

"It looked like him."

"Tell me precisely how it fell out."

She related the story and by the time it ended, he had that perturbed look on his face.

"Subtlety is certainly not your style, Miss Lassiter."

"Thank you. I've worked at that."

"Apparently. Did this person's image...waver at any time?"

"Not that I could see. One moment we're wrestling, and the next he's face down into the carpet with five guys on top of him."

"So he could have lost his concentration and no one would have noticed."

"What are you saying?"

"I do not believe this was Harter," Morrisey replied.

Cynda shouldn't have been surprised. Morrisey was all logic, but not necessarily when it came to Harter Defoe. Their friendship was renowned: the explorer and the geek.

She played devil's advocate. "All Rovers eventually snap if we keep going too long," she said gently. "Defoe's gone longer than the rest of us. Maybe the lag finally got to him."

"No," Morrisey said, his face tightening into a frown. "It's one of the reasons he went *walk about*. He knew he was reaching the end. He said he was going to find a quiet place and settle in for the remainder of his life, away from the adulation and the Vid-Net News reporters."

"If it wasn't Defoe, who else could've pulled this off?" she asked.

"I suspect this event was engineered from 2057. I think they utilized a Transitive to emulate Harter."

"Who are 'they'?"

"Most likely the Time Protocol Board, though the Government is quite capable of such chicanery."

"What's the payout?" she challenged. "TPB is making great money skimming off the top of the time immersion companies. Why screw with that?"

"The Time Protocol Board regrets allowing time immersion to become a public enterprise. There is -a drive to re-regulate the industry. There would be no recreational time travel, unless sanctioned by TPB."

"But not by Guv?" she asked, intrigued. He shook his head. "That's not good news. I don't like the Government any more than I like the TPB, but there has to be a balance of power."

"Precisely. At present, there is at least some transparency. My software monitors the timeline and, to some extent, the academics note when something is amiss. All of that oversight would end."

"And Guv's letting this happen?" she asked skeptically.

"Hardly. A showdown is in the offing. Which organization will win is up for grabs."

"So why didn't your software catch what happened at the party?"

"I have no idea. I have a team of analysts working through that very question as we speak."

She could well imagine how much that irritated him on a professional level. Defoe had been the one to hop through the centuries, to take the physical risks. Morrisey had bent the boundaries of time with his genius. Both had a lot to lose.

Morrisey cleared his throat. "You should be aware that TPB is making official noises about your stunt with Mr. Stone's ashes." She opened her mouth to protest, but he raised his hand for silence. "Their term, not mine. I firmly applaud your actions, Miss Lassiter. If you hadn't brought Chris home, our family would have had no closure."

Cynda relaxed. Cremating her dead lover and spiriting his ashes back to '057 against her former employer's orders had been a big no-no, but she'd gotten away with it. So far.

*And now for the million dollar question.* "Is Defoe a shifter?"

"He wasn't the last time I saw him." There was a noticeable

pause. "Yes, I am Transitive."

Morrisey's remarkable candor told her how much was at stake.

"We need to work both sides of this equation," he said. "See what you can find out about the Transitive population in '88 and whether any of them had contact with Harter in the past. Keep an eye out for him as well. He might know more about what is going on than we do, providing he's there."

"Okay. I'll also try to find out who the target was," she said. "That might give us an idea who was behind the gun."

"That's sound logic." Morrisey unfolded himself from the Lotus position and pulled on his boots. "Continue to hunt for Chris' watch. They'll expect that. Should you find something important, return to '057. Do *not* send the information over the interface. I'm working on a stealth version, but it isn't ready yet."

"Sounds illegal," she remarked with a smirk.

"Very," he replied. "I didn't think that would trouble you."

A broad grin spread across her face. "Not in the least."

"I won't be able to visit you in future. TPB found out about my other journey and issued a vigorous protest. Something about how a 'national treasure' should not be wandering through time. That's the same line they used with Harter. This trip will only settle the matter in their eyes."

Cynda hadn't thought about that. If Morrisey up and vanished, or took his vast knowledge into the past, that could cause some serious ripples, especially when the next software upgrade was needed. He was on an even shorter leash than she was.

Her boss retrieved his interface and began the winding procedure. "Mr. Hamilton sends his regards," he added, almost as an afterthought.

"Tell Ralph to watch your back."

Morrisey looked up, surprised, then issued a rare smile. "I would suggest you find someone to do the same for you, someone who knows the Transitives in this time period. This could get quite unpleasant before it's over."

*Ya think?*

⁜

Satyr liked to study people. It gave him an edge when it came to taking their lives. His attention to detail was why he was the Lead Assassin, the envy of the others. His failures were rare, his triumphs notable, his pseudonym a nod toward his sexual appetite, which was as legendary as his prowess as an executioner.

He'd once watched a tiger stalk and devour a villager in India, allowing nature's law to play out unhindered. In its own way, the creature had taught him a lesson in patience. It had waited among the grasses for a long time. Obscured until the proper moment, it leapt in a fury of teeth and claws, overwhelming its victim, dragging him down and dispatching him with a savage bite to the neck. Swift assault, swift death.

Like the tiger, Satyr made sure to blend into his surroundings. Those who passed him would not have noticed the man near the lamp post who observed people as they flowed around him on the street, hunting for weakness.

In the distance he spied the current Ascendant, the latest in a long line of men who had ruled over their kind. Like Satyr, he was *en mirage* in a form that would not have occasioned any notice. Well dressed, top hat in place, cane moving in time with each step, you would think him a banker or a well-heeled merchant.

When his leader drew near, Satyr inclined his head. Deference never went out of style. "Good morning, sir," he said.

"Mr. S.," was the quick reply.

They fell in step and didn't speak until they reached the door to the dining room on Rose Street. The moment they appeared in the entryway, they were waved into the private section. Breakfast was delivered immediately, for it was always the same. Then they were left alone. The staff would not intrude unless they heard the bell. To do otherwise risked decided unpleasantness.

"I did not expect to see you this morning," the Ascendant remarked. "What has happened?"

"There was an attempted assassination last evening at Effington's party."

"Who was the target?"

Satyr removed the lid of a Majolica bowl to reveal a selection of fat sausages. "Me, unfortunately."

"Good heavens. Who was the assassin?"

"He did not give his name," Satyr said, spearing a couple of links and placing them on the china plate in front of him. He always went for the sausages first.

The Ascendant frowned. "That is most disturbing. We don't need complications. Do you think he was sent by Mikhail?"

Satyr expertly sliced the pork into bite-sized pieces. "I don't think that's the case. The Mystic would want to kill me in person. It would be a matter of pride."

"Is this miscreant in custody?"

"He was," Satyr replied. "He's gone now."

"Gone? Gone where?"

"He vanished out of his cell. The Blue Bottles were in a fine frenzy."

"He's one of us?" the Ascendant demanded.

"Yes. I noted a slight waver in his form. I doubt anyone else saw it."

His superior's expression grew dark. "This person must ascend, Mr. S., and quickly. I will not have my authority challenged."

Satyr nodded. It was the Ascendant's prerogative to order the death of another. In this case, the order was justified. "It was quite amusing, actually. You should have seen the tumult around the prince. They had no clue he wasn't the target."

The Ascendant shifted two eggs onto his plate. "How did you escape injury?"

"That is the most surprising part of the story. It was Miss Lassiter. She threw herself at the fellow and drove him to the ground."

"Really? Now I wish I'd been there," the Ascendant replied, applying a pinch of salt to his eggs. "Perhaps it was of benefit that she was one of your rare failures."

Satyr bottled up his annoyance. "She is an exceptional case."

Sensing his irritation, his superior added, "She must be, or you'd not be Lead Assassin."

Satyr acknowledged the veiled threat, keeping his ire in check.

Apparently satisfied that his point had been made, the Ascendant added, "Of course, I was the one who suggested that you dispatch her in a subtle fashion. I quite liked your notion of chucking her under a beer wagon. That was inspired."

"Inspired, but ineffectual."

His superior grew solemn. "True. I am surprised you have not completed the contract. I've been meaning to press you on that point."

"An ideal opportunity has not presented itself," Satyr said. In truth, he'd rather have Miss Lassiter live for a bit longer. He found her unpredictability a challenge, one he relished.

"Make sure the opportunity arises *soon*. She worries me. Deal with her in a more...pronounced fashion this time."

"As you wish."

"Before you kill her," the Ascendant instructed, "learn what she knows about this new threat. Find out if the assassin's working for the Mystic or the Irishman."

*Neither.* "I will, sir."

"I have a new job for you." After a short pause, he continued, "One of your subordinates is a constable, is he not?"

Satyr nodded, his mouth full.

"I have a task for him, as well. But first, do pass those sausages before you eat them all, will you?"

✝

*2057 A.D.*

*TEM Enterprises*

Ralph remained on his cushion, unable to avoid the drama playing out in the chronsole room.

"How many of them are there?" Morrisey asked, annoyance in every word.

"Two, sir," his assistant Fulham replied. "They're from the Time Protocol Board. They insist they must speak to you personally."

Ralph smirked. The drones on the TPB were widely regarded as a waste of life force, at least within the industry. Most of them were political hacks with a child's understanding of time travel. Their current head, Davies, was deserving of a one-way trip to some time particularly unwholesome.

Ralph turned on his cushion to see what the verdict would be.

"Did they say what this is about?" Morrisey asked, his forehead furrowing.

Fulham shook his head. "I would, however, counsel you speak with them. They seem quite...intense."

Morrisey nodded reluctantly. "Put them in the tatami room. Don't bring in chairs; let them sit on the cushions like the rest of us. Make them as uncomfortable as possible."

Fulham smiled. "As you wish, sir." The door slid closed behind him.

"Anything I should know on the Vid-Net News?" Morrisey asked. "Something that might have precipitated this visit?"

Ralph turned and checked the online news organizations. "Nothing unusual. Stocks are down and there are complaints that Off-Gridders don't pay any taxes. Of course, they don't use any services, but hey, that's not the issue."

"Then it has to be about the '88 situation," Morrisey concluded. "I had hoped we'd have more time to figure that out without interference."

"No such luck."

Morrisey eased onto his cushion in the tatami room. He didn't possess the over-the-top reputation that Harter had garnered, but that was just as well.

Being a bit of a mystery put people off their game.

"What may I do for you gentlemen?" he asked.

The first man, a nondescript fellow with wavy hair, announced, "We have been sent by the Chairman, Mr. Davies, to lodge a formal complaint."

"And you are?"

"Mr. Davies' assistant."

"Your name?"

"Smith."

"And you?" Morrisey asked the other visitor.

"Jones," Smith replied. "He is *my* assistant."

*Smith and Jones? How unimaginative.* "What is the nature of this complaint?"

"You made another trip to 1888. You know our position on that."

"I am aware of your concerns."

"That time period is unstable at the moment. Why do you feel the need to place yourself in jeopardy?"

"I needed to speak to a Rover about a particular problem."

"Miss Lassiter?" Morrisey issued a curt nod. "What was the nature of the problem?"

"There was a time ripple. I asked her to investigate."

Smith waggled his finger. "Hardly a ripple, Mr. Morrisey. Perhaps you can explain why a Time Incursion Warning was not issued."

*How do you know all this?* "The software did not register the event as worthy of a T.I. Warning. I am reviewing the software code to determine why that happened."

"Perhaps the problem is not in the software."

Morrisey's jaw tightened. "Your implication is insulting. I would not suppress a warning for any reason."

"Mr. Davies thinks otherwise. He wonders if you are too close to Mr. Defoe to make a sound judgment."

"Why are you really here, gentlemen?"

"Defoe has gone rogue, and cannot be permitted to run around the time stream on his own. Any further infractions on his part will be laid at your doorstep."

"What else?"

"You must replace Miss Lassiter with a more reliable Rover who will find and return Defoe as quickly as possible. Her behavior in regard to Mr. Stone's death proves she is a loose cannon."

That raised Morrisey's hackles. "How so?"

"She defied her employer's direct order to discard Stones' remains in 1888," Smith replied. "She is not a Rover we can trust."

"*Discard* the remains?" Morrisey repeated.

"I realize he was your nephew; however, it was fiscally prudent to use this method."

Morrisey rose from his pillow in one fluid motion. "Miss Lassiter stays on assignment. When she finds Defoe, we will sort this out without your interference. If Davies has a problem with that, tell him to come see me—personally."

"I don't think—"

Morrisey was out the door before the sentence ended. He met Fulham in the hallway.

"Escort them out of the building. If they come back without Davies, don't let them in."

"Understood, sir."

Morrisey tapped his Personal Security Interface and then shook his head. He looked up at Fulham. "Find out their real names, will you? Evil craves anonymity. If you need anything, I'll be meditating in the pagoda."

5

*Friday, 12 October, 1888*
*Spitalfields*

"It's a simple request," Jacynda retorted. "I don't see the problem."

"You wouldn't," Alastair replied. He pushed the broom harder, raising a cloud of sawdust. Usually he'd have the door open, but not with the topic she'd raised. "Your problem, Jacynda, is that you do not listen. You just steam ahead as if there is no barrier you cannot penetrate."

She waved the dust away. "I cross centuries, Alastair. A simple 'no' is not a barrier to me."

"Therein lies your problem."

"I'm not here about *my* problems. I just need to know more about the shifters."

"I don't see that it is germane," he retorted. "You claim someone tried to kill the prince, at a party of all places. Why would that have anything to do with the Transitives?"

"He looked like one of ours, but a Time Rover knows better than to change history."

"Ergo, it has to be a shape-shifter?"

"I'm not sure. I need to check all possibilities."

Alastair made a couple wide swipes of the broom, kicking up more dust. He'd intended to tell her about the clinic's demise, but not now. Lord knows what she'd do with that tidbit of information.

He tried again. "This is not a course you want to pursue. The Conclave doesn't like Opaques asking questions. It's dangerous." He disliked using that pejorative term, but he'd hoped it might give Jacynda a sense of the disdain The Conclave held for those unable to shift.

She shook her head. "The Conclave won't do anything, now that you're a member."

"On the contrary, I suspect they would just go behind my back. You have to use some discretion, Jacynda."

Her anger faded into an expression he knew so well. She'd discarded his advice and was already plotting her next move.

"Jacynda, please, do not—"

"Good day, Doctor," she said, turning on her heels. The door slammed shut, pushing a small wave of sawdust across the floor.

‡

"Are you the copper who caught that anarchist?" the clerk asked, wide-eyed.

"No, I didn't catch him, though I did get close," Keats replied, not keen to have to relate the entire Green Dragon fracas yet again. The tale had grown from the initial newspaper report. The last he'd heard, he had single-handedly taken on no less than a dozen Irishmen. Ironically, it had only taken one to nearly put him in his grave. At least he'd gotten hold of one wagonload of explosives. That had pleased his superiors immensely. "Did you have any luck generating that list of former employees?"

The young clerk continued to stare at him like he was a god. That was unnerving.

"Is there someone else I can speak with?" Keats prodded. It was only half past ten in the morning and he was totally knackered. The sooner he was in his bed, the better. It would reduce the chances someone would discover he was out and about.

"I'll take care of this, Wilson," an older voice intervened.

Keats heaved a sigh of relief. "Senior Clerk Lowery, isn't it?" A nod. "I am trying to obtain a list of former employees who might have had knowledge of your invoicing process."

"I have it for you. I would have sent it out earlier, but Mr. Trimble objected."

"I see. I shall have a word in Mr. Trimble's ear about being a helpful citizen."

"Don't bother. He's gone. Packed up his things and left yesterday."

"Had there been difficulties before this?"

A shrug. "This way. I'm the new office manager. Word from the owner is that we are to help you in any manner possible."

"Excellent. You can start with Mr. Trimble's home address."

✠

Keats didn't realize he had a visitor until he noted the lithe, glaring figure loitering near his door. She held a pocket watch in her hand, a package tucked under one arm.

*Oh, no.* "Ah, Miss Jacynda, good afternoon." He tried to put on a brave face while digging his key out of a pocket. "I just stepped out to get a few papers," he explained, indicating the bundle under his arm.

A shake of the head. "According to your landlady, you've been out since this morning."

*An honest landlady is not always a blessing.*

He pushed open the door and crossed his sitting room, shedding his coat and hat along the way. Dropping the stack of papers on the floor, he sank into his chair with a weary sigh, waiting for the tongue-lashing that would follow. Instead, he heard the rattle of the kettle as it was plucked off the hob and then the sound of water being added to it. He watched as his visitor removed her hat and mantelet and carefully set them aside. The dark-blue gown accented her figure and made her light-brown hair seem somehow richer.

A very handsome woman.

Her glare returned. "What were you up to?"

"I wondered how it was that Flaherty knew which documents to forge to net him the explosives. That indicated he had someone on the inside, so I went back to the explosives firm and made further enquiries."

"Did you learn anything?"

"Yes. The office manager has abruptly resigned, which I find curious. I intended to visit his home, but grew too weary."

"That's a lot of footwork in your condition."

"Indeed." He smiled ruefully. "I would be grateful if you not mention my excursion to Alastair. He would be quite cross. Especially after—"

His guest's attention veered from the teakettle to him.

"After what?"

Keats stifled a groan. Jacynda was too sharp to miss such an obvious blunder. As he related the warning Alastair had received the night before, her face paled.

"Would Flaherty bomb the clinic?" she asked.

"Yes."

"No wonder Alastair was in such a vile mood this morning," his guest muttered, her glare mutating into a frown.

"You spoke with him?"

"Yes. At the clinic. He didn't say a thing."

"Most likely didn't want to alarm you."

The lid rattled sharply as she removed it to pour the hot water into the teapot.

"Fortunately, Flaherty is not aware of your name and to that end, I would suggest you not visit me for a time until things settle down."

She returned to her chair. He noted she hadn't agreed to his suggestion.

"I'm sincere about that," he said. "I don't want you in any danger."

"How's your head?" she asked.

"Better. However—"

"Good."

"Jacynda, I really—"

"I need your assistance."

Keats sighed. He'd done his best under the circumstances. "In what manner can I assist you?"

He listened in consternation at her activities of the previous night.

"Have you no fear?" Keats asked, shaking his head in amazement after she told him of the events at the party in Mayfair.

"Were you afraid when you tackled five Irishmen single-handedly?"

"Yes. Scared out of my wits."

"Well, this thing happened so fast I didn't have time to worry."

"So who was he after?"

"No idea. They all think it was the prince, but I'm not so sure."

"Is Fisher in on this?" She nodded. "Well, he'll sort it out."

"Not if he doesn't have a prisoner. He vanished out of the jail cell overnight."

"What?"

As she completed the tale, he leaned back in the chair, eyes half-closed.

"Home Office will be furious that a suspect of such importance has gone missing," he said. "Hulme must be beside himself." He frowned, though it pulled on his bandage. "Why were you visiting the prisoner in the first place?"

*Of course, he'd ask that one.* "I wanted to have another look at him. He seemed familiar in some way."

That seemed to mollify her host. It told her how weary he was.

"You say you saw something peculiar in the cell?"

"I thought I did. Sort of like a shimmer. I thought it was—" Cynda hesitated. She'd once told Keats she was from the future, and he'd chosen not to believe her. No reason to stir that up again. "A trick of my eyes."

"I wonder if it was a Transitive, " he murmured.

"You can do that shimmery sort of thing?"

"No, but others can."

"How?"

"It's rather complicated. Alastair hasn't told you about any of this?"

Cynda poured the tea and handed him a cup. "Alastair's been very unhelpful."

"Guilt, I suspect. I have a bit of it myself," he allowed.

"Guilt about what?"

"How you acquire your ability," he said, then took a sip of the tea. He added more milk. "Someone has to die for you to become a Transitive. In my case, it was my sainted mother. In Alastair's..."

"His lover," she said, eyes drifting downward. "He never told me the whole tale."

"I suspect there's a reason for that."

"Can you tell me what happened?" Cynda asked.

Keats shook his head. "I think it best you hear it from him. I will say that his lover was a Welsh gypsy and that she was murdered. He feels he should have prevented her death."

"My God."

Cynda took a gulp of the tea, then winced as it burned her tongue. A change of subject was needed. "Tell me more about the Transitives. I'd really like to understand all this."

"You put me in an awkward position. Opaques—those like you who are unable to change forms—are not allowed to know about us. In times past, Knowers, as they are called, were...dispatched."

"I accept the risk," she replied.

"You sound so sure. Once you start down this path—"

"I saw you shift in the carriage after you were injured. I want to know more about this, Jonathon. I'll get in less trouble if you tell me than if I keep asking questions."

He grew grave. "I had no idea I was that badly injured."

Their eyes met. "You were."

He sagged against the chair. "Well, then, I'll tell you what I can." He paused, gathering his thoughts. "My grandfather says we're a bit like cats. We are either somber, wild or furtive."

She cracked a smile. "Sort of like the rest of us."

He nodded. "To give you an example: the Wescombs would be what we call Solemns, the dignified, non-adventurous sorts. They shift at home and when in the company of other Transitives. Nothing flashy. The Pucks are the ones who are full of mischief."

He nodded before she could ask the question. "Yes, their name is from Midsummer Night's Dream. It's quite fitting. They are brash libertines. Virtuals, on the other hand, are capable of mimicking the scene around them and are the secretive ones.

Fortunately, they are rather rare."

"So you think what I saw was a Virtual?"

"Perhaps. If it were, the prisoner only need wait until he heard the guard returning before he went *en mirage*. Once the cell door was open, it was a matter of walking to freedom."

"Wouldn't someone have bumped into him?"

"That's always a danger. However, in the confusion, he could have easily assumed the form of a constable. No one would have noticed. They were hunting for a missing prisoner, not someone in uniform."

"Why didn't he do it at the party?"

"You threw yourself on top of him. He might be able to shift, but you were still impeding his ability to move, though your mind would say nothing was there."

"Then why not on the way to jail?" she pressed.

"If I were a constable, I'd have secured the fellow. Manacles would slow him down and he'd not be able to easily remove them."

"But he could hide them in an illusion," she said, intrigued.

Keats set his cup aside. "He could hide them, but they'd still be real. He'd have to drag them a considerable distance until he found a dishonest smithy to break him free."

Cynda groaned and rubbed her temples. "This is just so confusing. How did you learn all this?"

"Not an easy task. I interacted with some of the others. Well, actually, just the Pucks and the Solemns. Virtuals remain hidden, like the Mystics. I learned about them mostly by gossip."

"Mystics?"

"We are not immune to religious fervor," he commented with a droll smirk. "When you are given such a gift, some see it as a sign from God, so a minute number of us have taken the spiritual path. I find it fascinating how we always bend reality to fit our natures." He scratched just below his bandage. "Silly thing itches," he grumbled.

She set down the cup and rested her elbows on her knees. "Are there *that* many of you?"

"Not really. Still, we do form our cliques. I have spent some time with the Pucks," he continued, "however, their notions of entertainment did not interest me."

"Alastair said he could sense when a shifter is *en mirage*. Can you?"

Keats shook his head. "No. Alastair is a rare bird, one of the Perceivers. I think it has something to do with his Welsh antecedent. He's the only one I've encountered, or at least the only one who's admitted his ability in my presence. I can imagine that most prefer not to have that known."

"Why?"

"If you were up to mischief, would you want one of your own pointing you out? That is why Perceivers are not well regarded. They're seen as traitors."

"Like a taster for a king," Cynda suggested.

Keats issued a long yawn, followed by a look of chagrin. "Pardon me. I am quite tired."

"One last question: who do I talk with to find out if the assassin was a shifter?"

"No one!" Keats replied instantly. "That is a supremely bad idea."

"Look, I'm not going to tell the world. I just need to find this fellow."

"They won't talk to you."

"Then introduce them to me."

His uneasy expression changed to one of frank concern. "I am not up to that, at present. My health is not yet restored. Perhaps in a few weeks I can be of assistance."

*Funny, he was well enough to spend half the day investigating the Irishman.*

"Then I'll go on my own. Who do I talk to, Jonathon?"

"Why are you so intent on this?"

Cynda readied her alibi. "The police are asking questions about my involvement, especially when I'm present when Mr. Assassin goes missing at the jail. It looks like I'm an accomplice. I need to find out who this man is and make sure I don't get blamed in some way."

It worked. He shook his head in resignation. "I know a woman who has many...contacts within the community. She might be able to help us."

"Perfect." She smiled in triumph. That was easier then she'd expected.

"No, she's far from perfect. Nicci is extremely immoral, one of the worst of the Pucks. I hesitate taking you anywhere near her."

"It'll be fine. I'll ask a couple questions and off we go."

"No, you will not. I'll ask the questions. In fact, you'll wait in the carriage until—"

"No."

Another sigh. "She may demand proof you're one of us."

"No she won't. Not if I'm with you."

"I suppose you're right. I will smooth the way when we meet her. Pucks play wicked games and I do not want us at her home during one of the...gatherings."

Cynda filled in the blank. "Orgies?"

A quick nod. His protests had taken the last bit of energy. A protracted yawn overtook him. "I need to rest. Come back about nine. Nicci's day doesn't start until it is nearly over."

Cynda rose and handed him the package. "Thank you for recommending your cobbler. My new boots are heaven."

"That's very kind. I certainly didn't expect anything in return." He peeled back the wrapping and beamed. "*The Prince and the Pauper* by Mr. Twain. I have so wanted to read this."

"I found it at this great bookshop near the Strand. I'll have to take you there someday."

"I'd like that. I still owe you a trip to see the Crystal Palace," he replied, a brief sparkle in his eyes.

"We'll do it. Now have a nap and I'll be back later. You've overdone it again."

Outside, in the sunshine, she looked back up at Keats' window. *Pity you don't believe in time travel. It would make it so much easier.*

✠

Fresh from his shift at the hospital, Alastair made his way to the clinic. It was just after six and the streets were as crowded as ever. As he drew near, the clinic's new door mocked him. It should have been a sign of rebirth. Instead, it was a symbol of failure.

He unlocked it and stepped inside. The smell of wood and antiseptic greeted him. The room was as he left it this morning— newly constructed benches on one side and a small pile of lumber on the other. An imprint of Jacynda's boot in the sawdust caught his notice. Hopefully, she'd come to her senses and was enjoying a quiet evening at the hotel.

"She's probably not even capable of such a thing," he muttered.

He removed his coat, rolled up his sleeves and worked for the next hour completing the last two benches. He saw no reason to waste the lumber. As he hammered, he channeled his anger into each blow. Now that the clinic had to close, the Reverend Martin had offered to purchase the benches for his burgeoning congregation. In the same breath he'd cordially invited Alastair to attend services.

*Perhaps I shall.* It had been a long time since he'd been inside a church. He'd always found more value in doing God's work rather than talking about it.

He was partway through the sweeping when the landlord appeared in the door. A French Huguenot, he'd once been a weaver in the silk trade until the market collapsed. "I'm putting up the notice now," he said, waving a handbill. "I'm hoping to have the room rented right soon."

"That's fine. The benches will be out of here tomorrow morning.

A reverend will call for them."

The landlord nodded and tacked up the notice on the door with three loud thumps of his hammer. "Sorry you're leaving. You were doing good work here, Dr. Montrose."

"Thank you. I just don't dare take the risk now."

"I know," the landlord replied. "Doesn't make the decision any easier. Oh, and a young fellow came by this afternoon looking for you. Was interested in helping out at the clinic. I told him it was closing."

Alastair sighed. "It's a pity someone comes forward now that we won't need him." He went back to his sweeping. When he heard the door close, he paused, leaning on the broom.

A few months earlier, he'd resigned his lucrative position with Dr. Hanson in Mayfair so he could treat the poor as he saw fit. As Hanson had so rudely put it, "The self-righteous physician starving himself so he could treat the indigent and play God in the process."

Alastair shook his head and employed the broom once again. His work in Whitechapel had nothing to do with hubris. Penance came in many forms.

‡

Johnny Ahearn struggled to swallow. He felt weak in the knees, weaker in the bladder. The blade hovered only a short distance from his throat, a thin coat of oil glistening along its honed edge. Try as he might, he could only focus on that piece of steel, not the narrowed eyes of the man who held it.

He took a deep breath, hoping to draw in some courage with the fetid air. The other men in the shadows remained silent, their faces drawn. They would not interfere. At the far end of the passage, a wagon rumbled past, its wheels grinding against the pavement. Then the horse's clopping hooves faded into the night.

"What's wrong with ya, Flaherty?" Ahearn pleaded. "I'm doin' what ya asked."

"Are ya?" The whisper was razor-sharp, like the blade would be.

Ahearn blinked, confused. "Ya told me ta find yer girl!"

"And did ya?"

"Not yet, but I think I know where she might be."

"Where?"

"An old brewery. She's maybe in the cellar."

A queer smile marched across the lined face.

"Yer right."

Ahearn's eyes widened in comprehension, but the knowledge came too late.

"Oh, God, you're one of *them!* I thought you were—"

The knife flew forward, burying itself into the side of his throat. A deft, lateral movement, perfected by years of practice, severed the carotid artery and the windpipe, spraying a fountain of blood into the air. Ahearn gripped his neck, life spouting through his calloused fingers. A cavernous, choking sound gurgled past his lips. He sank down the brick wall, clawing at the air and the man who had cut him before he tumbled into a heap on the ground.

"Sweet Jesus," one of the witnesses murmured and crossed himself, followed by the second.

Satyr knelt to wipe the blade on Ahearn's coat sleeve. Once it was clean, he dropped it in his pocket.

"That's how it's done. Any questions?" Both men shook their heads, their faces ashen.

"Load him up. We're not leaving him here."

The pair encased the corpse in blankets and hauled it through the back gate to the waiting wagon. Satyr grunted with approval, savoring the expression in his victim's eyes at the very end. They all had that look. Didn't matter if it was a sheep or a man. Death made them equal under the caress of his blade.

6

"Dr. Montrose to see Lord Wescomb, if he is available," Alastair announced to the maid.

"I shall see if his lordship is at home," was the polite reply. Wescomb might be in residence, but not receiving visitors, and the verbal sleight of hand preserved the dignity of whomever came calling.

As Alastair waited in the foyer, he adjusted his tie and jacket. He noted another coat on the hall tree, along with a corresponding bowler. Wescomb had a guest. He sighed at his timing. Jacynda's assertion that the assassin might be a Transitive had rested heavily upon him all day. Unfortunately, the other guest would preclude asking his host questions in that regard, unless he knew them to be a shifter. He would have retreated, but there was another, more personal matter to discuss with Lord Wescomb. Once that was done, he would go the Artifice Club and confer with the other members of The Conclave. Perhaps they could offer some insights into the matter.

As he waited, he savored his surroundings. It had only been a few days since he'd been in this very house, ministering to Keats after his injury at the hands of the anarchists. There was a tranquility here that made him envy its occupants. Fresh flowers were carefully arranged in the lead crystal vase nearby. Meanwhile, he existed in a tiny boarding house room filled only with his medical books and his abundant dreams. What would it be like to come home to a warm hearth and a loving wife?

He heard a door open at the far end of the hall. Lord Wescomb's jovial face appeared. "Come in, come in," the elder statesman called, beckoning toward his study. "Your timing is excellent!"

After doffing his coat and bowler, Alastair hurried along the passageway and entered the lord's study as the maid took her leave. The room was as he remembered. A fire glowed in the hearth, casting shadows on the crowded bookshelves. Another gentleman lounged in a chair near the hearth, studying him with a bemused expression. He appeared a bit older than Alastair, with striking blue eyes and sandy brown hair. His luxuriant moustache bespoke a great deal of care.

"I apologize, my lord, I had no notion you were entertaining guests," Alastair said politely, as courtesy demanded.

Wescomb beamed. "Oh, goodness, this fellow isn't a guest; he's more like a dubious relative you can't shake loose." The visitor guffawed in response. "Come on in, my boy. You look as if you could use a drink."

Alastair took a seat as Wescomb poured him a brandy. He waited for his lordship to make the introductions, but waited in vain. The other guest chuckled, extending his hand in greeting.

"Dr. Reuben Bishop at your service."

"Dr. Alastair Montrose." They shook hands briskly.

"So you're the fellow Sagamor's been talking about."

Alastair blinked in surprise. Before he could answer, a substantial portion of brandy was placed in his hand.

Wescomb resumed his seat, performing the required tug on his waistcoat.

"Sephora is at one of her suffragette meetings. She'll be sorry she missed you. Reuben and I were just commiserating about what will happen when women obtain the vote."

"You believe it a certainty?" Alastair asked.

"In time," Wescomb replied. "All for the best, actually. We men have made a rather beastly job of it. Time to let the fairer sex have a crack."

"I agree," Bishop replied. "They can't possibly bugger it up any worse than we have."

It was clear that candor was going to flow as liberally as the brandy.

"How is Sergeant Keats faring?" Wescomb asked.

"Healing quite nicely while complaining about absolutely everything."

"No doubt displeased he is not in the thick of it."

"That would be the problem," Alastair concurred with a slight smile. "I suspect he will be back on duty in a week or so, one way or another."

"Excellent. I intended to write you a note tonight. Mrs. Vickers is a client of mine, a woman sincerely in need of a good physician. I recommended you, and she wishes you to call upon her."

"Most certainly, my lord. Does she have a particular ailment?"

"Declining health of an undetermined origin. Her physician is clearly stymied and, to be honest, I don't trust his judgment on the matter. I thought it might be wise to have a fresh approach. I'll supply the particulars," he said, moving to his desk where he extracted a piece of stationery from a drawer.

"Why didn't you tell me you had a patient that needed attending?" Bishop asked. "I am heartbroken you did not consider me, Sagamor."

To Alastair's immense relief, Wescomb laughed and shook his head.

"He's pulling your leg, Alastair. Unless you're dead, Reuben isn't interested."

"I'm a pathologist," the man explained. "I find it refreshing that my patients never complain about my treatment."

"How true," Alastair replied, warming to the physician's openness.

"So what brings you to my door tonight, Alastair?" Wescomb asked. "Not that you need a reason to visit, mind you."

Alastair placed his drink on the walnut table and removed a piece of paper from his pocket. "I come with a draft drawn on the Bank of England payable to you, my lord. I wish to return your donation to the clinic."

Wescomb frowned. "Why would you do that?"

"I've received a frank warning that if I reopen the clinic, the Fenians intend to destroy it."

"Good God," Bishop muttered.

"Although I am not particularly concerned about my welfare, I am truly worried about the danger to my patients if these people were to dynamite the place."

Bishop leaned forward, puzzled. "The newspapers claimed all the explosives were accounted for."

"They were instructed to say that to prevent public panic," Wescomb remarked as he rose from the desk. "It's far from the truth." He looked over at Alastair. "I am truly sorry it has come to this. I know how much the clinic means to you."

Alastair nodded gravely and placed the cheque on the table next to his brandy. "In time, perhaps I can reopen."

"I hope so," Wescomb said, handing him the patient's name and address. "You are sensible to take this warning seriously."

He then collected the cheque from the table, walked to the fireplace and dropped it into the flames. "I shall incur Sephora's wrath if I accept this," Wescomb explained. "Use the monies as you feel is proper for the unfortunates in Whitechapel. You are as honest a fellow as ever I have met. You will set it to good use."

"Thank you, my lord," Alastair said, taken aback. "I am honored by your trust."

"What will you do now that you've shuttered your clinic?"

Bishop asked, leaning back in his chair, fingers tented in thought.

"I still have my practice at the London Hospital, though my recent notoriety has caused some difficulties there. To be honest, I find the hospital atmosphere confining."

"Have you considered forensic medicine?"

Alastair sipped his brandy. "Odd that you should mention that. I just recently witnessed a post-mortem examination and found it most enlightening."

And disturbing. Though the findings revealed a murder, Jacynda's lover was not of this century, and neither was his killer. There had been no option to take the matter to the police.

"Sagamor's heard my speech on this subject a number of times," Bishop continued. "Nevertheless, I sincerely believe that forensic science will become a vital part of police investigative technique. Of course, the majority of plodders in the local constabulary just stumble over their own feet, but a few are bright enough to see the future. As you appear to be someone who is not afraid to become involved in police issues—"

A tap on the door.

"Oh, bother," Wescomb muttered. "Enter."

The maid opened the door, curtseyed and announced, "There is a constable here to see Dr. Bishop, my lord."

"Really?" Wescomb shot his friend a bemused look. "Speaking of the plodders. Show the fellow in, Marie."

"Yes, my lord."

"There goes my evening," Bishop said, draining his glass. "Oh well, it has to be an interesting case or they wouldn't send for me."

"Do the police usually track you down like this?" Alastair asked.

"I leave word with my housekeeper where the police might find me if needed. They don't call me out too often. Nevertheless, every now and then I get my fingers into some delicious crime or other." He beamed, clearly relishing this sudden development.

A constable appeared in the doorway, helmet in hand. The "D" on his collar told Alastair the fellow was from the Marylebone police division.

"Excuse me, milord, but I'm to find Dr. Bishop."

"I am he," Bishop said.

"I'm to escort you to the scene of a crime, sir."

"Really! Now there's a surprise." Bishop delivered a wink to Alastair.

The constable hesitated, clearly bewildered.

"So where's this one?" Bishop asked.

"Near the Tower, sir."

"Dicey one, huh?"

"I wouldn't know that, sir."

"Of course, you wouldn't." Bishop rose. "I'll be ready in a few minutes, Constable."

"Right, sir." The fellow trudged back the way he'd come.

Bishop turned toward their host. "Sorry, Sagamor, I was quite enjoying the evening."

"As was I, Reuben."

"Give my regards to Sephora, will you?" The moment Bishop reached the door, he turned. "I say, Dr. Montrose, would you care to come along? I warn you, it could be a bit graphic. They don't call me out on the routine cases, only those that have some unique element to them."

While Alastair deliberated, Wescomb added fuel to the fire. "Reuben is an excellent teacher. A bit over-the-top on occasion, but you'll learn something, that I can guarantee."

Alastair threw caution to the winds. He could call at the Artifice Club after this journey. "Well, why not? The clinic's closed for the time being. I might as well do something besides feel sorry for myself."

"There's a good sport," Bishop replied, clapping his hands together. "Come on, let's see what the Yard has turned over this time."

"The Yard?"

"Of course. The locals couldn't be bothered with me. It's Scotland Yard that pays my bills."

*Oh no.*

✝

From the grim expression on Keats' face, anyone would think they were going into battle. As the hansom headed west toward Mayfair, he leaned closer so Cynda could hear him over the rattle of the wheels.

Mindful of the driver, he lowered his voice, his breath tickling her ear. "I am against this adventure. I have no notion who may be present in that house. I am not in any condition to protect you—"

"No problem. I have a truncheon." She dug under her mantelet and produced it. "I had it shortened so it fits my pocket."

He smiled. "You took it off that fellow on Dorset Street, didn't you?"

"Yes, I did. Thanks for coming to my aid that night, by the way. I'd like to think I could have gotten out of that on my own, but I'm not sure."

"I was watching for Flaherty, not you. As to the truncheon, even if you were to employ it, Nicci would probably welcome the pain."

"I'm not worried," she replied, tucking the weapon back into the pocket.

He groaned in exasperation. "The only reason I am allowing this is because I fear you will try to find her on your own. That would be disastrous." He removed his handkerchief and mopped his forehead. "Alastair will have my guts for garters if anything happens to you."

"Then he must not find out about this little jaunt."

"At least we agree on that point." He fished for his notebook. "Now give me all the details of the assailant. I will be asking the questions, do you understand?"

"Whatever you'd like," she said. She reeled off Defoe's description and watched in amazement as Jonathon jotted them down despite the moving cab.

*That's gotta take some practice.*

"Anything else?" he asked.

"No, that's it."

"Good." He snapped the notebook shut, jammed it in his pocket and leaned back for a nap.


The butler eyed them with a jaded expression. "Yes?" he asked.

"We need to meet with Angel," Keats said in a muted voice. Cynda noted her escort had not handed over his calling card, as was Victorian custom.

"Your name?"

"Sir Galahad."

*Sir Galahad the Pure?*

"And the lady?"

"A friend," Keats replied.

The butler didn't blink. Such a request must be commonplace. This was getting more interesting by the minute.

They were left standing in the front hall. The house appeared ordinary—no racks or whips or other naughty items on display. Maybe Keats was overplaying the Pucks a bit.

She shot him a questioning look. "Sir Galahad?"

He fussed with his handkerchief. "It's her pet name for me."

The butler reappeared and motioned them forward. "The lady of the house has vouched for you, sir."

Keats didn't budge. "Is there a gathering in progress? We do not want to be involved in one of your mistress' soirees."

"The mistress is waiting," the butler gestured.

Keats' voice grew sharper. "Is there a gathering in progress?"

The butler shook his head curtly.

The sergeant sighed. "Come along, let's get this done. I don't want to be here any longer than necessary."

"Satyr?" Cynda asked.

Their hostess pulled her sideways a few steps and pointed through the crowd. There he was, with the usual accoutrements: pointed ears, tail, brown furry coat below the waist, goat hooves and a magnificent set of short horns. The mythological being was vigorously servicing a slim, youthful version of Queen Victoria.

Keats gasped. "My God, that's...that's...blasphemous!"

Nicci ignored him. "I can introduce you. You could be next."

"No, thank you," Cynda said. "After having a queen, I'd be a disappointment."

Nicci grew peevish. "Why are you here, then?"

Keats cleared his throat. "We need to speak to you somewhere a bit more...private."

"Only talk?" she replied. He nodded. "Well then, come along."

They found a reasonably quiet niche in an unused corner. There were a series of whips hanging on the wall behind them. One of them had fresh blood on it. Cynda turned away with a shudder.

Keats turned cop in an instant. "The Yard is investigating an attempted assassination at a party in Mayfair the other evening. It is believed that the prince might have been the target."

"Who was the host?" Nicci asked.

"Hugo Effington."

A half-smile appeared on Nicci's full lips. "Dear old Hugo. Now there's a rutting bull. I'm sorry I missed that occasion."

Keats flipped open the notebook and recited Defoe's description in clipped tones. "Does this sound like anyone you know?" A shake of the head. "Or anyone *en mirage?*"

Nicci's eyes slid to Cynda and then back. "No."

"Do you know anyone in our community who might be inclined toward committing such a rash act?" Keats pressed.

From somewhere in the room there was a shout of triumph and then applause. Cynda didn't want to know the reason.

"I don't see why this should concern us," Nicci retorted.

"The assailant disappeared from a locked jail cell. We both know how that can happen."

A silvery eyebrow arched as she waved a dismissive hand. "Oh, dear, you are so boring." She gave Cynda another long look. "If you're not willing to participate *fully* in our gathering, I think it's time for you to depart." She pointed at Keats. "Leave Galahad here. I've always wanted to break him in. He can tell you all about it in the morning, providing he'll be able to walk."

"He goes with me," Cynda said.

Nicci's eyes narrowed. She snapped her fingers and the butler appeared at her side.

"They're leaving." She waved an admonishing finger in Keats' face. "Next time, you're here as one of us."

"Point taken," he replied acidly.

As they headed for the door, Cynda glanced over her shoulder. Satyr had finished his task and was sipping from a goblet of wine, slaking his thirst after his exertions. He raised it in her direction, beckoning for her to join him.

She grabbed Keats' sweaty hand. "I've had enough."

7

Alastair maintained his silence during the hansom ride to the Tower of London, mentally preparing himself for whatever lay ahead. He also brooded on Bishop's offhand remark.

*Scotland Yard pays my bills.* It had been bad enough to blunder into Chief Inspector Fisher at Keats' rooms. Now he was stuck in a carriage bound for a crime scene where a member of the Yard would be present. Alastair had no doubt his name would be duly noted and written into some report which would eventually land on Fisher's desk. Fate constantly placed him under that man's scrutiny.

When they reached their destination, Alastair alighted from the carriage with considerable trepidation. The stench of the river instantly enveloped him. He instinctively turned to study the fortress behind them. They were near Traitor's Gate, through which many an unfortunate had been escorted to their imprisonment or death.

Alastair turned at the sound of his companion's voice.

"Where do we go now?" Bishop asked of a nearby constable, one of the Thames Police force. The doctor sounded keen to get on with it.

"The dead man's there, sir," the fellow replied, pointing across the expanse of dark water toward the twin pilings of the new bascule bridge.

Alastair had eagerly followed the newspaper accounts of each stage of the bridge's development. Now he'd be able to stand on one of the piers before it was complete. All it had taken was for someone to die.

"On one of the piers?" Bishop asked.

"Yes, sir. The night watchman found him."

"Snagged on the structure, was he?"

"No, sir. Lying on top."

"On top? A suicide?"

"I couldn't say, sir."

"You saw the body?"

The constable paled, then he swallowed. "Yes."

A pause. "How long have you been on the Thames River force?"

"Five years this December, sir."

"Ah, good man." Bishop turned to Alastair. "Come, let's find out what's got us away from Sagamor's fine brandy. The location is novel, at least."

Alastair wasn't a strong swimmer, and therefore did not relish water that rose much above his waist. As they walked toward the water's edge, he pondered how easily he could drown if he fell into the murky tidal flow.

"Is there a problem, Dr. Montrose?" Bishop asked.

Alastair leapt on the first thing that came to mind.

"Why did you ask the constable how long he'd been on the force?"

"Ah, that. It's my personal barometer. You noticed how he turned chalk-white when I asked about the body?"

"Yes."

"If he were new, I'd expect it. However, this fellow is a Thames copper, five years on. He's seen corpses in all conditions, many of them absolutely revolting. What his reaction tells me is this is going to be a right corker." A moment's pause and then, "Still keen to have a look?"

Alastair frowned and then nodded. "In for a penny..."

"Good. Hopefully you haven't eaten recently."

Near the water's edge, a pair of constables chatted among themselves in hushed tones while a waterman kept glancing toward the pier and back again, plainly wanting to be somewhere else.

Once they were in the boat, Bishop immediately engaged the fellow in conversation as the latter rowed toward the pier closest to the shore.

"How many have been out here?" he asked.

"Oh, about four or so, 'cludin' the big man."

"The one from the Yard?"

"That be 'im. The way the coppers are talkin', 'e's not one to muck about."

"Did you speak to the watchman after he found the corpse?"

"A bit. 'E kept goin' on and on what they done to the body."

Alastair and Reuben traded looks. "As in?"

The waterman paused in his rowing and leaned forward, whispering as if he was revealing a grave secret. "They cut 'im, cut 'im right wicked. I never 'eard of such a thing."

"Like the women in Whitechapel?" Alastair asked.

"Worse!" The man fell silent and put his agitation into the oars, the boat gliding smoothly across the inky water with each muscular pull.

*What have I gotten myself into?* He barely repressed a shudder.

As they drew next to the platform, it dawned on Alastair that the only way to the top consisted of a crude ladder secured to the side of the pier's wooden support structure. For those accustomed to climbing around on wooden scaffolding, the ladder was a luxury. For Alastair, it signaled an opportunity to plunge into the watery depths and perish before someone got around to fishing him out. He wet his lips and took a deep breath to control his fear. Neither action worked. When he muttered something about how precarious the ladder seemed, Bishop chuckled.

"Adds to the adventure," he replied exuberantly. "A tale to recount to one's grandchildren!"

While his companion negotiated upward, Alastair peered through the cross beams into the space beneath the structure. The pilings generated a series of eddies as the water flowed around the wood and concrete. Debris had wormed its way underneath the edifice and become trapped.

*Like I will if I fall in.*

"Your turn," Reuben called down from above.

As Alastair began the climb, he thought of Keats. This sort of nonsense was exactly the type of thing his friend would do without hesitation, relishing every moment of it.

Partway up, one of Alastair's buttons snagged on a rung and he had to arch himself outward to release it. The ladder gave an unnerving groan of protest.

"I wouldn't do that, if I were ya, sir," a bass voice called down. Above him, a massive head peered over the side of the structure. When Alastair reached the top, the voice's burly owner grabbed his arm.

"There ya go, sir," the fellow said, giving him a firm yank that helped him clear the ladder before he had the chance of plunging into the river.

"Good Lord," Alastair muttered and then remembered his manners. "Thank you, Constable."

"Right ya are, sir. His nibs is over there," he said, jerking a thick thumb toward the center of the piling. "Mind where ya walk."

Picking his way carefully across the wooden planks that constituted the present top level of the bridge, Alastair found Bishop in earnest conversation with a man clad in a black suit. When the figure turned at the sound of his approach, Alastair's heart sank.

*Fisher.*

Chief Inspector J.R. Fisher wasn't just from Scotland Yard, he was Special Branch. His presence on the pier was a bad sign.

"Good evening, Dr. Montrose," Fisher said, nonplussed as usual.

"Of course, you would know each other, wouldn't you?" Bishop asked, looking back and forth between them. "The explosives incident."

A brusque nod from the chief inspector. "Precisely."

In the awkward silence that followed, Bishop added, "I asked Dr. Montrose to join me."

Fisher grew pensive. "I wasn't aware you were acquainted with each other."

"We weren't until tonight. We met right before I received the summons. As Dr. Montrose expressed interest in my line of work, I thought it would be a good opportunity for him to observe a case firsthand."

The senior officer held his silence.

"If you prefer that I not be present, Chief Inspector, I will make my way back to the boat and wait there until Dr. Bishop is finished," Alastair offered.

After pondering for a moment, Fisher shook his head. "On the contrary, I believe you should be here, especially in light of the situation."

He waved them forward to a blanket-covered form some fifteen feet away. "The night watchman checks the piers once every few hours to ensure no one is messing about. A bit after nine, he noted a small fire on top of one of them. He rowed out to investigate."

Fisher gestured toward the burnt portion of the platform. "For a time, he thought some of the watermen where having him on, what with the fire and all. Then he saw the corpse."

"Suicide?" Bishop asked.

"Not likely," came the terse reply.

The senior officer knelt, then pulled the covering down to the corpse's waist. Details assailed Alastair's mind: a young man with red hair, thick build, shabby clothes.

"Is he the fellow who delivered the warning last evening?" Fisher asked.

Alastair swallowed heavily. "Yes, it is."

"The warning you spoke of at Sagamor's?" Bishop asked.

Alastair nodded grimly.

The chief inspector rose to his feet. "The constable who first examined the body found a scrap of newspaper in the dead man's hand. It was an article about the theft of the explosives. Both my and Sergeant Keats' names were circled in what appears to be blood. It's why I was summoned."

Bishop claimed a bull's-eye lantern from one of the constables and retreated some distance away. He swept the lantern back and forth like he was signaling a distant ship. He tipped up loose boards with the toe of his shoe, bending over to examine anything that caught his interest.

"What you are doing?" Alastair asked.

"Searching the scene. I know the coppers do the same thing, but I prefer to make my own examination. Often there is evidence left behind. Unfortunately, this location is particularly unfriendly for my purposes." Bishop stopped at the edge of the pier and shone the light on the water. "I wonder..."

The light illuminated off broken boards and other flotsam that slapped against the pier. Alastair joined him, though a step back from the edge. Alarmed when Bishop leaned further out, he grabbed onto the man's arm. "Careful!"

"Oh, right," the doctor said, clearly oblivious to the danger. He handed the lantern back to the nearest constable. Stripping off his coat, Bishop knelt next to the body and then beckoned the constable to move closer.

"Shine it on his head and slowly work your way down the body," Bishop ordered. Then he addressed Alastair, "I'll do a more thorough examination in better surroundings, but at present I wish to get a sense of what might have happened to the fellow."

Bishop tilted the man's head, displaying the gaping neck wound. "Throat cut to the spine. No marks indicating strangulation." He gestured to Alastair. "Roll him toward you."

Alastair knelt and did as commanded, feeling nauseous. The body was not completely stiff.

"Ah, as I thought," Bishop said. "You can let him back down again."

"What were you looking for?"

"Blood. You note there isn't much of it, other than the amount soaked into his shirt. I would suspect he wasn't killed here. He's cold, but that may be because of the ambient temperature. By heavens, it's chilly up here."

As Bishop reached to pull the blanket off the bottom half of the body, Alastair heard the constable shuffle backwards, the light moving with him. Bishop looked up and sighed.

"Fetch the lantern, will you, Dr. Montrose?"

Alastair secured the light and illuminated the body. A moment later, he heard Bishop spout, "My God. Did you find any of the...parts?"

"No," Fisher replied tartly.

The constable hurried away. Before long, the air was pierced by the sound of vigorous retching. Bile rose in Alastair's throat. He tried to keep his eyes above the bloodied mess that had once been the man's groin.

Bishop sent a look in his direction. "If you feel the need to join the constable, please do so away from here. We have quite enough contamination of the scene as it is."

"No, I think I'll hold up," Alastair replied, hoping his bravado was a match for his stomach. A further round of retching indicated another one of the Blue Bottles had found the emasculated corpse too much to handle.

The first constable returned, issuing a hoarse apology.

"Can't be helped, not with something like this," Fisher replied. "Find us more blankets and some rope so we can secure the body before we lower it over the side."

The constable hiked away at a brisk pace, no doubt pleased to be doing something that didn't involve staring at the dead man.

Fisher watched him depart. "There's something else you must see." He beckoned and they followed him. Near a charred section of the platform where the fire had been built, they found a long line of blood with an arrow at the end. It pointed across the Thames toward the white fortress and the portcullis near the waterline.

"So *that's* why he chose this location," Bishop said.

"I'm not following you," Alastair admitted.

Bishop pointed. "Traitor's Gate. The killer is leaving us a message."

"I fear so," Fisher said.

Bishop let out a deep breath. He slowly revolved in a complete circle, staring out into the darkness. "Your murderer is thumbing his nose at you, Chief Inspector. The victim was killed elsewhere, but hauled all the way out here to make a statement. He wasn't just dumped, but mutilated and a fire purposely set to attract the watchman's attention. The body would have been found in the morning for certain, but the killer wanted to orchestrate when you made the discovery. He is, in essence, saying that he can bloody well go anywhere he wants without fear of being caught."

"Sounds like Flaherty," Fisher muttered.

"Sounds like the Ripper, as well."

Alastair's observation earned him instant scrutiny from the other two men. He knew what was required of him, no matter what the consequences. "I wish to be an active part of this investigation, gentlemen. I owe it to the dead man. His decency may have cost him his life."

Fisher and Bishop exchanged looks. "I have no objections," the chief inspector replied.

"Neither do I," Bishop added. "I would appreciate the assistance. I should have a report by late morning, Chief Inspector."

"Excellent. Good evening, Doctors." Fisher tipped his hat and strode away, barking orders that sent constables scurrying in different directions like panicked sheep.

"It will take some time before the body is delivered. I would suggest you get some sleep," Bishop said, pulling a card from his pocket. "I'll be at this address at one, no...two in the morning. That should allow plenty of time for them to move the poor sod to Spitalfields."

Alastair stuck the card in his coat pocket. "Aren't you going back now?"

"No. I want to stay here while they move him."

"I shall be there at the appointed time."

Bishop took another look around. "What a place to leave a body. There's a cunning mind behind this murder. Is that what you'd expect of this anarchist?"

"He's cunning; that we've seen. But this is..." Alastair grew pensive. "I'd expect a man like him to cut the fellow's throat and leave him in an alley, not bring him here. That involved too much risk."

"Why would that be any more risky than obtaining explosives?" Bishop asked.

"All he needs to do is sit quietly until the time comes to set them off. Why taunt the coppers?"

"To feel superior?"

"Perhaps," Alastair replied. "I'm not sure."

"Well, get some rest. We'll meet in a few hours and see what this fellow can tell us."

As Alastair climbed down the ladder, he decided sleep was not needed. Keats had to know. Perhaps this news would drive him out of London and into the safe shelter of his family in Canterbury.

✝

"You didn't appear too shocked," Keats remarked, eyes closing as he sank deeper into the chair.

Cynda removed her outer garments before answering. "That isn't the first orgy I've attended."

Her companion's eyes flew open. "You mean you've actually—"

"No, no. Just watched."

"Oh."

He was at a loss for something to say, a rarity. "You've been to one of her parties as Sir Galahad, then?"

A reluctant nod. "It was a few years back. Once I realized what the Pucks were all about, I left as quickly as I could. It is not proper for a policeman to be at such a thing."

*Doubly so for a Scotland Yard copper.*

"Will you get in trouble for being there tonight?"

He was silent for a time, staring at the fire. "I hope not," he replied in a guarded tone. "The sort who attend Nicci's parties are not the kind to talk about it."

His uncertainty put her on edge. "How does she know what you actually look like?"

"We were introduced before, at a more conventional party. I failed to alter my voice when she met me as Galahad. She's very astute." His eyes weren't meeting hers now. There was more to this story.

"Why didn't you go *en mirage* tonight?"

He gave a one-shouldered shrug, still staring into the fire. "It didn't occur to me until it was too late."

*You're a lousy liar, Mr. Keats.*

"Who is the Satyr?" she asked, remembering how much the strange figure had unnerved her.

His eyes returned to hers. "I don't know. I'd never seen him before this evening."

"Would Nicci know?"

"Probably." He thought for a moment and then shook his head. "No, you cannot ask her. Do *not* go back there. It is clear that neither Nicci nor the butler is to be trusted. You could find yourself in the midst of those debaucheries. You heard her; next time you are expected to participate. They will insist, even by force."

She waved his protest aside. "I have no intention of going back there."

"Good." He noticeably relaxed. "Then that's settled."

*So you'd like to think.*

"That wonderful book you brought me is in my study. I'm just too weary to fetch it. Would you get it for me, please?"

"Sure."

Cynda entered the small room and lit the gas lamp. Her eyes skipped over the maps on the wall adorned with a myriad of colorful pushpins: Keats' unique method of tracking crime within London. Neat stacks of newspapers sat on the desk.

*A tidy room, a tidy mind.*

As she hunted for the items, she noted a magazine article in the center of the desk entitled, *How To Determine the Perfect Wife Through Facial Analysis: Ten Points to Consider.* She snickered until she saw his penciled notation in the margin.

*Jacynda – 9 points out of 10.*

"Oh, great." She was on the sergeant's short list.

He called from the other room, "Did you find it?"

"Ah, yes, I did," she said, grabbing the book. "Just admiring your, um, maps." Her mind was awhirl. She was becoming too embedded in this time period. Rovers roved. They didn't stay put and marry up-and-coming detective-sergeants.

She returned to the front room, a weight on her shoulders. Keats shot her a quizzical look. Had he sent her in there on purpose, knowing she'd see the magazine?

"I've quite enjoyed the story," he remarked, "providing I can stay awake to read."

"Glad to hear it." It was time to leave before the conversation veered in a more serious direction, like it had that time at the boarding house when he'd proposed marriage. Though he'd seemed oddly relieved when she'd refused his offer, that subject clearly hadn't been put to rest yet.

Cynda donned her hat and mantelet. Her host's eyes were closed again.

"Keats." No response.

"Jonathon?"

The eyes blinked open.

"You need to lock the door behind me."

He struggled to his feet.

"Has Alastair seen you recently?"

A nod.

"Did he say everything was fine?"

Another nod.

"You just look so tired."

"I am." After a moment's hesitation, he added, "There is something you should know, since Nicci made an allegation."

"Which is?"

He cleared his throat for effect. "I am most certainly *not* a virgin."

She grinned. "I never believed you were."

As she descended to street level, Cynda heard the locks engage. Once inside a hansom, she sent it south toward her hotel at Charing Cross. Something wasn't right with Keats. He had fallen asleep in the coach on the way back to his rooms, leaning against Cynda's shoulder. He'd murmured a word once or twice, but nothing more. He hadn't even *ventured*, like Alastair accidentally had on the return trip from Colney Hatch—the incident that had led to her discovery of the shifters. Instead, Keats just snored away like he hadn't had a wink of sleep in the last few days.

*Why didn't you shift?* It would have been perfectly acceptable under the circumstances. Keats' half-hearted claim of forgetfulness was just b.s.

Then it came to her in a flash.

She'd treated him with twenty-first century technology the night the Irishman had bashed in his skull, saving him from a choice between blindness or death. In her haste to help him, she may have somehow compromised his ability to shift. It had been a decision she'd not thought twice about.

Until now.

8

*Saturday, 13 October, 1888*

Satyr was currently *en mirage* in one of the two forms that Hugo Effington knew. Like an actor changing characters between scenes, he switched forms at will to keep his quarry off guard. It was highly amusing—Effington actually thought he was a thespian and all this was makeup. The truth would have made the fellow wet himself.

The bully was always easy to locate: he was either at one of his warehouses, at his club, or warming some tart's bed. As of late, there'd been less of the latter as the funds grew tight.

He could tell the moment Effington spied him. There was a slight hitch in the man's gait.

"Good evening, Hugo," Satyr said, knowing how he hated the name.

"What the hell do you want?"

Satyr fell in step, keenly aware of the man's hulking menace. Effington was prone to employ his fists rather than his brains. If he got his hands around your neck, there was little you could do.

Unless you were Lead Assassin.

"How is the *project* progressing?" Satyr asked evenly.

"It is moving forward. I told you that a few days ago."

"All will be ready in time?"

"Yes."

"Is the Irishman behaving himself?"

"Yes. You've got him by the bollocks; he has no choice."

"Much like you."

His companion's gait faltered again. "What do you really want?"

"I heard there was an incident at your party last evening."

Effington's forehead took on a sheen, though the night was chilly.

"It was nothing," he replied. "The police are sorting it out."

"Who was the assassin?"

"I don't know. He was not on the guest list."

"So how did he get in?"

A noticeable pause, which told Satyr that a lie was in the making.

"The butler admitted him. I sacked the fellow for it," Effington replied.

"Really?" Satyr inquired. "Was your butler always so...inefficient?"

Effington didn't respond.

"I see," Satyr said. "You asked what I want: find out the identity of the assassin and where I might locate him."

Although a man of bulk, Effington stopped instantly in his tracks. "He's in jail."

"No, he's not. He escaped overnight."

Effington turned pale. "Good God. I won't be a party to murder."

"Oh, don't trouble yourself, Hugo. Right now, murder is the least of your worries."

Satyr executed a one-eighty and headed in the other direction, ears pricked toward any sudden movement behind him. Instead, he heard Effington swearing under his breath and stomping away. When a hansom rolled by, Satyr turned and watched as Hugo hailed it down and jumped inside, issuing a torrent of abuse at the hapless jarvey.

*He's an absolute barbarian.*

A thought sprang into his mind, causing him to smile. When the time came for Hugo Effington to shuffle off this mortal coil—which would be soon—Satyr knew the perfect ending for such a vile man.

*All I need is a bit of tinder...*

‡

Cynda stared at the gaudy tinplate ceiling above her bed, counting the individual tile squares in each direction as their images wavered in the firelight.

*Seventeen by twelve equals...*

No clue. She tried again. Still nothing.

"Two hundred and four," Mr. Spider offered, perched atop the wooden headboard.

"Thanks," she muttered. It was a sad day when your hallucinations had to do the math for you. Lately, she found herself thinking about how to lace her boots, walk down stairs. She'd hoped the respite in Victorian England would mitigate some of the time lag. It hadn't. She was one step away from forced retirement, despite her boss' claims to the contrary.

The evening had set her nerves on edge, robbing her of needed sleep. Transitives like Keats and the Wescombs didn't trouble her. They were benign. The Pucks, on the other hand, were like piranhas that lurked in the shadowy depths, waiting for you to wade into the water so they could devour you a bite at a time.

She forced her mind back to Defoe. How to find a time traveler who doesn't want to be found? He wasn't like the tourists. They didn't stray very far. He could be anywhere. He could even be back in 2057, and Morrisey might not know.

"Or he could be preparing for another assassination attempt," her delusion suggested helpfully.

"Thanks," she grumbled.

She thumped her pillow in aggravation, further fueling her desire to flip open the interface and vanish. That's how she'd always dealt with the restless feelings—keep on the move.

Despite her increasing delusions, she couldn't bail out of the job when she returned to '057. Morrisey had paid for her medical care after she'd been knifed by Dalton Mimes, a rogue tourist. She owed Morrisey.

*Which is probably why he saved me.* He was adept at manipulating people.

She flopped onto her back, staring at the ceiling again. A quick look up at the headboard revealed that Mr. Spider was gone.

*I can't even maintain a decent hallucination.*

Her interface erupted underneath the pillow, sending vibrations into her molars. She pulled it out and popped open the cover, hoping it wouldn't require her to get out of bed. A couple of quick stem winds activated the screen.

Glowing letters marched across the dial like iridescent ants.

*TPB has issued an official recall for Defoe.*

✠

The nondescript brick building near Bishopsgate Police Station had most likely been used as a warehouse in a previous incarnation. The only thing that made it different from its neighbors was the constable standing at the door.

"Sir?" the fellow asked, his voice betraying his boredom.

"I'm Dr. Montrose," Alastair said. "Dr. Bishop is expecting me."

"Right you are, sir. He's inside."

"Thank you, Constable." Had Keats once drawn duty like this? Surely he had. Still, it was hard to imagine his friend breaking up fights and hauling drunks to jail.

To Alastair's surprise, the building's interior was nearly one hundred feet square, accessed by a set of twin doors. Lit by ceiling-mounted gas lamps, the room emitted a sharp, antiseptic smell, counterpointed by the earthy odor of fresh sawdust rising from the floor. Countless footprints marred the uneven surface. An examining table sat directly under two of the lamps, currently occupied by a sheet-draped form. Nearby, Reuben Bishop looked up from sorting a mound of instruments.

"Ah, there you are. Any difficulty finding the place?"

"No. I've been by here before. I had no notion it was a morgue."

"There are a couple of us who use the building. I occasionally teach classes here, in the vain attempt to entice more students into the profession."

"May I ask..." Alastair hesitated, unsure how his question might be received.

"Go on."

"Why are you not affiliated with St. Mary's, or one of the other institutions?"

Bishop weighed his reply. "That's a fair question. I'm a bit of a maverick, and I can irritate the hell out of certain people. I find I work best outside the framework of an institution, though I have no qualms about St. Mary's."

"You work alone, then?"

"For the most part."

*Then why do you want me here?*

"Why does Scotland Yard use your services instead of the Home Office coroner?"

"You are full of questions this morning." Reuben moved a knife from one position to another. "Did you get some rest?"

Noting that the doctor had not answered his query, Alastair dropped the subject. "Instead of rest, I decided I should let my friend Keats know of Ahearn's death."

"How did he take it?"

"He wasn't at home. No doubt he's on the streets, pushing himself when he should be recovering. I fear complications will arise if he doesn't obtain proper rest."

"Some of us are more driven than others. Personally, I relish nothing more than a leisurely Sunday in bed, preferably with entertaining company." Bishop waggled an eyebrow.

Alastair chuckled. "I can't afford entertaining company."

"Every man can afford a mistress," Bishop replied.

"Not this one."

"Well, while you were attempting to be a loyal friend, a constable located this fellow's priest and he identified the body. Apparently, the deceased's wife is with child, and it was felt that it was best she not see her husband in such a condition."

"A decent precaution." Alastair removed his hat and coat, hanging them on pegs near Bishop's own. He rolled up his sleeves and scrubbed vigorously in the basin of clear water nearby.

"Most don't believe it worthwhile to clean themselves before they conduct a post-mortem. You do. That bodes well, Doctor."

The praise felt genuine. "Please call me Alastair."

"Reuben," was the instant reply, accompanied by a smile. "You said you'd attended a post-mortem in the past?"

"Yes. I watched a few in medical school."

"Well, I do them a bit different than most, so please bear with me."

"I shall."

"Remove the sheet from our poor deceased friend, obtain his height and estimate his weight, make note of any injuries, bruises and such."

Alastair pulled off the sheet, setting it aside. Gazing at the dead man's face and the bloody gash beneath his chin, he murmured, "May God have mercy on your soul."

"Amen," Reuben replied and returned to sorting instruments.

Hours later, Alastair stood in the open doorway, stretching his hands over his head to ease the cramp in his back. The audible crack he elicited did nothing to rouse the dozing constable, still leaning against the brick wall. That had to be an acquired skill.

In the distance, Alastair heard the clock at the Black Eagle Brewery tolling the hour. Six. Just near dawn. He watched an older woman hurrying along with a basketful of fresh flowers, then a lad bent nearly double by the heavy bag of newspapers he had to sell. It reminded him of Davy Butler. He'd not seen much of the boy and his mother in the last couple days. Probably best to check on them to ensure her lung infection had cleared properly. Then there was Lord Wescomb's referral. It seemed his days were filling up, even without the clinic.

Alastair was weary but mentally invigorated. Wescomb had been correct—Reuben Bishop was an excellent instructor. The post-mortem had unfolded at a snail's pace, yet he had learned more in these few hours than he felt his mind capable of grasping.

Behind him, Reuben penned notes at a battered desk. "Once I

am finished, I would like you to review the document. I want to ensure that I did not overlook anything."

"I doubt you did. You are the most thorough of individuals."

"It may not seem so once I am called to give testimony at the inquest."

Quietly closing the door so as not to rouse the snoring constable, Alastair returned to the corpse, arranging the sheet over what remained. They had examined every major organ, including the brain and lungs, dissected the heart, the liver, and removed the stomach and intestines. In many ways, they had completed the mutilation the killer had begun.

Reuben blotted the final sheet of paper and handed the pages to Alastair. Leaning against the wall, as there was no chair available, he studied the report.

As he read of the injuries, images paraded through his mind. Single, lateral incision to the neck, severing the left carotid artery, resulting in syncope, the drop in blood pressure that led to the victim's demise. Extinction of life came shortly thereafter, secondary to massive blood loss. Bruising on the right shoulder. Genital mutilation conducted post-mortem. Incisions were neat, indicative of an assailant who had experience with dissection. Last meal was of potatoes and beef. Lesions on lungs indicative of early-stage tuberculosis, evidence of healed burns on both legs. Time of death estimated sometime between five and eight in the evening.

"I have no issues with the report," Alastair said, placing it on the table.

"Excellent. If you are amenable, I would like to include your name on it."

Alastair hesitated. "I'm not sure, to be honest. If I sign the report, I may be called as a witness. It would deeply trouble me if my somehow inadequate testimony allows this fellow's murderer to go free."

Reuben nodded sagely. "That, you see, is the cross we bear for peering inside God's handiwork. If we are inadequate to the task, an innocent may hang or a killer go free. It is a sobering responsibility."

Should he sign? Ahearn had gambled more than his reputation when he'd delivered the warning. It was only fair that Alastair saw this through to the end. He took up the pen and added his name to the report.

Reuben beamed. "Well done. You've taken a decisive step toward a new career, should you decide to pursue it. I've seen physicians refuse to sign the forms, fearful it would somehow damage their careers should they be required to substantiate their claims in court. You seem not to suffer from that malady."

"My career is already at sea. Besides," Alastair motioned toward the corpse, "he deserves justice."

"You will be compensated for your assistance in this case."

"I hadn't anticipated that. That's very generous."

"Don't be too grateful. We don't get that much per case." Reuben smirked. "Certainly not enough to support a mistress."

He pointed at the pages. "This is a dull recitation of facts. For the moment, let us consider who would most fit the profile of our murderer, given his expertise with the knife."

"Expertise?"

"A single slice, perfectly aligned to sever the artery," his companion observed. "No digging around or hacking like an amateur. This fellow has experience in swift executions, whether of livestock or people."

"I agree," Alastair replied. "There was minimal bruising on the body other than the right shoulder."

"Yet the victim was not beaten senseless, then dispatched. That implies he knew his killer."

"Flaherty," Alastair murmured.

Reuben leaned forward. "You mentioned the Whitechapel killer while we were on the pier. Do you believe this to be his handiwork?"

Alastair shook his head, and then frowned. Perhaps he was overly fixated on the anarchist. "At least I don't believe so."

"Why?" Reuben had asked that question countless times during the post-mortem, pushing Alastair to think through each new finding, each blanket statement he made. In his own way, Reuben was rehearsing for the inquest.

"As far as we know, all of the Whitechapel murder victims were female. They were strangled before their throats were cut. This fellow's hyoid bone was not crushed, though it did show signs of being nicked by a sharp instrument. He was not disemboweled."

"Your conclusion?"

"I do not believe it is the same man. Flaherty..." He caught himself. "Whoever wielded the knife wanted Ahearn to feel the blade as it cut his throat. He wanted him to suffer. Yet, he was castrated after death, which makes little sense." Alastair stifled a yawn with the back of his hand.

"Cutting a throat is much quieter," Reuben remarked, drawing his finger dramatically across his neck. "If someone intended to remove my privates, I would be shouting so loud they could hear me in Mile End."

"Not a total sadist, or at least a cautious one."

"Come, let's rouse the constable and make sure the body is

tended to. Then I'll make copies of this report before we hand it to the proper people."

"Do you always do that?" Alastair asked, surprised.

"Yes. Proper recordkeeping is just as important as good forensic technique. You'd be amazed at how often papers get lost, on purpose or otherwise."

This time, Alastair's yawn broke free. "I apologize."

Reuben contributed one of his own. "A good night's work, Doctor. You have definite potential."

Alastair nodded wearily at the compliment. He paused at the doorway and gave the shrouded corpse one last look.

What if that were Keats lying there? Would he have been able to cast aside his emotions and perform the final medical rite upon his friend?

*Dear God, never let it come to that.*

✦

Satyr and his superior pulled their chairs up to the laden breakfast table.

"Magnificent spread," the Ascendant observed. "What news of Miss Lassiter? I did not note an article in the paper reporting her demise."

"She is still alive," Satyr said, for the moment ignoring the sausages. "There are mitigating circumstances."

"Such as?"

"I shall get to that in a moment. You should be aware that I attended one of Nicci's gatherings last evening."

The Ascendant sighed. "Another one of Miss Hallcox's bacchanals, I gather?" Satyr nodded. "I do wish the Pucks would learn to restrain themselves."

"Not likely."

"You'd say that, of course. You're one of the worst, Mr. S."

Satyr executed a lecherous smile. "I enjoy life."

"You know my dislike of such behavior; I have lectured you on that often enough. How does this relate to Miss Lassiter?"

Satyr gave his report of the party and its unexpected guests. Only after completing it did he reach for the sausages and eggs.

The Ascendant dabbed at his mouth with a linen napkin. "Sergeant Keats, you say? Why would the man not be *en mirage*? That is most intriguing."

"That was a puzzle. From his startled reaction, I suspect he did not know a gathering was in progress."

"Ah, that might be it." The Ascendant placed the napkin into his lap. "I surmise the only reason the previous Ascendant allowed Miss Hallcox to play her games is that he received sexual favors from her."

"He did," Satyr replied, "and that made him vulnerable to her blackmail."

A knowing nod. "I shall not make the same mistake. Deliver my personal warning that she is not to have further contact with anyone at Scotland Yard. She must fall in line, or pay the price."

Satyr quirked an eyebrow. That would be an interesting kill. His mind began running through potential scenarios.

Unaware of Satyr's mental foreplay, the Ascendant continued, "As to Miss Lassiter, end her life today, will you? Make it look like an accident."

"On the contrary, sir, I heartily recommend you allow the woman more time to find the fellow who tried to kill me. She is tenacious. If she does not uncover him, I can fulfill the contract. If she does, then I'll kill them both."

The Ascendant's brow furrowed. "I am not sure if I agree with your suggestion. Like the proverbial cat, Miss Lassiter appears to have nine lives, and if she continues in her investigations she may cripple our efforts."

"I would not let her get that close, sir."

"I find it remarkable how you seek to delay the inevitable when it comes to this woman."

Satyr opted for honesty. "I will sincerely regret the day Miss Lassiter is no longer among us. I sense there is more to her story than we perceive. To that end, I would prefer not to rush her execution."

"You must do better than that, Mr. S. You are sounding almost...sentimental."

"The assassin called Miss Lassiter *a fool*. From her reaction, I swear she knew him."

"Troubling," Ascendant replied. It was one of his favorite words. He dumped three lumps of sugar into his tea and stirred it while he thought. He was not an impulsive man, not like their previous leader, which meant he'd probably last longer. "Very well, let Miss Lassiter live for the time being."

"Perhaps this new menace, as you call him, may just terminate her for us."

"That would be ideal. The perfect kill is when the blood is on someone else's hands."

"You sound like an assassin," Satyr said with some amusement.

"That is a compliment from someone of your accomplishments."

"Thank you, sir." His hand wavered over the choice of

marmalade or fresh grape preserves. He chose the latter. It was always good to embrace new experiences.

"Keep an eye on Sergeant Keats. Should he become troublesome, do the honors...as Flaherty, of course. In that way we can assure he will have no mercy from the police when the time comes."

"Indeed, sir," Satyr replied.

The Ascendant changed direction, as he often did without warning. "What of the Irishman?"

"He continues his tasks. I did have to remove one of his subordinates. The fellow was trying to find the girl and getting too close for my comfort. I used him as an example for some associates I am training at present."

"Excellent," the Ascendant replied, nodding his approval. "What of Hastings? How is he managing The Conclave?"

"Fairly well. Dr. Montrose remains a thorn in his side."

"No doubt. And Mr. Livingston?"

"He's quiescent. Nothing much out of him. Nothing that ruffles Hastings' feathers, at least."

"That troubles me. Quiet men hatch plots."

"I have someone watching him," Satyr replied. *Someone he would never suspect.* "I had a word in Effington's ear last night."

"Is he staying in line?"

"At present. I don't trust him. Mrs. Effington went missing right after the party. From what I overheard at the jail, the police believe she committed suicide in the Thames."

That stopped the Ascendant in mid-chew. He washed down the food with a gulp of tea. "How extraordinary. Do you think perhaps the assassin was after Effington instead of you, and that she assisted in some manner?"

Satyr felt affronted. "I doubt it." He lifted the toast halfway to his mouth and then paused. "Oh, and that office manager Trimble met with a hideous end."

"What sort?"

"His body, or what's left of it, will be found on the train tracks near Brixton Station. A suicide. Or at least that's the way it will appear."

"How dreadful," the Ascendant replied with false sincerity. "Anything else I should know?"

"We're out of toast," Satyr replied.

"Then do ring the bell, will you?"

9

Scotland Yard was a rat's nest of constables, detectives and inspectors, all entombed in a mausoleum of paperwork. In stark contrast, the interior of Chief Inspector Fisher's office confirmed that its occupant possessed an ordered mind. Stacks of paper were arranged in neat columns along one wall. The desk was immaculate, and the single window clean enough to allow a few rays of muted sunlight to make their way inside.

As he waited in the relative quiet of the office, Alastair glanced at his companion. Reuben looked exhausted, but a twinkle still resided in his eyes. There were footsteps outside the door, voices, and then the senior police officer entered the room.

"Sergeant Keats will not return to work anytime soon. That is all I am willing to say on the matter, Inspector."

Now that he knew the conversation was about his friend, Alastair turned to study the large man standing at the door.

"Shirking his duty, I'd bet," the fellow said. "Like as not he's with some whore in a knocking shop, banging away and bragging about his exploits. You don't see him for what he is, sir. I do. He's nothing more than a puffed-up garden gnome—"

Alastair rose from his seat. "You must be Inspector Ramsey. Keats has spoken of you...repeatedly."

Ramsey expelled an explosive grunt. "I can just imagine what that pretty boy has to say."

"As Sergeant Keats' physician, I assure you that his head injury precludes such vigorous activity."

A snort. "I doubt it. He's a clever one. Likes to play his games."

The chief inspector interjected, "I will inform you when Keats is ready to return to duty, Inspector. That will be all."

The glare deepened. "As you wish." The door thumped closed behind him.

Fisher sank into his chair as the sound of receding boots filled the hall. "I can't leave the two of them in the same room, they so detest each other."

Alastair took his seat. "It is easy to see why. You'd think the inspector would have the good sense to acknowledge that Keats is his intellectual superior."

"Not every case is solved by outsmarting the criminal. There are times when plodders like Ramsey have their place. If I could only get Keats to see that."

Reuben sniggered. "Plodders," he murmured. "I never thought I'd hear you employ *that* word, Chief Inspector."

An arched eyebrow. "I'm aware of what the public thinks of us, Dr. Bishop. I read the papers. *Punch*, in particular, seems to delight in rendering us as inefficient, bumbling morons. I grow weary of it."

"Then let us help you," Reuben said, pointing toward the papers in the center of Fisher's desk. "Our report on the Ahearn post-mortem lies just there."

The chief inspector pulled the papers closer and read each without comment. To keep himself occupied, Alastair tried to disconnect a loose thread from the cuff of his coat. The cuff was wearing thin, even though this was his best suit. He disliked the idea, but he would have to spend a portion of the money Cynda had given him on a new coat, if only to maintain a professional appearance during his hospital duties. He dared not give his superiors further cause for displeasure.

"Death caused by syncope secondary to the severing of the left carotid artery," Fisher recited. "Mutilations to the genitalia were conducted post-mortem." He leaned into his chair, tenting his fingers in front of him. "Well, that is a blessing, at least."

"If there can be a blessing in a man's death," Reuben replied.

A solemn nod from the chief inspector. "Your report states you believe the killer is right-handed."

"Indeed. The killing stroke was clean and sure, from the front, the cut deeper on the right. He knew what he was about. I would hazard a guess that he's a slaughterman or a butcher."

"A butcher, no doubt, whether by trade or avocation," Fisher remarked. "I appreciate your work on this, Dr. Bishop." The chief inspector's eyes darted to the other man. "And yours as well, Dr. Montrose."

The chief inspector stood, signaling Alastair and his companion to do the same.

As the doctors reached the door, Fisher added, "Flaherty was once employed on a cattle boat. According to a few of our sources, he can kill and gut a cow faster than any man out there."

"It may be that his talent is not confined to animals," Reuben observed.

"Does Keats know about this?" Fisher asked.

"No, not yet," Alastair replied, not caring to reveal that the sergeant was willfully disobeying orders. "I shall see him this afternoon and relate the news." *And give him a piece of my mind.*

To Alastair's surprise, Fisher accompanied them outside the building and into the courtyard. Noise poured out of the Rising Sun, a nearby pub.

"Excuse me, but I need to speak to Dr. Montrose...in private," Fisher explained.

Reuben accepted the abrupt dismissal with a graceful tip of his hat. "As you wish." With a nod toward Alastair, he set off.

"Walk with me a bit, will you, Doctor? We need to discuss a matter out of the earshot of Scotland Yard," Fisher said.

They covered a considerable distance before the chief inspector spoke again.

"Are you aware of the attempted assassination the other night?"

"I seem to remember hearing something about it," Alastair evaded.

"There's scant mention of it in the papers, though that will surely change once the Fourth Estate learns more of the details."

"Why does this concern me, Chief Inspector?"

"Because your Miss Lassiter was involved. She was the one who kept the assassin from completing his task."

Jacynda had not mentioned that stray detail. "Tell me what happened," Alastair said, steeling himself for what would follow. He listened to the chief inspector's tale in consternation, growing more agitated with each passing moment.

"As if that wasn't astounding enough," Fisher continued, "the assailant vanished from his cell the very moment Miss Lassiter came to visit him."

That he already knew, but it came as little consolation. Why hadn't she told him the whole story?

Fisher's tone turned flinty. "This is all very troubling, Doctor. What do you know about this woman?"

"That she is from New York," was Alastair's guarded reply.

"And?" Fisher prodded.

"Very little else, Chief Inspector." *At least nothing you'd believe.*

"Could she be involved with anarchists?"

Alastair worked to keep his tone neutral. "I doubt that very much."

"Well, to resolve my curiosity, I shall be sending an enquiry to America to learn more about her business here in London."

"I do not feel she poses a threat, Chief Inspector. She is more a well-meaning busybody, if anything." Alastair could only imagine Jacynda's response to that description.

"I see. Nevertheless, on the more critical matter, if this would-be assassin is one of yours, he must be returned to our custody in short order."

Alastair's chest tightened. So *that was the purpose of this little chat*. "Who do you believe was the target?"

"The odds-on favorite was the prince, which should indicate to you the degree of pressure we are under. I have already been called in front of Police Commissioner Warren, twice, lest I fail to comprehend the gravity of the situation. The Queen is demanding answers. Prisoners do not simply disappear from jail cells, Doctor. It's not done."

*What a disaster.* "I shall speak to my counterparts to see if they know anything of this incident," Alastair said, his mind reeling.

"Do that. I will not tolerate assassins of any stripe, be they Irish, American or otherwise. I intend to convey that message to Lord Wescomb as well, in the strongest possible terms."

"I understand."

Fisher relaxed slightly. "Do you have any notion why Miss Lassiter always seems to be in the middle of significant events?"

"To be honest, Chief Inspector, I believe she seeks to be in just such places."

A shake of the head. "Extraordinary," Fisher muttered before hiking in the direction of Scotland Yard.

"Foolhardy is a better word," Alastair said softly.

‡

Keats' door opened to a narrow chink. The resident gave Alastair a bleary-eyed stare, creasing into a deep frown. His right hand held a partially obscured truncheon.

"What do you want?"

"I have some news," Alastair replied, mindful of the neighbors.

Keats continued to eye him warily. "Prove you are truly Alastair."

"We proposed marriage to the same woman, and were both denied."

Clearly disgruntled, Keats jammed the truncheon into the umbrella stand near the door and waved his friend in.

The doctor engaged the locks as Keats sank into his chair. "Where were you last night?" Alastair asked.

"Umm...I...spent some time with Jacynda."

"I didn't think you were well enough to court," Alastair replied briskly.

"I wasn't courting her. She had questions about the Transitives, and I was attempting to be of assistance."

*I should've known she'd try that.* Alastair glowered. "Would this have something to do with Jacynda's involvement in foiling an assassination?"

"So you've heard about all that, have you?"

"Not from her—she was scant on details when we last spoke. Fisher told me everything, including what happened at the police station. He is convinced the fellow is one of ours, as he put it."

Keats groaned. "He may be right. Given the mysterious circumstances of the escape, I suspect it was a Virtual."

Alastair's mouth dropped open. "Do you mean to say they really exist?"

Keats nodded.

"Well, that might explain why there are times that I have sensed someone on the street, but been unable to pinpoint the source. Most unnerving."

"Oh, they're around. I've never met one, at least not that I'm aware of." He scratched near his bandage. "So what brings you to my doorstep in such a disagreeable mood? "

Alastair sat in the chair nearest the fire, warming his hands and doing his best to snuff out the flash of jealousy that had nearly overtaken him a moment ago. He and the sergeant had agreed to undertake a friendly rivalry for Jacynda's affections. Now that it was playing out, he disliked the bargain intensely.

"Johnny Ahearn is dead," he finally replied. "His body was found on one of the Tower Bridge piers last evening."

"My God." Keats shook his head in dismay. "He has a wife. She's pregnant with their first child. He told me he was selling information so he could afford to move his family out of Rotherhithe to somewhere less..." Keats' voice faltered. "Damn." He wiped the back of his hand over his mouth, staring into the fire. A thin wisp of smoke curled upward from the flames.

"How did he die?" he asked.

"His throat was cut and his genitals mutilated."

Keats' face flushed with anger. "That bastard Flaherty!"

"He may not be the killer," Alastair said, echoing Reuben's caution.

"Of course he was. The man's a vile beast. I swear I will see him hang at Newgate for this!"

"I assisted at the post-mortem this morning," Alastair continued, ignoring his friend's outburst. "He died quickly. The mutilations occurred after his death."

"You? Why were you involved?"

The doctor related his encounter with Reuben Bishop and the events that led to his time on the bridge pier.

Keats' anger faded into sadness. "That brings me some comfort, at least. I have heard Fisher speak well of Dr. Bishop."

Alastair took a breath and slowly let it trickle out. "As a friend, I implore you to leave London."

"So you can have more time with Jacynda, I suppose?" Keats delivered with a flippant smirk.

His weak attempt at humor sliced to the bone. "I don't want to be the one to tell her you got your throat cut," Alastair retorted.

The sergeant leaned back in his chair with a lengthy sigh. "Perhaps I shall visit my family in Kent," he said in a low voice. "It would be advantageous to all."

Their eyes met. "I should go. I have a patient to call on," Alastair said as he rose. "Send a note round to my boarding house if you decide to leave. If not, I'll come see you tomorrow."

A nod. "When is Ahearn's funeral? I'd like to arrange a donation to the widow. I don't want her to have to walk the streets to put food in her child's mouth."

"I can handle that for you."

A smile of relief. "Thank you."

Alastair reached the door, and then turned. The sergeant was watching him through bloodshot eyes. "Have you been resting?"

"It's been hard. My head hurts too much."

"You are taking the headache powders?"

"Yes."

"Then let me put it bluntly: stop being a fool and allow yourself time to heal, do you understand? There are others at the Yard who can find Flaherty."

"Ramsey couldn't find his arse with both hands!"

"Inspector Ramsey isn't the only one at the Yard," Alastair shot back.

Keats sagged further in his chair. "I suppose it doesn't matter either way. I still can't go *en mirage*."

"Just allow yourself time to heal. I spoke with Lord and Lady Wescomb about your problem, and they said it often accompanies a head injury. Rest is the best cure." Alastair paused. "I do have one further request. If you have any influence with Jacynda, please try to have her be more circumspect. She ignores my pleadings."

"As she does mine," Keats commiserated. "She is keen to find the missing assassin for some reason or another."

"Jacynda's always keen to find something or someone. She's not using her head."

Keats let out a bitter laugh. "Who are we to talk? I am hunting a monster, you're chasing a dream and she is pursuing a phantom. I think we all need a holiday in Kent."

With a jolt, Alastair realized how much his life had changed in only a few weeks, how far it had drifted from that dream Keats had spoken of.

‡

Per Morrisey's order that she keep hunting for Chris' watch, Cynda was out on yet another wild-goose chase. She might be one of the best Rovers in the business, adept at finding people in all time periods, but locating Chris' interface was only one step less impossible than finding the elusive Defoe. She'd already lost count of how many shops she'd visited over the last week. There were so many, she now had a script of how the visits played out, lest someone in 2057 ever made a VidBio of her exploits:

*Cue intrepid Time Rover—enter watch/pawn shop door. Bell above door jingles, clangs, falls off its chain and lands at Rover's feet. Resident cat hisses at, trips or ignores Rover.*

*Cue the owner. "Mornin'/afternoon/evenin', miss. How might I help you?"*

*Rover responds: "I'm looking for a unique pocket watch."*

That was where it always fell apart. To Victorians, a unique pocket watch had curious engravings or a particularly stylish dial or had once been owned by the Duke of Wellington. She never believed that last one. If the duke had owned all the pocket watches attributed to him, he'd have had one for each day of the year.

She'd study the different watches, shake her head and leave. Sometimes it was an easy exit; sometimes she had to get huffy if the owner wouldn't leave her alone. The pawn shop owners were the worst. Once you were in their shops, they expected you to buy something just for breathing their air.

Cynda pushed opened the door to yet another shop. Five minutes later she was on the street again, empty-handed.

"Maybe it *is* at the bottom of the Thames," she muttered.

As she headed down the street, her shadow was still under the lamp post, supposedly enjoying the latest edition of the *Times*. He'd followed her from the Charing Cross Hotel. *TPB or Guv?* It was hard to tell nowadays.

She purposely walked past him, waiting for her interface to sniff him out. Nothing. That meant he still could be from the future, just minus an Essential Records Chip. Illegal, but it had been known to happen.

*Or a Victorian who just doesn't fit in.*

A block later, her shadow was gone, as best she could tell. Didn't mean he still wasn't there.

"Paranoia, thy name is Rover," a voice said near her ear.

She angled her eyes sideways to see Mr. Spider riding on her shoulder.

Now that was just too weird.

‡

The grim news of Ahearn's death was too much for Keats to take sitting down. Despite the doctor's warning, the "invalid" was back on Flaherty's trail. This time, he was in search of the office manager from the explosives company: the one who had so conveniently resigned after the forged orders came to light.

When he finally found the boarding house and introduced himself as a copper, the landlady didn't have good news.

"Mr. Trimble left yesterday," she said, swiping a worn broom over the front stairs.

Keats let his disappointment show. "Did he say where he was going?"

Swipe, swipe. "No, sir. Just paid up and went. That's the way all of 'em should be," she said. She moved down a stair.

"Any notion where he's from?" he persisted.

"No, sir. Didn't stay that long, really. Came here right after the Summer Bank Holiday."

"Did he leave anything behind?"

A shake of the head as she leaned against the broom. "He went off with a constable."

*What?* "Did you see his number?"

"Didn't care. He said he'd come to collect Mr. Trimble, and off they went. I don't know anything more. Now good day to you." Her sweeping resumed with agitated strokes.

Keats walked wearily toward the omnibus stop. The facts didn't add up. Trimble started work in early August and the break-in occurred at his office in late September, but supposedly nothing was stolen. Then Flaherty acquired three loads of explosives without paying a single pence, using the stamped stationary from Trimble's office as promissory notes. Nearly a fortnight later, the office manager gave his notice and vanished with some constable. Because of the anarchists' involvement, this was clearly a Special Branch investigation.

"Why would someone else be working this case?" Keats muttered.

If he reported this new development to Fisher, his superior would be furious that his sergeant was out there taking unnecessary risks. If he didn't let Fisher know the latest, it might hamper the hunt for Flaherty. As a copper, Keats had little choice. He'd write up a report tonight and send it to the chief inspector. If he were lucky, it wouldn't result in anything more than a tongue-lashing.

While waiting for the omnibus, Keats purchased a *Daily Telegraph* and sifted through the pages. There was a small article about a supposed assassination plot at a Mayfair residence. The police had no comment at this time. He found an article about Johnny Ahearn's death. An inquest was scheduled for Monday next. If by then he could go *en mirage,* he would attend.

After more page flipping, an article on page ten caught his interest.

### Local Clerk Found Dead on Railway

The omnibus came and went as he stood there, riveted by the gruesome story. Mr. Harrison Trimble, of Hinchley Wood, had flung himself off a train near Brixton Station late last evening. A suicide note in his pocket claimed extreme depression.

"How convenient," Keats grumbled, folding the newspaper and jamming it under his arm. Another lead had evaporated like mist under a full sun. Even more disturbing was the realization that Flaherty might have a constable under his control.

10

If the hotel maid was troubled by the fact that two men had called upon Cynda in the course of one evening, she did not betray it. Her discretion was rendered all the more extraordinary by the fact that the first caller was a royal equerry bearing a gift box from His Royal Highness the Prince of Wales.

The upshot of the first visit was a necklace. It nestled at the bottom of a velvet-lined case, a single large pearl set inside a circlet of gold. Time Immersion rules said it was illegal to bring such a gift back to 2057. Cynda decided to keep it anyway. Returning it to the sender would raise too many questions.

Her second visitor of the evening wasn't nearly as polite.

"Dr. Montrose says he must speak to you on a matter of your health, miss," the maid said, waiting primly at the door for Cynda's verdict.

*Health?* "Allow him to come to my room." Cynda closed the door and parked herself in the chair near the fire and her cup of tea. Keats' welfare flitted through her mind. She shook her head. Alastair had said something about a matter of her health.

The doctor was shown in a few minutes later, wearing a perturbed expression that told her she should have left him cooling his heels in the lobby.

"Want some tea?" Cynda asked after the maid had curtsied and left.

"No."

She knew that clipped tone. There were a number of reasons as to why he might be peeved. She'd have to wait until he revealed his hand, or risk fanning his ire.

Alastair removed his outer coat, hanging it and his bowler on the coat tree and then strode to the couch opposite her. As he sat, his brown eyes remained fixed on her. The bags underneath them were more pronounced.

*Best to get this over with.* "So what have I done this time?" she asked.

A frown formed. "I heard an amazing tale about a young woman who, in the midst of a party, grappled a man to the floor after he shot at the Prince of Wales."

She put on her game face. "Really? Sorry I missed it."

The doctor's moustache twitched. He rose from the chair. "Oddly enough, I spoke with that young woman the morning after the incident, yet she failed to mention her involvement. I had to learn of it from Chief Inspector Fisher."

*Fisher again.* "You sure you don't want any tea?"

"No, I do not want tea!" he barked, now pacing back and forth between the window and the chair where she sat. He reminded her of one of those windup toys kids used to have before everything went robotic. "You're acting so oddly, you have Fisher wondering about you. He's issuing official enquiries to determine your background."

*Ah, dammit. I'll need a back story if I stay here much longer.*

"Why didn't you tell me what really happened?" he pressed.

"I didn't want to get another one of your lectures about my unladylike behavior."

His eyebrow crooked upward. "I wasn't aware that I was so inclined. You make me sound like a tyrant."

*No, just a pain in the ass.* "Where I come from, the rules are different. We both know I fall considerably short of the Victorian ideal of womanhood."

He halted near the window, back to her, posture rigid. "That is not the issue and you know it."

"Then tell me what's bothering you."

"Your attitude. You demand I help you, then give little in return."

There was more. "So what's the real problem, Doc?"

When he turned to face her, he looked older. "Keats might be Flaherty's next target. The man who warned me about the threat to the clinic has just been murdered. According to him, Flaherty is also hunting for our friend."

"Does Keats know?"

"Yes, he does. I'm surprised he didn't mention it to you last night."

Inside, she fumed. *You idiot. Why didn't you say something?* She never would have hauled him out on the streets if she'd known—especially if he weren't *en mirage.*

"He didn't bother," she said. "No matter what, I have to find out what's happening, Alastair. Something doesn't feel right about all this."

The doctor took a step toward her, his face set. "The Conclave will not hesitate to rid themselves of someone they consider a threat. They will not act as boldly with me now that I'm a member. If you agree to stay out of this, I shall make further enquiries on my own."

"No deal."

"Jacynda—"

"This is my job, Alastair. I don't tell you how to be a physician."

He shook his head in frustration. "So be it."

A moment later, Alastair was out the door, barely taking the time to gather his hat and coat.

She let out a whoosh of pent-up air.

"Well, *that* was enlightening," Mr. Spider said, crawling along the top of the couch. He settled on one of the carved rosettes. "The doctor lectures you; you skewer his ego. Doesn't that sound familiar?"

"No, it doesn't," Cynda retorted.

"Your brother always treated you the same way," the arachnid observed.

Before she could deliver a comeback, the blue illusion was gone.

✚

Desmond Flaherty sought refuge from the streets. Scores of candles flickered inside the chapel, yet they seemed to hold little of the darkness at bay. It was late evening, and there were only a few parishioners present: an old lady, a young couple, and a grubby vagrant, snoring with his mouth open.

Flaherty genuflected and crept toward a pew near the front. Just because this was God's house didn't mean some bastard wouldn't try to kill him on hallowed ground. After another look around, he knelt, crossed himself and closed his eyes.

*Sweet Mary, help me. I can't find her. They'll kill her sure as anythin', once I'm no use. Mother of God, save her.*

Fiona. Just sixteen, with the face of an angel and the will of a warrior. Like her mother, God rest her. He'd never have let his only child near that bastard Effington if he'd known. He'd have killed anyone to protect her, sacrificing his soul to hellfire for eternity to keep her safe.

And he'd failed. Paddy hadn't been able to find where they'd taken her. So far, neither had Johnny Ahearn. He crossed himself again, lowering his head.

Flaherty felt someone slip into the pew next to him. He slid his fingers into a pocket, touching the reassuring steel of the knife.

"Good evening, my son."

Father Nowlan. Flaherty left his hand in place. With the *strange ones*, you never knew. They could look like anyone. He only knew the one with the voice of the devil, the one that held his daughter's life in the balance. That bastard could be sitting next to him at this very moment.

"Good evenin', Father," he replied cautiously.

The cleric caressed his rosary and kissed it, twice. It was truly Nowlan. That was the sign they'd set between them. Flaherty let his caution drop a notch.

"Have ya found her yet?" the priest asked.

"No, Father. Johnny's lookin' for her. I saw him yesterday mornin'. He's gettin' close, he said."

"Too close." Father Nowlan spoke gently. "The rozzers found him last night. His throat was slit."

"Oh, sweet Jesus," Flaherty whispered, crossing himself. He wiped a grimy hand across his moist eyes. "It's my fault, Father. I kept pushin' him."

"He did it of his own will," the cleric replied.

"True enough, but it still cost him dear." He looked down at his hands. "These *strange ones* are crazy bastards. Ya never know who they'll look like."

"I've heard talk of them before," Nowlan replied. "I never believed in all that...until now."

Flaherty rubbed his stubbled jaw. "I have to do what they tell me, or they'll cut her up and leave her naked on the street, like one of the Ripper's whores." He shook his head in frustration. "I don't dare cross 'em."

"Do ya have any notion what they're up to with the explosives?" the cleric asked.

Flaherty shook his head. "I wager it's somethin' bad, though."

"They're closing that clinic on Church Street. There was talk about bombing it."

"I heard the rumor. I had Johnny warn the doc, easy-like. Told him to use my name if he had to scare him some."

"Why?"

"A few pieces of dynamite are missin' from the load. I got no love for anyone who helps the rozzers, but I'll be damned if I'll let anyone blow up a bunch of people just to get to one man. That ain't right."

Nowlan placed a comforting hand on Flaherty's arm. "I'll keep praying for yer daughter. Just remember that God sends us aid in very strange ways. Maybe yer help is already here, and ya don't know it."

Flaherty shook his head. "I don't know about that." He began to quake. "I'm so afraid for her, what they've been doin' to her..."

The priest's grip tightened. "God never turns His back on any of us."

Flaherty crossed himself and shook his head in despair. "Will you hear my confession, Father?"

"Of course, my son."

Desmond Flaherty retrieved the silver cross from under his shirt and kissed it, tears filming his eyes. It was his wife's. He'd carried it with him ever since her death that day in Belfast. The day the rozzers killed her.

He swallowed hard and began. "Forgive me, Father, for I have sinned enough for ten men, and my evil has come back on my dear Fiona."

✚

No matter how many times Alastair entered No. 43, the building continued to confuse him. As was customary, the Artifice Club's first-floor steward escorted him to the appropriate door. Like some child's parlor game, the door changed each day. Only the steward knew which door belonged to which social organization.

Alastair marched up the two flights and into the antechamber. Ronald, the Eighth Room Steward, welcomed him warmly, his royal blue livery turned out to perfection.

"Good evening, Ronald." He removed his coat and bowler and handed them over. "Are the others here?"

"Indeed they are. There was, however, some discussion as to whether or not you would be present this evening, sir."

"As in, they hoped I would not be?" Alastair queried.

A nod, accompanied by the faintest of smiles.

"Well, then, I am pleased to disappoint them."

The smile widened. "As always, sir."

Upon hearing Alastair's arrival announced, three heads swung in his direction. At least this time they weren't *en mirage* as the Horsemen of the Apocalypse.

George Hastings lounged in his chair, brandy in hand. From the reddish glow on his face, it wasn't his first. He sucked on a cigar, expelling smoke into the air like a coke furnace.

"Ah, there you are," Hastings greeted him in his characteristic booming voice. "I thought you'd decided not to join us."

Alastair let the jibe pass. Cartwright, seated to the right of Hastings, watched the doctor nervously. When they'd first met, he'd adopted Pestilence's form. Cartwright took his cues from

Hastings, who'd been War.

Alastair settled into his predecessor's chair. Stinton had resigned, choosing to tend to his Satsuma pottery collection rather than deal with The Conclave's convoluted politics. In many ways, Alastair envied him.

"Good evening, gentlemen," he said.

The fourth member of The Conclave finally spoke. "Good evening, Doctor." Malachi Livingston was *en mirage* again—not as Death this time, but a human form. Alastair had never seen him as he truly was. He wondered if any of the others had caught on.

"Mr. Livingston," Alastair replied politely. Turning toward Hastings, he asked, "Do we have any business to attend to?"

"Not as such," was the brusque reply.

"Then I have something that needs our consideration." An indifferent shrug came his way.

Alastair selected his words carefully. It was paramount that Fisher's knowledge of the Transitives remain hidden. The more highly ranked and powerful the Knower, the more likely The Conclave would demand some overt action. Discovery remained their most potent fear. If the assassin were truly one of their own, this might prove the final blow to their anonymity.

Alastair laid out the bare essentials—the attempted assassination, who the target might have been, and that the would-be killer might be a Transitive.

One of Hastings' bushy eyebrows rose dramatically. "Our sort do not go about assassinating royalty, Doctor."

"Well, there was that attempt on—" Cartwright interjected.

"*English* Transitives do not do such things," Hastings replied, putting an end to his cohort's protest.

Alastair pressed on. "After his arrest, this fellow vanished from his cell. The police are at a loss as to how he escaped."

"How did you learn about this, Doctor?" Livingston asked.

Alastair embroidered the truth. "I was at Scotland Yard and overheard a conversation."

"Why were you there?" Hastings asked suspiciously.

"I assisted with a post-mortem for one of their cases."

Hastings chuffed in disapproval, an explosion of smoke exiting his nose and mouth. "This has nothing to do with us. If the fellow has gone missing, someone must have slipped him a key or bribed one of the jailers."

Alastair bluffed. "If he were a Virtual, then all he'd need is an open door."

"Nonsense," Hastings retorted. "They don't exist."

"Are you sure?" Livingston asked, leaning forward.

A gruff shake of the head. "They are mere legends. No one would care to endure the *Rite de la Mort* twice." Hastings turned back to Alastair and tossed the cigar stub into the fire. "This is not our concern, Doctor."

"Then what is our concern, sir? As I remember, you were quite keen to involve yourself in my affairs."

"We felt you presented a threat."

"Yet this assassin does not?"

"You do not understand how we work, Doctor," Hastings replied. "Your...abrupt addition to The Conclave has put us at a bit of a disadvantage."

"A disadvantage of your own making," Alastair said. "If you hadn't been intent on destroying my clinic and running me out of town, I wouldn't be one of you now."

A snort, followed by a long drag on a new cigar. "You pushed your way in, so now you have to deal with the consequences."

"Which are?"

"Behaving like a gentleman."

There came a low chuckle from Livingston. "Come now, Hastings. If that were a requirement for membership, you'd have been out long ago."

"I dislike your tone," Hastings growled.

"I dislike you, so we're on even footing," Livingston shot back.

Ronald entered, added more wood to the fire and then exited, breaking the tense moment. Alastair wondered if he'd done it on purpose.

Livingston leaned back in his chair. Hastings continued to glower.

"Despite the fact that we cannot tolerate each other, the attempted assassination is the most important matter facing us at present," Alastair said. "Discreet enquiries need to be made."

"That is not our purview," Hastings replied. He waved his cigar hand dismissively, scattering ashes across the floor. "Others will handle that."

"Who else is there?" Alastair quizzed.

Hastings muttered something under his breath. "If you will excuse me, I have more convivial acquaintances with whom to spend my time." He glared at Alastair. "You're pushing too hard, Doctor. Sit back and enjoy the brandy. We don't need crusaders in our midst."

As Alastair opened his mouth to respond, Livingston's hand gently touched his sleeve.

Hastings departed, Cartwright following in his tracks. As the pair collected their garments in the antechamber, Livingston rose from his chair and gestured to the gaming table.

"Chess, Doctor?"

"No."

Livingston ignored his warning tone and crossed to the table. "I think a game would do you good, help you focus your displeasure."

"I am not interested in games, Livingston."

Livingston sat down at the table with a sardonic grin. "Don't be boorish."

Alastair grudgingly hauled himself across the room. There was the sound of a door closing and then footsteps on the stairs as the other two members departed.

"Ah, that's better." Livingston adjusted a white knight so that it sat precisely in the center of the chessboard. "I have no intention of us actually playing, Doctor. I just wanted to distract the others."

"Why are you always *en mirage?*" Alastair demanded.

A blink of surprise, followed by brief hesitation. "To be otherwise invites...repercussions."

"Of what kind?"

"The fatal variety." Livingston raised the knight and then set it down again. "I might suggest that you do not let others know of your ability. Perceivers have a short lifespan in some circles."

Before Alastair could reply, Livingston raised the knight again. "For a moment, consider this as representing George Hastings. What does that suggest to you?"

"That he moves in set directions, and so is somewhat predictable."

A nod of respect. "And?"

"And what?"

An annoyed sigh. "Clear your mind, Doctor. What else does a knight do?"

"He can jump over other pieces in his path."

"And his greatest enemy?"

"A well-played pawn."

Livingston returned the piece to the board. "You are that pawn, Doctor. Hastings fears you because you cannot be cowed."

"The same could be said of you, sir."

"Ah, but you are more...belligerent. That annoys him."

"What is the purpose of this lecture?"

"Virtuals do exist, contrary to Hastings' dismissal of their existence. Too hasty a dismissal, which in its own right is telling."

*First Keats, now Livingston.* "You've seen one?"

"Yes, as it were. They make the perfect assassins. However, if this fellow were a Virtual, why did he choose to make his move in front of witnesses? That's not their style."

"Perhaps to send a message to others at the party," Alastair mused.

"Perhaps. How was the shooter thwarted? Did someone intervene?"

*No one I ever want you to meet.* Alastair shrugged. "I heard it was some American. It really doesn't matter."

Livingston leaned back in his chair in thought, tapping the top of the chess piece with a finger.

"Is there another entity *above* The Conclave?" Alastair asked.

"Not that I am aware of," Livingston replied, still deep in thought. "Unless..."

The heavy silence made Alastair edgy. He stood, clearing his throat. "I must be going. It has been a long day."

Livingston's pensive expression disappeared. "Why are you closing your clinic? Lack of funds?"

The shift in topic caught Alastair unawares. "I received a death threat. If it remained open, it ran the risk of being bombed."

Livingston eyes widened. "Hastings' thugs?"

"No. This came from one of Flaherty's men."

"I see. How is Sergeant Keats?" Livingston asked.

This was beginning to feel like a police interrogation. "He's healing."

"Good. There are those who do not like the idea of having our kind in Scotland Yard, but I think it is a grand idea. It may be the Yard that keeps us all from being hung as traitors."

When Alastair reached the door, Livingston called out, "Have a care, Doctor. You've raised warning flags in Hastings' mind. That might prove a danger."

Alastair turned. "How do I know that you are not playing me for a fool?"

A wry grin. "Perhaps I am. That's your puzzle to unravel."

"And here's yours. What if the assassin were a Virtual, and his target the prince?"

Livingston's expression grew somber. "Then he has opened Pandora's Box, and the evil unleashed will kill us all."

11

"There's a fellow to see you, miss," the maid said as Cynda leaned against the door, half-awake. She'd just fallen asleep.

"If it's the doctor, tell him to go home." She'd had enough of Alastair Montrose for one day.

"It's not, miss."

A glance at the calling card. "Oh, great." *What is he doing out at this hour? If Flaherty spots him, he's a goner.*

"Miss?" the maid asked.

"Let him come up."

"Do you wish tea?"

"No, he's not staying that long."

Cynda closed the door and dragged herself to the chair near the fire. She supposed it to be sometime after nine, but felt too lazy to pull the pocket watch from under the pillow to check. A long yawn engulfed her. Right before she'd dived into bed, exhausted, she'd sent a terse message to Morrisey asking for a *back story*, as Rovers called it. Something to cover her tracks with Fisher. She wondered what Morrisey would come up with.

There was a tap at the door.

"Come in," she called.

She'd intended on giving Keats a royal ass-chewing, but the expression on his face stopped her cold. As he sank onto the couch, bowler in hand, she was reminded of when he'd proposed to her at the boarding house and she had turned him down. A gallant misunderstanding: he'd thought her pregnant and offered to make her child legitimate.

"What's wrong?" she asked.

"I have been given Hobson's Choice."

"What do you mean?"

A sigh. "I went to see Nicci tonight. She sent me a note."

"Why?" Cynda demanded. "You know you can't trust her."

"She said she had information on my 'explosive Irishman.'"

"And you believed her?" Cynda asked, amazed. "Come on, Keats, you know she's—"

He waved away her objection. "I know. I, too, was concerned it was merely an attempt to trap me at one of her orgies, but that was not the case. She was able to tell me precisely how many explosives and of what type had been stolen. None of that information was made public."

"So what does she want?" Cynda prodded.

"If I agree to spend time in her bed, allowing her to do whatever she chooses with my person, she will reveal the locations of *all* the stolen explosives."

Cynda could only blink.

"If I refuse, she threatened to make the Yard aware of my presence at her debauchery."

*The bitch.*

Cynda moved to the couch, taking his cold hand and nestling it between her palms. "But you didn't take part in it. We left as quickly as possible."

He shook his head.

"You were on official business."

He shook his head again. "I am on medical leave; I had no legitimate reason to be there. Therefore, my presence would indicate that I am a man of baser morals, one amused by watching others in the throes of sexual congress. It is not what the Yard expects of their men."

"Why didn't she try this trick the last time you were at one of her orgies?"

"I was a mere constable then. Now that I'm with the Yard, the stakes are higher."

"I still don't think she'd be so stupid. The Conclave will go after her if she opens her mouth. They don't want one of their own under scrutiny from the law."

"I pointed that out. She laughed at me. Nicci believes she is invincible. Remember, we have no notion who was at the gathering. There could easily have been one of The Conclave, a Member of Parliament or a peer of the realm among those debauchers. She's probably blackmailing the lot of them. They will protect her at all costs to save their reputations."

"I never thought of that." Cynda squeezed his hand. "Could she really have information on Flaherty?"

A half-hearted shrug.

"So what do you intend to do?"

"I could refuse her, and perhaps nothing will come of it. Or perhaps Flaherty will detonate his explosives and kill hundreds. Would not those lives be of more importance than the moral discomfort of spending a night with her?"

Cynda held her silence. This was not her decision.

"If I do what she wishes and the information leads to Flaherty's arrest and retrieval of the explosives, I will most certainly advance in rank. It will be a major coup."

"And for the rest of your life you will always know that your greatest accomplishment came from..." She cleaned up her language, "bedding that...woman."

A grim nod. "I would be on a short leash, and every time she wished to have a man in her bed, she'd just give it a tug. I would not be able to refuse." He shuddered. "She'll hold it over my head for the rest of my life."

*You are so screwed.*

Cynda tried to sound reassuring. "If she can find this information about Flaherty, so can you. Don't sell yourself short, Jonathon."

A wisp of a smile. "She has many more...contacts than I do."

She chuckled. "Then you need to make love to all the Irish girls in Whitechapel," she said, trying to lighten the moment. "*Somebody* has to know where he is."

"There is another I'd rather spend my time with," he said.

She smiled at the not-so-subtle come-on. "You'll make the right decision, I know it." She looked away for a moment and then back again. "I'm so sorry, Keats. I shouldn't have pushed you so hard."

He shrugged. "And I should have been honest with you that I cannot go *en mirage*."

"True." His admission didn't diminish the guilt, especially since she still wasn't sure if his *en mirage* problems were her fault. "Is there anything I can do?"

"No. However, I value your counsel. I appreciate having someone to unburden myself to. I dare not tell Alastair. He would be appalled that I have been anywhere near the Pucks." He rose. "I do hate keeping secrets from him. That is not how a friendship should work."

After he left, she locked the door behind him and banged her forehead on the wall a few times. Then she retreated to her bed, swearing with each step. She'd gotten Keats into this mess at the exact point in his career when a vulture like Nicci could do the most damage.

Time Rovers weren't supposed to get involved.

*To hell with that.*

Miss Hallcox was due a visitor in the morning, one who had a lot less to lose than Sergeant Keats. Little Miss Nicci needed to learn there was a price for playing head games.

‡

From the edgy looks of Desmond Flaherty's accomplices, it was obvious none of them were keen to be there. Standing within a few feet of forty-eight half-size barrels of gunpowder, each capable of blowing a man to hell twice over, was enough to make anyone piss himself. Except Flaherty.The Irishman inhaled deeply, savoring the scent of powdered destruction. "Is that all of them?"

The man who'd been packing the barrels nodded and wiped his forehead, leaving a grimy black trail in its wake. He coughed deeply from the dust.

"I'll be damned glad to get away from this stuff," he said. "Never liked it."

Flaherty snorted. "If ya gotta die, it's better'n hangin'. That's a slow business. The rozzers make sure of that." He gestured toward a wooden crate. "Pull out five sticks of dynamite. I've need of 'em."

The fellow did as he was told, laying them gingerly on a bed of straw. He wiped his hands on his trousers and rose, giving Flaherty a puzzled look. "You want me to tie 'em together? One stick isn't going to do much."

"Depends on where ya put it."

"If you say so."

Once the task was completed, Flaherty waved him over. Pulling a coin out of his pocket, he explained, "Heads, ya live. Tails, we cut yer throat."

"What?"

"Ya heard me. Let's see if yer lucky tonight."

The coin whirled overhead and Flaherty grabbed it in midair, slapping it down on the top of his left hand. He kept it covered. "Call it."

"What the hell is this?"

"If ya call it right, ya'll live to see tomorrow."

The man blanched. "But I did what you asked."

"Call it!" Flaherty shouted. The man swallowed and started to back away. He stopped abruptly when he found the others ringing him now, knives drawn.

"Oh, sweet Jesus." He murmured a brief prayer. "Tails."

Flaherty bounced the coin between his palms like a conjurer and then displayed the coin. "Damn, what luck." He flipped it to the astonished man, who fumbled but caught it. Pointing to the door, he ordered, "Best be out of London before midnight, or one of these gents will find ya and gut ya slow-like."

The man fled, his feet skidding on the straw-covered floor. Flaherty squeezed the coin's double-sided mate in his left hand, there just in case the fool called heads. Fear was a crop he had to fertilize frequently. He didn't need to kill them—just let them think he would.

There was a throaty chuckle. "I figured ya'd do him like Ahearn," one of the fellows said, folding his knife and tucking it away.

Flaherty glowered at his accuser. "Don't believe everythin' ya hear."

The fellow cocked his head. "Yer sayin' ya didn't kill Johnny?"

"That's what I'm sayin'." The men glanced uneasily at each other. "Is the little sergeant still wanderin' around Whitechapel?" Flaherty asked.

His accuser nodded. "Down by the White Hart. Couple of us are watchin' him."

"Silly bugger, isn't he?" Flaherty muttered. "It'd be a service to tie him to one of these barrels and blow him to bits. That'd be a fine day's work."

"Coppers would go mad tryin' to find ya."

"It'd be a merry hunt." He surveyed the barrels. "Have these taken to the warehouses in small batches, no more than four at a time. Ya know where they go."

"Yeah. I still think yer takin' a risk doin' it this way."

"Risk is what makes life sweet, Tommy. Now get to it. I want all of 'em gone before morning. Then sweep down the place, lay new straw and have the slaughterhouse bring twenty head of cattle in here for a day or so. Pay 'em whatever they need."

"Cattle? Why?"

"If the rozzers find the place, they won't want to go diggin' in the shite to find out what we've been up to."

"Yer a right clever one, Flaherty. What about the rozzer?"

"I'll take care of him. Just get this done proper," he said, gathering up the dynamite and dumping it into a sack. As he reached the door, he looked back at the barrels and took one last deep breath.

Instead of heading toward Bloomsbury and the comfort of his

rooms, Keats caught a hansom as far as Aldgate Station and the refuse heap known as Whitechapel. Anything to avoid Nicci's shameless offer. He'd keep off the worst streets: Thrawl, Dorset and Flowery Dean, as the locals called it. Instead, he concentrated his efforts along the south end of Brick Lane and to the east. It was still a rough area, but he might be able to get in and out of the area without Flaherty taking notice.

*Might.*

A futile attempt to go *en mirage* in a dark alley had only given him an upset stomach and sparked a headache. It also reinforced a disturbing reality: how much he'd come to depend on shifting to do his job. Was his ability the only reason he'd advanced so rapidly within the ranks? He would find out soon enough, for now he was on even footing with every other copper, just when he needed that edge the most.

As he neared the White Hart, he spotted one of the "unfortunates." Everyone had a euphemism for the prostitutes: daughters of joy, prossies, dolly-mops. Each one obscured the desperate women beneath.

He stopped in front of Red Annie, whose perpetually rosy cheeks resembled crisp apples. "Evening, Annie," he said.

"Oh, it's you. What you want?"

He angled his head toward the alley.

"You tryin' to trick me?"

He shook his head, hoping to get her off the street so they could talk.

"Well, I ain't goin' until I see the brass," she said.

He flipped over his palm to reveal a shilling's worth of coins. A gap-toothed smile erupted. "This way, luv. I'll do you right proper for all that."

He waited until they were in the darkest part of the alley before he broke the news. "Don't want a knee-trembler, Annie. I need information."

The woman halted in her tracks and turned, glowering. "I knows what happens to folks who talk to you."

"The money will get you three nights in a doss house, where old Jack can't find you." He hated that he had to play upon every prostitute's deepest fear.

"I heard he's gone to America," she bluffed, but shuddering nonetheless.

"I doubt it."

"How I know you ain't him? Rozzer would be just the sort, I'd say. Nobody'd dare accuse you, or they'd end up in the clink."

"You *don't* know. That's why you should stay inside at night, not going with men."

"I got to," she said, puffing up in indignation. "I got no choice."

*No, you probably don't.* "I need to know about an Irishman named Flaherty. He stole a bunch of explosives."

She looked around and dropped her voice. "Someone said he's hidin' them here and there, both sides of the river. Don't ask me where. I don't know."

"Who told you that?"

"I heard it in a pub. I was gettin' a wee nip to warm me up."

*Lots of wee nips.* "Is that all you know?"

"I heard he's lookin' for someone. I didn't catch a name, but word is that he's right keen to find her."

*Her?* "Anything else?"

She shook her head, the tattered flowers on her hat flopping forlornly. "I'd still like to earn that shillin'," she said, reaching for her skirts.

"No, Annie. Not like that." He handed her the coins. "Get yourself inside where it's safe, you understand?"

There was a long pause. "I heard this Irishman wants your bollocks."

"I've heard that too."

"Then why are you out where he could find you?"

Keats offered his arm and walked her toward the street.

"Much like you, Annie, I have no choice."

‡

The gentleman rapped on the front door of the Hallcox residence. There was no answer. He rapped again, but nothing came of it. No doubt Nicci's butler was deep in his mistress' drinks cabinet, watering down the scotch. When he tried the door handle, he found it locked, as would be expected.

After a look around, he set to work. In a short time, the door swung open. Locks were like people: you just needed to know how to push them the right way.

He entered the foyer without calling out, scenting the air for danger. There was none. Without doffing his hat and coat, he ascended the stairs to Nicci's bedroom at a measured pace. It was a location he'd visited on more than one occasion, though he'd never paid for the privilege. Near the top, he heard the butler call to him. He didn't stop or return the greeting.

The moment he appeared at Nicci's bedroom door, the seduction was a *fait accompli*. Nicci gave him a triumphant smile and rapidly divested him of his hat and coat. She licked her full lips in anticipation.

"I knew you'd come back, Keatsie." She issued that ridiculous giggle of hers. With little ceremony, she pulled him toward her bed, throwing her dressing gown aside, exposing her voluminous breasts and those invitingly wide hips.

*Such a gilded whore.*

Satyr played the innocent sergeant to perfection, allowing Nicci to coax him into forbidden pleasures that he knew so well. He feigned reluctance and astonishment at her crude demands, reveling in the ruse and the fury it would spark when it all ended.

Later, as he lay reasonably satiated on top of her, Nicci issued a low moan.

"I knew you'd be worth the wait, Keatsie," she said, trailing a hand through his hair. She tugged the calling card from under the pillow and gave it a kiss. "My first Scotland Yard detective. I'll add you to my collection. I knew you wanted me from the first time we met."

"Why did you think that?" he asked in a bored tone, rolling away from her. Now that the seduction was over, she disgusted him. They always did.

"I saw it in your eyes."

"I must admit you've proved diverting, though a bit overrated, I think."

She frowned. "That's a rude thing to say." Nicci pulled herself out of bed and donned her dressing gown. As she walked away, she turned and gave him a skeptical look. "You are Keats, aren't you?"

"Who else would I be?" he asked.

"It's just that you seem familiar. Some of us like to play games with our forms."

"Some do."

Satyr tugged on his clothes, timing the instant when he would make the shift to his own form and deliver the Ascendant's message.

Nicci retreated to her dressing table, wedging the card under a jewelry box. "I suppose since you've kept your part of the bargain, I must as well."

*Bargain?* He hesitated, holding himself in the sergeant's form. Ah, yes, her bait. Just what had she dangled in front of the sergeant besides a night in her bed?

"Indeed," he hedged. "It is only fair, after all I've done for you."

"I was impressed. You're better than I thought you'd be." She waved an envelope in the air. "When you make inspector, remember how you got it. If I ever need your assistance, you have no choice but to grant whatever I ask, or I will bring you to your knees."

The envelope landed on the bed. He pulled out the contents.

What he read sent a chill through him. A consummate actor, Satyr donned a bright smile, as would be expected, and tucked the page back into the envelope. Setting it on the bed, he went to her, kissing her intensely, fondling her, distracting her. As he did, he playfully tugged the corded sash out of her dressing gown.

"You are remarkable, Nicci. You have astounded even me."

"I knew I would," she said, leaning into his kisses. "Catch your anarchist and then come back to my bed. I like you."

"How did you learn all that about Flaherty?" he asked, nuzzling an ear.

A shake of the tousled hair. "I never tattle."

"Pity."

After a brief deliberation, he decided to let Keats do the final honors. It would be so much more delicious that way.

He gently turned her around, leaning her back against him. His body responded, like it always did. She purred, no doubt thinking along the same lines.

Ignoring his rising desire, he slid the cord around her neck. Initially she didn't resist, no doubt believing it to be another erotic game. He constricted it again, and she began clawing at the fabric in blind panic. Sure to keep his hands out of reach, he constricted the sash a bit more.

Oh, he remembered the feeling so well, the incising pain, the mind-numbing terror. The lack of oxygen, the arousal it brought. He arched his hands upward, lifting her so her feet wouldn't drum on the floor and tightened the cord one last time.

He could hear the question screaming in her mind.

"Why?" he whispered near her ear, employing Keats' voice. "Because, dearest Nicci, not all obsessions are meant to be fulfilled."

As she flailed, he whistled a tune he'd recently heard in a music hall. It was quite a lively one.

He was still whistling when she stopped moving.

Satyr shifted into nothing on the stairs, pausing to note the butler and a plump maid in a tense embrace at the far end of the hall.

"Come on, girl, we got time."

He held himself motionless until he was sure their attention was fully engaged, then quietly opened the door. As he walked, invisible, into the night, he gazed up at the window where his latest accomplishment lay in death's repose. He touched the envelope buried deep in his pocket.

"Serendipity," he murmured, "with a bit of drama at the end. Well done, Mr. S."

✠

A kick caught Keats in the thigh, narrowly missing more vulnerable parts. Cursing his stupidity, he tried to rise. A strike in the ribs made him double over, wheezing.

"That's enough," a familiar voice ordered.

"We're just havin' a bit o' fun," one of his assailants protested. "Gettin' a boot in, like the rozzers always do."

"This one's not like other coppers. Help him up, or ya'll be takin' his place."

Rough hands yanked Keats to his feet. He worked his shoulder. Nothing felt broken. Mercifully, they'd left his head alone.

Flaherty stepped closer, flanked by two men. That meant there were five, counting the pair that had just jumped him.

"What are ya doin' here, little sergeant?" Flaherty sounded drained, unlike the last time they'd met.

"Hunting you, of course."

"Now why would ya want to do that?"

"Something to do with the explosives, perhaps?" Keats suggested as a line of sweat trickled down his back.

Flaherty gave a thick snort. "Yer damned stupid for a copper."

"At times." This was one of them. *Bluff.* At least that way, he'd go down with some style. He raised his voice authoritatively. "Listen up, gents. If you'd all be so kind as to consider yourself under arrest—"

A couple of the Fenians guffawed.

"Yer a right clown, Sergeant," Flaherty replied.

Keats shrugged. "Had to try. If you intend on killing me, I would appreciate it if you refrain from mutilating my body like you did Ahearn's. My grandmother's health is poor, and the sight of my filleted body would send her to the grave. The family doesn't need two funerals to plan."

Flaherty frowned. "Why do ya think I killed Ahearn?"

"Only a heartless bastard leaves behind a pregnant widow."

Flaherty's face clouded, and a knife appeared in his hand. He waved the other men back. "He's mine. His lyin' tongue is the first that I'll take out."

As Keats' heart rammed inside his chest, Red Annie's words came back to him. It was an insane gamble, one that might make his death even more excruciating if he got it wrong.

"You cut me up, and there'll be no one to help you find...*her*."

The Irishman hesitated. "What ya know of it?" he asked, his scowl deepening.

Keats studied his foe in the dim light. Who was this woman? A missing lover? No, that didn't feel right. Someone closer to his heart.

"You come in with me and we'll talk. I'll do what I can. I found you in Green Dragon Place, didn't I? If I can find you, I can find her."

Flaherty held himself motionless for a time, deep in thought. His men shifted uneasily behind him, puzzled at this change of events.

Keats pressed his luck. "None of the other coppers will help you. I will."

"Ya swear it?" Flaherty demanded.

"On my sainted mother's grave," Keats replied, reflexively crossing himself. He meant every word. He'd help Flaherty as long as it took to deliver the Irishman and his explosives into the Yard's hands.

The Fenian's expression clouded again, and then he abruptly crossed himself in response. "On yer sainted mother, ya bastard. Damn, the priest was right."

Before Keats could ask what that meant, the Irishman waved forward a fellow the size of a small mountain range. The huge man bent over and Flaherty murmured something in a low voice. A nod. More instructions, all below Keats' ability to overhear. The big man shot his boss a startled look. "Just do it, ya hear?" A resigned nod.

The anarchist turned toward Keats, folding his knife and returning it to a pocket. "Consider this a warnin', little sergeant. Ya come after me again, and I'll gut ya, no matter the health of yer gran."

He spun on a heel and strode down the alley toward the street, the others following. Only the huge dockworker stood between Keats and his quarry.

*What just happened?*

"Damn you, come back here!" Keats called.

A rough laugh echoed off the brick walls. "Ya never learn, copper."

"Move out of my way!" Keats bellowed, desperate to find a way around the big man. The human barrier held his stance, hands bunched into fists the size of Keats' head. There was no other way out of the alley except through him.

"I order you to move!"

Flaherty stopped when he reached the street, gave a salute and then disappeared around the corner, his bewildered men straggling behind him.

"Oh, bugger!"

Keats charged at full speed. A fist caught him straight on the chin like a sledgehammer. He was unconscious before his body hit the refuse-strewn cobblestones.

# 12

*Sunday, 14 October 1888*

"Is it one of my patients?" Alastair asked through a barely cracked door, followed by a wide yawn.

His landlady shook her head. "No, it's a constable. Said he was supposed to fetch you on order of some chief inspector."

The image of Ahearn's mangled body came to the fore. *Oh, God, not Keats.* Alastair started to close the door when he remembered his manners. "I shall be down directly."

He was still adjusting his braces as he clattered down the front steps toward the carriage. The constable opened the door and gestured to him.

"Where am I going?" Alastair asked, pulling on his coat.

"I have no idea," a familiar voice called out from inside. "Come on, the more the merrier."

Alastair took a seat across from his mentor. The door slammed and the carriage lurched forward after the smart crack of a whip.

"Dressed in a hurry, did you?" Reuben asked with a grin.

"Too fast, I'd say. Do you know what this is about?"

"A woman has been murdered."

Fear charged into Alastair's heart; his hands faltered as he buttoned the top of his shirt. "Do you know her name?"

"No, but we're going to Mayfair, if that helps."

It didn't. Jacynda could be anywhere. When he raised his eyes, he found Reuben watching him intently.

"Is something wrong?" his companion asked.

"I'm concerned for an acquaintance of mine. She has a habit of getting into dangerous situations."

Alastair stared out the carriage window. Images blurred. He

braced himself as the carriage surged around a corner, then looked back at Reuben. "Have you ever known a love so intense that you fear it might consume you?"

"Yes, I have. I suffer from the same malady."

"How do you bear it?"

"I don't, at least not very well. I pray I warrant that love come the next sunrise. The day it ceases to be mine, I fear I may perish, dramatic though it sounds."

"We are of like mind," Alastair said.

"What is this lovely maiden's name?"

*Hardly a maiden.* "Her name is Jacynda. She is from New York."

"Ah, yes, Sagamor spoke of her in glowing terms. Which, if you are not aware, indicates he holds her in the same awe as he does his wife. Few women approach that pedestal, let alone ascend it."

"High praise, indeed. Lady Sephora is a most remarkable woman."

"I wish you good hunting," Reuben replied. "Be sure to invite me to the nuptials."

"I sincerely doubt that will ever occur. My friend Keats has a much better chance than I. He has a solid job and a promising future. I'm just a poor doctor whose patients can't even afford to eat properly."

"Miracles do happen," Reuben offered.

*Usually to someone else.*


Alastair did not recognize the house, but that did not ease his worries. He noted the movement of a curtain at the window of the dwelling next door. The presence of police in the middle of the night never heralded glad tidings.

Clearing his throat, he asked the constable, "Who lives here?"

"A lady named Hallcox, sir."

He heard a groan issue forth from his companion.

They were met at the bottom of the staircase by another constable, this one older and with a ruddy face. He had that stern, all-business expression that indicated there was a superior within earshot.

"Upstairs, sirs. Last room on the right." As they mounted the stairs, Alastair thought he heard the sound of weeping.

They were met by yet another constable outside the specified room.

"A veritable swarm of Blue Bottles," Reuben remarked dryly, then addressed the constable. "Drs. Bishop and Montrose, as requested."

The constable opened the door and stood back. Alastair's first impression was oppressive red: the walls a deep burgundy, the curtains crimson, and the carpets of ruby and dark rose.

"Looks like a Turkish bordello," Reuben remarked.

Chief Inspector Fisher was inside, standing between them and the bed.

"Well, well, your favorite inspector again," Reuben whispered, and then strode into the room. Another dark-suited policeman stood near the dressing table. He was rolling a pencil between his fingers in agitation.

"Close the door," Fisher ordered.

The moment Alastair complied, the senior officer stepped aside, revealing the corpse.

"Oh, Lord, it *is* her," Reuben said, moving forward until he stood near the bed.

"You are acquainted with this woman?" Fisher asked.

"I have seen her at an occasional party or two. I know her more by reputation."

"Which was?"

Reuben sighed. "She is known among her circle as *Allcocks*, a play on her last name. It is appropriate because she has...had an insatiable appetite for men of all stripes."

"Have you ever been with her?" Fisher demanded.

Reuben gaped and then shook his head. "God, no. What a question."

Fisher gave Alastair a penetrating look. "You?"

"No, I've never seen the woman until this moment."

"Excellent. I need both of you completely free of attachment so that the post-mortem findings will be as impartial as possible. There are enough entanglements with this murder as it is."

"May I ask why you're present, Chief Inspector?" Alastair queried. "Is this woman somehow connected to anarchists?"

"Just do your work, Doctors," Fisher retorted.

The rebuke caught him off-guard. Stung, Alastair moved to the bed, across from Reuben. Bending over, he studied the dead woman's face. If it had been pretty, it was no longer so. She bore the classic signs of strangulation, a cord tied around her neck in an obscene bow.

"I believe we can rule out suicide," Reuben murmured, moving to the end of the bed.

Alastair undid the sash, carefully laying it aside. An ugly stricture mark marred the pale flesh.

"Step back here," Reuben ordered, gesturing. "What do you see?"

Alastair moved to the spot his fellow physician indicated. Observing the scene from this new vantage point, his mind rebelled. "I hesitate to say..." *They will think me perverted.*

Reuben turned toward him, his eyes aglow. "Go on."

Alastair cleared his throat and after an anxious glance at Fisher, composed his thoughts. He'd encountered the vile serpent of human nature often enough in the East End. In the West side of London, it felt more profane.

"The hands are placed on the breasts in mimicry of ecstasy. Her legs are parted and the fireplace poker points toward her female regions as if positioned for entry. It's...an obscene parody of the sexual act."

"I agree with my protégé," Reuben said. "The murderer arranged the scene to discomfit us."

"Do you think she was interfered with?" the younger copper asked, stepping forward.

Reuben gave him a quick glance. "I didn't catch your name."

"I apologize. Inspector Hulme. I'm the local inspector."

"As to your question, Inspector, we'll be able tell more during the post-mortem, though I don't note bruising in the areas one would expect. It is possible, given her libidinous nature, that she invited her killer to bed and after a vigorous romp, he took the matter a bit further than she could have imagined."

"Why?" Hulme asked. "If she were willing—"

"There are many means of sexual arousal, not all of them decent. Fortunately, that's your problem to decipher." Hulme colored. "Don't take that as chastisement, Inspector. Frankly, I'm happy all I have to do is tell you how this poor lady died. I'd not want your job for anything."

"There are days I feel the same," Fisher said.

"Who found her?" Reuben inquired.

"Her ladies' maid, curious as to why her mistress didn't ring for her sleeping powders," Fisher replied.

"And the fire? Was it like this at the time, or has the maid built it up since then?"

Hulme shook his head. "I'm not sure, Doctor. I will ask."

"Good. It is overly warm in here, and that will affect our estimated time of death."

"We already know that, Doctor," Hulme replied. "The butler made note of her last paramour and the time he arrived. That was right before eleven. The maid came upstairs at half past midnight."

"That's roughly an hour-and-a-half window, providing the woman was alive when her paramour entered her room."

Hulme frowned. "Surely if the fellow had found her dead, he would have raised the alarm."

"You sound so certain. What if he were married or a prominent member of society?"

"I hardly think that's relevant."

"On the contrary, Inspector. Would you want your name splashed across the newspapers as having visited a woman of loose morals and finding her strangled and positioned in such a way? I certainly wouldn't."

Fisher nodded. "Unfortunately true, Inspector."

Reuben stepped forward and examined each of the woman's hands in turn. "No evidence that she scratched her assailant. Pity." He returned them to their exact positions. After a moment's pause, he asked, "I must pose the same question as Dr. Montrose. Why is Special Branch interested in this case?"

The two inspectors traded looks. "It is not important you know that at present," Fisher replied. Without another word, he swept out of the room, causing the constable on guard to jump. The moment the door closed, the junior inspector let out a stream of air.

"What a nightmare."

"Shan't argue there," Reuben replied, sketching the position of the body on a notepad with precise strokes. "When you move her," he instructed Hulme, "bring the sheets up and enfold her within them. We will want to see what we can find on them. And bring the gown, the cord and anything else you think of value."

"Certainly."

"After the body is removed, post a constable at the door. I want the opportunity to examine the room during the daylight before some maid goes trying to clean it up."

"As you wish."

Reuben added a few final touches to the drawing and closed the notebook. The physician gave Alastair a wan smile. "Let's meet at six sharp. We'll need clear heads for this work."

Reuben turned for one final inspection of the late Nicci Hallcox. "What a way to die," he said in a low voice. "First bliss, then horror."

"Much like life," Alastair murmured.

☦

Keats awoke with the taste of blood in his mouth, shivering from the cold. He had a gag in place and his hands were tied in front of him. A jarring bump slammed him into the side of something wooden. A container of some sort, he thought. He heard the creak of a wagon and then he faded out again.

When he next awoke the cold was worse, causing shivers to engulf him. He was in a wooden box. A coffin, by the shape of it. He smelled fresh pine and then the unmistakable scent of damp earth. He panicked, shrieking into the gag at the prospect of being buried alive.

His frantic screams and contortions only exhausted him. He sagged, forcing himself to breathe through the panic. It was difficult to hear anything over the thump of his heart. As minutes passed, he waited for the clods of dirt to hammer on the lid. None came. His terror gradually began to subside.

A faint owl-hoot. Then scratching on the outside of his wooden prison, followed by a snuffling noise, like a curious beast assaying its next meal. More scratching.

He was above ground. Keats wept for joy. The tears ran down his face, stinging the abrasion on his jaw.

*I must stop reading Poe.*

After much squirming within the confined, stuffy space, he pulled off the gag and shouted for help. The creature fled. He shouted again. The owl hooted in return.

"Oh, bugger."

Using his teeth, he worked hard on the knots and after considerable time and abraded lips, managed to get free. Trying to force open the top of the coffin did no good, so he kicked at it until the wood splintered. Whoever had confined him had not nailed the lid tightly. More kicking finally brought a stream of fresh air. He gulped it hungrily, offering a prayer of gratitude.

Dazed, he climbed out. His right foot caught on the edge of the coffin and he plowed face-first into the moldy forest floor.

*Nightmares are better than this.*

He slowly sat upright, groaning as he moved, clutching his jaw. He felt like he'd drunk a whole barrelful of bad gin. In fact, he felt worse.

Gingerly swiveling his neck in either direction revealed nothing familiar. No streets, buildings, gas lamps or people. Why had the huge oaf carried the coffin out into the middle of nowhere?

The owl hooted again, filling the night with a deep, mournful sound.

He rose from the ground, woozy. He brushed the dirt out of his hair and beard, noting his bandage was gone now. Wondering how many hours had passed, he fumbled in his coat, but didn't find his pocket watch. The loss was a deep blow. It had been a present from his grandfather when he'd taken his position at the Yard, specially engraved to commemorate the occasion. Only a few pence resided in his pocket. No calling cards, nothing that proved he was a detective-sergeant with Scotland Yard.

"Damn, damn, damn!"

The owl hooted three times in response. After more curses that seemed to melt the moment he uttered them, he grumbled, "At least they left me my boots."

Branches flagellated his face and hands as he shoved his way through the undergrowth. Staring upward, he couldn't see the Northern Star, only a thin quarter-moon. London could lie in any direction; it was pointless to go on until daylight. When he found a copse of trees, he settled into a niche formed by thick bushes and dried leaves. Hunching up against the cold, he tightened himself into a ball to try to conserve body heat.

As he shivered, one question kept stampeding through his brain. *Why didn't you kill me?*

✝

J.R. Fisher stared into the dying coals in the hearth. He had no energy to rebuild the fire. He should retire to bed, but he lacked the will to climb the stairs. He was vaguely aware of his wife calling his name. When he didn't answer, she entered his study.

"J.R.?"

"Yes."

"Why haven't you come to bed?" she asked softly. "Has something happened?"

She knelt near his chair, a heavy robe over her nightdress. Her hair lay in a long plait down her back, tied with a ribbon. He remembered when it was like rich chocolate. Now it was woven with silver, even more beautiful in his eyes. He took her hand and kissed it.

"Yes, Jane, something has happened. After this evening, I am seeing my future guttering like that fire."

She rose and took the chair closest to him. "Tell me."

"My sergeant has been implicated in a murder, one involving a woman of dubious repute. She was strangled after he visited her tonight. He is not in his rooms and cannot be located."

"Which sergeant?" she asked.

It was only then he realized he'd not mentioned a name, as if he had only *one* sergeant. That was telling. "Keats."

"Do you think him capable of such a monstrosity?" she asked.

He looked up into her eyes. "My heart says no."

"And what about your head?"

"Another no. Neither of those matter; I must treat him as any other suspect. I fear..." He sighed low and long. "I fear that if the truth is not uncovered, he will hang."

"My God," she whispered. "He is such a bright young man."

"Yes, he is. I remember you were quite taken with him when we had him round for dinner that evening."

"I liked him very much, quite genial company," Jane replied. "Very earnest and intelligent."

"I cannot lose him now," he murmured. "Not now."

"You have others who can succeed you, J.R."

"None like Keats."

"Is the Home Office still pressing you about that missing assassin?"

"Yes. I'm not out of the woods yet. Warren is very incensed."

"No doubt, since he's receiving his own hiding from the press over those killings in Whitechapel."

He nodded. "I'm an ideal scapegoat at the moment."

When he said nothing further, Jane kissed him on the cheek and left him alone. She'd always understood his need for quiet reflection.

In the darkness, the chief inspector grimly reviewed the facts. All pointed to his sergeant. That meant one of two things: either someone had carefully fitted Keats for the noose, or he'd committed the crime himself.

In the chief inspector's experience, neither scenario brought any sense of hope.

⁜

"She is wearing barely more now than she usually did in life," Reuben observed, studying Nicci Hallcox's sheet-draped body. Her hair fanned around her in a blonde halo, her vacant eyes staring at the gas lamps, unseeing. "Whenever I saw her, she was dressed scandalously."

"In what way?" Alastair asked.

"If her nipples weren't peeping out of the top of her bodice, she would adjust her gown until they were. It had the most dramatic effect on almost every male within sight."

"But not you?"

A quick shake of the head. Reuben raised his head from the methodical instrument arranging. "Ever witnessed a female's post-mortem?"

Alastair nodded. "In medical school."

"That was in Baltimore, wasn't it?"

"You seem to know a great deal about me."

"Sagamor, for the most part. And others. You've cut a path, though you don't realize it."

"Not one most would envy."

"Those who are breaking new ground do not follow convention."

Alastair lowered his eyes to the notebook in his hand. "I once attended an inquest where the coroner spoke of the details of a young woman's death with such coldness I felt nauseated."

"You knew the lady?" Reuben guessed.

"Yes. She was my lover. She was murdered."

"Ah, that explains it," his companion replied. "A matter close to the heart. Did they convict the person or persons who killed her?"

"No. He was already dead." Alastair set down the notebook and squared his shoulders. "If you're ready, Doctor."

His mentor studied Alastair's detailed notes, then grumbled under his breath.

"It's damned irritating that she was so libidinous. Three different-colored strands of hair in the sheets, besides her own? We must check with the maid and find out the last time the linens were changed."

"If she were so inclined, they might have been changed daily, which would mean that she had three different men in her bed in the course of about twelve hours," Alastair conjectured.

Reuben leveled a look in his direction. "Just men?"

"Surely you're not saying—"

"From what I can gather, Miss Hallcox was interested in everyone if they were above ground."

"Were you totally honest with Fisher when you said you'd never had relations with this woman?"

A startled look. "Definitely. Why do you ask?"

"It seems that you are, in some ways, more affected by her murder than I would anticipate."

"The death of a woman always troubles me." Reuben resumed looking at the document. "You might want to make further note of the angle of the ligature marks on the back of her neck and include a diagram with detailed measurements. Those may prove important. Other than that, well done." He handed the sheets back to Alastair.

"Thank you."

"You have a definite future in forensic medicine. If you decide otherwise, at least I know one Whitechapel physician who won't let a suspicious death glide past him on the way to the grave."

Alastair chuffed. "I wonder how many I've missed so far."

Reuben fixed him with a sobering look. "You'd be astounded."

13

With relief, Satyr observed the church doors opening and the first trickle of parishioners exiting the sanctuary. A few minutes later, his superior shook the reverend's hand. When the Ascendant saw him, he raised an eyebrow and then nodded slightly—the signal that Satyr might join him.

Instead of hailing a hansom, they set a course for the graveyard. Once out of earshot, the Ascendant said, "You know I prefer not to do business on the Sabbath."

"I know, sir, however, this is very important." He reached into a pocket and handed over the paper he'd received from Nicci. The Ascendant peered at it. His rhythmic steps faltered, then came to a halt.

"My God. Where'd you get this?"

"Nicci Hallcox," Satyr said, lowering his voice. "I went to deliver your message last evening in my own fashion. After a bit of..." he waved a hand, knowing his superior would be revolted by the details, "she announced that since I'd kept my part of the bargain, she would keep hers." He gestured at the paper. "This is what she handed me."

"Who did you *present* as? Yourself?"

*Hardly.* "No. Sergeant Keats."

The Ascendant's face paled.

"I knew that Nicci was keen to bed him. I thought it would be a lark to appear as him and then deliver your message. I even had a calling card printed just for the occasion. As luck would have it, I'd caught him paying her a brief visit an hour or so earlier. I would surmise that her offer revolted him."

The Ascendant scanned the page again and then hid it in a pocket. "Is this the only copy?"

Satyr nodded. "I searched her room."

"I trust I will read of her untimely demise in this morning's paper?"

"Yes. However, that presents a complication. It is possible the sergeant may be blamed."

The Ascendant stared into the middle distance, brow furrowing.

"You did say that the perfect murder is one in which the blood is on someone else's hands," Satyr went on. "You have often stated that you felt he presented a threat to your future plans. This will remove the sergeant from our concerns."

"I believe you may be right. If they find him blameworthy, it will occasion an uproar in Scotland Yard, keeping them too busy to annoy us. Indeed, I think we have fallen on our feet."

Satyr executed a slight nod and a mental sigh of relief.

"Where would she have obtained this information?" his superior asked.

"I doubt Flaherty would be visiting a West End strumpet. It has to be Effington. He knows where the *merchandise* is stored, and he was known to use her every now and then."

The Ascendant adjusted his gloves. "It's not time for him to ascend yet, though this debacle certainly warrants it. Give him another warning, more graphic this time."

"Yes, sir."

"What of the Irishman?"

"I reminded him of his daughter's fate if he displeases us," Satyr replied.

"Excellent. And what of his tasks?"

"Nearly complete. I did have to remove one of his subordinates. He was trying to find the girl and getting too close for my comfort. I made it look as if Flaherty had killed him and used him as an example for two *associates* I am training at present."

"Excellent." The Ascendant nodded in approval. "Well handled." He adjusted his top hat against a slight puff of wind. "I thank you for reporting this development. However, in future, do be more circumspect."

"As you wish, sir," Satyr said, instantly discarding the advice.

✝

Her ruined night's sleep now behind her, Cynda rose early and set off for Mayfair, keen to start Nicci's day with a bang. As the horse-drawn hansom clattered its way west, she unfolded and then struggled to read the note that had appeared under her door that morning. It was written in Alastair's expressive handwriting, every letter perfect.

*My dearest Jacynda,*

*I offer my apologies for my behavior last night. Worry for you clouds my mind and I do not always act a gentleman. I shall endeavor to be less antagonistic in future.*

*As to the other matter—my superiors purport to know nothing of the event the other evening and are not interested in pursuing the matter. I shall speak at length with Lord Wescomb and see if we may decide a further course of action.*

*With sincere affection,*
*Alastair*

"I'll be damned. He apologized. That's gotta be a first."

She jammed the note in a pocket, shaking her head. After a long yawn, she collapsed against the seat and closed her eyes.

"We're 'ere, miss," the jarvey called out.

Cynda yawned and then stared. Twin constables flanked Nicci's doorstep like blue-suited gargoyles. There was straw spread on the street in front of the house to muffle the traffic and all the shades were drawn. Clearly, there'd been a death in the household.

"Ah, I've changed my mind. I need to go to Bloomsbury."

"Right you are, miss," the man said, snapping the reins.

To her displeasure, there was no Keats to be found. Instead, she encountered a hand-wringing landlady.

"They kept asking all sorts of questions about some woman in Mayfair and where the sergeant was," the woman said, mangling a handkerchief in her hands. "I haven't seen him since yesterday afternoon. I kept telling them that. They went all through his rooms. It's a mess! He'll be very upset."

*Some woman in Mayfair?* Cynda's stomach started churning. "Was the woman's last name Hallcox?"

"That sounds like it. They say he might have killed her! Sergeant Keats is not that sort. He's a decent, good man. He brings me flowers and always pays the rent on time."

Cynda left the landlady to her distress and retreated to the hansom waiting for her at the kerb, her mind awhirl with dread.

*Could he have done it?* All it would take was Nicci playing her trump card and his beloved career was over.

*And that, gentlemen of the jury, is known as motive.*

The horse flicked its ears at a persistent fly. "Miss?" the jarvey nudged.

"Ummm, I need to go to Marylebone next."

"Whatever you wish, miss," he said, clearly not upset at the steadily rising fare.

As the hansom headed west again, Cynda replayed her conversation with Keats. Though there had been an undercurrent of righteous anger when he'd left, he wasn't seeking revenge against Nicci. Instead, he seemed keen to do what he did best—work the case on his own. However, if Cynda's hunch were correct, it meant someone had gone to an extraordinary amount of work to put the noose around her friend's neck.

Lady Sephora took one look at her and beckoned her to take a chair in the dining room.

"You are so pale," she remarked with concern. "What has happened?"

There was no nice way to do this. "Keats is implicated in a woman's murder."

Sephora sank onto her chair. She stared at her hands as Cynda told her about Nicci Hallcox's devious offer and the threat to Keats' career.

"It's not him; it can't be," Sephora said at last. "I do not believe it for a minute."

"That isn't the way the cops will see it."

Sephora blinked her eyes repeatedly, trying to forestall tears. Drawing herself up, she asked, "Shall I have Mary bring you some breakfast?"

"No, thank you. I don't really have an appetite right now."

Sephora busied herself by stirring milk into her tea in slow, clockwise motions. Victorians were masters of dealing with the horrific by taking refuge in the small details.

"I've met Miss Hallcox, you know," she admitted. "Her life defined immorality. For her to make such an offer to Keats is detestable, but not out of character. There are a number of men who have fallen into her bed and are now literally paying the price."

"Blackmail?"

"That's what I've heard, and from more than one source. She kept trying to entice John. He ignored her, but she wouldn't step back. Finally, I warned her about the perils of continuing such behavior. She treated me with contempt." Sephora's cheeks were red now, her eyes flashing at the memory.

Cynda cocked her head, wondering if she'd misunderstood. "You threatened her?"

Sephora delicately dabbed at the corner of her mouth with a linen napkin. "Not in a violent way."

*Right.* Victorian manners were in their own way a polite violence. Words were as sharp as daggers and often more deadly to a reputation than a well-placed bullet. Unless you were Nicci Hallcox. She had no reputation to guard. Sephora's threat was just fuel for the fire.

"Deidre was convinced her husband partook of Miss Hallcox's...generosity from time to time," Sephora continued. "He denied it, of course, but she'd noticed some of her jewelry had gone missing. She suspected it might have been used as payment of some kind."

"Could Effington have killed her?" Cynda asked.

Sephora's eyes widened. "That is a possibility. He has the temperament for it."

Cynda didn't bother with the niceties. "Is he one of your...folks?" she asked. When there was no immediate answer, she added, "If you can't say, I understand."

Sephora gave a shrug. "I don't think he is, or Deidre either."

*So much for that angle.*

"If Keats did not return to Miss Hallcox's residence after he sought your advice, where do you think he would have gone?" Sephora asked.

"I'd bet on Whitechapel, trying to find Flaherty on his own. It was the only way to avoid Nicci's trap."

"That's a very dangerous move on his part."

"No other choice, I think."

"You said he took you to one of her debauches." Sephora lowered her voice and leaned over the table. "Are they as, well, I've heard stories."

"Twice over."

"Good heavens," she said, leaning back and tucking the napkin in her lap.

"I'm going to talk to Effington's butler and then make a trip to Rotherhithe to see where Deidre supposedly ended it all."

"Perhaps she's absconded with her lover," Sephora offered.

"So she had one, then?"

"Yes. A young fellow. He was at the party, I gather, though I'm not sure which one he was. She did not introduce us."

"Deidre invited her lover to the party?" *That took some stones.* Maybe she wasn't as mousy as she appeared.

"You will not find their butler in residence. Effington fired him the night of the party. Apparently, there was a terrific row between them."

"Then where do I find him? Is there some place they go when they're out of work?"

"I'll find out for you." She rang the bell and Mary appeared shortly thereafter.

"Please ask Cook to come up. I have a question to put to her."

"Yes, milady." A curtsey and the girl was gone.

"For my part," Sephora began, "I shall make enquiries in my circle as to whom may rejoice at the loss of Miss Hallcox. I suspect there will be a considerable number."

A tap at the door. "Enter."

The cook came into the room, her massive white apron starched to perfection. No doubt she'd donned it right before she headed upstairs. "How may I help, milady?" she asked.

"You are in contact with Mr. Effington's cook, Mrs. Rogers, am I correct?"

"Yes, ma'am."

"Do you have any notion where Miss Lassiter might locate Boyles, their former butler?"

The cook's face grew pensive. "Well, ma'am, I understand that he is well out of it. Mr. Effington's given him a black mark and he's not been able to find work. Last I heard, he spends his time at the Dog and Duck. Some relative of his owns it, I gather."

"Good Lord," Sephora murmured.

"I met him once. Right nice fellow. If I may be frank, milady, it's a pity he's being treated this way for doing his job."

"I agree, Mrs. Griles. I'll talk to you this afternoon about the menu for the dinner party for Saturday next. Thank you. That will be all."

"Yes, milady."

The door closed behind her. Sephora took another sip of tea. "When you find Boyles, tell him I wish to speak to him. We've not had a butler since Stamford died. If Effington is willing to cast aside a seasoned butler, I'm not averse to taking advantage of that error."

"I will." Cynda rose. "Thank you for the help."

Sephora nodded and escorted her to the door. Her face brightened. "Surely by this afternoon Keats will have reappeared and presented a suitable alibi. Then the police can focus on the real killer."

Cynda forced herself to nod encouragingly. "From your lips to God's ears."

She didn't believe it for a moment

.

‡

Something tickled Keats' hand, jerking him awake. After some searching, he finally spied the intruder—a black beetle skittering away across the leaves. Above him, the birds issued a few tentative chirps. His breath formed clouds in the frosty air. Yawning loudly, he rose from the ground, stiff and sore. Daylight hadn't improved his situation. There was no beaten path to be seen.

*No food, no idea where I am. What a cock-up.*

Another yawn, followed by an intense stretch that did nothing to ease his stiff muscles. *I bet Flaherty's having the laugh of his life. Probably all over the pubs by now.* He'd never live this one down.

Keats executed a three-hundred-sixty-degree turn and then stopped in his tracks.

"Pick a direction," he uttered aloud, "and three out of four guesses will be wrong." He could be anywhere outside of London. He suspected it wasn't too far, but far enough that he had no frame of reference.

Talking to himself seemed to help, so he added, "Just walk until you find someone. There's got to be a cozy farmhouse with lots of food and a pretty girl to cook it for you. Always happens to lost heroes in fairy tales."

Hours later, when the sun was straight overhead, Keats found the train tracks. He looked one way and then the other. No sign of life in either direction. Feet burning and stomach shriveled in a knot, he chose south, continuing his lonesome trek toward civilization.

✝

Livingston found his assistant, William, waiting in the far corner of the dining room. His eye was not on the door, but on a young lady a few tables over. Her older escort, no doubt a mother or aunt, had carelessly left her unattended for the moment. He assessed the situation like a hunting dog left alone with a fresh ham.

As he sat down across from his assistant, Livingston gave the girl a nod and then dropped his gloves on the table.

"Oh, sorry, sir," William said, rising.

"Not at all, William. I note you had your mind elsewhere."

"Yes, sir." A sideways glance. "Fine-looking filly, she is."

"No doubt with a father who would cheerfully gut you if you ruined her marriageable qualities."

A roguish smile. "If he caught me," William said.

"I assume the reason you now work for me is because you did get caught with your hands...or some other part of you...somewhere it shouldn't have been."

The smile widened. "Quite right, sir. I don't regret it a minute."

"I see. However, I would prefer that you keep your mind on business from now on." He pulled a calling card out of a pocket and penciled a name and address on the back. Pushing the card across the table, he whispered, "To that end, this lady is quite discreet. Her services are expensive, but she is healthy and very talented. I'll be happy to pay for a once-a-fortnight visit should you find your attention wandering."

"A prostitute?"

Livingston grimaced and leaned in closer. "If you call her that to her face, I can promise that you'll never service a woman again once I finish with you. It would be like calling a fine bottle of French wine frog piss. I urge you to employ the word *courtesan* while in her presence."

William tugged the card away. "Thank you, sir. Now what may I do for you?"

"Have you heard any rumors about an attempted assassination in Mayfair?" William gave a quick shake of the head. "Curious, that. Little in the papers, either. Someone has been exercising considerable influence in that regard."

"Why?"

"That's one of my questions. I want you to find out everything you can about the event. It was at a party held at Hugo Effington's house. I particularly want to know who stopped the assassin. I have a hunch..." He tapped the table with an index finger. "Talk to the servants. They know everything."

"I will, sir." A quick glimpse at the young girl, and then back. "Anything else?"

"No, that will be it for the time being." Livingston rose. "Do be cautious, William. I would hate to lose you."

"Yes, sir."

Once Livingston reached the door, he turned to study his assistant as he donned his gloves. The young girl was sending admiring looks in the young man's direction. To Livingston's relief, William was already scrutinizing the back of the card with considerable interest.

"Good. Very good."

Adelaide would see to William in ways that a pale virgin could not begin to imagine, learning more about this ambitious young man in the process. The fellow was a rough gem destined to become a fine jewel, providing his rutting instincts didn't put him in the grave.

14

Just as Sephora's cook had said, Cynda found Effington's former butler at a table in the corner of the Dog and Duck, an empty pint in front of him. He wasn't drunk, but the scowl on his face told her this wasn't going to be a slam-dunk.

"Boyles?" she asked.

His eyes narrowed. "You're the lady from the other night, aren't you?"

"Yes."

"You ended up costing me my job."

"No, the fellow with the gun did that."

"Right, but he's not here."

It was a threat, but she didn't sense any violence behind it. He just needed some way to vent. "How about I buy you a pint?" she offered.

He thought for a moment. "In exchange for what?"

"What really happened at the party."

The eyes narrowed further, but he nodded. "You got yourself a deal." He waved at the barman and pointed at his glass. "Another one." Looking back at her, he said, "My name is Brown, Howard Brown. They didn't like the name, so they stuck me with Boyles. Sounded awful." She gave a nod of agreement. "Aren't you having one?"

"No. Alcohol and I don't do well together."

"Teetotaler, are you?"

Cynda pulled out a chair and sat down. "No, just don't want to get drunk on my bum."

Brown gave her a hint of a smile. Maybe this wasn't going to be as hard as she thought. She handed the coins to the publican as he set the foamy pint in front of them.

"So what do you want to know?" Brown quizzed.

That she hadn't anticipated. Butlers were usually very close with information, especially when it related to their employers. It was a hallmark of their profession.Unless they'd been treated like peons.

"Why did you get fired?"

"Mr. Effington," he said, adding a fair degree of acid to the name, "accused me of allowing that man in without an invitation. That, and his nibs was really put out when I sent for the police."

"Why didn't he want the cops involved?"

"Effington's not on the up-and-up. He's involved in shady business dealings. Probably figured the coppers would find something out and put him in the clink."

"How do you think the assassin got in?"

"I've no idea. He didn't come in the front door or below stairs. Unless Effington or the mistress let him on the sly, I'd say he just appeared out of nowhere."

*A genuine possibility.* "Had he been at the house before?"

"No, never saw him before that night."

"Did you catch his name?" Another shake of the head. "Who do you think he wanted to kill?"

Brown took a long sip of his beer and then smacked his lips. "Well, now that's a puzzle, isn't it? They were all bunched together near the fireplace like a covey of quail. Could have been any one of them. The way the mistress acted, you'd think he was after her."

Cynda took the opening. "Could he have been?"

Another long sip of beer. "Possible. Things weren't right between the master and the mistress. He always had a string of ladies, even with his first wife. The latest Mrs. Effington knew about them, and it didn't set well."

"Do you think Effington would hire someone to kill her?"

"No better place to do it, wouldn't you think? It would look like the killer was aiming at one of the nobs and accidentally hit her."

It was an intriguing notion, but it didn't play out. "Hired assassins like to live to see the next day," she said. "Effington could just claim not to know him and it'd be the killer who ended up with the rope around his neck."

Brown drummed a finger on the table, brows knit. "Maybe it was just some lunatic."

"What happened to Effington's first wife?"

"Died right sudden. She was the mistress' sister."

Cynda smirked. "Keeping it in the family."

"Keeping the *money* in the family is more like it. Effington doesn't have any, at least not anymore. His warehouses aren't doing too well. He's been living off her for some time. You can imagine that didn't set with him."

"I understand she has a lover."

Brown nodded. "She'd been going out twice a week, just taking the air, she said. Bert, one of the groomsmen, said she was meeting some young jack. She'd be inside a hotel for a couple of hours and then out she'd come, all smiles."

"Young jacks can do that for a woman," Cynda said.

Brown grinned. "Best the master never find out who he is," he added. "He's a vicious bastard and I'm not apologizing for saying that, either."

"I heard her lover was at the party."

"Might have been. I noticed she was talking to a gent for quite some time. Whether it was him or not, I couldn't say."

A thought nudged her. "Young fellow, mid-twenties or so? Wore a red rose in his lapel?"

"That was him."

*Mr. Macassar Oil, the guy who helped her up from the floor.*

Brown leaned across the table. "You've not said why you're interested in all this."

"Lady Wescomb and I are worried about Mrs. Effington." *And now for the million-dollar question.* "Any notion where she is at present?"

His expression grew guarded. "In the Thames is what I hear."

They eyed each other. Cynda leaned over the table. "Come on, we both know that's not likely."

He gave a sigh. "I don't know for sure. She might have done herself a mischief. For God's sake, don't go to the house and ask any questions. Effington will find out. If she's still alive, he'll take care of that problem right proper."

"I won't. You helped Mrs. Effington escape, didn't you?"

He took the time to drain the remainder of his beer, weighing the question. Cynda held her breath. Finally, he nodded. "She pleaded with me to help her. She was afraid the master would blame her for what happened, beat her to death. He was that angry."

"How'd you do it?"

"Spirited her out below stairs through the tradesmen's entrance."

"In one of her nice gowns?" A nod. "Did she take a bag or something with her?" Another nod. *Maybe she had a change of clothes.*

"I hope she didn't do it. He isn't worth it, I can tell you."

Cynda smiled. "You're a good man, Mr. Brown."

"I like to think so. I'll be blunt. If I can do anything to get up that bastard's nose, I'm happy to oblige."

*Hell hath no fury like a butler sacked.*

She tried a new tack. "Is Mr. Effington involved with a woman named Hallcox?"

A quick nod. "He saw her regular. She was a tarted-up whore if there ever was one."

"Nicci Hallcox was murdered last night."

Brown looked surprised. "I hadn't heard that."

"She was probably blackmailing your former employer. Do you think Effington might have killed her?"

"If she was battered and bruised, I'd say he's your man."

She'd gotten what she came for. Now it was time for the quid pro quo. Cynda dug Sephora's calling card out of a pocket. "Lady Wescomb wishes to speak to you about a position, if you're interested."

Brown looked at her, down at the card and then back again. "You're pulling my leg, right? All those toffs stick together."

"I think you'll find the Wescombs are of a different stripe," Cynda said. *They're not jerks, for one.*

"Well, I'll talk to her ladyship. Don't know if anything will come of it, but it won't hurt to have it known she wanted to speak with me."

Cynda rose. "Thank you, Mr. Brown. You've been a considerable help."

"You've been the same, miss." He tucked the calling card in his pocket. Giving her a serious look, he cautioned, "Be careful. I don't want to read about your death in the paper."

"That makes two of us."

✠

In the daylight, the murder scene didn't look any less garish.

"Exactly like a Turkish bordello," Reuben muttered under his breath. He turned to the constable at the door. "This will take some time."

"As you wish, Doctor," the fellow replied. The door closed.

The two doctors traded looks. After a moment, Reuben stripped off his coat and started at the far corner of the room, upending furniture as if it were moving day.

"What *are* you doing?" Alastair asked.

"What did you think of Inspector Hulme?" Reuben replied.

It was astounding how the man could deflect one question with another.

Alastair didn't hold back. "Certainly not as seasoned as Fisher. Didn't ask the questions I thought he should."

"Precisely!" Reuben replied, launching a finger into the air for emphasis. "He asked if the victim had been interfered with, but nothing more. If I had a chance to impress a chief inspector, I'd have been flying questions around the room like a drunken swallow. Instead, you'd think he'd been asked to investigate someone stealing a wormy apple from a costermonger's cart."

"That still doesn't explain what you're doing."

"Looking around the scene for whatever the police might have missed."

"Under the furniture?" Alastair asked.

"Evidence goes in mysterious directions. I once found a cufflink at the bottom of a chamber pot. Fortunately, the killer hadn't been able to find it. It cost him a trip to the gallows." Reuben paused in front of the victim's dressing table. "Would you join me so that you can watch me rifle through her things?"

As if reading his assistant's thoughts, Reuben explained, "It is best that you have a second person present if you're going through someone's possessions. That way, you will not be accused of theft should a piece go missing."

"Good Lord, I never thought of that."

"You shouldn't have to, but you'd be surprised what families will say after the fact."

"Has that happened to you?"

"Yes, damn them."

"Surely they wouldn't have arrested you," Alastair protested.

"There was some discussion about it. Fortunately, a maid found the missing item a few days later. Still, the accusation did nothing for my reputation, though it was eventually retracted."

*Is that why you don't have a Home Office position?*

Reuben opened drawers and then sneezed when he encountered loose face powder. "God gives women natural beauty, and they insist on messing about with all this. Do you realize some of this muck has arsenic in it? How absurd." He opened the jewelry box and whistled in appreciation. "It would appear our Miss Hallcox had admirers who were willing to pay the freight."

"Or she invested in jewelry," Alastair said, though he doubted that was the case.

Reuben gave him a strange look and then an affirming nod. "Quite right. I stand corrected. I can hardly harp at you to keep an open mind and then assume the lady received jewelry in exchange for sexual favors."

He delivered a quick wink before dumping the jewelry on the table. Instead of examining the horde, he rattled the case. "Aha, what is this?" He dug around until the false bottom sprang open, sending a cascade of calling cards to the ground in a white shower.

"Women do like to hide things, don't they?" As Alastair retrieved them, Reuben replaced the jewelry in the box and snapped it shut. "So who has been calling on our dearly departed?" his companion asked.

Alastair peered at the names, flipping over card after card. "A peer of the realm, a couple members of Parliament, a judge, another judge, someone at the Home Office..." The back of one card caught his notice. "Good Lord, there are a series of date."

"Tallying up their visits? How quaint," Reuben remarked, now lifting up bottles and studying their contents. He opened one and did a test sniff. "Rose. Very nice."

Ignoring the running commentary, Alastair thumbed through more of the cards, astounded at the clientele the dead woman had acquired. Then he stopped abruptly at one. He flipped the card over. All the dates were within the last few months, one just the previous week.

*You perfidious bastard.*

Oblivious to Alastair's consternation, Reuben observed, "It seems Miss Hallcox knew everyone, both socially and biblically. Do jot down the names and the dates and then we'll turn the cards over to Hulme. I want to ensure that Fisher sees the list, as well."

Alastair looked up, surprised. "You don't think Hulme will share the names?"

"Just being cautious. If we find pressure being applied to our work in any manner, we will at least be able to determine if it is courtesy of one of Miss Hallcox's paramours."

Alastair parked himself in the nearest chair and began his transcription as Reuben continued to search the room. A tour through the wardrobe resulted in a lively critique on the dead woman's choice of clothing. Then Alastair heard the rattle of the commode. His fellow physician was consummately thorough, if nothing else.

"Anything?" Alastair asked, looking up.

Reuben shook his head. "When you're done, let's move the mattress and see what we find."

Alastair continued his efforts, making careful notes, his emotions still at full boil.

‡

Standing in the entrance to the Bury Street hovel, Cynda was summoning the courage to make the ascent up the stairs. They might as well have been Everest. The holes were still there and seemed larger than a couple of weeks earlier. She knew from experience that the parts that seemed intact were actually spongy wood eager to snap an ankle or topple you headlong to the floor below. She noted with some disgust that the cat corpse near the bottom of the stairs was now reduced to a pile of bones. The maggots had moved onto fresher edibles a few feet away.

*How do people live like this?*

They didn't, not in the usual sense. Children died more often than not as their parents slowly worked themselves to death. The only reasons Davy and his mother had survived up till now were their tenacity and Alastair's care, though often the doctor had little more to eat than his patients. If not for his expert care, Mrs. Butler's recent her chest infection would have been fatal.

Cynda managed only two steps up when her skirt caught on one of the broken boards.

"Oh, crap," she muttered, not keen to tug on it or she'd rip the fabric. It was her Whitechapel garb, bedraggled clothes most folks would have pitched into a bonfire. Still...

"Miss Jacynda?" a young voice called behind her. She heaved a sigh of relief. The climb would not be needed.

"Come unhook this skirt, will you?" she called.

"Be right there!" He scurried up and in a moment had it free, then helped her down.

"Hello, David Edward Butler," she said, knowing how much he liked it when she used his full name. He delivered a gracious bow. As usual, his face needed washing despite his mother's supreme efforts. He was taller than most kids in Whitechapel, with sharp eyes and a sharper mind.

"G'day, Miss Jacynda. What brings you to my crib?" he asked, beaming.

"I wanted to check on your mother. Is her chest better? I forgot to ask Alastair the last time I saw him." *We were too busy getting on each other's nerves.*

"Much better. The doc says it's almost clear. He saw her a few days back."

"That's very good news." The best kind of news. Mrs. Butler had come close to dying from a chest infection. Alastair had pulled her back from the grave.

"It's not all good news. She's sellin' apples now."

"Why?"

"Her boss gave her the sack. Said she was too sick to work for him."

Scalding words formed on the tip of Cynda's tongue, but she

swallowed them in deference to the kid. "I'll see if I can find her something, I promise."

"That'd be good. I can't earn enough."

Cynda knelt, taking Davy's rough and grubby hands into her own. She saw tears forming in the corners of his eyes.

He shook his head sadly. "Mum won't let me tell the doc. She knows he'd pay the rent, and she don't want that."

"Well, you won't have to. I'll pay you two shillings a day for the next week. I need you to do some work for me."

His eyes widened as he labored to do the math. "Four...eight...fourteen shillin's? That's a fortune!"

"It's going to be a bit dangerous, that's why I'm paying so much." *And I want your mother off the street.*

Davy's amazement faded to a cynical frown not usually seen on a twelve-year-old boy. "What you want me to do?"

"Escort me to Rotherhithe to start with. I need to go to Church Stairs."

"Rotherhithe? You bein' a lady and all? They'll have you in a flash. They're all sailors and they have no law."

"We'll go during the day and we won't stay long."

"Why you want to go there?"

"I need to find out if someone killed herself or not."

"Why?" he persisted. "That's what rozzers do."

"Because it's very important, Davy. If the woman didn't commit suicide, I fear her husband will find her and harm her." Deidre was the key. She might even know the assassin.

The kid's face sobered. "You mean he'll hit her?"

"Yes." *Or worse.*

"I hear that sort of thing at night. Me dad never ever raised a hand to me mum and if he had, I'd a stopped him. It ain't right."

*God, you're a good kid.* "No, it's not. Will you help me?"

His face screwed up in concentration. "Does the doc know what you're about?"

*This one oughta be a lawyer.* "No, and he better not find out."

"Two shillin's a day?" he asked.

"Yes. I'll pay you half now," she said, kneeling to dig the money out of her right boot after a quick look around.

"I'll have to let me mum know where I'm goin'. That way, if I don't come home, she knows where to look."

For half a second, Cynda thought he was teasing her. Then she saw his face. There was no hint of jest, only grim determination.

15

Reuben Bishop yawned into the busy Scotland Yard hallway, covering his mouth belatedly.

"I do hope these late nights abate for a time," he muttered.

Alastair nodded while clenching his teeth together to stifle his own yawn. "Fortunately, we had lunch when we did," he observed. He was as tired as Reuben, barely keeping his eyes open. What they'd discovered in the course of the post-mortem had put sleep out of reach.

Reuben went into lecture mode. "First rule of the business: eat whenever you have a chance. Blue Bottles have their own notion of how long matters should take and to hell with everyone else."

"So I've noticed."

As if on cue, a constable trotted up. "The Chief Inspector will see you now, sirs."

Fisher waved them into his office. "I apologize, Doctors. Other issues are pressing us at this point."

Reuben handed over the report and outlined the results of the post-mortem in a clipped style with no verbal flourishes, an indication of his weariness. Summing up, he added, "We found three different sets of hairs on the sheets, besides the victim's: light brown, gray and black."

Fisher nodded. "That follows the maid's testimony. Miss Hallcox had a busy social schedule: a peer of the realm in the afternoon, a magistrate right before dinner and then her killer. I see you estimate death somewhere within that ninety-minute span." A shuffle of papers. "No other signs of violence?"

"None. There is one point, however. Miss Hallcox had the French Disease."

"Syphilis? Not too surprising, given her randy nature."

"No, but it might be to those who availed themselves of her charms."

"Perhaps it was a reason for her murder, as well," Fisher observed. He tossed the report on his desk with a disgruntled sigh. "I had hoped for more."

"In what way?" Reuben inquired.

Fisher tented his fingers. "Oh, that the killer stands six feet tall in his stocking feet, has a slight limp, smokes Alexandria cigarettes, dotes on his mother and is prone to bet on the ponies."

"There are limits to our abilities, Chief Inspector," Reuben replied peevishly.

"So it appears. A question for you, Dr. Montrose. Was Keats in the habit of attending debaucheries?"

Alastair started in surprise. "Keats? Heavens, no."

"Miss Hallcox's butler insists that my sergeant was present at a *soiree* Friday last. From what I gather, the deceased was known to host orgies."

Alastair shook his head. "I sincerely doubt Keats would do such a thing."

"Well, it may well be that we are misinformed," Fisher replied. "Unfortunately, the chief suspect in this case *is* my sergeant, gentlemen. He visited Miss Hallcox for a brief period of time last evening, departing in a *fine fury* as the butler put it. A short time later, he returned and spent time in the company of Miss Hallcox, in her bedroom."

Alastair could do nothing but stare. Reuben shifted uncomfortably.

"To sum it up," Fisher announced, "if what the butler said is true, then my sergeant was the last person to see Nicci Hallcox alive."

"Surely he has a suitable alibi," Alastair retorted. "What has he told you about it?"

"He left his lodgings early last night and has yet to return."

"My God," Alastair murmured. "I cannot believe this."

"According to the butler, my sergeant attended the debauchery accompanied by a young woman whose description is eerily familiar."

Alastair's throat tightened. "In what way?"

"She sounded a great deal like Miss Lassiter. Have you spoken to her recently?"

"Last evening, but she made no mention of this."

"Ah, well, there we are again. Events seem to swirl around this woman like leaves in a gale."

Fisher leaned back in his chair, tented his fingers again. Alastair noted a fine tremor that the chief inspector could not conceal.

"Personally, I am not convinced of the butler's veracity. At first, he claimed he did not need to speak with us because of Miss

Hallcox's connections with numerous important personages. After more pressure, he stated he saw Keats leave right before the maid went upstairs. However, after close questioning, he finally admitted he had not seen my sergeant leave at all and was, in fact, involved in an assignation of his own. He admits to a weakness for drink. It is very clear he holds animosity toward Keats, though he would not state the cause."

"He's correct about the important personages," Reuben said, handing over the list Alastair had so carefully compiled. "We found calling cards in the false bottom of Miss Hallcox's jewelry case, quite a number of them actually. We sent the cards to the inspector. We thought you might like a list."

Fisher looked surprised, a rarity for him. "I wonder how Hulme missed that."

"To be candid, he didn't seem engaged," Reuben said.

A rueful nod. "I fear you are correct." Fisher studied the list. "Are these...dates?"

"Yes. We suspect those are when the cards' owners spent time in Miss Hallcox's bed. We also suspect she did not note them purely out of nostalgia."

"Good heavens," Fisher said, blinking in surprise. "I had no idea that an eighty-year-old lord could be so invigorated."

"We all should hope for such stamina at that age," Reuben replied.

"Keats' card was found underneath her jewelry case," Fisher said. "It didn't have any notations on it, which could mean he'd not been with her, or..." he trailed off.

"Or he killed her before she had time to make the note," Reuben said.

Alastair shuddered. This was too close to home. A few weeks earlier he had faced the dock over a false murder accusation when Jacynda had been attacked by one of her tourists. When she'd disappeared into the future, he was left behind with bloody hands and a ravening mob on his tail keen to extract street justice. Thankfully, Jacynda had returned alive, healed of her hideous injury, and the charges were dropped. He'd even been touted as a hero for saving her life.

That wouldn't happen to Keats.

"It appears my sergeant is in august company," the chief inspector remarked, dropping the list on his desk as if it had somehow soiled his hands.

Alastair gestured toward the paper. "If Keats is considered the prime suspect in this murder, he holds the least rank of the lot. I am concerned that he will take the blame to avoid exposing the others to social ridicule, or a possible murder charge."

"That is my concern, as well. I will do my best to ensure the murderer is found, be that my sergeant or a peer of the realm. I've never allowed rank to affect my judgment."

"You may not, but there are those in the government who are prone to do just that," Reuben observed. "You are taking a sizable risk being involved with this case. There may be accusations that you tampered with evidence if it goes to trial."

"I know," Fisher replied, his voice tense like stretched wire.

"This may cost you your career, Chief Inspector."

The two men eyed each other.

Fisher abruptly rose. "It's worth the risk. Thank you, gentlemen, I appreciate your work." He stuck out his hand and shook each in turn. "I will keep you apprised of the investigation as it unfolds."

As they exited the building, Reuben suggested they make their way toward The Clarence for a drink.

"Why there, if I may ask?"

"Police like the place. We might hear a few rumors."

Alastair's mood darkened. "Rumors will not save my friend."

"No, but they won't hang him, either. They're just a weathercock."

"From what I can feel, the wind's blowing toward the gallows."

"Often the wind is fickle, just like a woman. We may yet see a fair breeze clear your friend of murder."

Once they'd bought their pints and found a remote corner in which to enjoy them, Reuben spoke up. "Frankly, I am confused. Fisher knew last night his sergeant might be the killer. Why did he call us in on the post-mortem? I certainly have no attachments to Sergeant Keats, but you are his close friend. That is a direct conflict of interest."

"I had no notion Keats was in the picture," Alastair protested.

"No, neither of us did. Nevertheless, that will not stop speculation that we may have mussed about with the evidence in some manner to save your friend's life. I just hope Fisher has something up his sleeve, or this is going to be damned awful for the lot of us."

Alastair shook his head in despair. "There is another moral dilemma, Reuben. It's about the cards."

"You seemed rather distracted after you began transcribing the names. Did you recognize one?"

Alastair nodded. "He is the fiancé of a woman I hold in fond regard."

"Who is this lady?"

"Dr. Hanson's daughter, Evelyn."

"Oh, him. Arrogant sod. Thinks his opinions are personally delivered on a silver platter from God himself."

Alastair smiled ruefully. "You know him well. Evelyn and I were once engaged. Her father and I had a disagreement, and it broke us apart."

"Disagreement? I heard you told him to go hang himself."

Alastair started in surprise. "How did you know about that?"

"Sagamor. He thought it was absolutely brilliant on your part. I agree. Nevertheless, back to your dilemma. How do you propose to handle the situation?"

"I thought a discreet visit to Lord Patton was in order. He may not be aware he has been exposed to the disease."

"Or ignored the symptoms when they first manifested. The young can be quite ignorant when it suits them."

"If Dr. Hanson learns of my intervention, he will believe I am doing this solely to ruin Evelyn's future happiness," Alastair admitted.

"Saving her life is more like it. To that end, I'd be happy to accompany you."

That brought comfort. "I will take you up on that offer. I sincerely appreciate this, Reuben."

"Drink your pint and we'll make a social call on the young libertine. Let's hope he thinks with more than just his cock."

‡

*What am I doing?* She had asked that question countless times since the train pulled out of Liverpool Station and headed south under the river toward Rotherhithe. Next to her, Davy craned an eager face to peer out of the closest window. Not that there was anything to see—the train was currently thousands of feet beneath the Thames.

*Well, maybe not thousands.* It was still inside the Thames Tunnel, something built by Victorians that could drown them like a litter of helpless kittens if it collapsed. Even though the tunnels were still in use in '057, it didn't make her feel any more secure. Salvation would only be found when she reached daylight.

"We're under the river!" the boy exclaimed. "I never thought I'd be on a train. Wait 'til I tell me mum!"

Cynda kept the fixed smile pasted on her face. A glance toward Davy told her why she'd been so determined to do this—his face was aglow, his nose pressed firmly against the window.

"I think I saw a fish!" he said, and then turned toward her with a mischievous wink. She delivered a mock glare and then chuckled. He read her like a book.

Rotherhithe was a grubby and bustling district, the shop signs betraying the maritime blood in its veins. Shipwrights, barge builders, timber agents and ship chandlers rubbed elbows with pubs and ropemakers. Sailors and dockworkers were everywhere. Some ignored them; others gave Cynda an appraising eye. There were women as well, for sailors and soldiers always drew females desperate for a few coins. In that way, Rotherhithe was no different than Whitechapel.

A glance behind them revealed no sign of her *shadow*, as she called him. She lost him at Pratchett's Bookshop and he'd stayed lost, though it was only a few blocks from the hotel. The gregarious bookseller had rented her the room, which had a back entrance, for executing the switch from Miss Lassiter to a denizen of Whitechapel. Certainly beat wandering in and out of the upmarket Charing Cross Hotel dressed as a third-class citizen. Pratchett had no qualms about the use of his room for such a change of costume. A well-read mind was a fertile one.

At an intersection, Davy paused for a moment, then tugged on her arm.

"Church Stairs is that way," he said, pointing left.

"How do you know?" As far as she knew, the kid had never been on this side of the Thames before.

"I asked Mr. Riddle."

"Who?"

"He's a mapmaker. I went to his shop and asked him how to get to Church Stairs. He said he'd tell me for a shoeshine."

*Enterprising kid.* "Well done, Davy."

After more walking, she spied the pub's sign: Spread Eagle and Crown. It was a plain three-story affair compared to the likes of the Britannia or the venerable Princess Alice.

Ignoring Davy's protests, she left him outside. The interior was as packed as the watering holes in the East End. She noticed the black wood paneling and oak beams right off. There were built-in settles, or alcoves, each full of patrons swilling, swearing or smoking. The pub had been here when a group of parochial Pilgrims set sail for America. No doubt at least some of the locals had wished them good riddance. As far as she knew, the pub was still there in '057.

The ambient noise was too much for carrying on a conversation with the publican about a dead woman, so Cynda pushed her way back out. No easy feat. She found Davy loitering just outside the door, leaning up against the wall, kicking it with the heel of his boot.

"Nice pub. Crowded," she said.

"So you say," he said with a frown.

"So where is Church Stairs?"

He jerked a thumb to his right.

Of the many set of steps that led to the river, Church Stairs wasn't much to shout about. Once she reached the bottom, she looked out over the broad expanse of the Thames. The tide was going out, and children scampered in the mud hunting for items to scavenge. Boats slid through the dark and oily water. A steam launch chugged by, generating a wake that made the smaller boats rise and fall like yo-yos. On the far side, she saw a cluster of masts near Shadwell New Basin and the rum and sugar warehouses.

Time slid into the past. She stood a bit further upstream, on Bankside in Southwark, with a British historian named Max. The year was 1666; the entire northern sky lit with the glow of destruction.

"My God," Max whispered as if they were at a funeral, unaware he was clutching her hand in a death grip. "You can read about the Great Fire and look at the sketches, but...my God."

"It's the like the end of the world," she murmured, stunned as sheets of crimson flame billowed into the night sky like dragon's fire.

To them it was. Thirteen thousand houses, nearly ninety churches, even the great St. Paul's was consumed by the blaze. Twenty-first-century scholars still had no notion of how many died. The poor wouldn't have a chance to escape, cremated in the firestorm. It was literally hell on earth.

"Miss Jacynda?"

She blinked. In the distance, London stood whole, no glow in the sky. The Rovers had a name for what she'd just experienced: *time slipping*. It was a very bad sign, the next to last domino before retirement.

"Yes?"

"I asked a few of the mudlarks about the lady's clothes."

Cynda blinked again. Just how long had she been slipping? That sort of inattention could be life-threatening.

"What did they say?"

"That anythin' left on the stairs woulda been nicked and sold. They watch for things like that." He flipped open his muddy hand. "See, I found me a penny and a clay pipe."

"Good for you, Davy."

He pocketed his treasures as if they were made of the purest gold.

An old sailor met them at the top of the stairs, his weathered face textured by decades of salt spray. He puffed on a pipe and studied Cynda with a jaundiced eye.

"Ya lookin' for somethin', miss?"

She connected the face—he'd been inside the pub, standing by the door. A local who probably didn't miss a thing.

"A posh lady was supposed to have waded out into the water and drowned herself the other day. Did you hear about it?"

"Yah," he said, a cloud of aromatic pipe smoke surging upward in the air. It smelled heavenly.

"Did you see her?"

"Nah."

"How did you hear about it?"

"Rozzer told me. He didn't see her neither. Just found her clothes."

"What kind were they?"

"Fancy ones, he said."

"Do many people come here to drown themselves?"

"Nah. It's better off the bridges. Ya drown faster."

That wasn't something Cynda had considered. Would Deidre have had the nerve to wade into the cold and filthy water, feeling it advance up her body until it reached her chin? If so, why take off her heavy clothes? They'd have sped her demise.

"I couldn't do it," she murmured, shivering.

"I'd hang meself first. Quicker."

Neither method sounded appealing.

Another puff of the meerschaum pipe. It had a buxom mermaid carved into it. From behind her, she heard Davy call out that he'd found another prize along the shoreline. At least he was enjoying himself.

"Ya say she was a posh bint?" the sailor asked.

"Yes, from Mayfair."

He spat and shook his head. "The rich ones don't kill themselves around poor folks. Looks bad."

Sound logic. "Do you know where I could find that constable?"

"Just saw him up by St. Mary's. PC Walker's his name. He's tall and got carrotty hair. Ya'll be able to spy him a mile off."

She fished in her pocket and handed him a half crown. "Have a few pints on me."

A craggy grin. "Thanks, miss." He looked up at the sky. "I'd be headin' back to wherever ya came from. Night's here soon, and ya don't want to wander around these streets then."

"Whitechapel isn't much better," she said.

He stopped puffing and spat again. "Whitechapel, ya say? Then ya'd best stay here. That's the devil's playground."

As he turned away, she asked, "What tobacco is that?"

A toothy grin. "Jolly Sailor. Best there is." He stomped off, smoke marking his trail.

She looked over at Davy, who had rejoined her. "Come on, let's go find us a red-haired rozzer."

A short time later, they were on the train for the return journey to Whitechapel. Davy had his nose against the glass again; Cynda closed her eyes and held it together until they pulled onto solid ground.

The constable wasn't much help, though he remembered that evening well enough. He'd had to lecture a pair of extremely drunk Portuguese sailors about trying to out piss each other on a brick wall. Then he'd checked out Church Stairs and found the discarded garments. When Cynda asked if the clothes had been warm as if recently worn, he shook his head. Any dampness at the hem of the skirts? Another shake of the head. And there'd been no sign of anyone entering the water.

That settled the matter for her.

"She's done a runner," Cynda murmured. Hopefully, old Hugo wouldn't find out, or there'd be hell to pay.

16

The duke's household was in an organized uproar with his return from the country. Servants hustled by with harried expressions, barely noting the two visitors.

By the end of an hour, Reuben was grinding his teeth and popping his knuckles in the way he only did when agitated. Alastair's nervousness had taken residence in his intestines. His clear duty as a physician warred with his regard for Evelyn. What if she learned of his visit? Would she think this petty revenge on his part?

He had to admit that he still cared for her. When she passively accepted her father's decree that their engagement be broken, it had been a blow to his pride and to his heart. Jacynda would have laid the man out flat for such a suggestion. Yet, there was a softness, a tranquility to Evelyn that was noticeably absent in Jacynda's character. He longed for that peace, that lack of emotional conflict. Two ends of the scale: Jacynda's vibrant intensity and Evelyn's calm acceptance. In between the two extremes resided the perfect wife for him.

The butler opened the door to the sitting room and gestured with a gloved hand. "This way, gentlemen. The duke and his lordship will see you now."

"About damned time," Reuben whispered.

The duke made no effort to rise from behind his mahogany desk. His eldest son, Lord Patton, stood near the fireplace. He was more handsome than Alastair had anticipated: in his early thirties with an aquiline nose, good posture and a dour look worthy of his family's ten generations. His father wore the same expression. Apparently it was hereditary, like the nose.

As previously agreed, Alastair took the lead. "Your Grace, we are here on a personal matter."

"Which is?" the duke asked with more than a hint of irritation.

"We have cause to believe that Lord Patton has been..." Alastair cleared his throat and plunged on, "exposed to syphilis, your Grace. If your personal physician has already treated you, then our call is unneeded. However, if you were unaware of this exposure, it is best that you seek an examination as soon as possible."

A light laugh issued from the young lord. "Is business so slow that you must come door to door to find new patients, like a patent-medicine peddler? How vulgar."

Reuben bristled. "No, your lordship, we are attempting to circumvent a tragedy."

"I don't consort with slatterns, Doctor," the young man shot back. "I have standards."

"Is this a clumsy attempt at blackmail?" the duke demanded.

Before Alastair could speak, Reuben touched his arm and interceded. "No, your Grace, it is not. We have no monetary interest in this situation."

"Then how are you privy to this information?" the duke asked.

"Miss Hallcox was murdered last evening, and we were called to perform the post-mortem. Your son's calling card was found in her bedroom, along with a number of others. Your card had the dates of your assignations noted on the back. We thought it would be best to bring this matter to you in a private fashion, rather than have it appear in the papers."

The young lord noticeably flinched.

"Our concern is that you may already have this disease and be unaware of it, my lord. Worse, you may pass it on to your bride and afflict your future offspring. It is not an illness to be ignored," Reuben explained.

The duke rose, his eyes pinned on Alastair. "That's where I've heard the name before. You were Miss Hanson's fiancé. You're the fellow Hanson sent packing because he wouldn't follow orders."

"My history with Dr. Hanson and his daughter is not the issue, your Grace. Our concern is for your son's well-being." *And that of Evelyn.*

The butler appeared the instant the duke rang the bell. "The doctors have delivered their scurrilous rumor. They are no longer welcome."

"Please do not dismiss our warning, your Grace," Reuben urged.

"I do dismiss it out of hand. Now good day."

Alastair turned to the young lord, praying he could reach the man's conscience. "Lord Patton, if you care for Evelyn, don't harm her because of your folly."

The young lord's sneer deepened, but he did not reply.

As the front door closed firmly behind them, Alastair let loose a rare stream of vitriolic oaths.

Reuben raised an eyebrow. "I agree. At least we tried."

*Not hard enough.*

‡

Keats found the transient camp a few hours before dusk. If it hadn't been for the dog barking and the crackle of the fire, he probably would have missed it in his exhaustion. It was set back from the tracks a good distance and consisted of a few patched lean-tos and a fire pit tucked in a clearing. A quartet of ragged men huddled around the fire. A pot bubbled above the flames. No matter how stark the scene, it looked like heaven in his eyes.

The tan dog barked again. "That'll do, Rupert," someone called out, slapping his thigh. "He's not a rozzer." The dog returned to his side, its three legs giving it a queer gait.

Keats took the hint. "Afternoon, gents." He halted a short distance away, showing some respect. "Mind if I share your fire for a bit?"

"Where ya from?" one of the men asked.

"London."

"Why ya here?" another asked.

His mind spun into action. "Got drunk. Got robbed and dumped in the middle of nowhere. Won't have a job by the time I get home, and that's a right bugger."

There were hearty guffaws all round, and a hand waved him forward. He sat near the blaze, welcoming the warmth. A cup was dipped into the pot and handed over to him. It was weak tea.

"No sugar," the man with the dog said. "Ran out this mornin'."

There was more laughing.

"It's all the same," Keats replied, keeping his speech as plain as possible.

"What's your name?" the man asked.

"Jon."

"I'm Old Bill and this is Kipper, Roger and Fat Mike," the man said, gesturing around the circle.

"Pleased to know you, gents."

Kipper leaned forward. "I bet it was a bit of bad gin that got ya here, wasn't it?"

Keats shook his head, blowing on the tea to cool it. "*Irish* whiskey," he said. "Stuff always gets me in trouble."

As they continued to banter back and forth, he studied his companions. Old Bill had craggy features and the build of a sailor.

His gnarled hands told Keats that his working days were over. Kipper was rail-thin with ferret's eyes that were always on the move. Fat Mike wasn't rotund in the least. It made Keats wonder if he'd once been hefty and the life along the tracks had whittled him down to size. Roger was very quiet, not jesting with the others. He kept his eyes lowered to the cup in his hands.

In the distance, a horse neighed. The dog started up again.

"Go see who it is, Kipper," Old Bill ordered. Kipper hurried through the bushes while the other men rose, picking up stout and branches.

"Trouble?" Keats asked, loath to set down his cup of tea for anything short of a riot.

"From time to time, the lads in town like to pay a visit. They think it grand fun to trouble us."

Fat Mike spat on the ground. "Bastards give us a hard time. They should live like us for a day."

Kipper reappeared. "It's the vicar and the lady. They've got stuff in the cart for us."

The men relaxed, assuming their former positions around the fire.

Before Keats could ask, Old Bill explained, "The vicar likes to come and save our souls. The lady, bless her, comes with him every now then. She's a good Christian soul and brings us food and clothes. It never hurts to have a bit of prayer said over you, but I prefer the grub."

Kipper grumbled, "Pity they don't bring no drink."

"Last thing you need," Fat Mike said, rolling a cigarette in his grubby hands.

Keats turned around as the pony cart pulled up. The vicar was quite young, no doubt just out of seminary.

"Good afternoon, gentlemen," he called out cheerfully. He hopped off the seat and helped the lady down. When she tipped back the hood of her cape, Keats beheld golden hair in a tight bun and deep brown eyes.

"Good afternoon, miss," Old Bill called out. "And you too, Vicar," he added.

"We've brought stew and some blankets. We thought with winter coming on, you would need them," the young woman said. She was pretty in a simple way, her voice low and soft, carrying a power that Keats would not expect in one so young.

The vicar set the cast-iron pot near the campfire and opened the lid. The scent caressed Keats' nose and his mouth began to water, making him forget everything else.

Kipper reached toward the pot with his cup, and got his hand slapped by Old Bill.

"Wait for the prayer," the old sailor murmured.

They bowed their heads. The vicar offered a mercifully short blessing, for which Keats was grateful. The smell was irresistible: his stomach growled loudly. He waited as the others were fed, Old Bill doling out equal portions.

*More civilized than Whitechapel.*

The young woman placed a blanket on the ground and then sat near the fire. That astounded him. He'd expected they'd hand out the charity and leave, not wanting to socialize with tramps.

*What sort of woman would do this sort of thing?*

"You're a newcomer," she said, addressing him.

He stammered, "Ah...um...yes."

"He's from London," Kipper said around a mouthful of stew.

"What brought you here?"

*Playing the fool.* "A misunderstanding," he said.

"I see." She leaned closer, studying his forehead. "It appears you have taken some injury."

He fingered the thick ridge of the healing scar. It still hurt. "A while back."

"I have some salve in the wagon," the vicar offered, hopping to his feet. "It cures nearly everything. I make it myself."

Once the exuberant cleric headed toward the wagon, Old Bill leaned closer.

"Ya must be careful, Miss Lily. Not all of us are good people. Not all of us understand that yer here to help. Ya being so pretty and all. I'd not want to see ya come to harm. Ya understand me?"

"The vicar is with me," she said simply.

"No offense, miss, but he'd not be much in a fight. The old vicar, they respected him. This new one's too green, if ya get my meaning."

She studied Old Bill with a thoughtful expression. "I know. I keep my faith in God, and all will be well."

"God's good in His own way, miss, but he wants us to use our heads. I'm just warning ya to be careful."

"I understand, and I thank you for your concern."

Keats' stomach rumbled loudly again and he apologized, embarrassed. As he ate, he savored each bite of stew. It had chunks of lamb, potatoes and carrots. A feast.

"Is it to your liking?" the young lady asked. Her voice continued to enchant him, a blend of honey and sunshine.

"It's very good."

"What is your name?"

"Jon."

The vicar returned with a small tin. Their benefactress wetted a cloth from a flask and said, "Lean closer and I will clean the wound before I apply the salve."

Keats didn't hesitate to comply, even though it would slow down his progress on the stew. There were worse things than being tended to by Lily.

As she cleaned, he grimaced. "I apologize. How did you receive such a vicious injury?"

"I was attacked and robbed."

"Oh, dear." She continued her ministrations while Keats gritted his teeth. "There, the salve is in place. That should help."

"Thank you very much, miss," he said, truly grateful.

She handed off the tin to the vicar and then wiped her hands on her apron. "I have paper and pen with me. If you wish, I will write to your family. I often do this for some of the others. Or if you wish to write yourself, I will post the letter. It always helps if your kin know you are alive and reasonably well."

A plan formed in his mind. "I would like to write them, thank you."

"We'll come back in two days' time. I can pick it up then. You'll be here?"

"No, I'll be leaving at dawn tomorrow."

"Then write it quickly and I'll take it with me."

As he turned away, he caught a glimpse of Roger's face. Seething jealousy. He'd seen that look on Alastair once. Perhaps it was good he said he was leaving in the morning.

Keats took possession of the writing materials the vicar offered, retreating a short distance away to compose his letter in the dimming light. As he worked, Lily wrote out a note for Old Bill's daughter, since he could hardly hold a pencil.

"She's in Whitby, Yorkshire," he said, "Right fine gal."

"I will send it tonight," Lily said, pencil moving.

"Bless ya."

The moment Keats finished his own correspondence, he tried to press coins into her hand for the postage.

"No, let me do this," she said. "Seeing that you were robbed, it's the least I can do."

*How true.* "You are a blessing, miss."

A soft smile. A short time later, Lily and the preacher left the campsite. It felt colder now.

"Never met someone like that before," Keats said.

"Make someone a right fine wife." Old Bill looked around the group and shook his head. "Won't be one of us. We're not good enough."

"I doubt if any man is," Keats said. Roger gave him a penetrating look and then an understanding nod, the jealousy gone.

Old Bill handed him a couple of the new blankets and Keats curled up at the base of a tree. The dog came by, licked his hand, wagged his tail a couple of times and then went to join Old Bill in the lean-to.

As he lay looking up at the darkening sky, Keats thought of his rooms in Bloomsbury, how luxurious they were compared to this rough place. He had a home to go to. These men had little else but the hard ground beneath them and the sky above.

Maybe someday he'd come back and pay his respects to the golden-haired lady who believed that all men deserved respect, even those who owned nothing but their name.

‡

Flaherty looked up from the crates of dynamite as Paddy lumbered in the warehouse door. He heaved a sigh of relief. Paddy was one of the few he could trust.

"How'd it go?" he asked and then lowered his voice. "He's still alive, isn't he?" Often Paddy didn't know his own strength.

The dockworker nodded his thick neck. "Kickin' inside the coffin. Right put out."

Flaherty laughed at the thought. It'd been a foolish gamble, but something told him to leave the copper alive. *Damned priest.* Nowlan had gotten his hopes up again with all that talk of God's love and such.

"Ya did leave it so he could get free?" he asked.

A nod. "I hit him pretty hard; thought I broke his jaw there for a time."

"How far out of London?"

"North of Stock. I stripped his pockets like y'asked, but left him his boots."

"Why?" Sometimes it was hard to follow Paddy's reasoning.

"It was real rough where I dropped him. Couldn't leave him with no boots, even if he is a filthy rozzer."

Flaherty smiled. "Ya've a good heart, Paddy."

"Why didn't ya leave him in that alley?" the man asked, puzzled.

"I needed some time to get things right." He gestured. "Now give me his stuff."

The large man dug in his pockets and pulled out odds and ends, dropping them on top of one of the crates. Flaherty looked at the collection and snorted. "Not much, is there? Ya'd think a copper would have better geegaws in his pockets." He rummaged through the pile: a pocket watch, a folded note, a bit of money, a few calling cards. Flaherty popped open the watch and shook his head in disappointment. The dial was shattered, the hands stopped at three before eleven.

"Must a happened when I hit him," Paddy said a bit sheepishly.

"Shame. It's a fine watch. We coulda got good brass for it."

"Ya can't pawn this one. It's got his name in it. They'll track it right back to ya for sure." He squinted at the cursive script. *To Jonathon D. Keats, Detective-Sergeant, Scotland Yard, Jan. 1887.* Flaherty looked up at his men. A couple of them were watching him closely. "It's for when he started at the Yard." He huffed. "He was a boil on my bum even before that."

"So why didn't you lance that boil, Flaherty?" one of the men asked. "You cut Ahearn to pieces, but you let that stinkin' pig live. Why?"

"I have my reasons," Flaherty replied.

"Some might say you've lost your nerve," the man said.

Eyes swiveled toward him. The threat of violence flared.

Flaherty dropped the watch and the rest of the copper's possessions into a pocket. "Finish unloadin' these crates as fast as ya can, then lock down the warehouse and hide the wagon." As he walked by the man who'd challenged him, he brandished a brief flash of steel. Then he was out the door.

His challenger stared down at his coat in horror. It had a long rent across the heart, but not deep enough to penetrate the vest or shirt beneath.

"Hell, he nearly killed me!" he spouted.

Paddy shook his head. Lifting two of the half-barrels at once, he observed, "Flaherty never nearly kills nobody."

On the street, Flaherty kept to the shadows, a stick of dynamite hidden under his jacket. It was his dream to light it, stuff it in the *strange one's* trousers and watch him soil himself trying to put it out before it sent him back to Hell.

Pausing only for a second, he pulled the envelope from under his coat and dropped into the letter box. Then he moved on as if it was nothing, just another note to a friend in Ireland. It would be waiting for the little sergeant once he returned from his time in the woods. Flaherty had kept the note blunt; no need to be all flowery about it. If the little sergeant found Fiona, he'd reveal the location of the explosives and turn himself in. After that it wouldn't matter if they hung him or threw him in Newgate forever. As long as Fiona was safe, the rest of the world could rot.

17

The moment she opened the door, the expression on Alastair's face made Cynda's heart sink. He methodically took off his hat and coat and then sank onto the couch.

"Do you have anything to drink?" he asked.

"Tea?"

"Something stronger."

"There's some whiskey over there in the cabinet."

Alastair rose and poured himself a liberal portion.

*This is gonna be ugly.* She'd been fearing this moment. "Do you know about Keats and the Hallcox woman?"

Alastair nodded somberly. "I was called to assist with her post-mortem. We delivered our findings to Chief Inspector Fisher this morning."

*Why you?* "Have they found him yet?"

"No. I sincerely hope he turns himself in before the inquest. Perhaps we can get some of this cleared up and avoid his name being mentioned in open court." He rolled the liquid in the glass. "While I was at the Yard, Fisher asked me if Keats was the sort who attended orgies."

*Uh-oh.*

The doctor looked up. "In the same breath, he mentioned your name, as well. Were you at this debauchery he spoke of?"

"We were both there, but not as participants. We were trying to find out about the assassin. Keats thought Miss Hallcox might know."

"I asked you not to do this, Jacynda."

"I know."

"And yet you went to Keats, behind my back."

She could only nod. If it had turned out differently, she would have been defensive.

He shook his head in disapproval. "Blast his soul! I told him to stay at home and recuperate. He should have refused to help you in any way, if nothing more than for his health.'"

"I know," she murmured. "There were mitigating circumstances."

His eyes narrowed. "How did you learn of Miss Hallcox's murder?"

She told him about Nicci's offer and Keats' dilemma.

"Good God," he muttered. He took a deeper pull of the whiskey, wincing as it burned its way down his throat. "Keats shouldn't have gone anywhere near the woman, no matter what outrageous claim she made."

"That would be like asking you not to visit a sick patient just because she's a prostitute. Keats is a cop. His job is to find the bad guys, no matter where they might be."

That didn't earn her a scowl like she expected.

"I spoke at length with Lord Wescomb," he continued. "He has made private enquiries, and no one believes that the assassin was a Transitive."

"Well, if that's true, it's back in my lap again."

"Lord Wescomb's sources could be wrong."

"That's possible. But there's a lot of politics going on in 2057, and some of it might be playing out here."

He glowered. "Wouldn't that violate some rule or something?"

"It would. Doesn't keep it from happening."

He lowered his eyes again. His jaw was so tight she could see the muscles twitching.

Something else was troubling him. She waited him out.

He took another gulp of the whiskey. "Miss Hallcox had syphilis. She kept records of her various customers. One of them was..."

"Hugo Effington."

"I see." He hesitated and then continued, "Lord Patton."

The name did not ring any carillons. "Who is he?" she asked.

"He is betrothed to Evelyn Hanson, the woman I once planned to marry."

*That's going to mess up the honeymoon.*

"Reuben and I spoke with the lord and his father this afternoon. We were treated abominably. Patton denies he was ever with Miss Hallcox and refuses to be seen by a physician. It is my belief that they will not be forthcoming to Evelyn or her father about the situation."

"Why not?" Cynda asked.

A pained sigh. "Often when a man proposes marriage, the young woman's father will have a private conversation with him to ensure he is not diseased. If the truth is offered, it's a godsend. Most times it is buried. The end result is that the woman contracts syphilis in the marital bed and when she goes to a physician to seek help for her symptoms, she is told it is merely female hysteria."

Cynda took a series of deep breaths to forestall the verbal explosion building inside her. The breaths only made her lightheaded. "That's insane. Talk to Evelyn's father."

"It would be of no help," he replied in a pained voice. "He and I disagreed about informing women of the true nature of their illnesses. He said it would only bring marital disharmony."

"*Marital disharmony?*" Her voice rose in incendiary fury. "You've got to be kidding me. A woman is infected by her bastard of a husband and she can't be told the truth? That's...*murder*. Any society that condones that is barbarous."

His head jerked up, eyes ablaze. "I know we seem primitive to you, but it is the way things are here. We are trying to improve, grow more sensible about such things. It appears we are eventually successful, since your time is so damned *perfect*." He shot the last two words at her like bullets.

Before she could retort, he rose and began to pace. "We never invited *your* people into our century. We are not simpletons or savages to be studied and lectured for our quaint ways. You treat us as if we're inferior beings."

Cynda rocked back in shock. She had never thought of it from *their* perspective. A Rover wouldn't. It was just a job. *Here today, dead tomorrow*, as their black humor put it.

From his perspective, the time immersion industry was the equivalent of the asylum tours in the eighteenth century. The rich paid money to go see the mad people so they could laugh at their bizarre antics. Though the 2057 academics used terms such as "immersion research" and "intra-societal studies," it was the same. Humans always hunted for a reason to feel superior. Sometimes they had to cross centuries to find it.

"I'm sorry. I'd never seen it that way before."

As she struggled to put his observation in perspective, one message came through clearly. All of this was about Evelyn. *He still loves her.*

Perhaps that was for the best. Evelyn was from his century, and though she wasn't a barnburner from what Cynda had heard, she would treat him well.

*But would she ever love him?* Cynda put her own emotions aside. He needed her help. "Do you want me to talk to Evelyn?"

The doctor started in surprise. "I don't..." He thought for a moment and then shook his head. "I doubt she would listen to you."

"It's worth a try."

"No, you two will not see eye-to-eye. Besides, there is no certainty that her fiancé is infected. If he is not, it will crush her to learn he is of that nature and would think so little of her to risk her health."

"She deserves the truth."

He took another long belt of the whiskey. "It may be too late. If the young lord has already convinced her to submit to his passions, she may be infected. If her affliction is made public, the engagement will be nullified and she will find no future suitors."

Unmarried women, the scourge of Victorian culture. Better married and dying than single and healthy.

"Would *you* still marry her?" she asked.

He blinked at the audacious question. "I am not sure. I do not fear the disease, for I know how it is transmitted and we could take precautions. I suspect we would be comfortable together. We never argued like you and I. She wouldn't have stood up to me in any way."

"Too bad. She should have called you on the carpet every now and then."

"Perhaps not as often as you do," he said.

She shrugged as he quaffed the last of the whiskey and rose on unsteady legs. "I must rest. I've been late to the hospital twice this week and have been warned that further infractions will lead to my dismissal. As if that were the worst of my problems."

After collecting his hat and coat, she caught his hand.

"You did the right thing."

That deep well of regret flared in his brown eyes again.

"It will be of little consolation if she dies demented and paralyzed because of that arrogant...person." She heard a stronger word hanging in the air between them.

"In many ways, her death would be on my head. If I hadn't confronted her father, felt the need to assert my authority, we'd still be engaged."

"And Keats would have died because you wouldn't have been in Whitechapel to save him."

His expression flattened. "Is this what you contend with? Do this and one lives, do that and another dies? It's worse than my profession."

She nodded, thinking of Kate Eddowes at Mitre Square. One word might have saved her from the Ripper. The same word might have killed someone else.

"God help us both, then," Alastair said, raising her hand to his lips.

✝

Monday, 15 October, 1888

It was with some reluctance that Keats left the tramps behind. There was an odd feeling of camaraderie among them, though he suspected Kipper would have knocked him over the head and stolen his boots if Old Bill hadn't been around.

Following the directions he was given, he set off along the tracks, aiming for Ingatestone before sundown. The going was rough and he made poor time. A few hours in, he heaved a sigh of relief when he found a path running along the railroad tracks.

*If I were king, there'd be signposts in this damned country.*

There were signposts, of course, but not where he was. As he walked in the clear air, birdsong around him, he tried to work out all that had happened in the last day or so. It was an amazing jumble.

When he returned to London he'd give Fisher a full report, though it would probably earn him an ear-chewing and perhaps a note on his record. He needed his superior's analytical skills. The missing woman was the key to the equation, but he had no notion who she might be. As far he knew, Flaherty had no relatives in London, most of them living in Belfast. Perhaps he could check the Newgate Prison records, see if anyone wrote to Flaherty during his incarceration. Whoever the woman was, she'd inadvertently saved the sergeant's life.

When he wearied of the topic, he set his mind on two more pleasant topics: Jacynda and Lily. Either one would make a splendid mate. Jacynda would be a bit more high-spirited and prone to oaths. Although she had turned down his recent proposal of marriage, he held hope that might not be the case the next time around. Meanwhile, Lily had a simple charm all her own, and a generous heart. Jacynda was thinner, Lily well rounded. Either could easily bear his children. He could well imagine the pleasure they'd have creating them.

*Like you're such a catch*, his mind chided.

"I've got a steady job and a good income," he retorted, bored enough to start talking to himself again.

*You're a copper. You're out all night with whores and cutthroats. What kind of woman wants to marry a man like that?*

"I'm good at what I do. I'll be chief inspector some day."

*If you're so damn good, what are you doing out here, huh?*

To shut down his nagging conscience, he began to whistle a song he'd learned as a kid. In time, he was singing to himself to ease the loneliness. The sound of an approaching train caused him to pause as the cars rattled by him. Faces peered out of windows and a couple of the passengers waved.

He gamely returned the wave and continued his journey, another tramp left behind.

‡

They adjourned to the pub the moment Johnny Ahearn's inquest ended.

"You did well," Reuben said, looking at Alastair over the top of a half-full pint of ale. "You detailed Ahearn's visit to your clinic quite succinctly."

Alastair's eyes focused on the bubbles rising through glass. "His widow kept watching me. All I could think about was her husband's mutilated body."

"Thank God they asked the women and children to leave before I had to testify about the post-mortem details, though some of them were incensed at the idea."

"The widow wasn't," Alastair said. He would always remember her hollow-eyed stare, trembling hands clutching her rounded belly.

"I had expected the jury to find sufficient evidence to implicate Flaherty in the death. I was mistaken," Reuben mused.

"Willful murder by person or persons unknown," Alastair intoned, still focusing on the table. "It cannot be any more impersonal than that."

"Since we're discussing legal matters, do you intend to tell me what haunts your past, or do we save that for another time?"

The door was open. It was time to step through.

"I killed a man in Wales." Reuben whistled under his breath. "He stabbed my lover to death. I saw only red haze. Others pulled me off him, but he was mortally wounded."

"Apparently, the jury did not find you culpable," Reuben replied softly.

"No, they did not; however I wonder if that verdict was correct."

"You still carry that guilt? You'd have been better off if they'd hung you. At least you'd be at peace."

Alastair chuffed. "I fear you're right."

"Personally, I am glad they found the truth," Reuben said. He raised his glass. "A toast to Johnny Ahearn, who did the right thing."

"To Johnny Ahearn," Alastair said, "and for swift capture of the man who killed him."

✝

The pub was quiet this time of day. Malachi Livingston had a pint of ale in front of him, more for appearances than anything. "You're sure it was Miss Lassiter?" he asked.

William nodded and took a gulp of his own pint. "I heard it from one of the maids. She was in the room when it happened."

Livingston tapped the head of his cane in thought. *Why didn't Montrose tell me?* Surely he'd have known. "What did the assassin look like?" he queried.

"Distinguished gent, graying hair. American, they say. They had no notion how he got in. No invite, that's for certain." After another sip, William continued. "Mrs. Effington went and tossed herself into the Thames after the party. The maid said she wasn't surprised. The master is a mean bastard, she said. He beat her all the time."

"Attempted assassination followed by a suicide?" Livingston thought for a moment, his cane-tapping growing more agitated. "Where'd they find the body?"

"Haven't yet. Did the deed in Rotherhithe. Could be out to sea by now."

"Peculiar choice of location. What else have you heard?"

"Effington is nearly out of money. He's been working with shady characters, running illegal goods and skimming off some of the loads. He's got a couple of high-ranking toffs in his pocket, or at least he did until the brass ran thin."

"Thief and wife-beater. He's not going to be up for sainthood soon, is he?"

William grinned and took another pull on the ale.

"I want you to find out why Mrs. Effington vanished on *that* particular night. I want to know if it is possible she hired someone to kill her husband."

William blinked in surprise. "I hadn't thought of that. I figured the assassin was after one of the bluebloods."

"Might have been." Livingston took a sip of his ale. Though he didn't like the stuff, it was a shame to waste it. "See if you can get a guest list. That'll tell us something. Also, see if you can find the names of those high-ranking toffs. I like to know who we're up against." He shoved the drink toward William. "Oh, and do be careful. Keep an eye out for Effington. From what I gather, he's volatile."

"Yes, sir."

Livingston slid a sovereign across the table. "Have you visited the courtesan yet?"

A manly smile flooded the young man's face. "Last night. Very fine lady," he said. "Very fine. I thank you for that, sir."

"Anything to keep your mind on business," Livingston replied, rising. "Oh, and check if Miss Lassiter is still in residence at the Charing Cross Hotel. I might need to speak to her in the days to come."

"I will, sir."

Once he reached the street, Livingston adjusted his cape and hat. There were so many pieces in this puzzle, and that made him ill at ease. Until they were sorted out, he'd not know who was behind this bold move.

He consulted his pocket watch. He had time to visit The Artifice Club before his assignation with Adelaide. As he walked, he picked up the latest newspaper. The lead article might prove an excellent weapon against that old warhorse, George Hastings.

18

"Sorry, miss. Don't have anything like you're asking for," the watchmaker replied. It was as if he were quoting from the same script the previous two and a half score of his brethren had used.

"Thank you anyway," she said, forcing herself to be polite.

"You might try Oddegocker's over on Leadenhall Place. Honest chap. He carries different sorts of watches. I buy stock from him now and then." She hadn't been there. With a name like that, she'd remember.

"Thank you very much."

"Good day, miss," the fellow said, turning his attention to the watch in his hand, probing the interior with a fine screwdriver.

Instead of trekking all the way to the aforementioned street, she parked her bustle in her favorite dining room, seeking solace in tea. Her interface had been depressingly silent except for the "Found missing interface yet?" message she'd received this morning, clearly issued by her boss to keep the bureaucrats from learning what she was up to.

So what was she up to? Davy hadn't been able to get a lead on where Deidre Effington was hiding, but he'd promised to continue to watch Effington's house and follow any maids who came and went. Maybe one of them might lead him to their missing mistress. It was a long shot, but Cynda was hopeful that Mrs. E. knew something about either the assassin or the target. Going from boarding house to boarding house trying to find an elusive Rover was a nonstarter, as they said in these parts. All in all, she had nothing to work with. It wasn't a situation she relished. She knew the Powers That Be were keeping score and right now she was in the negative digits. Morrisey pulled a lot of weight, but TPB held the ultimate authority over her Time Immersion license.

Cynda had just stirred milk into her tea when someone halted near the table. She looked up, half-expecting to see Alastair, since he'd been the one to introduce her to the place. The buzzing of her interface told her she wasn't close. A quick tap and it fell silent.

Frank Miller executed a wide smile. "Tag, you're it."

She stared, openmouthed. Three years back he'd been a quick fling, which had abruptly ended when she'd found out he'd been flinging with two other women at the same time. She'd never been good about sharing.

"What brings you to London?" Cynda asked, gesturing toward the empty chair.

"Vacation." He waved over a server and ordered a plate of tarts. They were instantly delivered.

"Vacation?" she asked, thinking she'd heard wrong. Rovers didn't take vacation in the time stream. It'd be like a plumber spending his holiday in a toilet factory.

"My employer offers side trips to interesting time periods in lieu of vacation pay. I thought I'd check out Ripperland."

There were so many things wrong with that explanation, Cynda didn't know where to start.

"Would you like some tea?" she asked, falling back on Victorian courtesy to buy time. Serving tea allowed one to regroup. Allowed one to figure out how old Frank had found her tucked away in the back corner of an obscure Whitechapel dining room. Her ESR Chip would rat her out on his interface, but he had to be within twenty feet or so for that to happen. That meant he knew where to look.

Frank chuckled and lowered his voice. "Sure, I'd like some tea. And a lot more than that, if you're game."

The offer wasn't surprising. In the past she'd have opted for just that sort of "attitude adjustment," as she called it. A quick roll in the hay, and everything would be all right in the morning. He wasn't a tourist or a local, so it was kosher. No one would care.

But she would. After Chris, that sort of sleazy encounter didn't appeal anymore. He'd upped the stakes, and old Frank wasn't even in the running.

"I agree," Mr. Spider said, wandering out from behind the sugar bowl.

"So how goes it?" Frank asked through a bite of tart, quickly washing it down with a gulp of tea.

"Okay, considering," she lied. "How about you?"

"Not bad. Got a divorce a couple of months ago. Ex couldn't handle my traveling."

"I didn't know you'd gotten married."

"Yeah, about a year back."

He demolished more of the tart. "Pity about Chris Stone, by the way. Nice guy. We worked together at ETC," the voice went even softer, "before I moved to Time In Motion."

That she hadn't known. "I miss him," she said.

Out of the corner of her eye, she watched three blue legs extricate a lump from the sugar bowl. Mr. Spider methodically unwound the lump from its distinctive blue paper wrapper and then lobbed it into her tea.

"Hey!" she said.

"Another one?" he asked, noticeably proud of his accomplishment.

She nodded. *How does he do that?* When she looked back in the bowl, none of the cubes were missing.

"Cynda?" Frank asked.

She shot him a nervous glance. If it got back to '057 she was seeing things, they'd yank her license in a second.

"Hmmmm?" she responded, as if she'd been daydreaming.

"I said, there're a lot of rumors floating around about Chris' death. Some say he killed himself."

She shook her head. "The tourist killed him." *Tortured and killed him. And I let the bastard live.*

"You sure it wasn't Defoe? I've heard he's gone over the deep end."

"No way."

Mr. Spider had another cube in his hands...feet...whatever. The sugar neatly arced into her drink. *That's enough.* An exasperated sigh came from the arachnid, who was clearly enjoying himself.

"So what's this about Chris' watch?" Frank asked.

That brought her back to the moment. "What about it?"

"I heard it was missing and that you brought Stone back in an urn. All the Rovers are talking about it."

She nodded, a suspicious knot forming in her stomach.

"Any idea where the watch is?" he pressured.

Mr. Spider twisted around the sugar bowl to stare at her companion with his compound eyes.

"No clue." *Why do you want to know? Why are you here?*

"Poor guy." Frank shook his head. "He said you two were screwing like a pair of rabbits."

Her fingers tightened on the cup handle, turning as bone white as the china. Chris would have never said that. Mr. Spider fetched another sugar lump, but didn't unwrap it. Instead, he weighed it in his hand, attention firmly on their tablemate.

Frank pressed on. "I'm in London for the night. How about you and I go back to your hotel and shag off some lag?"

*How do you know I'm staying in a hotel?* Rovers usually bunked in boarding houses. She'd only moved to the hotel to put some space between her and Alastair's increasing interest. And the service was top notch.

"I'm still not over Chris yet," she said. Which was the truth.

Frank delivered a libidinous smile, unaware that his seduction was failing miserably. "Oh, I understand. Still, nothing like getting laid, is there?" The sugar flew through the air and caught Frank square on the forehead. He didn't flinch as he reached for another tart. Pity her delusion wasn't real.

She turned her full attention to the annoyance across the table currently wiping crumbs off his waistcoat. "So who sent you to play Spanish Inquisition?"

"I'm not—"

She leaned over and dropped her voice to a near whisper. "Cut the b.s. You don't do this location. You're more a Mesopotamia kind of guy."

"I go where I'm sent," he said, parroting the Rover mantra.

*Which means you're not on vacation.* "Well, here's the message. I don't know where Chris' watch is. I don't know where Defoe is. Tell your handlers that."

"You're taking this all wrong."

"I don't think so. Your bosses work for the Politicos."

"You're working for the Genius. You don't think he's up to his ass in weird shit?"

"Could be. Don't care. Just stop talking about Chris, okay?"

"Fine, whatever you want." He took a sip of tea and then set the cup down with a rattle. "Any chance of hooking up tonight?"

"Go the hell away, Frank."

He rose and then bent over the table with a smirk. "You're in it deep, Cynda. I was your last chance." He was out of the dining room before she could think of a comeback.

"What an arse," Mr. Spider observed. "Don't know what you saw in him."

"No idea myself," she murmured.

The server hurried over with a chagrined expression. True to form, Frank had stiffed her for his portion of the bill.

‡

"I trust you've seen the newspaper?" Livingston asked, dumping the latest edition on George Hastings' lap.

Hastings tossed it aside with a snort. "I have. There's nothing else to read."

Cartwright looked up briefly from his crossword puzzle, then went head down again.

Once Livingston settled into his chair, Ronald handed him a glass of brandy and offered a cigar. He declined the latter.

"I am surprised The Conclave allowed Miss Hallcox such latitude over the years," Livingston said.

"Just a fancy whore, nothing else."

"From what I hear, she's been pushing her luck for a very long time."

"Familiar with her, were you?"

"Only by reputation," Livingston replied. "Still, it does beg the question why we would waste our time harassing someone like Dr. Montrose when Miss Hallcox was a genuine threat to our anonymity."

"She was under control," Hastings said. He took a swig of brandy, followed by a long intake on his cigar. The smoke flowed out, hanging in the air like a disoriented wraith.

"Under whose control?" Livingston challenged.

"What is a nine-letter word for extortion?" Cartwright asked, tapping his whiskered cheek with a pencil, oblivious to the rising tension in the room.

"Blackmail," Livingston said, "deriving from both Old and Middle English." His eyes never left Hastings.

The warhorse looked away first, confirming his suspicions.

"Of course. Thank you," Cartwright replied, penciling in the letters.

"My pleasure."

Hastings cleared his throat. "If Sergeant Keats is named as the killer, that will complicate the issue."

*Keats?* Perhaps there was more here than Livingston realized. The newspapers hadn't mentioned a suspect by name. "Why do you think it is the sergeant?" he hedged.

"I heard it from someone at Home Office. He said that the sergeant was Miss Hallcox's last assignation that evening. The Yard is keeping it quiet, but they are running out of time with the inquest on for Friday."

*Just how high in the government had Miss Hallcox extended her reach?* "Who is this person who chose to be so candid?" Livingston asked.

"Oh, an assistant of some sort," Hastings replied, waving a hand dismissively. "He prefers to remain anonymous."

"I wouldn't doubt that."

"I never did like the idea of one of us being at the Yard,"

Hastings remarked. "Too dangerous. Perhaps now is the time to sever that connection."

"Too dangerous for whom?" Livingston asked.

Another puff of smoke. "You sound like the doctor. Perhaps both of you should take some time away, Livingston. Go to the Continent."

*So that you can play executioner?* "I shall consider it," Livingston lied. He quaffed the brandy and made it to the door before his companions knew what he was about. "Good evening, gentlemen."

On the street, he hiked until he found a hansom and set it toward the West End. He would be early to Adelaide's, but that was of no concern. Besides her amatory talents, she was a keen judge of human nature. He'd be willing to bet a fine meal at Simpson's that the events at Effington's party and Nicci Hallcox's death were related, and that Hastings was somehow involved.

✝

Frank's sudden appearance had sparked a swarm of questions in Cynda's mind. Despite Morrisey's assertions to the contrary, Chris' watch was growing more important by the minute. "Find it and you'll know why," her delusion remarked from his place on her shoulder.

She jerked her eyes toward him. "Why are you sitting there?"

"Your hat's not that comfortable," he replied.

"Of course. Silly me."

Cynda turned her mind back to the problem. The way the watch was constructed, no one in this century would know what it was or how it worked. Despite all of TPB's posturing, the loss of one interface was not as big a deal as one might expect. Even if a Victorian figured out how to trigger the interface, all they had was a pretty colorful watch. If that industrious person then managed to accidentally transfer to another time period, a clean-up operation would be mounted. The failsafes were built in.

Losing a Rover, on the other hand, rated far higher in Cynda's book.

"Not to the bureaucrats. People are always replaceable," Mr. Spider remarked.

*Are all spiders so cynical?*

"Only the blue ones."

With the Whitechapel killer on hiatus, the streets were anything but empty. Besides the ubiquitous newslads and working girls, there were costermongers with their carts and slaughtermen on the way to their homes, clad in shirts and pants splattered with fresh blood.

"No wonder they never found the Ripper," Mr. Spider observed. "Everybody here looks like they just killed someone."

"Got that right."

There was a commotion on the street ahead of them.

"Come you lads, give it up!" a cop ordered.

When one of the combatants lunged in his direction with a knife, the constable let loose with a piercing two-tone shriek from his whistle and waded in with his truncheon. The battle was on.

A few moments later, another constable pounded past Cynda. By the time she reached the scene, both of the fighters were in custody and the first constable was holding a handkerchief to a wound on his hand. Some of the bystanders booed, and one brave soul threw a rotten apple.

*Just another night in Whitechapel.*

Cynda headed west along Aldgate. As she neared Mitre Square, her mood darkened. A fortnight before, Kate Eddowes had died there.

She kept a small piece of the dead woman's skirt, not as a memento, but more like a memorial—a reminder that for every bit of history a Rover kept on track, someone paid a price. Because Cynda hadn't warned Kate not to take that last walk into the square, history had remained unchanged. In many ways, a part of her had perished with Kate.

On impulse, she cut right onto Duke Street. She'd come this way on *that* night, seen the man who'd kill Kate. The Ripper. At the time, she'd feared it to be Alastair Montrose. To her relief, it hadn't been. That hadn't been any consolation to Kate Eddowes.

The solitary gas lamp at the entrance to Church Passage had little effect on the gloom, its sooty glass holding most of the light hostage. Cynda stood there for some time, drawing the courage to go forward. It wasn't that she believed in ghosts, but this place held a certain horror for her.

*Come on, just do it.*

The moment she entered Church Passage she felt cold seep into her spine, as if evil still resided in the stones. As she stepped into the open square, her eyes went immediately to the corner where Constable Watkins had discovered the mutilated body.

Each of her footsteps echoed across the open ground. As she drew near, she saw the wilted flowers. Cynda knelt and touched a faded rose that had molded itself over the bricks.

"Rest in Peace, Kate," she whispered. "They never caught him.

I'm sorry."

A solemn "Amen" came from her shoulder.

There was a clamor of footsteps, and then a voice erupted from the passage that led to Mitre Street. Cynda rose and headed toward the noise, displeased at the interruption.

The voice continued on in a monotone from a gentleman who had his back to her. He was clad in a somber black suit, like an undertaker. A group of six clustered near him, listening eagerly. One of the women kept adjusting her hat, like Cynda had when she'd first come to 1888.

"Tourists?" Mr. Spider asked, peering at them intently.

*Can't be. No ESR Chips. This time period is still a "no go" zone because of the murders.*

"Your former employer didn't care about that," the spider replied. Waiting in the twilight, she strained to hear the group's leader.

"Just a few yards from here, Catherine Eddowes died in Mitre Square. She was arrested earlier in the evening of the twenty-ninth of September for drunkenness and taken to Bishopsgate Police Station. When released, instead of heading for her lodgings, she made her way to this area, where she met her end at the hands of Jack the Ripper."

*A Ripper tour? Already?*

In years to come, the tours would be commonplace, an oral history of the Ripper's legacy. But this, so soon after Kate's murder, seemed sacrilegious.

There were murmurs in the group. One of the men held a glossy brochure that looked too fancy for this time period. Her former employer used to hand out sales literature like that.

An "Oh no" came from her shoulder.

The guide continued in his monotone. "The next development in the case is when George Lusk receives a package containing a portion of a kidney preserved in wine. An accompanying note claimed it came from Eddowes and that the murderer fried up the remainder of the kidney and made a meal of it." One of the group gasped.

*Lusk?* Cynda couldn't remember when he'd received the package. Maybe it was all kosher.

The guide continued, "From the night of the Double Event to the ninth of November, there were no murders that could be attributed to the Ripper. There is speculation that he may have been in jail, in hospital or an asylum during that period of time."

Cynda's mouth dropped open. No one else in this time period knew of Mary Kelly's death—three and a half weeks *before* it had taken place.

"No!" she said, stepping out of the shadows. A couple of the tourists shied backwards, as if she held a blade in her hand. "You can't do this!"

The tour leader turned toward her. "Is there a problem, miss?"

She dropped her voice to a lethal whisper. "Who the hell do you think you are? You can't talk about...*November!* Not *now!*"

The guide's jaded expression did not waver. "And you are?"

"I'm Jacynda Lassiter. I'm a Time Rover with TEM Enterprises."

One of the tourists went "ohhh," and there was the flash of a nano bulb and the whir of a shutter. Mr. Spider ducked under her mantelet, complaining about his many eyes.

"Oh, come on! You can't use that here!" she said, her own eyes watering.

"I think I've heard of you," the tour guide replied. He sounded sincerely unimpressed, despite her reputation within the industry.

"You shouldn't even be here. This is a restricted time period."

"It is not restricted anymore," the guide replied.

*Not restricted?* "So why didn't I register you...or them?" she demanded, giving a sweep of her hand to encompass the tourists.

He crooked a bushy eyebrow. "We have a special license to travel with muted ESR's."

"What?" Nobody was allowed to hide an Essential Record Chip. It was a Class Three Felony. "Who gave you that license?"

"It's not your concern."

"It *is* my concern. I'm the one who has to clean up after you if you make a mess of it. Who gave you the damned license?"

The guide sniffed. "Time In Motion is my employer. If you have any concerns, speak with them." He pointedly turned his back on her. "Let's see, where was I? Ah, yes. There has been a recent development involving a Dr. Montrose, a Whitechapel physician, and for a time it was believed he was involved in the killings. Alas, that proved to be a hoax perpetrated by a twenty-first century publishing house to promote a new book." He gestured down the passage. "Now if you'll come this way, I'll show you the actual location where Catherine Eddowes met her grisly end."

Cynda sputtered in rage as the group filed around her, some of them shooting her wary looks. As they passed, one of the women said to another, "I told you we should have waited until they opened that new tour. We could have been right there in Miller's Court when it happened. We could have seen the killer for ourselves!"

*Oh, God.*

19

There was a protocol to be followed when one visited Adelaide Winston, and Livingston was always careful to follow it. You arrived at a side entrance to preserve your anonymity, were shown to a private room where fine brandy and cakes were available, and waited. Adelaide was a courtesan, one of the *grandes horizontales* whose talents should be esteemed, not demanded in a drunken or rowdy voice. Miscreants who behaved otherwise, be they lord or prince, were firmly escorted out the side door and told not to return.

Adelaide no longer charged for his presence in her bed, deeming him a lover, not a customer. She did not keep him waiting long, but then her schedule on Mondays was always light. He was her only visitor.

"Malachi. Welcome," she said, floating into the room like a silk-gowned vision. Her rich auburn hair glinted in the gaslight, flowing down her back as she knew he loved it.

"Dear Adelaide. It seems like forever." He meant it.

"Do you wish to talk or go up right away?"

"Talk can come later," he said, laying a delicate kiss on her neck. He felt her shiver underneath him in anticipation.

"That is how I feel," she said. They touched hands in a certain fashion, then he made a mark in her palm and she returned it. They smiled at each other, having established that each was indeed who they appeared to be. It was too dangerous otherwise.

"Come along, Malachi," she said, taking his hand. "I do not wish to wait another moment further."

Once they had reignited their passions and consumed them in a heady rush of pleasure, she laid her head on his chest and snuggled close, her hair draping down her shoulders in a wavy cascade. He craved these moments, knowing them to be so rare.

"You are troubled tonight, Malachi. I sense it."

He was immediately chagrined. "I am so sorry, Adelaide. I hope I did not slight you in any way."

"No, you never do. I so look forward to our time together." She planted a kiss on his cheek. "What is troubling you?"

"Nicci Hallcox."

She stiffened slightly. "I do hope you will not be telling me you actually went with that person."

"No, I have not been with her. What I wish to know is who would most want her dead."

Adelaide's tension eased. "About anyone who'd had relations with her, I would think. She was a vile creature."

"I believe the man they will name as her killer may be innocent. My guess is that someone presented as him so that he would be found guilty of the crime."

She raised her head. "Who is this innocent person?"

"A sergeant at Scotland Yard. His name is Jonathon Keats."

Adelaide returned her head to his chest. "I read about him in the papers when those explosives went missing. Quite an intriguing fellow."

"Quite a dead fellow if this charade continues. Have any of your...sources given any notion why this murder was committed?"

She sat up, pulling the sheet close to her body. "No, they have not. In fact, there has been scant talk of this in my presence, which is quite unusual."

"Perhaps they do not wish to upset you," he replied.

"I do not think that's the issue. I believe they are nervous about exposure. One of my regular gentlemen alluded to his activities in my bed and the potential for blackmail on my part."

Livingston frowned. "Did you demand he issue you an apology for such an insinuation?"

"No. However, I will be occupied whenever he attempts to make an appointment with me in future."

"Good." Livingston huffed. "Some men have no manners."

Adelaide smiled softly. "Most, actually. You being one of the exceptions, Malachi."

He inclined his head at the compliment.

"What does The Conclave say about all this?" she asked.

"If you mean Hastings, he's already hinting about Keats' eventual *accident*. No doubt it will be of the fatal variety."

"You once said you felt Hastings was not his own man. I agree.

I think the Ascendant is pulling his strings."

Livingston blinked. "I thought the position of Ascendant was discarded in the Middle Ages."

"On the contrary, there has always been an Ascendant, but it has been merely a figurehead—someone who enjoyed the title, but did not take it literally. It was just recently that the power of the position has increased. The Seven Assassins have been reinstituted once again."

"The Seven," Livingston murmured. "All Virtuals?"

"A few, I gather, including the Lead Assassin, as is tradition."

"Who is the Lead now?"

"Someone who calls himself Satyr. He is an abomination, from what I've heard."

Livingston shook his head, astounded. "How did you learn all this?"

"Being a Transitive has it bonuses. Our people are often very open about such matters if they feel you are discreet. One of my gentlemen is a member of the Twenty: those who select the next Ascendant. I have found him quite talkative when he's in the right mood."

"I thought they were sworn to silence."

"They are. However, he had aspirations to become the new Ascendant and so he's displeased at being passed over."

Livingston pulled her back onto his chest, covering her with the thick counterpane to submerge the gooseflesh that had appeared on her soft skin.

"I wonder who the assassin was at Effington's party," he murmured.

"I've not heard. However, there is speculation that his target was the Lead Assassin."

"That's intriguing news."

The smell of her perfume performed its magic. His body told him it was time to move to more pleasant pursuits.

"Let us forget all this for the rest of the night," he said, smoothing a finger down her soft cheek.

"One last thing. You must be cautious of William."

"Why?" he asked, his temper stirring. "Did he act inappropriately with you?"

"No, he was amiable sport, but I sense his loyalty is divided. He was too curious about you. Usually men are considerably more engaged in the moment, if you understand my meaning."

"I do," he said, putting her warning away for later consideration. He had already made up his mind he would recommend no more men to Adelaide's bed.

She trailed a hand down his chest. He moaned at her touch and smiled. "You are a menace, Adelaide. I would spend my life making love to you if I didn't have this work to do."

"Someday I shall retire, dear Malachi. That day comes soon. I have my fortune and I want a quiet life. Perhaps you'll be there to share it."

He looked into her eyes and saw a future he might not live to enjoy.

"I adore you, Adelaide," he whispered.

"I know, dear Malachi, I know."

✝

Cynda didn't bother to remove her hat or her shawl, her fury exploding in a torrent of typing the moment the interface logged on.

*What the hell is going on here?* she demanded.

*Cyn? What's happened?*

*Why are there tourists running around '88?*

*Shouldn't be, not with TIC out of business. The others got the message.*

*Didn't work. I just heard a tour guide tell his group about the last Ripper murder three weeks IN THE FUTURE.*

*Sh\*t!*

*Yeah, double dose. They masked their ESR Chips. I just happened to stumble over them.*

There was a significant delay, no doubt to allow Ralph time to relay this information to their boss.

Then he was back. *What company were they with? We'll file a grievance.*

*Time In Motion. The guide said he had a license to do this.*

*We'll check it out.*

*Sounds like they're planning trips to 9 Nov for a ringside seat to the Kelly killing. They're making this a freaking sideshow!*

*Hold on.* More silence. Cynda paced, waiting for the response. Mr. Spider was sitting near the keyboard, entranced by the words hanging in the air above it.

"Why are they doing this?" she demanded. "This is everything we Rovers try to prevent."

"Perhaps it's like the Defoe-as-assassin incident," Mr. Spider observed.

She sank into the chair and gave him a long look. Having an astute delusion wasn't a bad thing.

"Makes sense. If it blows up, they can blame recreational time travel and shut it all down, just like Morrisey said." She nodded appreciatively. "Have I ever told you you're a devious little spider?"

"No, not once," he said, looking extremely flattered.

The screen lit up. *New regs out a week ago. '88 has been opened up by order of TPB. We didn't receive notice of the change.*

"Probably because Morrisey would have been kicking someone's ass over it," she said. Her hallucination nodded in agreement. A thought occurred and she put it into a question. *What other time periods are open?*

*Only 1888 so far.*

"Only '88." In case someone was tapping the line, she added, *Still looking for Chris' watch.*

*Good deal. Keep us posted.*

*Log Off.*

*Logged Off.*

"Why not another time period?" she pondered.

"Perhaps it's not so much the time period, but the people within it," Mr. Spider suggested.

Cynda nodded. "Defoe. It keeps coming back to him. We gotta find Deidre and figure out who the assassin was trying to kill. Then I might get a clue to what's going on."

‡

*Tuesday, 16 October, 1888*

Though John Patrick Ahearn was past caring who attended his funeral, Alastair was still wary. Not all of the deceased Irishman's friends or family might take well to his presence. He kept a discreet distance from the coffin as the priest droned on. Standing near the open grave was the widow, a pale and weeping figure. Though his knowledge of the Catholic religion was scant, Protestants were no strangers to grief. A few of the mourners cast suspicious glances his way. He ignored them. If Flaherty had the guts to try to kill him here, so much the better. It'd save them having to cart the anarchist's body to the graveyard.

Once the funeral had ended, a solemn line of mourners marched toward the closest pub to drain a pint in the deceased's honor.

Alastair introduced himself to the cleric.

The priest was unimpressed. "I'm Father Nowlan," he said, his brogue thick as a London fog. "I saw yer name in the newspaper. Ya were in that fight in Whitechapel."

"I was."

Alastair looked down into the grave where the plain coffin awaited burial. "Do you know how he died?" he asked in a low voice.

"I heard."

"The majority of the people I treat are Irish, and they can't afford to pay. I don't care where they come from or how they worship; I just know they need help. Ahearn warned me that Desmond Flaherty was going to bomb my clinic. He paid a high price for his humanity."

The cleric went still.

Alastair pulled an envelope from his pocket. "This money is for the widow. It comes from Sergeant Keats and myself, in acknowledgement of her loss. If you think it's best she not know where it came from, we're agreeable. We don't want her on the streets, not in her condition."

The man thought for a moment and then took the envelope. "So what's yer sermon, Doctor?"

"Flaherty's mission is to kill. It does not matter who is in the way. We need help to stop him."

The priest leveled his dark eyes on Alastair. "Then here's mine: the devil ya see is not always the devil ya should fear. There's more to it than just Flaherty, sir."

"So tell me what all this is about."

A shake of the head. "I can't. I'm bound by God's law. For once, I wish I weren't."

As the cleric strode out of the graveyard, coat flapping in the breeze, a large raven settled on a tombstone a few rows away from the open grave. It sharpened its beak on the stone, eyeing Alastair. When the gravediggers moved forward to finish the job, the bird gave a throaty call and took to the air in a dark blur of wings.

20

"Does this train go under water at any time?" Cynda asked.

The conductor's elegant handlebar moustache waggled at the question. "No, miss. Just on to Canterbury and Dover. We stop before we reach the water."

"Excellent," she replied. Cynda popped for a First Class ticket to Canterbury and settled into one of the compartments, tucking her skirts around her like a proper lady. Even though it was highly unlikely that Keats was visiting his family in Canterbury, they might be able to provide her with clues as to where he was hiding.

Her journey was one of pique. Lots of pique, actually. The changes in 1888 had rattled her. She'd sacrificed five years of her life and so much more to keep time on track. Dedication to that quest was in the lifeblood of every Rover, including Chris. Now some marketing department jerk was willing to run roughshod over it all to earn a few more bucks.

The more troubling issue was Keats' silence. Why hadn't he turned himself in, or at least contacted her? Didn't he trust her to help him?

Cynda removed her hat and placed it in her lap. That wasn't proper, but the thing bugged her as much as the bustle. She was acutely aware that in a million little ways she wasn't Victorian. That was becoming more obvious with each passing day. She'd pick up some social skill, only to have a hundred other discrepancies thrown in her face. Her time at Effington's party had been a depressing case in point, though people were polite or merely stared at her when she did something odd.

*Like tackling Defoe, or whoever that guy was.*

To her relief, there'd been no mention of her in the press in any substantial form. That probably wasn't Inspector Hulme's doing, but someone higher on the food chain, which meant there were some serious players involved.

Bored with the wait, Cynda turned her attention to the passengers pressing toward the train. A little girl held a birdcage, its occupant a skylark nesting on a small section of turf. She was kneeling by the cage, talking to the small bird while her parents arranged for a porter to handle their luggage.

The carriage door slid open and a man in a well-tailored suit entered, bowler in hand. He had brown hair and a moustache, with a fringe of gray at the temples. "Do you mind if I join you, miss?"

She shook her head, gesturing toward the bench seat across from her. He settled, crossed his legs and then peered out the window.

A minute or so later, the train pulled out of the station and headed east. The grimy city slowly evolved into late autumn countryside. It was a welcome sight. She'd always loved rural England.

"The hops picking has not been good this year, I hear," her companion said flatly while flicking a bit of dust off his knee. He had intelligent eyes.

"No, it hasn't." She'd learned that tidbit from one of the Ripper's victims. "Hard on the local economy, I gather."

"Indeed," he concurred. "Are you an American?"

"Yes."

"From New York?"

She paid more attention now, her caution rising. "Yes, how did you know?"

"A fortunate guess."

He returned his gaze out the window. Taking that as a sign of disinterest, she did the same.

For the remainder of the journey to Canterbury, they held their silence. Though she'd not intended to, she actually dozed, her head against the side of the carriage. When she woke, her companion was watching her intently. "Sorry," she said, straightening herself and then replacing the hat. "Travel always does that to me."

He smiled benignly. "I can't sleep on a train. Quite annoying when you're going a great distance. Consider yourself fortunate."

The moment the train halted, he led the way, helping her down the stairs and onto the platform.

"Thank you, sir."

"Good day, miss. Enjoy your visit to Canterbury." He tapped his bowler and set off at a brisk pace.

Using the address supplied by Keats' landlady, Cynda took a hackney toward London Road. His family's house was a three-story white structure, a bit larger than its neighbors. A cascade of flowers hung like colorful bunting under the broad bay window, despite it being mid-October.

"This is it, miss," the jarvey said, pulling the horse to a halt. "You want me to wait?"

"No. I have no idea how long this will take." She paid the sum and the cab rolled away.

Readjusting her hat, Cynda took a deep breath. This could be awkward, especially if they did not know about Nicci's death. She tapped on the door and waited. The maid answered.

"Yes, miss?"

"I'm Jacynda Lassiter," she said. "I've come to..." she rummaged for how Sephora would say this, "call on Mr. Jonathon Keats, should he be in."

A look of panic, quickly submerged. "Oh, ah, one moment, miss. Let me see if he's, ah, available." The door closed.

Cynda groaned. Usually, domestic servants parked you in one of the front rooms while the owners of the house decided if they were well and truly home. In this case, she'd been left on the front steps like a beggar. Sephora would not have stood for this. Cynda resisted the temptation to hammer on the door and demand entrance while they worked out what to do with her.

A carriage went by, then another. She bit her lip, counting slowly to thirty. The door reopened. This time the maid had a sheepish look, no doubt roundly chastised for the lack of courtesy.

"Please come in, miss. Mr. and Mrs. Fitzgerald will see you now."

"Thank you."

Cynda was escorted to a sunlit room at the back of the house—a pleasant change from the dark and cluttered rooms she'd seen in other houses. Victorians had the habit of buying enough stuff for four houses and trying to cram it all in one. This room looked like an extension of the lush garden just outside the double doors. Pleasant and welcoming.

She was met by an older couple, Keats' grandparents. He'd spoken of them often during his recovery, and they matched what she imagined they'd look like. Mr. Fitzgerald had a full beard with pure white, bushy eyebrows. His eyes reminded her of Keats—mischievous. He rose stiffly to greet her. His diminutive wife remained seated, a carved mahogany cane resting at her side. She had silvery gray hair and bright eyes.

The older gentleman beckoned Jacynda forward. "Miss Lassiter, please do come in."

"I'm sorry for intruding." Cynda wasn't particularly sorry, but it had to be said. She sat as primly as possible in the proffered chair.

"You must accept our apology as well," the woman replied. "We did not realize you were coming, or we would have met you at the station." It was odd how this century apologized for nearly everything, whether they were responsible or not.

"No, no, it is not your fault. I made the trip on a whim. Jonathon mentioned he might come for a visit."

The old couple traded looks.

She had so hoped Keats was here. There was something restful about this house that would help him heal. Maybe it was all the flowers. Far better than hunting around the East End for that phantom Irishman.

The old man nodded politely. "One moment." He gave a silver bell a shake, then sank onto the couch next to his wife.

*He's here?* She smiled at the thought. That would be a good start.

"Jonathon wrote about you. He said you were very brave that night he was injured," Mrs. Fitzgerald commented.

*He wrote you about me?* "It really was nothing. It was his bravery that mattered."

"Jonathon thinks very highly of you, dear. He is quite taken with you."

"He is a very wonderful person," Cynda replied, and meant it.

"He said you are aware of our...unusual abilities."

*What hasn't he told you?* "Yes, I am."

"You are not so inclined?" the woman asked.

"No, not at all." She had enough trouble with hallucinations without becoming one.

The door opened, and after a moment's hesitation, Keats entered. He was beaming, and his eyes sparkled far merrier than last time she'd seen him. As she rose, he took her hand and kissed it.

"It's so good of you to visit us, Miss Lassiter. I had hoped you would come to Canterbury."

"My pleasure. I see you are *much* better."

"Oh, I'm doing very well, thank you."

*Now for the coup de grace.* "Is your knee still troubling you?"

A startled look and then, "What? Oh, no, much improved."

"I see. I was concerned, given how badly it was injured during the fight."

"Oh, it's right as rain, as they say."

"Then how about we do the introductions again."

"Pardon?"

She held out her hand. "I don't think we've met. I'm Jacynda Lassiter. And you are...?"

He shot the older couple a desperate look.

Mr. Fitzgerald gave a wheezy sigh. "Jonathon said you were a very perceptive woman. What gave it away?"

"The location and size of the bandage. Jonathon's is on his upper right forehead, not near his temple. He always calls me Miss Jacynda, and he didn't hurt his leg in the fight."

A conciliatory nod. "Shut the door, Roddy. We owe the lady an explanation. Oh, and ask the maid to fetch us some tea and brandy. I, for one, could use a snort."

After the tea had been delivered, Roddy shifted back into his own form. He was at least a decade younger than Keats.

"I'm Jon's cousin," he explained. "When we received a letter from him asking for our assistance, we determined I should portray him for any visitors."

Cynda's teacup halted halfway to her mouth. She set it down with a clunk.

"Have the police been here to speak with you?"

"A constable came to the door a couple days ago. He asked if Jon were home. I told him that as far as we knew, he was in London. Now that we've received his letter, we know he's not."

"When did you receive it?"

"Just today," Roddy replied. "He must've written it in a hurry, because his handwriting is usually more legible."

"May I see it?"

At a nod of approval from Keats' grandfather, the letter was fetched. The envelope was badly wrinkled and smudged with dirt.

"Ingatestone," Cynda mused aloud. "Where is that?"

Roddy grinned. "I had to look it up on the map. It's northeast of London."

*Why are you outside of the city?* "Does he know someone there?"

"Not that I am aware."

She skimmed the brief letter. Keats reported that he was involved in a special investigation and that after a slight mishap, he was back on the anarchist's trail. He was quite concerned that Fisher might learn that he was disobeying orders and asked his family to act as if he were visiting them in Canterbury, should anyone make inquiries about him. Afterward, he spoke of how devastated he was at the loss of the watch his grandfather had given him on the occasion of his promotion to Detective-Sergeant.

Bewildered, Cynda read the letter again. "He doesn't know," she whispered.

"Pardon?" the young man asked.

Cynda returned the letter to its envelope. When she looked up, three pairs of eyes were riveted on her.

She turned to Roddy. "It is very dangerous for you to go about looking like your cousin right now."

The young man's eyes widened. "Good heavens, why?"

"Jonathon has been..." *God, this is hard.* "The police wish to speak to him about the death of a woman in London."

Keats' grandfather leaned forward. "Do you mean that Jon is somehow *involved* in this woman's murder?"

"That's what the police wish to find out," Cynda replied. "According to the woman's butler, he was the last one to see her alive. He's been missing since the night she was killed."

"When was that?"

"Last Saturday evening."

"Oh, dear," Mrs. Fitzgerald murmured, crumpling a handkerchief in her pale hands. "If that is the case, why didn't he go to them and clear up this misunderstanding?"

"I don't know." Cynda gestured toward the letter. "From the look of things, he may not know the cops are looking for him."

Mr. Fitzgerald asked in a lowered voice, "How was the lady killed?"

"She was strangled. She was of..." Cynda struggled for the right words, "a woman of low morals. Chief Inspector Fisher is doing what he can, but until Jonathon tells his side of the story, it looks bad."

Fitzgerald leaned back, his snowy brows furrowed. "Ah yes, Chief Inspector Fisher. Jon mentions him frequently. He says he's an excellent policeman."

"From what I hear, the praise fits." She took a sip of tea, minus the brandy.

"Well, he'll turn himself in, I'm sure," Mr. Fitzgerald said. "Until that time, at least no one will be able to recognize him. That's a comfort."

A comfort Cynda wasn't willing to snatch from them. Hopefully, Keats had healed enough he could go *en mirage* now.

After a tap on the door, the maid entered. "Sir, there's a police officer at the door. Says he wishes to speak to you." She handed over a card.

Mr. Fitzgerald groaned and read aloud, "Chief Inspector J.R. Fisher of Special Branch, Scotland Yard."

"What does he look like?" Cynda asked, a suspicion forming in the back of her mind.

"Very distinguished older gent."

"Brown hair with gray at the temples, wearing a black suit?"

The maid nodded.

*The guy on the train who knew I was from New York.*

Cynda shoved her teacup at Roddy. "I'll take that brandy now."

After she polished off the tea in two gulps, she slipped out a side door and walked a couple of blocks to try to calm her nerves. Finally, she hailed a cab for the journey to the railway station.

It was no great surprise when a certain distinguished gent took his place next to her on the train platform a half an hour later. He doffed his hat in respect and offered his card. She gave it a quick look and pocketed it.

"I am pleased to finally meet the infamous Miss Lassiter," he said. "You have quite a reputation for adventure."

"And I hear you're an excellent copper," she said.

There was a hint of a smile.

"Did you read Keats' letter?" He nodded. "I don't think he knows what's going on."

"I had the same thought, though it begged incredulity. Keats always reads the newspapers. He has to know of Miss Hallcox's death."

"What's he doing in Ingatestone?" she said. "Could Flaherty be there?"

"Our sources say he's still in London, though precisely where has eluded us."

Fisher extracted a pocket watch and triggered the cover. After scrutinizing the time, he snapped it shut. In the distance, she heard the sound of a train whistle.

"I had so hoped he was here and that his family could provide a suitable alibi," he said. "It would have settled the matter."

The train halted in front of them. Doors sprang open and passengers alighted onto the platform. Once the way was clear, the chief inspector assisted her up the stairs and followed her to a First Class carriage. She took off her hat, tossing it on the seat. Fisher set his bowler in his lap, dusting it expertly with a cuff.

"You intrigue me, Miss Lassiter. You have a decided taste for danger."

"I lead a full life," she admitted.

"'Full' is hardly the word. First you were knifed in a Whitechapel alley, then you were involved in that altercation in Green Dragon Place. Most recently, you foiled an assassination."

Cynda shrugged, not knowing what else to do.

"All of this leads me to wonder what sort of person you are. To that end, I've made enquiries."

She offered a harmless smile as her stomach began churning.

"However, the mystery is now solved." He paused, but she didn't take the bait. "To my amazement, I received a cable this morning from New York stating that you are in the employ of the Pinkerton Agency."

*You think you're surprised.* Pinkerton's was the premier

detective agency in America, well known even in England. That had to be Morrisey coming through with her back story. Pity he hadn't bothered to tell her what it was.

"Well, now you know," she said.

"Are the Wescombs aware of your profession?"

She shook her head.

"How about the doctor or my sergeant?"

"No. I was ordered to keep a low profile," she said.

"So it would seem." He gave her a stern look. "Did you know there would be a murder attempt that night at Effington's?"

"No."

A skeptical look. "I am told Miss Hallcox's parties were always rife with sexual licentiousness, and that my sergeant attended one a few nights before the woman's murder. Is that correct?"

*Might as well be straight.* "Keats took me to see Nicci only because he thought she might have information about the assassin. Unfortunately, she didn't. She was hosting an orgy, but we didn't know that until we arrived. The scene revolted him."

"Not you?"

"I'm not easily shocked, Chief Inspector."

"Miss Hallcox attempted to seduce my sergeant while he was at the debauchery. At least that's her butler's claim."

"She did, and failed miserably."

"Perhaps Keats changed his mind, and that led to his visit last Saturday evening."

Cynda shook her head vigorously. "Not the way he looked at her. He was repulsed."

"Repulsed enough to strangle her?"

*This man's a menace. He twists words so easily.*

"No. Keats wouldn't waste time on Nicci. He's after the explosives."

"Then why do you think he went to see her?" he pressed.

*The butler must've told him about the note.* "I think you know."

An imperceptible nod. "Do you know what the correspondence said?"

"I didn't see it, but Keats told me Nicci claimed to have information on the whereabouts of *his explosive Irishman.*"

The chief inspector's mouth pursed. "So you spoke with my sergeant Saturday evening."

This guy was too quick. No wonder he'd made chief inspector. "Yes. He visited me at the hotel."

"What was the purpose of that visit?"

"Keats asked for my opinion on what to do about Nicci's offer."

Fisher shifted positions on the seat. "Was she blackmailing my sergeant?"

"No." *Please don't ask.*

"Did she threaten to blackmail him?"

*Damn.* She didn't want to lie, but she didn't dare tell him about the threat to Keats' career. That would be like handing him a ready-made guilty verdict.

She cleared her throat, framing her reply with care. "The deal was simple: if Keats bedded Nicci, she'd tell him where Flaherty could be found. She made it plain she'd own him from that day forward."

Fisher eyed her, and she returned his gaze. He knew she was shading the truth.

*Don't push it any further, not if you care about your sergeant.*

Fisher turned away and stared out of the window at the passing landscape. Cynda found she was clutching the edge of her mantelet so tightly, her fingers felt on fire.

"Who do you think did the deed?" the cop asked. When he looked back, there was a question in his eyes, and it wasn't just the one he'd asked.

*Does he know about the Transitives?*

"Perhaps the butler didn't get a good look at the murderer, or...thought he saw Keats when it was actually someone else."

Their eyes connected. She put it as plainly as she dared. "Sometimes, not everyone is as they appear."

The chief inspector visibly relaxed. "Was Miss Hallcox one of those?"

She nodded.

"Then I shall be equally candid. I am aware of my sergeant's unique abilities and those of Dr. Montrose. They both have been shielding me so that certain authorities within their group do not feel it necessary to kill me. Have they done the same for you?"

"Yes."

"Are you one of them?"

"No, thank God."

"Well, that's a relief. I was beginning to think I was about the only one around here who wasn't."

Cynda let loose with a smile. "I had no notion they existed until I came to London. Shocked the hell out of me."

Fisher's eyebrow went up at her choice of words, but he nodded nonetheless. "Despite your employer's reputation, I must issue a warning. If I find you present a threat to the Crown, I will have no choice but to throw the full weight of Scotland Yard upon you."

The warning was delivered smoothly, but she felt the teeth behind it. "I'll remember that."

"When Inspector Hulme learns that my sergeant is not in hiding with his family in Canterbury, the hounds will be set loose.

His picture will appear in the newspapers. Up to this point I have shielded Keats, but now there is nothing further I can do."

*How much has this cost you?* "If they print his picture, someone will sell him out and he'll end up with his throat cut."

"Not if he hides his identity. He seems quite capable of that."

"Not anymore. Since his injury, he hasn't been able to shift forms."

The cop slumped. Clearly, the news was a personal blow.

"Should my sergeant contact you, please urge him to turn himself in."

"I'll try. I doubt he'll listen."

"In that case, I would appreciate if you would serve as a...liaison between us."

She didn't say anything for a time, knowing what Fisher's request entailed.

His voice went sharp. "I cannot promise you will not be charged for aiding him."

"I'll take the risk."

That earned her a look of deep respect.

She asked the question that had been eating at her all along. "I know you're fond of Keats, but why are you risking your career for him?"

Fisher opened his mouth as if to give a patent answer and then shook his head. "I first met Jonathon in Whitechapel five years ago, in Arbour Square. He was a constable then and a bright one. He'd just nicked a ring of thieves and he'd done it by using his intellect. His superior wasn't that impressed. I was. I marked him for Scotland Yard then and there."

"Sounds like Keats," she said.

"Nevertheless, that is not the answer to your question. I have risked everything because Jonathon was to be my legacy. I wanted to leave a bit of myself behind, and he was it. Do you think that arrogant?" he asked, cocking his head.

"No. He's the best choice for your job."

"At one time, that was true. Unfortunately, even if we determine he's not involved in the murder, there is the issue of his personal habits. The knowledge that he attended Miss Hallcox's debauchery will affect his chances at promotion."

"Not if he arrests Flaherty and locates the explosives."

A nod. "That may redeem him. Finding the failed assassin will do as well."

Cynda's heart sank. *You might as well be looking for the Lost Ark of the Covenant.*

*Wednesday, 17 October, 1888*

21

Keats had arrived in Ingatestone at dusk the night before, too late to barter his boots for money to wire his family. Unable to buy food or even a pint, he found a dry corner of a stable and curled up under one of the thick wool blankets. It stank of horse sweat. It didn't matter. Despite his burning feet, he was asleep in minutes.

Once the shops opened, it had taken Keats a good bit of haggling to get a tolerable price for his boots. It wasn't anywhere near what he'd have gotten in Whitechapel, but it would suffice to send a telegram to his family and to buy him some breakfast, with a bit left over to purchase a broken-down pair of boots.

*Only temporary*, he reassured himself. He certainly didn't want to lose his new boots now that he'd found a pair that actually fit. He ate a meat pie while lounging against a wall and heard the cry of a newspaper vendor. By force of habit, he brushed the last of the crumbs off his trousers and waved down the lad.

He surveyed the front page, eyes skimming over articles one after another. Rampant speculation as to the Ripper's whereabouts was the prime topic, along with the Whitehall torso murder. The Parnell Commission was still in session.

He flipped the paper over. A picture beneath the fold caught his notice. He stared, his mouth falling open. Unholy panic exploded in his chest. He forced himself to remain calm, tucking the paper under his arm and strolling away from the center of town.

Minutes later, he stopped near a pond and sank onto the ground, his back against an oak tree. Unfolding the newspaper, he reread the headlines in disbelief.

Mayfair Slayer On the Run

SCOTLAND YARD DETECTIVE SOUGHT IN HORRIFIC MURDER
SAID TO HAVE STRANGLED VICTIM AFTER ARGUMENT

Keats' hands shook so furiously it was difficult to hold the newspaper. He read the article twice...a third time, and then dropped the newsprint on the ground, hands still quivering. He closed his eyes and leaned against the tree, working through the facts as he now knew them. Nicci had been murdered after an apparent assignation the very night he'd visited her. Her butler claimed Keats was the last person who had seen her alive.

*Why would he lie? Who was he protecting?*

He picked up the paper again, tracing along the rows of type until he found what he wanted. "She died Saturday night," he whispered, "somewhere between half past ten and midnight." He'd visited Jacynda at—he frantically rifled through his memories— about nine. From there he went into Whitechapel. He remembered hearing one of the clocks chime ten after he'd talked to Red Annie near the White Hart. He'd been near Old Montague Street when he'd been caught by Flaherty.

Reality struck him like a sledgehammer, causing his stomach to roil.

"Oh, dear God," he whispered. He clapped a palm over his mouth to keep from retching.

Desmond Flaherty was his alibi.

⁜

"Well, this is a mess," Mr. Spider commented as Cynda tried for the fifth time to flag down a passing hansom. "You should have stayed in the hotel."

*Can't. I need to go to the watch shop and then I'm meeting Davy at the Aldgate Pump at noon. He'll be there no matter what.*

"Well, you might not be."

Another hansom driver ignored her. Cynda swore under her breath. She'd passed on breakfast for this torment, barreling out of the hotel at a furious clip shortly after the maid had announced the arrival of a "pea-souper."

This London "particular" was a sickly byproduct of coal fires spewing zillions of pounds of pollutants into the air. She'd heard of them, but never seen one. It hung like a curtain over the city, a heavy pall of greasy yellow-green air that burned the eyes and stung the throat.

"Rule Britannia."

When Cynda finally caught a cab, the driver grumbled at the address she supplied.

"Gonna take a right lot of time, miss," he complained.

"Then let's get going."

More grumbling before he set the horse in motion. As they moved forward at a snail's pace, sounds grew muffled as if they were trapped inside a box packed with cotton. Ghostly forms materialized out of the fog and then vanished again. Street lamps were barely visible. Disembodied voices called out to one another like sailors lost at sea.

Once they arrived, she gave the grumbling cabbie a nice tip and stepped out into the venomous cloud.

"I don't like this at all," Mr. Spider announced. "Ideal for thieves and murderers. You'd never know what hit you."

Her delusion had it dead right. This was like the blackouts in 2023 when whole cities became hunting grounds for the *predatory classes*, as Dickens once called them.

The moment she stepped inside Oddegocker's watch shop, she sighed in profound relief. Even if this was a wild-goose chase, she felt safer here. She posed her question and waited.

"Something unique?" Oddegocker asked, scrunching his brows in thought. He seemed a pleasant fellow, his wispy brown hair defying gravity like a young Albert Einstein. "I have a couple of pieces that might interest you."

He returned with a blue cloth in his hand and revealed a watch made of the finest silver. "Quite a sad story with this one," he said. "It was pawned because the owner's wife had died. She bought it for him right before she fell sick and didn't have time to get it engraved with his name. Afterward, he could not bear to look at it."

The tale sounded genuine, not some made-up provenance to add sentimental value to the item. She popped it open. There was an intricately engraved oak tree on the back. It was exquisite. "It is very nice."

"I have this one, as well. It's also quite unique, but it has some damage to it. I have been unable to figure out how to open the back. It defies all my efforts. I've never seen one like it before."

The fabric fell back, revealing a pocket watch with a dent in its cover. Holding it up so Oddegocker couldn't see the dial, she gave it a particular set of windings. The dial lit up. She twisted the stem again and it darkened.

*The lost is found.* Somehow, it didn't feel as good as it should. She fought to keep tears from forming in her eyes. They'd prove hard to explain to the watchmaker.

Instead she forced a polite smile. "Very different indeed. How did you come by it?"

"From Mrs. Pearson, at the end of the street. She owns a rooming house. Some fellow left it behind in a box under his bed. When he didn't return, she put a notice in the paper, but nothing came of it. She sold it to me, as she had no use for it."

So that's where Chris' killer had been hiding out when he wasn't her neighbor at Annabelle's Boarding House. Mimes had used the second location as a place to change disguises, masquerading as Alastair in an effort to create the illusion that the doctor was actually the Ripper. At least he'd not been a Transitive or she'd never have caught him.

*The things some authors do to make themselves famous...*

Cynda pointed at the timepiece in her hand. "I'll take this one."

"Not the other one? It is very handsome, and the case is not damaged."

A wild thought came to mind. "I'll take that one, too, and I'd like it engraved."

Oddegocker fetched a pencil and paper. "Just write out what you'd like. It'll be done tomorrow. What with the fog and all, it'll be a quiet day."

At the mention of the weather, Cynda shot a look out the front window. A figure passed in the yellowish brown haze and then disappeared a short distance away.

"It's not getting better, is it?"

"No. Probably won't, not this time of year," Oddegocker replied.

As the watchmaker wrapped up Chris' interface, she fretted over the wording for Keats' watch. She hoped it sounded right. If things went well, she could deliver it to the sergeant in person.

By the time she reached Aldgate Pump, her nerves were history. Mr. Spider had sought shelter under her shawl and refused to come out. At least that had stopped his near-constant bitching about the fog. She'd been bumped and jostled so many times she'd lost count. Two of them had been attempts to pick her pocket. Her interface was in her right boot, Chris' in the left. They rubbed against her ankles, but at least they wouldn't disappear without a trace.

Reduced to feeling her way down the street, she finally gave in and hired a young lad to lead her to the pump by the light of a flickering torch. That had cost her a few pence, but it had been worth it.

In 1888, the Aldgate Pump was a concrete edifice. The location had been a landmark since the 1700s. Locals collected water from in a pail or a jug, or just took a drink. Some congregated and chatted among themselves, swapping gossip. There was little of that activity today. The locals were either at home or hurrying that way. The thickness of the mist around her felt like a hundred-pound weight on her chest, an oily ooze that sank into her clothes and made her shiver.

*Come on, Davy. I want to get out of here.*

As if he'd heard, Davy appeared in front of her, a torch in hand. He was grubbier than usual, with a scarf tied around his mouth. She could have wept for joy.

"Right murky, isn't it?" he asked in a muffled voice. "Not the worst I've seen, mind you. You should have a scarf on you. This stuff'll tear your lungs apart."

"Will it go away soon?" she asked.

A shrug, barely visible. "Maybe."

"Did you find out anything?" she asked, trying to talk around the handkerchief.

He nodded and then tugged down the scarf a few inches so she could hear him better. "One of the maids went out yesterday for a time. She was dressed proper, like a ladies' maid."

"Where'd she go?"

"A shippin' office and then she posted a couple letters."

"What kind of shipping office?"

"Passenger ships. Their sign says they got boats that go all 'round the world," he replied. "I'd like to get on one of them some day."

"You will, I'm sure of it. Just don't get on one that says it's unsinkable." She blew her nose on her handkerchief to stop the burning sensation. It didn't help. "Did the maid buy a ticket for her mistress?"

"I think so. They were talkin' about a ship to America. Leaves tomorrow night. I didn't hear much more—one of the clerks called me a scamp for hangin' 'round and sent me off with a flea in me ear."

"Did you hear what class she booked?"

"First. The clerk was tellin' her about the 'lectric lights and fine fripperies they got."

"That's got to be for Deidre. A ladies' maid wouldn't spend that kind of brass." She put her arm on his shoulder, his clothes feeling damp to the touch. "Good job, Davy."

The kid beamed. "You want me to watch the house some more?"

"No, I think you've got what I need."

"I still need to earn the rest of me money," he said with a note of concern.

"Don't worry about that. What shipping line was it?"

He dug inside his shirt and produced a wrinkled handbill. *"Norddeutscher Lloyd Express Mail Steamers. Shortest Route from*

*London to New York."*

She looked up. "You're great, Davy." His smile grew even wider. "Oh, I almost forgot. There is a Mr. Pratchett who manages a bookshop in the Strand. He needs a delivery boy. I recommended you."

"How much is he payin'?" the lad asked dubiously.

"Don't know. Go talk to him after you bathe. You're too much of a grimy urchin right now."

A lengthy sigh. "Me mum says I should have a bath every other day!" He shuddered.

"Your mom and I agree. Except I'd say *every* day."

"Oh, that's not right," he replied, shaking his head. "Not right at all."

"You'll make more friends if they don't have to stand upwind of you." He wasn't that bad, but it was fun to play with his head.

Davy laughed and capered around, holding his nose. Then he grew serious. "You goin' back to the hotel now?"

She studied the handbill again. *Special train from Waterloo Station every sailing day at 12:35.* If Hugo knew what Deidre had planned, this could get ugly. Cynda needed backup on this job, and she knew just the guy to ask.

"I need to go to Annabelle's Boarding House. Will you help me get there?"

"Right as rain," Davy replied. "Just hold onto me hand and don't you dare let go."

*Not for the world, kid.*

‡

It might as well have been night when Davy deposited her on the boarding house steps. Thank God he'd been with her, or she'd have ended up under the wheels of an omnibus. It'd loomed out of the fog like a freighter bearing down on a small fishing boat.

"Now you're safe," Davy said.

"Bless you. I couldn't have done that on my own." He puffed up with pride. "You're going home now, aren't you?"

He shook his head immediately. "Not while there's money to be made. I can sell torches and make four or five pence a piece. That's good brass! It'll go on all day and night."

*What a kid. He'll own all of London someday.*

"Be careful!"

He winked and then scampered down the stairs, his torch enveloped by the yellow gloom a few steps later.

She turned to rap on the door. No doubt Alastair was still at the

hospital, but Annabelle wouldn't mind an opportunity to stuff her
with some of those excellent scones.

The landlady opened the door and beckoned her in. She didn't
seem surprised to see her.

"Oh, you've come. I was hoping you'd got my note what with the
fog and all," she said, a frown gracing her face. "He needs to talk
to someone."

"I didn't get a note," Cynda responded, baffled. "I haven't been
at the hotel all day. Is something wrong with Alastair?"

Annabelle looked upstairs and nodded. "They gave him the sack
at the hospital."

"Why?"

"Some duke complained about him. I asked, but the doctor
wouldn't say what it was about." Cynda groaned. "He was furious
when he came home this afternoon," Annabelle continued. "He's
been in his room ever since. Every now and then, I hear him
cursing. He never does that."

*Oh, not good.* "I'll go talk to him."

"Thank you, luv. I don't know what to say to him."

"How's your leg?"

"Much better. Mildred went home two days ago. I miss her. She
sure was a help around here. I miss you, too. You're always a
bright soul." Annabelle looked upstairs again, her worried
expression deepening.

Cynda patted the landlady's rough hand and headed up the
stairs. It felt odd to be here again. A few weeks earlier, she'd lived
in the room next to the doctor's. Chris' murderer had been right
across the hall.

She tapped on the doctor's door.

"I'm not in the mood for conversation!" Alastair boomed.

"Fine by me. I'll just sit and watch steam come out of your ears."

There was the sound of footsteps crossing the room, and the door
jerked open. The doctor's hair was askew, his jaw set, eyes blazing.

"Good evening," she said, pushing by him before he could send
her packing. She removed her hat. "I hear you're job hunting."

He slammed the door and glared at her. "Lord Patton's father
complained to my superiors. Now I'm out of work. Damn the
bastard. I try to save his son's miserable life, and he treats me like
a dog. Damn him to hell!"

She cranked an eyebrow. "So what do you intend to do?"

He paced the length of the room, all of about ten feet and then
back again. "I shall accept Reuben's offer tonight. He is in need of
an assistant to aid him with the post-mortems. Unlike the

hospital, he doesn't care if my name is in the newspapers."

"Who's Reuben?" she asked, puzzled.

"Doctor Reuben Bishop. He's been pressing me to consider a career in forensics. I found myself quite taken with the idea after—" He shot her an anxious glance. "After a recent post-mortem."

*Chris' autopsy.*

"That sounds like a good idea," she said, trying to sound encouraging.

"There is a small stipend and I would receive additional payment per case, though it isn't much. I will continue seeing patients. Perhaps between the two I will make ends meet."

"If you find you don't like forensics, you can always get on at another hospital."

Another reluctant nod. "I was offered a position at Great Ormond Street a few months back. I suspect that offer might still be open, provided the duke doesn't interfere."

"So what is bad about all this?" she challenged.

"My professional reputation has been sullied by a highborn bully. I find that unconscionable."

"True, but there's not much you can do about it short of calling him out for a duel."

"Dueling is illegal," he retorted. "You know that."

"So? Doesn't keep you from shooting him."

He settled on the chair, his frenetic energy dissipating. "Violent and practical." To her relief, his anger dampened another notch.

Cynda dug in her pocket. "The lost is found," she announced. "It's Chris' watch."

He took it from her, rubbing a thumb over the dent.

"It just seems I have lost so much recently." His tired eyes met hers. "Now you will be going, as well."

Ouch. That was one hundred percent guilt and it stung. "I won't be going that soon," she replied, collecting the watch. *Not until I find out what's up with Defoe.*

A spark of hope flashed in his eyes. "Perhaps one day you'll tell me about some of the times you've visited. In the past, of course. I realize you can't speak much about the future."

She'd wondered when he'd start asking questions. It was a miracle he'd waited this long.

"Someday," she hedged. "In the meantime, I need your help now that you're not gainfully employed. My guess is that Hugo Effington's wife is leaving for Southampton tomorrow. She's catching a ship for New York."

"I'm not following you."

She caught him up on Deidre's recent history.

"Rotherhithe, eh? Fisher didn't mention that tidbit. At least she's alive. That is a blessing."

"I'm guessing she is. I haven't seen her yet. I intend to catch up with her on the train and ask a few questions before she sails away."

"So what do you need me to do?"

"Ride shotgun."

"Pardon?" he asked, puzzled.

She put it in Victorian English. "I need someone to watch our backs on the way to Southampton. If I can figure out her plans, so can Effington."

"When do you need me?"

"There's a special train from Waterloo at half past twelve."

"I shall be there."

It was time to share the bad news. "Keats isn't in Canterbury," she said, "and his family has no idea where he is. He wrote them a letter, said he was hunting for Flaherty. I don't think he knows what happened."

"Is that possible?"

Cynda shrugged. "I met Fisher on the train back to London. He's at the end of his rope. He admitted to me that he knows about the shifters."

Alastair frowned. "I'm surprised he did. He must trust you."

"No, he's running out of options."

"Just like the rest of us," he replied, rising.

"Tomorrow at the train station?" A nod. "Thanks."

He brushed a finger along her jaw line in his signature gesture. His eyes sought hers. "We have been at odds recently. I hope this discord between us will pass."

"I'd like that," she replied. It'd been better between them when they'd first met. Maybe it could be that way again.

He cocked his head. "Then you promise to listen to me more often?"

She gave him a lopsided grin.

"I thought so," he sighed. "Let me help you find a cab. It's too dangerous for you on the streets when it's like this."

For once, Cynda didn't argue.

‡

Blindsided by the news of Nicci's murder, it took Keats some time to regain his emotional balance. Flaherty might be his alibi, but there was no likelihood that the Irishman would step forth and save his nemesis from the rope. It was certain his men wouldn't dare defy him to save a copper's life. They'd end up like Ahearn if they did.

Once Keats regained control, he painstakingly formulated a plan. He dared not contact his family in Canterbury; now that he was a wanted man, no doubt their house was being watched, perhaps even their mail searched. Fortunately, he'd not hung about in the transient camp so the police had no way to trace his whereabouts from the letter Lily had posted for him. He would only put Alastair's career in jeopardy if he asked for his assistance. Jacynda was his only hope.

He composed the letter in the post office, his nerves shredding by the minute lest a constable spy him. Using some of his precious coins, he handed it over to the mail clerk.

*She has to help me. No one else can.*

"No return address, sir?" the clerk asked. Fortunately, he was paying more attention to the envelope than to the man who was mailing it.

Keats shook his head. "I'll be on the move. Thank you for asking."

Fearing to use the train, he set off on foot toward Montnessing, hoping to make London by the next night. He would meet with Jacynda, secure some money and then disappear into the bowels of the East End. He could hide as well as any ruffian in that neighborhood.

He knew that finding Flaherty would not likely save his skin. All Keats could hope for was that he'd have company on that scaffold in Newgate.

‡

"Time to let go," Cynda whispered. "Come on, you can do it."

Chris' watch nestled in her palm, her thumb repeatedly rubbing over the dent in the case like it was a worry stone.

"He's gone. He's telling his silly jokes to the other angels. It's time to let go." The tears flooded for the second time since she'd begun this ritual.

"The man who killed him is in an asylum," she murmured through her tears. "You caught him. It's time to put Chris to rest."

That was the problem. Once she sent his interface, the last bit of him was gone. She had his funeral picture and some VidMail messages in 2057, but that was it.

Christopher Stone, her lover, was no more.

The sobs tore through her like a storm.

Cynda let the grief own her until there were no more tears. Then she wiped off the watch with her handkerchief, performed the winding maneuver and set it in front of her on the floor of the hotel room. Instead of shielding her eyes when the transfer came, she watched the lights dance and whirl and shimmer inches above the carpet. Then they dimmed and were gone.

"Rest in peace, Chris. You're still alive as long I can remember you."

22

*Thursday, 18 October, 1888*

The chief topic of those on the train platform was the weather. The pea soup had drained away, and for that, Cynda was profoundly grateful. From the gist of the conversations around her, it could have lasted for days.

Cynda watched Alastair enter the First Class carriage, just as they'd arranged. Armed with a description of Mrs. Effington, he'd vowed to keep an eye on her if she was in that section.

To Cynda's surprise, Deidre Effington wasn't with the toffs, but back with the poor folk. It took Cynda some time to recognize her. In stark contrast to the elegant woman she'd met at the party, the Mayfair matron was now the picture of destitution; mussed hair, mottled bruise on her cheek, shabby clothes and a large, ratty suitcase at her feet. Even her boots sported holes in the sides. It was an excellent disguise.

To the casual observer, Cynda didn't look much better. She'd resurrected her working-girl outfit, muddied it up and donned a second-hand straw bonnet. Her red shawl stood out more than she liked, but it fit the image.

She sat a few rows behind her quarry, on the alert for trouble. An inventory of their fellow passengers didn't ring any alarm bells. There were surly characters in their midst, but not someone from Mrs. Effington's world.

*Anyone I should worry about?*

Perched on her right shoulder, Mr. Spider pointed with his foremost leg. "Only that gent three rows away."

*Lucky I brought my truncheon.*

"Better to have a poisonous bite."

She stared at him. *You can do that?*
"Perhaps."
*Just what I need—lethal delusions.*


After the nearly hour and a half it took to reach Southampton, Cynda was eager to get off the train and into the fresh air. As the carriage emptied its passengers onto the platform, she made note of the fellow Mr. Spider had pointed out. He was trudging away, paying no further attention to Deidre.

Unsure of where Alastair was in the throng, Cynda trailed the forlorn figure as she headed toward the docks. Deidre stopped only once, apparently asking for directions. After that she shied away from anyone she met on the street, her movements tense. She looked like the perfect victim.

The guy from the train made his move only a few blocks away. In a heartbeat he cut in front of her, brandished a knife, and forced the stunned woman down an alley before she could cry out.

"Damn!" Cynda took off at top speed, nearly overshooting the alley in the process. By the time she slowed down, she found Deidre up against a wall, the knife near her throat. Her assailant was groping her breasts, saying something under his breath. Deidre shook her head, tears filling her eyes.

The knife was the problem. Cynda needed to distract him long enough to let the truncheon do its work. She hid the weapon behind her back and sauntered up like a dolly-mop in search of a customer.

"Oy, luv, fancy two of us?" she called out, using her best Whitechapel accent.

The man jumped. "Go 'way!" he shouted, glaring at her. More importantly, the knife moved from Deidre's throat.

"It's more jolly that way, luv," Cynda continued. She tugged up her skirt with a free hand to reveal a bit of ankle. "I'm sure she'll share ya, won't ya dearie?"

Deidre's eyes widened. She'd remembered the face from the party.

"Of...of course," she stammered.

"See, luv? Why make 'er do all the work?"

"I don't need you 'ere," the man said, waving the knife in her direction, his other hand gripping Deidre's shoulder. She looked inches away from fainting.

Cynda moved within blade range, mindful of her previous encounter with a knife. "Don't be that way. Ya look like a fine gent."

"I said go 'way!" He jabbed at her with the knife for emphasis. The moment the blade was farthest away from his body, the truncheon came down on his wrist. She distinctly heard bones snap. He howled in pain as the knife descended to the ground.

"Bitch!"

"Is there a problem here, ladies?"

*Now the doc shows up.*

"Just a discussion about proper etiquette," Cynda replied, discarding the accent.

Alastair studied her to see if there was any blood and then stepped forward and put himself between the whining bully and Deidre. With a kick, he sent the knife out of reach.

"Are you injured?" he asked. Belatedly, Cynda realized the question wasn't for her.

Deidre shook her head, incapable of words. Satisfied, he returned his attention to Cynda. "May I?" he asked, gesturing toward her truncheon.

She shrugged and handed it to him. This might prove educational.

Alastair moved closer and lightly tapped the wounded man's chest with the weapon. The ruffian lurched backward, eyes darting around for an avenue of escape. There was none.

"Who sent you?" the doctor asked, menace lurking beneath his manners.

A blistering oath split the air. That earned him a stronger poke in the chest. "You've still got one good wrist," Alastair observed. "Don't make me change that."

The man spat, fortunately missing his target.

"Your time grows thin," Alastair threatened, giving him another jab.

"'E said it'd be easy. Just grab 'er off the train and cut 'er throat, plain and simple. Said to make it look the Ripper got 'er. Said I could 'ave 'er if I wanted; 'e didn't care as long as she was dead."

Deidre began to waver on her feet. Cynda slipped an arm around her.

"Who sent you?" the doctor repeated.

"Posh gent, a big bastard, evil look in the eyes. Didn't say 'is name. Gave me ten quid to do it."

*Only ten?*

"Hugo," Deidre murmured, sagging heavily against Cynda.

Alastair heard her. "How did you know she'd be on the train?"

"Been following 'er maid for a week. Finally got lucky." He winced, gripping at his wrist tightly. The fingers didn't move right. Maybe she'd been a bit too harsh on the guy.

*Nah...*

"Let him go," Cynda said. "He's paid his penance."

Alastair stepped back and waved to indicate the fellow was free to leave. The rough didn't hesitate, cradling his arm as he fled.

"I figured you'd argue with me," Cynda remarked, claiming her truncheon.

"It's very unlikely he'll be able to use that hand again. I think that was more than enough punishment."

She bit back a retort.

Alastair gently took the frightened woman's arm to steady her.

"Do I know you, sir?" Deidre asked, her face pale, tears glistening on her cheeks.

Cynda made the introductions.

"Madam," Alastair said, inclining his head politely.

"How did you find me?" Deidre asked.

"The same way as the guy with the knife," Cynda explained. "I had someone following your maid. I figured if you were still alive, your husband might try to remedy that problem."

"So it appears." She looked up at Alastair. "Thank you for your intervention, Doctor."

"You owe me no thanks, madam. I am pleased to assist in your escape and to provide for your safety," Alastair replied gallantly.

This was rapidly devolving into a scene from Jane Austen.

"Can we go now?" Cynda prodded.

"Most certainly. Come along, Mrs. Effington, I'll see you safely to the ship."

"Oh, thank you. You are most kind." There was a significant hesitation and then Deidre added, "I thank you as well, Miss Lassiter. That was very brave, like the other night at the party."

The expression on Alastair's face said he didn't agree.

As the pair walked to the ship, Deidre on the doctor's arm and her suitcase in his free hand, Cynda trailed in their wake like an unwanted kid sister. Once the matron had regained a bit of composure, Cynda caught up with them.

"I have some questions, Mrs. Effington."

"I will answer whatever queries you put to me," the woman replied, her arm still linked with Alastair's. "I owe you the truth."

Cynda cut to the chase. "Was your husband having an affair with Nicci Hallcox?"

A frank blush bloomed on the woman's cheeks. "Yes."

"You know she's dead?"

"I read about it in the papers. She was blackmailing Hugo. He would give her my jewelry, at least until she refused even that in payment."

*Aha.* "What did she demand when the jewelry wasn't enough?"

"I am not sure."

"Did you hire the assassin to kill your husband?"

"Heavens, no!" A look of chagrin crossed her face. "I admit, I wish he had died. Hugo is such a monster."

"Then who do you think the assassin was trying to kill?"

Deidre's blush turned deeper crimson. "For a time, I thought the fellow was aiming at Reggie."

"Reggie is your lover?" Cynda guessed.

"Yes. He told me I was wrong, but I saw it happen. Reggie was standing exactly where the man was aiming his gun."

"What's your lover's full name?"

"Reginald Fine. He's a solicitor at a law firm. He is a wonderful man and I love him deeply. He treats me with such respect. He promised to join me in New York once legal matters are sorted out."

"How did the gunman get in the house? Could Hugo have let him in?" Cynda quizzed.

"No. He was very upset. He kept saying it would ruin everything. I think it is because he fears the—"

Deidre hesitated, raising her face to the doctor. He gave her a reassuring smile in return.

"Well, you should know all of it. There is a man that Hugo deals with who is very...frightening. Hugo calls him Mr. S. He came to the house, twice I think, something to do with Hugo's business. I learned that it was best to depart as soon as that man appeared at the door. My husband was especially violent after their meetings."

"What did he look like?" Cynda asked.

"Never the same. He wore disguises, very good ones. I only recognized him because of his voice and the way Hugo reacted to him."

Cynda and Alastair traded a look over the top of the woman's head. Deidre had just described a Transitive from a layman's point of view.

"When one of our maids disappeared after the last meeting," Deidre continued, "I grew afraid. I thought perhaps she had overheard something."

"Did you contact the police?" Alastair asked.

"No. Hugo would not let me. He said she'd run away, but I didn't believe him. Fiona wasn't that sort. I liked her. She knew how to make me laugh." The woman's eyes misted again. "There was so little mirth after I married Hugo."

In 2057, the law rested firmly on the side of a battered spouse. Not so in Victorian England. Deidre had few options, most of them dismal. Cynda took her arm and gave it a squeeze.

"Why did you fake your suicide?" Alastair asked as they turned onto the street that led to the docks.

"I was afraid of my husband. I thought he had hired that man to kill Reggie, and that he would kill me. Our butler helped me escape, God bless him."

"So where were you hiding?" Cynda asked.

"In a brothel, of all places." The woman shuddered. "One of our former maids hid me there. She...works there now after Hugo debauched her."

They stopped at the end of the gangway. Cynda found herself in the midst of a very tight hug. She returned it and whispered in the woman's ear, "Start over. Not all men are like your husband."

Deidre pulled away. "I know." She turned toward the doctor and asked, "Would you escort me aboard, sir? I suspect there will be difficulties as to my dress when I try to claim a First Class Cabin. I appear as if I belong in Third."

"Certainly," Alastair replied, nonplussed. Cynda watched them ascend the gangplank. As Deidre had suspected, it took some time to get her passage sorted out. Eventually, the pair disappeared into the ship.

Unable to pace due to the crowd around her, Cynda fussed with the fringe on her shawl. Time passed, over an hour and a half by her watch. The luggage was on board. Shouted orders sent sailors scrambling. A sharp blast from the ship's horn made her jump. Still no sign of Alastair.

"Come on, come on," she grumbled. *You can't go to New York with her. I need you here.*

She stopped fidgeting, shocked by the inadvertent admission. She *needed* Alastair. She was learning to trust someone other than herself. It wasn't a comfortable realization.

"You trust Ralph," she heard from her shoulder. Of course Mr. Spider would have to hear that admission.

*I've known him since pre-school. That doesn't count.*

Another thunderous blast of the ship's horn cut off his reply. Passengers lined the railings, calling to their loved ones. Next to her, a man held up his young daughter. She waved at someone on the ship.

"Mama!" she called, as if her mother could hear over the tumult.

*Mama!* Another voice called in Cynda's memory. It was a child, clinging to a ship's railing as the deck rolled underneath her tiny feet. *Mama!* Smoke billowed past her tear-creased face the moment before the stern plunged under water, taking her to her grave.

Shivering violently, Cynda pulled her shawl around her. Another time slip. They were never pleasant memories, only ones of destruction. A touch on her elbow jerked her back to the present. Alastair was standing next to her. He peered down at her, then bent closer.

"Are you ill?" he asked. "Your face is very pale."

"No, just...remembering something." She shoved away the images of that day on the cold Atlantic waters. "What kept you? I thought you were going to New York."

"It took some time to sort out her luggage. Apparently, someone had arranged for a trunk to be delivered, I'm not sure who. The steward was having difficulties locating it."

From the look on his face, Cynda could tell that wasn't the only problem. He drew her further down the pier, away from the crowd. Once they were more isolated, he explained, "Mrs. Effington asked that there be some documentation of her injuries. She was concerned her husband would claim she was of unsound mind, given her feigned suicide. She asked me to catalog her wounds."

*Catalog?* "You mean you examined her?"

A brusque nod. "So there would be no hint of bias, we asked another physician on board, one from America, to assist. His wife was of particular comfort to Mrs. Effington. It was a most difficult thing we asked of her."

"I can imagine." *Strip down and show us how much your husband despises you.*

"We made copies of the findings, which we all signed."

"That'll be hard to ignore in a court of law."

"That was our strategy. She promised to send a cable to the police once the ship was at sea so they will know she is alive."

"Did you tell her about Nicci's disease?"

Alastair issued a tormented sigh. "Yes. We had a frank conversation and she promised to be fully examined upon arrival in New York. It is my hope her husband did not contract the disease so that she might not have to pay for his vulgar behavior."

Cynda squeezed his hand and then turned toward the ship. It was edging away from the dock. The final lengthy blast of the ship's horn made the air around them vibrate. He searched the railing until he found Deidre and pointed her out to his companion. They waved together, and the woman blew them a kiss.

"Don't worry. Karma will even the score with Effington," she said.

"Karma? What is that?" he asked.

Cynda turned toward him. "It's an East Asian philosophy. Karma says that what you do in this life will catch up with you. If you do good, then you're okay. If you're a fiend who beats people, like Effington, your life will be a living hell."

"We should be going. I will secure us a hansom to the train station."
He hurried into the crowd before she could ask what was wrong.

They had compromised and bought tickets in Second Class. He fit
in, she didn't. Though a few of their fellow passengers gave her
disapproving looks, Jacynda ignored them. It wasn't until they were
in the carriage that they spoke about other than trivial matters.

"What was wrong with you at the pier?" he asked. "You looked
so distant."

She thought about his question and then nodded to herself as if a
decision had been made. "I'm...time-slipping. It's not a good sign."

"I don't understand what that means."

"I'm reliving places and times I've visited. Very few of them are
pleasant. Tourists don't like to pay a lot of money to be bored.
They want a bit of excitement. If they attend a coronation, it had
better include an assassination for the same price."

"So what sorts of things are you seeing?" he asked, fascinated.

Jacynda removed her hat and scratched her hair. "I'm going to
need a bath once I get back to the hotel."

He tried again. "Please, I'd like to know what it is you see," he said.

"It's in the future, Alastair."

"Then don't tell me dates, or anything else like that. The look
on your face was so horrifying I feel I should know what it is you
must cope with...offer whatever comfort I can."

She fiddled with the fringe on her shawl for a while and then
nodded. "This time, I was on a ship in the Atlantic. It was sinking.
It had been hit by a...bomb."

"A warship of some sort?"

"No. A passenger liner. They got caught in the middle of a war."

Cynda and the tourist had boarded the ship in New York. As
the academic took notes, she tried to make polite conversation
with people who would be dead in a few short hours. The tourist
had found it an immense lark. They always did, until the end. His
casual humor vanished the moment the torpedo impacted under
the bridge, sending smoke and terrified screams into the air. He
began to weep when the secondary concussion blew out the
starboard bow. He and Cynda were pulled into the future as the
ship's stern heaved upward into the air, taking the little girl and
the *Lusitania* under the waves for eternity.

"I thought civilians were protected during conflict. It would be
heinous to kill non-military personnel," Alastair observed.

"That's the way it used to be. The rules change."

"How many die?"

"Twelve hundred."

He looked away, sickened. "How soon?"

"I can't tell you that."

"Then tell me it's the last war we fight."

The laugh was bitter. "I'd be lying, Alastair. It's just the start."

"I see why you aren't keen to talk about this. Why did you become one of these Rovers in the first place if it's all horror and death?"

"There wasn't much else I could do unless I wanted to become a doctor like my father. That didn't interest me. Being a Rover lets me go to all sorts of places and times. We're famous where I come from, sort of like nobility."

"Well, that would be some incentive, I guess. How long have you been...traveling?"

"Five years. Only the last year has been awful. I spent a year in training, then the next year with a Senior Rover at my side. Now they just throw the new ones in and let them work it out for themselves."

"I would think you would be afraid of altering time," he said. "Is that not a distinct possibility?"

"The theory is that time is pretty elastic. It snaps back along the same or a similar course if something gets screwed up."

"So I was supposed to lose my job at the hospital and begin a career in forensic pathology?"

Jacynda started twiddling with the fringe on her shawl again.

"Was this supposed to happen to me?" he pressed.

"I didn't do a full search of your timeline, or Keats' either. I didn't want to know."

"So you have no notion if what has happened is correct or not?" he asked, baffled.

"No. My boss keeps track of that."

"I see." That was little comfort. What if he was supposed to have married Evelyn or retain his position at the London Hospital? What if all that had been somehow altered just by meeting Jacynda?

*What an unnerving thought.*

The fringe-fiddling stopped. "Anyway, once *they*," she continued, waving a hand in a vague motion, "realize I'm slipping, I'm out of a job. It means my brain has sustained too much damage."

"What will happen to you?"

"I don't know, Doc. Most Rovers quit before they reach this point."

"But not you."

She grinned and shook her head. "That would be giving up."

He took her hand and kissed it. "Well, should you find yourself out of a job, have them send you here. Reuben keeps telling me I need a mistress. Perhaps I'll come into some money someday, and then I can buy you a fine house with a garden and a maid to cook your meals. You could read books all day and eat as many scones as you like."

Her laugh was lighter than he'd expected. "A mistress? That's an interesting job title. Jacynda Lassiter, Kept Woman."

"I could visit you on the weekends, we could go for rides in the country," he said. Part of him wished it were so.

Jacynda's eyes shone. "That's the nicest offer I've had in a long time, Dr. Montrose, but when I'm done here, I'm due back in 2057. The way things are going, I'm willing to bet they won't let me return to 1888."

*Then don't leave.*

Alastair put his arm around her and Jacynda leaned on his shoulder. He felt the slight tremors running through her body.

Instead of speaking his heart, he hugged her tighter.

23

2057 A.D.

TEM *Enterprises*

Tracking his boss' movements through the chronsole room, Ralph revolved on the low pillow. It was a skill acquired only with considerable practice. Morrisey sat behind his low desk, executed an overhead stretch, and then glowered.

Ralph's curiosity got the best of him. "So why did TPB want to see you, sir?"

Morrisey's eyebrow arched in disdain. "It was about my nephew's interface. They had issues, they said."

"What sort of issues? Cynda found it, you gave it to them. End of story."

"On the contrary, they accused me of defying their authority. They say they never received Chris' interface, even though I personally handed it to their representative."

"That's bull. The guy was TPB. His credentials ran though SecurNet with no problem."

"Apparently, he does not work for them. Word is the Government now has the interface. The chairman of the TPB is livid. He blames me for the *double-cross*, as he put it."

Ralph leaned back against the desk and adjusted his glasses. "Why is Chris' watch such a big deal?"

"Exactly my question. Mr. Davies wouldn't answer that, of course, just spouted some nonsense about time integrity and all that. I intend to put that exact question to the Government, though I doubt I'll learn any more from them than I did from Davies."

"Well, at least they can't blame this on Jacynda."

"She's not out of it yet. This turf war between TPB and Guv is heating up, and the Time Rovers are in the middle of it. Miss Lassiter is widely despised at TPB. I worry they may go after her in an effort to discredit me. For the time being, she's safest in 1888."

Ralph frowned. "Now that's a very disturbing thought."

"I couldn't agree more."

⁂

*Thursday, 18 October, 1888*

*London*

Malachi Livingston detested hospitals. They reeked of death and carbolic acid. Clutching the note Ronald had handed him upon his arrival at the club, he hurried along the hospital corridor until he found a nurse mopping the floor with scant enthusiasm.

"I am here to see a young man named William," he consulted the note, "Cavendish. He was brought in earlier this evening."

She leaned against her mop and then arched a thumb toward a set of double doors at the far end of the hall. "Likely down there, sir."

"Thank you, madam." She snorted in reply.

He encountered a physician along the way and received the verdict—cracked rib and bruised kidneys. Then he found his assistant lying on a bed in the corner of the ward, covered by stained sheets.

William's face was untouched, only a scratch on his chin. Livingston rejoiced in that, given the young man's vanity. There his good fortune ended—there were vicious bruises from the neck down. Each breath seemed a monumental effort.

Livingston sat by the man's bed, guilt churning. Though Adelaide had warned him to be careful of William's motives, he had caused this. He'd sent the fellow nosing around Effington, knowing how dangerous it might be.

"William?" he said.

Eyes fluttered open and then took some time to focus. "Sir?"

"I just got your note."

"I have...the guest list, sir."

Livingston leaned closer. "Yes, yes, but what happened? Tell me all of it, man."

"Effington caught me...talking to one his grooms. Gave me a thrashing. I thought he'd kill me."

*That sonofabitch.* "Do you wish to file charges?"

William shook his head. "Do no good. He's a toff."

"You do not deserve this," Livingston replied sharply, his hand gripping his cane. "He is not above the law."

"It won't help. He owns judges." William swallowed with considerable difficulty. "He'll get off, clean and simple."

"When did this happen?"

"Tonight, just after dark. I thought he'd gone out."

"Who witnessed it?"

"Groom called Bert and a stable boy. They pulled him off me."

As his anger turned molten, Livingston swept his eyes around the ward and made a decision. "Where do you live, William?"

"Seven Dials, sir."

"Do you live on your own?"

"Yes, I have a set of rooms, sir. Nice place, not like most of them."

"What's the address?"

His assistant supplied it through cracked lips.

"I shall have you transported to those rooms and arrange for a private nurse to stay with you until you are up and around. You must get out of this place as quickly as possible."

William did not argue. Instead, he pulled something from under the covers. He offered it to Livingston with a hand that bore a whip mark. "The guest list, sir," he croaked. "I hid it under my shirt so Effington couldn't find it. I tried to put marks next to the names of the toffs he owns."

There was dried blood on the paper. "Good God, what this has cost you," Livingston whispered. "I shall make the bastard pay, I swear it."

"He's worth sending to hell."

Livingston shook his head. "He'll beg for hell once I'm done with him."

He swept out of the hospital like a dark omen, causing people to stand aside as he passed. His first stop would be to arrange for William's care, then the police station in Mayfair to swear out a complaint. They'd not ignore him, despite his assistant's belief. Then he needed to do more research into Hugo Effington's affairs, beginning with those who were at the party.

William's beating was a personal challenge. It was time to teach the bully a well-needed lesson.

✣

Jonathon Keats completed his journey to London in style. The farmer hadn't charged him anything for the ride from Ilford, but it had meant he'd had to sit in the back of a wagon only inches away from the penned-up sheep and their woolly stench. When they reached Mile End Road, he hopped off, gave the farmer his hearty thanks and headed north. Once the wagon was out of sight, he turned south and set his feet toward Whitechapel.

Though he needed to hurry to make the rendezvous with Jacynda, he dared not call attention to himself. Blending in was the key. He'd spied many a suspect just because they acted nervous. His heart sank when he reached the street in front of the dining room and she was not to be seen. After over a half an hour with no sign of his savior, gloom descended. Knowing he should not stay much longer in a fixed position, he took one last look around and set off into the night, heart sinking with each step.

*Why didn't you come? Did Alastair stop you?* No, Jacynda would not have mentioned his letter to the doctor, knowing the consequences. *Perhaps you didn't receive it in time.* Yes, that had to be it. To think otherwise would mean he was truly alone.

Though he had a few pence, he decided not to kip at one of the doss houses. Someone might recognize his face under the grime and turn him in, though there was no love lost between the constabulary and the common dosser.

When Christ Church's clock reached midnight, he abandoned his search for Flaherty and headed for an abandoned slaughterhouse. He settled into a corner near the rear fence. The stones beneath him reeked of stale blood and offal, but the yard was deserted. He curled up and tried to sleep, despite the aching cold.

Inspector Ramsey had always told him that he was a cocky little bastard, that some day he'd fall hard. Even Ramsey hadn't realized how far one man could descend in the matter of only a few days.

Though it was hard for him to admit, his personal ambition had been his undoing. He'd been blinded by the need to capture the Irishman, to make the grade so he could advance in rank. His unwavering pursuit of that goal had clouded his mind to other dangers more insidious than that of a Fenian rebel.

Although he now saw the light, he still had no choice but to follow the path of blind obsession, wherever it might lead.

☩

*Friday, 19 October, 1888*

Reuben had insisted they review their post-mortem findings before the inquest began, to refresh their memories. They'd met at a dining room, Reuben's favorite. It was of no consequence how good the food might be; the conversation did nothing to improve Alastair's appetite.

"They will only call me to give testimony," Reuben said, taking a second helping of eggs.

"That would be for the best," Alastair replied, absentmindedly stirring his tea though he'd added nothing to it as of yet. He'd eaten only part of his breakfast, his stomach in a queasy knot. "It is very hard to be objective when it's your best friend who faces the long drop at Newgate."

"Have you ever seen a hanging?" Reuben inquired.

"No, thank God."

"I have, more than once. It all depends on the skill of the hangman. If he is good, the drop is precisely calculated and the neck broken instantly. From what I hear, our executioner, Mr. Berry, is very good at his trade and—" Reuben halted and then swore under his breath. He touched Alastair's sleeve in contrition, his face crimson. "My God, I apologize."

Alastair pushed his full teacup away. "No apology needed. It's what I've been thinking ever since this whole mess began."

When they reached the street, newsboys shouted the headlines: they were all about Keats. Newspapers were rapidly purchased and scrutinized with inordinate interest.

HALLCOX INQUEST TODAY
HUNT FOR MISSING SERGEANT CONTINUES
REWARD OFFERED FOR CAPTURE!

"Since the Ripper has taken a holiday, now they have a new bone to chew, at least until he resumes his activities," Reuben noted.

"You believe he will?" Alastair asked, pleased with the change of subject, no matter how morbid.

"Most certainly, unless he's dead or incapacitated. He has a frenzied mania to his killing. That doesn't pass overnight."

"Do you think it's a surgeon?"

"That or a butcher. You've seen the size of a non-gravid uterus. Try finding that little bit in no light while keeping an ear cocked for the sound of a constable's boots. The man's sheer nerve astounds me."

"I thought I might attend the Stride inquest on Monday," Alastair replied.

"Excellent idea. I hear Wynne Baxter's officiating. No better way to learn than to listen to your fellow colleagues, good or ill."

Once inside the building where the Hallcox inquest was to be held, Reuben elbowed his way through the scrum. "They love a show, don't they?" he grumbled. "Come on, we have seats near the front."

It took some time before they reached their destination. Lord Wescomb was already in place. He rose and shook hands with both of them.

"I didn't know you'd be here, my lord," Alastair said. Wescomb was a barrister, and that provided a thin ray of hope.

"I thought it best that I attend. Keats will need an advocate for the trial."

"That's very thoughtful of you."

"One should plan for the worst. I gather there's been no news of him?"

"None."

Wescomb peered through the crowd. "Ah, there's Fisher. Perhaps he has some news."

The chief inspector paused for a moment to speak to a constable and then joined them.

"Lord Wescomb, Doctors," he said. From the dark circles under his eyes, it appeared that sleep had become a stranger.

"Chief Inspector," Wescomb replied. "Any news of your sergeant?"

A shake of the head.

"Sorry to hear that. I had hoped he would turn himself in and we could sort through this."

Fisher glanced around. "Jury viewing the body, I gather?"

Wescomb gave a nod. "This is as sensational as the Whitechapel murders, unfortunately."

Fisher turned his attention to Alastair. "I trust if my sergeant has contacted you, you would have the decency to let me know."

Rather than be insulted, Alastair heard the desperate plea. Fisher was at the end of his tether. If the papers were correct, Home Office was making life unbearable for him.

"He has not contacted me, Chief Inspector. If he does, I will do everything I can to persuade him to come to you immediately."

A small sigh, nearly lost in the clamor of the crowd. "Thank you." Fisher swept on and took his seat in a rigid manner.

"Another personal hell," Reuben remarked.

It was nearing four in the afternoon when the inquest ended. It had gone quickly, methodically laying out the guilt of only one man, based solely on the butler's testimony. Numb, Alastair remained in place, staring into Keats' dire future. He was vaguely aware when Reuben rose to talk to the chief inspector. Behind them, reporters scampered out of the room to file their stories.

Within the hour, the headlines would proclaim a charge of willful murder had been brought against his closest friend.

Alastair rose in abject despair. A quick survey of the diminishing crowd did not reveal Jacynda. His heart sank further. Wescomb joined him, his face drawn. "I saw a few points that I find are inconsistent, but on the whole, the case looks reasonably solid *if* you believe the butler. Of course, we both know that might all be an…illusion."

Alastair nodded. "Indeed. I think it is time for me to put more pressure on our *superiors* as to who may be behind this charade."

"A wise move. I shall make enquiries at my level. If Keats comes to you, let me know instantly. I wish to be with him when he turns himself in."

"I shall, my lord."

"Keep faith, Alastair," Wescomb said, touching his arm in a comforting gesture.

"I shall try, my lord."

Despite the considerable distance from Mayfair to the boarding house, Alastair hiked briskly while he mentally reviewed the case. There was a dearth of physical evidence. Though Nicci Hallcox's maid had testified that the bed linens had been changed the morning before the murder, the hairs found within were not of Keats' coloring when compared to those removed from the hairbrush in his rooms. From the physical standpoint, other than his calling card, there was no indication that he had ever been in Miss Hallcox's bedroom.

It all fell upon the butler's veracity. The fellow had sworn under oath that Miss Hallcox had sent Keats a note that had occasioned his visit to her residence, though he did not know the contents thereof. After a disagreement, the sergeant had stormed out of the house in a foul temper. Then, inexplicably, Keats had returned some time later and spent a lengthy time in Nicci's bedroom before her body was discovered. None of the other staff had seen his friend during the second visit.

"Too thin," Alastair murmured. "There is no physical evidence proving that Keats killed her." He pondered on that. Perhaps there was some bit of evidence that proved the sergeant was *not* the murderer. He made a mental note to review his notes yet again.

Behind all this was a Transitive, bent on destroying his friend. He just needed to find out which one.

24

Cynda loitered outside the dining room, attempting to look nonchalant. She'd switched clothes at Pratchett's, pointedly dressing down for the location, so nervous it had taken her three tries to button her bodice.

*What if he doesn't show up?*

It took a great deal of effort not to pace in nervous anticipation. Instead she tapped a boot underneath her skirt.

*Come on, Keats. You've got to trust me.*

She was aware of the passage of a constable, who gave her a look that indicated he didn't want to see her the next time he came around. Just down the street, one of the newsboys was shouting the results of the inquest. It was bad.

She bit the inside of her lip, drawing blood. The last report she'd received from Ralph was that TEM was slowly stewing in hot water over Chris' watch, caught in a catfight between Guv and TPB. He'd pointedly not called her home, a hint that she should keep up her hunt for the assassin, no matter how futile.

Across the street, she spied someone of Keats' height. Other than that, she wouldn't have recognized him. He had a limp, his beard was a shabby tangle and his clothes only one step above what a ragpicker would consider a lost cause.

He crossed the street some distance ahead of her and leaned against a lamp post, adjusting a boot. She walked slowly toward him, wary of any sign of a trap. When they met, he gave her a leering smile. His face was filthy, his hair disgusting. He smelled awful.

"Come with me, luv," Cynda said, employing her best working-class accent. "I got us a room."

They walked in silence to the rundown hotel Cynda had scouted out earlier in the day. His limp became more pronounced on the stairs.

The moment they were in the room, he sank against the wall, sighing in relief.

"Thank God," he muttered. "I swear every copper in London is out there."

She threw the flimsy lock and removed her shawl. "I'm sorry I wasn't here last night. I didn't get your letter until this morning. I was afraid you wouldn't show up."

Their eyes met. His were bloodshot. "I thought you'd—"

"Never, Jonathon," she said. "Never."

"I'd give you a kiss in gratitude, but I'm—" he said, gesturing at himself with revulsion.

"I picked a room with a decent drop to the ground in case you have to hoof it."

He looked impressed. "You think like I do."

"Alastair reminds me of that regularly. I brought food for you." She angled her head toward the battered washbasin. "There's soap and water. You didn't ask for it, but I brought tooth powder and a hair brush."

"God, you're a wonder." He stripped off his filthy coat and headed for the basin like a man possessed. The water sloshed inside and then he halted right before diving in.

"Maybe I'd better not. If I get too clean..."

"I bought some theatrical makeup. You can wash yourself up and then add back whatever grime you need."

The look she received was pure adoration.

"You heard about the inquest?" she asked.

"Who hasn't?" Keats muttered. "It's in every damned paper, along with my picture. They're offering a reward now! You'd think I was the Ripper."

She sank on the bed, waiting for the explanation.

In between scrubbing and brushing came the words she'd expected. "I didn't kill her."

"I know. I wouldn't be here otherwise."

Keats turned his face toward her, droplets of water caught in his beard. "It had to be a Transitive. The papers make it sound like she was servicing most of London. Why pick *my* form?"

"To keep you from finding the explosives?"

He gave a grunt. After more ablutions, he sank on the bed next to her smelling like strong soap, tooth powder and sheep.

"So what happened to you that night?" she asked.

"Can I have some of the food first? I haven't eaten much since yesterday morning."

"Oh, sorry."

He watched her rummage in a bag and pull out a large cloth. She set it on the bed and unwrapped it to reveal dark bread, a thick hunk of cheese, some beef. More digging unearthed a bottle of ginger beer. He took it from her as she pulled the creaky chair closer and sat, watching him intently.

He unstoppered the bottle and took an immense swig of the beer and then smacked his lips. "That tastes so good." He set it on the floor and ripped off a hunk of bread. Mouth mostly full, he began, "I left your hotel and went into Whitechapel. Flaherty found me."

"What? And you're alive?"

"Yes, if you can believe it. Flaherty could have left me as gutted as a Christmas goose, but instead he had some hulk of fellow pop me on the jaw, jam me into a coffin and drop me in the middle of nowhere.

"I found myself in the middle of a forest, up near Stock. It's northeast of London. I had to kick the lid off to get free. When I crawled out, it's all trees and owls and brambles." He dove back into the meat, tearing off chunks with little delicacy. "I ended up near Ingatestone with a bunch of tramps. I walked for nearly a full day until a farmer offered me a ride back to London."

"Someone with sheep?" she asked.

A grin. "Yes. I'm sorry, I'm not pleasant company."

"Doesn't matter. Why didn't Flaherty kill you?"

Keats took another pull of ginger beer. He tried to stifle the burp, but failed. "I have given myself a headache pondering that very question. I heard on the street that he's looking for someone, a woman."

"Who?"

"I have no notion. For a while I wondered if he was trying to find you, because of what you did that night to save my life."

Jacynda shook her head. "He could have just followed Alastair around and eventually he'd figure out who I was."

"That's what I thought. So I ran a bluff—I told Flaherty I'd help him find *her* if he turned himself in. And by God, he didn't cut my throat. He wouldn't have passed on that opportunity unless she was someone very important to him."

"That was a big gamble," she said.

He shrugged it off. "I was dead otherwise, might as well take the chance. What I don't understand is why he didn't tell me the woman's name."

"Maybe the guy who put you in the coffin was supposed to tell you."

Keats shook his head. "I was unconscious and if he left me a note, I wouldn't have seen it unless it was stuffed up my nose. It was pitch black out there. Makes you appreciate gas lamps."

"When did you find out about Nicci?"

"Yesterday morning. I saw the papers and realized I couldn't contact my family for money or I'd be traced." He tore off some cheese and mated it with the beef. "I pawned my new boots. It didn't leave much for food."

After a few chews, he continued, "I didn't dare contact Alastair. It would ruin his career if he were found helping a criminal. It was enough of a gamble for you."

"His career's hit the rocks anyway. He got the sack at the hospital. He's working with some doc named Reuben Bishop full time now."

Keats nodded his approval. "Excellent. He'll do well."

"I agree. He assisted with Nicci's autopsy. She had syphilis."

He stopped mid-chew. Talking around the food, he said, "Thank God I didn't go with her."

"I visited your family in Canterbury. Fisher showed up right after me. They know what's going on."

"This must be hell for them."

She smiled at a memory. "They're very sweet people. I read your letter. I brought you a new watch."

He looked up at her, genuinely surprised. "Thank you, that is very kind. I think Flaherty or his oaf must have the other one." He paused and then his face saddened. "I can only imagine what the chief inspector thinks of this."

"It's hard for him. He knows you're innocent. He said that if you wanted to pass information to him to do so through me."

His surprise deepened. "You realize the risk in that? It was bad enough to have you meet me tonight."

"You're worth it."

That warmed his heart. *What an amazing woman.* "I'll keep that offer in mind."

He finished off the beer and cheese while she told him of her trip to Southampton the night before.

"Thank God Alastair was with you. That was very dangerous to do on your own."

Jacynda shrugged. "It wasn't too bad. There are a few things you should know. Nicci was blackmailing Effington. I think he paid her with information about Flaherty when he ran out of money."

"Ah, so that's where it came from."

"I did some checking—some of Effington's warehouses are in Wapping, though most are in Rotherhithe."

"They're the perfect place to hide explosives. I've heard that Flaherty hasn't been seen in Whitechapel since the night I was sent into the forest. There's a connection, I can feel it. If I just had a list of those warehouses..." he said, frowning. "Oh well, I'll do it the old-fashioned way—boot leather."

"Heading for Rotherhithe next?" she asked.

He nodded. "I'll try to get a job at one of the warehouses. Even if I don't, I can watch the loads, see if I recognize someone. All I need is one witness from that night who can lead me to Flaherty."

"That's taking a huge risk, Jonathon. You're not that healthy. Wouldn't it be better to turn yourself in and let Fisher substantiate your alibi?"

Keats shook his head immediately. "I have only one chance at this. The longer I stay free, the more likely I will find Flaherty. I know how he thinks, at least until the other night's bizarre behavior."

"And get yourself hung or knifed in the process?" she asked in a near whisper.

He put his hand on hers and gave it a light squeeze. "It's the bargain I accepted when I took Nicci's note seriously."

She averted her eyes. "I shouldn't have pushed you so hard. I got you into this."

"I don't blame you."

"You should," she said.

He shook his head. "Let's agree we're both fools and leave it at that."

That didn't seem to mollify her. "Can you shift now?" He shook his head. "You're a sitting duck, Keats."

"No, I'm not. I know the docklands and I'm good at what I do. I'll prevail."

She pulled on her shawl. "The room's paid for. Stay here tonight. There's more food in the sack and..." Bending over, she dug in her boot and extracted an envelope. "Here's twenty pounds. If you need more, send me another letter."

When she reached the door, he caught her arm and turned her toward him. The kiss wasn't rushed.

"When I find Flaherty and this is all over, I promise to take you to the Crystal Palace to celebrate. We'll spend the whole day there. I will be the most fortunate man in all London, as you'll be on my arm."

Jacynda blinked her eyes to hide the sheen of tears.

"I'll hold you to that promise, Jonathon."

‡

After changing clothes at the bookshop and dodging a very chatty Pratchett, Cynda set her feet toward the hotel, her mind a jumble.

"You should have made him turn himself in," Mr. Spider chastised. Cynda couldn't see the creature, but he was somewhere nearby. "He'll just get himself killed. He has too many enemies."

"And if he turns himself in, they'll hang him," she muttered, settling the argument. There was more to his "Sir Galahad" nickname than he might admit. From what she remembered, Lancelot's son had dogged determination and that's what had led him to the Holy Grail.

*He just might pull it off.*

"And if not?" her personal delusion inquired.

"Go away. I don't want reality right now."

"How about a primate? I'd say the timing is good."

The moment it saw her, the organ-grinder's monkey aimed his tiny feet toward Cynda, knowing her to be a soft touch. About once a week she encountered the little fellow and couldn't resist dropping a few coins in his tin cup. Once the coins had been paid, he doffed his hat and then scampered back to the organ-grinder, who gave her a knowing nod. She responded with a wink.

"He's so cute," she said. She remembered the first night she'd seen him. Keats had given her spare change so she could continue to enjoy the little fellow's attentions. That memory only made it hurt more. So much had gone wrong in the last few weeks.

"Quite lively," someone said. The accent was American.

Cynda turned, then stared at the man standing next to her. She blinked again in case he was a lag-induced hallucination. He was still there.

"That is a White-headed Capuchin. They are from South America," he added. "They live to be fifteen to twenty-five years old in the wild."

Her interface remained silent. *Another muted ESR Chip?* She examined his face. It was a bit younger than the night at the party and seemed...off in some way. Moreover, he wasn't the least bit upset by her presence, unlike the last time.

"Yes, quite cute," she replied, frantically working through her options. *How do I find out if you're for real?* "Ah, I don't believe we've met," she bluffed.

"No, we haven't. I would remember a pretty face such as yours."

Maybe this was the real Defoe.

"So, are you the man most of the universe is looking for, or a clever imposter?"

His eyes twinkled. "What do you think?" He delivered a bemused smile and offered his arm. She accepted it and they strolled through Whitechapel like any other couple. She kept the other hand near her truncheon, just to be safe.

*How do I sort this guy out?*

"So what color are your delusions?" she asked.

She got a confused look in response.

A Senior Rover would have replied instantly—hot pink zebras on flaming ice skates, hordes of neon prime numbers. Whatever plagued them. Harter Defoe had coined many of the terms used in the time immersion industry, including time lag and lag lightning. He'd documented the advanced effects of time travel on the human brain as he'd experienced them. Defoe's delusions would have their own hallucinations. She bet they were damned colorful.

"You're not the one," Cynda said, genuinely disappointed. She pulled her arm out of his and stepped back a pace or two, fingers resting on top of the weapon underneath her shawl.

Her companion gave a short bow. "No, I'm not the *real* one. However, you do get something in return for spotting me."

He produced something from his pocket and offered it to her. She took it with a great deal of caution. It was a token.

"This will get you an entry into a very special contest worth," he lowered his voice, "one million pounds."

"A what?" Maybe she'd misunderstood.

"It's a promotion, you see. I'm an actor and move from location to location. When someone spots me, I give them a token. There'll be a drawing in three months' time."

"You're an advertising campaign?" A nod and a toothy smile. "Is that why you're, ah, masked?" Another nod. "Time In Motion, right?"

"You are quite clever," he said. He winked. "I hope you win." After a tip of the top hat, the faux Defoe ambulated down the street, swinging his cane with exaggerated ease.

*You've got to be kidding.* First the Ripper tour and now this. Victorian London was getting too weird. She dropped the coin into her pocket and headed for the hotel.

She was within a block of Charing Cross Station when someone called to her. Figuring it was another marketing scheme, Cynda turned toward the inquirer in a foul mood. Her interface vibrated, announcing someone's future origin. She tapped it and then it vibrated again. This time, the tap was a lot stronger.

The man who'd called to her was one of a pair. He was ramrod-straight, as if under inspection by a superior officer. The other had more of a slouch to him, and wore a Rover's insolence.

"We need to speak privately," Ramrod said.

"And you are?"

"I would prefer that we discuss that somewhere else."

She shook her head and planted her feet.

"I go nowhere until I know what is up."

The amused fellow suggested, "Consult your timepiece, Miss Lassiter. No doubt that will help remind you of your appointment."

*Appointment?*

She retrieved the interface from its hiding place beneath her mantelet. Winding the chain around her wrist lest some street urchin try to do a snatch and grab, she popped open the watch's cover.

The words scrolling across the screen made her swear.

*Retrieval Order—Jacynda Lassiter. Return for TPB Hearing 11/02/2057 @ 14:30.*

She raised her eyes as the cover snapped shut in her hand.

"What is this about?"

"We have questions about your last assignment," Ramrod replied.

"I returned Chris Stone's watch; what else do you want?"

A shark-like smile came from Ramrod. "You."

*Can't leave now, not with Keats on the run.*

"Now is not the best time for this. I'll return in a couple of weeks."

Ramrod shook his head.

"A week?" Silence. The pair trailed after her like a shark following a wounded dolphin. If Morrisey hadn't been able to circumvent this retrieval, that meant it came from the highest level. He might not even know about it. Excrement was flying in all directions, and a sizeable chunk had just landed in her lap.

Ramrod would have followed her to her room and watched her pack if she hadn't ordered him to stay in the lobby.

"Your watch," he said, extending a hand.

"What?"

"Hand over the watch. That way, we know you'll not try to do a runner on us."

"It'd look really bad if you tried to wrestle it from me in the hotel lobby."

He removed his other hand from a pocket, displaying a metal box. "Not if you fainted. Then, I'd only be helping a lady in distress."

*Neuro-blocker. End of discussion. This one's playing hardball.*

She pulled the watch out and tossed it at him. He nearly dropped it.

"Give me an hour."

"Half an hour or I'll come after you," was the curt response.

Jacynda set the hotel maid to packing her dresses into a paper-wrapped parcel while she penned notes to deal with her sudden departure. *Burning your bridges* is what Rovers called it, though the majority never stayed in one place long enough to build any.

In Lady Sephora's note, Cynda pleaded a sudden trip to the country to visit a sick friend. She had no way of telling Keats what was up, and that worried her. Who would help him once she was gone? She didn't dare ask for Alastair's help, not in a letter. Someone else might read it, even if she tried to be cryptic with the message. Besides, she had no idea where Keats would light in Rotherhithe.

That left the doctor's note. Of the trio, Alastair would understand this brief journey might prove to be for a lifetime. How would he react? Would he think she'd left this way to avoid saying goodbye?

She phrased the note carefully, indicating she had to leave suddenly because of *business*. Maybe he'd understand what she meant. She asked him to check in at Pratchett's to collect her clothes should she not return in a couple of days. That might keep the bookstore owner from contacting the police lest he believe she'd fallen victim to some heinous crime.

"Not too far from the truth," Mr. Spider remarked. "Don't forget Fred," he added, pointing with a leg.

She glared at him and started to pack her Gladstone. Fred went in last after a quick kiss to his furry head. Before she snapped the top shut, Mr. Spider crawled inside.

"Whoa, it's dark in here."

Cynda rolled her eyes. Then the truth hit her like a shot in the gut—she might never travel again. This could be a one-way trip.

No, she couldn't think of it like that or she'd do a runner. She was a Rover, a good one. They'd have to let her continue her work. This was just administrative b.s. It'd be cleaned up in no time.

Cynda offered the maid the envelopes. "There are a pair of gentleman waiting for me downstairs. I do not want them to know about these notes, do you understand?"

"As you wish, ma'am." The maid stuck the letters deep in a pocket.

Cynda handed her a sovereign. "That's for the gallons of hot water you've brought up those stairs for me."

The woman looked up with a puzzled look. "They're making you leave, miss?"

*Yes.* "No, I just need to settle some matters at home, that's all."

A nod of understanding. "Thank you, miss. You've been right nice to me."

Cynda gave her a smile and sent her on her way. In many ways, she was just as much an indentured servant as the young girl in the starched white apron.

The two Retrievers stood near the fireplace, talking quietly. Ramrod was clearly ill at ease, tugging on his coat repeatedly. The other seemed at home in the time period.

225 |  *Virtual Evil*

*Definitely a Rover.*

"Here," Cynda said, shoving her Gladstone and the parcel into Ramrod's hands. "Earn your keep." A sour frown formed as he juggled the items.

"Burned your bridges?" the other man asked.

"Yeah, I've torched 'em. Let's get this done. I want to be back by dinner."

A low chortle from Ramrod told her she was going to be sincerely disappointed.

25

"Why won't you let me enter?" Alastair demanded.

Ronald, the Eighth Room Steward, put a finger to his lips and barred the doorway. He had a panicked expression on his usually taciturn face.

"You dare not," he whispered. "They are one member short. If you are present—"

"Who is missing?"

"Mr. Livingston." Ronald urgently pointed toward the outer door. "You must leave now or—"

Alastair pushed his way through.

George Hastings began talking the moment the door opened.

"About time, Livingston. We need to get this issue settled before Montrose—"

"Before Montrose does what?" Alastair shot back.

Hastings colored and took a long sip of his brandy, then glowered. "You're earlier than usual."

"You still haven't answered my question," Alastair retorted.

Hastings puffed his cigar, sending a blue haze into the air. Alastair waved it aside as he sat in the chair where Livingston usually resided, near the fireplace. Cartwright clutched his crossword tightly in his hands.

*No wonder Livingston sits here.* The chair afforded an excellent view of the others. It had always struck him that the most enigmatic of the quartet was judging them. From this chair it was entirely possible.

"I hear you continue to be involved with Scotland Yard," Hastings remarked.

"Yes. I was summoned to aid them in two murder investigations." A nice shading of the truth, but it would hold water.

"I would advise that you limit your interaction with them in future."

Alastair opened his mouth to challenge the order and then changed his mind. He would learn more if he played along. "I shall take it under advisement," he replied. It was the sort of response Livingston might make.

"Humph. Well, that's not why we're here, anyway." Hastings glowered at Ronald, who was poised in the shadows. "As long as there are three present, we can vote. In fact, this will work in our favor."

"Vote on what?" Alastair asked.

"The matter regarding Mr. Keats."

"His rank is detective-sergeant."

"Yes, yes," Hastings said, waving away the protest. "We must determine how to proceed."

"Proceed on what?"

"On the matter of his termination."

Alastair shot a look at Ronald. The steward lowered his eyes. *That's why you tried to stop me.*

Hastings continued, "A warrant has been issued for Keats' arrest. His name and his picture are in the newspapers. He cannot be taken into custody."

"How else can he prove his innocence?" Alastair said.

"Innocence is not the issue, Doctor. The revelation of our existence is. He must be tidied up before the coppers get hold of him. In an effort to save his own skin, he may reveal more than is prudent."

"Tidied up?"

"With the allegations hanging over his head, it is possible that we can make it look like suicide."

"You would have him killed like a stray dog?"

"Oh, no. We'll make it as quick and painless as possible. He cannot be allowed to remain on the streets."

"I refuse to allow this."

"You have little choice. And, to be honest, neither do I. I suggest we vote on it," Hastings said.

"You are voting on a man's life! Do you think you're some Roman emperor who can just drop his thumb and send a man to his grave?"

"Of course, this is dearer to your heart than for the rest of us, but you must see the sense in it. I was against Keats joining Scotland Yard in the first place. He ignored my advice. Now see what has happened. We have no other choice."

"You could let him go to trial, present his case."

"And if he's found guilty, then what? Men who find their future involves a rope often do very rash things."

"This cannot be happening."

"Regretfully, I vote that Keats be...removed," Hastings said and then promptly took a large swig of brandy.

Alastair riveted his eyes on Cartwright. The man was sweating profusely. He pulled a handkerchief from a pocket and dabbed at his face. After wiping his lips, he said, "I vote for removal."

"Damn you, Cartwright," Alastair seethed. "I vote nay."

"Two for—"

The door swung open. Malachi Livingston strode in, as if late for the theater.

"Ah, there you are, Ronald." He handed over his top hat and cane and then turned to his companions. "Midst of a vote, are we?" Before Hastings could close the ballot, he added, "I'm against termination. Two against two. It's a draw, Hastings."

"By God, you know better than to challenge—"

"I will not send a man to his death just to make your master happy."

*What master?*

Livingston continued to stare into his adversary's eyes. "Since the vote has been taken, it cannot be brought before this body in future. However, since you are always eager to bend the rules, know there will be repercussions if anything happens to Sergeant Keats."

Hastings' usually florid face went pale. "It's not me behind this, Livingston. You should know that."

"Oh, I do. Do you think *he'd* not hesitate to kill you, as well? I wonder which of the Seven they'd send to do the deed. Perhaps the Lead Assassin. I hear he's particularly lethal."

Hastings' knuckles whitened on the glass.

Out of respect, Alastair rose from the chair, but Livingston waved him down.

"Stay there. You look comfortable. I'll sit here by Cartwright and help him with his crossword." The man shrank back, as if Livingston intended to dive for his throat.

Hastings dropped his cigar and ground it out on the carpet. "To hell with you, Livingston." The warhorse lumbered out the door, Cartwright scurrying behind him like a terrier.

"Well, that was amusing, wasn't it?" Livingston said. "Some brandy, please, Ronald, and a cigar."

"For me, as well," Alastair said. "I apologize for not listening to you, Ronald."

"No apology needed, sir," the steward replied. "It worked out for the best."

After the cigars were lit and the brandy poured, they were left alone.

"Who is this master who pulls Hastings' strings?" Alastair asked.

Livingston produced a perfect smoke ring that hung in the air. "Later. Any notion where Sergeant Keats is?"

"He's hunting Flaherty. The Irishman's his alibi."

"You're joking." Alastair shook his head. "Bloody hell," Livingston muttered. "Is Miss Lassiter trying to find him?"

"How do you know her name?" Alastair asked, eyes narrowing.

"I have known about her for some time." He leaned over and tapped his cigar on the andiron, sending a cascade of fine ash onto the hearth. "I have a patient I'd like you to attend," he said, suddenly shifting topic. "He was beaten quite viciously."

Alastair struggled to catch up with Livingston's mental leapfrog. "Is he in hospital?"

"Not now. I had him moved to his rooms, and a private nurse is attending him."

"What sort of injuries?" Livingston told him. "I see. There are complications we must watch for. Young or old?"

"Young fellow." Livingston paused. "I think you will find this case of particular interest. His assailant was Hugo Effington."

Alastair's eyes snapped up from his drink. "Is Effington in custody for the assault?"

"Not yet, but I'm working on that." Livingston pulled out a piece of paper and handed it over. "The young man's name is William Cavendish. He is my...assistant. He gathers information for me. Unfortunately, Effington caught him at it."

"I shall see to him at no charge."

Livingston gave a nod of respect. He tossed his cigar into the fireplace and finished off the brandy, followed by a deep sigh of appreciation. "Being a member of this snake pit does have its rewards."

Alastair jammed the paper into a pocket. "We've accomplished nothing. They will still go after Keats. Our little sham vote isn't about to stop them."

"Indeed. Which is why I suggest you find him as quickly as possible."

"I am too well known. They will follow me and kill us both."

"Not if you go *en mirage*."

Alastair's face clouded. "You know my thoughts on that. If I begin to go about *en mirage*, The Conclave will have won. I do not wish to be part of this nonsense."

Livingston chuffed. "Then it is up to you to determine what is more important—your pride or the life of your closest friend."

Alastair bristled at the rebuke. "If you're lying to me, playing me in some grand game, I swear you shall answer for it."

A thick chortle. "Good Lord, that's not a threat, my friend."

"I hardly consider you a friend."

"You'd best get used to the notion. We both have so very few of them left." Moments later, Livingston was out the door and down the stairs in a flurry of movement.

The silence of the room bore down on Alastair. He had no notion what Hastings and Livingston had been discussing. He'd purposely kept himself isolated from the Transitives, praying they would ignore him. The more he shied away from them, the further he was pulled into their sordid politics. He should have demanded Livingston explain what was going on, who these Seven were.

Alastair finished off his brandy and threw the remainder of the cigar into the fireplace, its taste foul.

As he donned his coat in the antechamber, he hazarded a question. "You've been around a great number of individuals in your line of work, Ronald. How do you judge Livingston as a man?"

"In complete candor?" the steward asked.

"Yes, please."

Ronald took his time to answer. "I am not exactly sure what kind of man he really is. Nonetheless, at the center of him, I sense decency, though he cloaks it very well. I would say that if I was in a tight corner, the two men I would want by my side are you and Mr. Livingston, sir, for both of you are moral men with indomitable spirits."

"I am not as moral as you might believe," Alastair replied, brows furrowed, "though I thank you for that. I just do not know how to judge our Mr. Livingston."

"Perhaps that is because he is too complex to read as a simple man. The same, I might add, may be said of you. I trust him, though I have no idea why."

Alastair smiled and nodded. "Thank you very much, Ronald; I appreciate your wisdom."

The steward bowed and opened the door to the hallway. "As ever, it is a pleasure to be of service, Doctor."

## 26

Livingston was waiting for Alastair at the kerb, sitting inside a carriage. "Come on. Nice night for a ride," he said, gesturing toward the open door.

Alastair took the risk and climbed in. He'd barely shut the door when Livingston delivered two sharp raps on the roof with the top of his cane, setting the carriage in motion.

"Now will you tell me what is going on?" Alastair demanded.

"Not yet. Somewhere more private. Hold your silence until we reach our destination. One never knows who is listening."

Alastair leaned back and folded his arms across his chest. He kept his eyes on his companion, who seemed unusually pensive. To his relief, the journey did not take long. Livingston exited the carriage first. Alastair gasped as he stepped into the open. The stone walls of the Tower loomed behind them. Ahead lay the Thames and the twin piers of the new bridge, one of which had served as a bier for Johnny Ahearn.

"Why here?" he challenged.

"I'll tell you later." After paying the driver, Livingston set off at a brisk clip toward the river, leaving Alastair to follow with increasing anxiety.

By the time he joined his companion at the water's edge, some arrangement had been made with one of the watermen. For an undisclosed sum, they had the use of the boat for one hour. Livingston crawled into the craft without any apparent trepidation. Alastair was not cut of the same cloth. He entered it gingerly, fearful of tipping it over. He heard the waterman muttering at his antics, but ignored him.

The moment he settled inside, Livingston ordered, "Row us out to one of the piers. I want to be out of the flow of water traffic, but not close to shore."

After much hard work and with sweat rolling down Alastair's face and back, they reached the closest pier. He was relieved when Livingston raised a hand.

"This is suitable." Livingston took a rope from the bottom of the craft and tied them off to the pier. "That'll keep us from drifting to Gravesend."

Alastair shipped the oars and let the craft drift. The line played out and went snug. "Why out here?" he asked, eyeing the dark water uneasily.

"It affords complete privacy. Though our kind is capable of amazing feats, we have yet to learn how to walk on water." Livingston paused and then added, "Thank God."

"So what is this all about?"

Instead of answering, Livingston removed his pipe from a pocket and began to pack the bowl. Only when it was full and the pipe lit did he reply. "We are here because of the Ascendant. I believe he is the one dictating Hastings' decisions."

"Who is this...Ascendant?" Alastair asked, his eyes on a broken barrel as it floated past. His stomach rolled at the sight.

Livingston didn't seem to notice his distress. "I have no idea of his actual identity. It changes rather often."

"What is his purpose?"

"For centuries, the Ascendant was the final authority over our kind, at least those who acknowledged him. He is called the Ascendant because he alone is given the right to choose who will die or ascend, as they call it. He is chosen by a score of men and serves at their whim. When they no longer have confidence in him, it is the responsibility of the Lead Assassin to eliminate him. It is also the Lead Assassin's responsibility to keep him alive until that moment arrives. Failure in that task is always fatal."

"Why?"

"It prevents the Lead from usurping the Ascendant's position. The Lead Assassin is always Virtual, one of the Seven, as they are called. Virtuals make formidable assassins. By the time you realize one of them is trying to kill you, you're already headed to your grave. Near invisibility has its merits."

A steamer chugged up river, churning waves that rippled across the dark water and lifted their boat in a series of undulations. Alastair's gut somersaulted as he tightened his grip on the sides of the boat.

"What has this got to do with Keats?" he asked through gritted teeth.

A billow of aromatic pipe smoke rose from the bow. "I believe Keats was set up as Nicci's killer to rid our community of a very astute Scotland Yard detective, one that might prove a threat to the Ascendant in some manner."

"If this assassin is so good, why put Keats through such hell? Why not just kill him outright? They could always blame it on the Fenians."

"I have done a great deal of thinking on that very question." A spiral of smoke climbed upward and then caught the wind, trailing away. "What was Scotland Yard's preeminent case until the Hallcox murder?"

"That's obvious—the Whitechapel killings."

"Precisely. Since the killings started, the furor at the upper levels of government has only grown tenfold with each additional murder. The Yard is turning over every brick and cobblestone in the East End to find that butcher. Then the very moment the clamor begins to diminish, Miss Hallcox's death is laid neatly at the feet of a Scotland Yard detective-sergeant, one of their best, no less. I dislike coincidence."

Alastair reluctantly released his grip on the boat. "My God, you see this as some grand conspiracy," he replied, shaking his head. "That's too far-fetched."

"Is it? Scotland Yard is clearly overwhelmed by the response to these crimes. They have hundreds of plainclothes coppers wandering around in search of the Ripper. What if the Whitechapel killings and the Hallcox murder are being employed as diversions? Is this not a perfect opportunity to do something daring while everyone is looking the other way?"

"To what purpose?" Alastair asked, leaning forward.

"The Fenians are not the only ones who see a prime opportunity to overthrow the monarchy."

A slight breeze shifted Alastair's coat, sending a shiver up his back. Not all of it was from the cold.

Livingston relit his pipe with some difficulty. "To bring about a revolution, there has to be a catalyzing event, like the assassination of a monarch or something of that momentous nature."

"Then you really believe the man at Effington's party was after the prince?"

"If so, why do such a thing in front of all those people?"

"Desperation?"

"Exactly. It reeks of it, and that's what troubles me. Desperate men do not think of consequences. We do not need a revolution in this country, Doctor. England *must* remain a monarchy."

"Why?" Alastair demanded. "It is certainly not a just system at present, certainly not for the poor in the East End. They work for twelve, fourteen hours a day and still starve to death. What kind of government allows such a travesty?"

"One that is infinitely better than the alternatives," Livingston replied hotly.

"I'm not convinced about that," Alastair said.

"Are you a socialist, doctor?"

"No, a humanitarian."

"Ah, one of *those*." Livingston puffed on his pipe in agitation.

Alastair scrutinized the man more closely. "How do I know you're on the level?"

"If I were a threat, you'd be dead by now, if only to preserve my anonymity. I noted your fear of the water just now. I, however, am an excellent swimmer."

His companion's gaze grew steely. "I'd be sure to take you to the bottom with me."

Livingston laughed. "I believe you would. You're far more useful to me alive, Doctor. Your talent as a Perceiver is a potent weapon against those who wish to remain hidden."

Alastair reluctantly nodded. "That still doesn't make me want to trust you."

"Then tell me what it will take to gain that trust. Our hour on the water is drawing to an end. This must be resolved tonight."

"It's simple. Tell me who you really are."

"Malachi Livingston."

"I still don't believe you."

Livingston groaned. "You are a stubborn man, Doctor. Very well, I can tell you this much. I am the man who prevented Miss Lassiter's death that night near the Paul's Head Pub."

Alastair went still. "So prove your claim. Tell me exactly what happened."

"Miss Lassiter met you on the street for a very poignant farewell scene, and then entered the Paul's Head. She was carrying a Gladstone that appeared quite heavy. I suspect her lover's urn was inside. A while later, she met a man on the street, and they took a turn down an alley. By the time I caught up with them, he'd already stabbed her and—"

"Where was her injury?"

"Her chest. She was clutching it. By the time he attempted to cut her throat, I was there to intervene."

"I didn't see you. Why didn't you reveal yourself?" Alastair demanded.

"No need. You came charging down the passage like an avenging angel, so I went after the attacker. I figured you'd see to Miss Lassiter."

"Where'd he go after that?"

Livingston frowned. "I lost him, unfortunately."

"Why were you following her in the first place?"

"Because she intrigued me, much like you and Sergeant Keats do. I thought her capable of handling the situation, or I would have involved myself sooner."

That didn't ring true. Alastair had one last question. "There was another injury. Where was it?"

Livingston closed his eyes in recollection. "On her neck, the right side. When I hit the fellow, the knife knicked her."

Alastair shifted on the hard plank. Livingston had been in that alley, one way or another. If he hadn't known for sure that Jacynda's assailant was from her time, he'd have suspicions about the man sitting across from him.

Livingston leaned forward in the boat, a self-satisfied smile firmly in place. "One other minor point. I was the person who appeared at the Bishopsgate Police Station in Miss Lassiter's form to reassure the police you were not a murderer. Once they knew she was alive, the charges against you were dropped."

Alastair gaped. "I always wondered who that was. For a time I thought it was Jacynda, but she denied it. Why did you go to such effort on my behalf?"

"I had no desire to see you up on charges. I especially did not want to appear in court just to save your life."

Alastair sighed. "Thank you for that."

"Think nothing of it."

The doctor grasped onto a slim reed of trust. He marshaled his thoughts and told his companion about the evidence they'd found in Miss Hallcox's room, Mrs. Effington's escape and her husband's involvement with the dead woman. When he finished, Livingston was nodding to himself.

"Did you find Hastings' calling card at the Hallcox residence?" he asked.

Alastair shook his head.

"How about someone from Home Office?"

"Yes, there was one. I don't know if I can reveal his name at this point. The case is still under investigation."

"I understand," Livingston said. "You say there were a number of high ranking officials that partook of her flesh?"

"Yes. Quite a few." Alastair gingerly leaned back. To his relief, the boat did not tip over. "Do you think Effington's involvement with Flaherty is that catalyst you spoke of?"

"It could well be. Our difficulty lies in the fact we have no notion of

Flaherty's target. It could be an edifice or a monarch, for all we know."

Alastair pulled his coat closer. The breeze was cutting through the fabric now. Livingston opened his pocket watch, consulted the dial and then snapped it shut again.

"Best head for shore. The waterman will be reporting the boat stolen if we don't arrive on time."

After the line was untied, the doctor eagerly plied the oars.

Livingston repacked his pipe. "Has Miss Lassiter had any luck locating the man at Effington's party?" he asked.

"No. Not yet."

"Warn her to be on her guard, and you as well. Effington will be furious his wife has absconded. He will not hesitate to harm either you or Miss Lassiter."

"We will be careful."

"One additional warning. If the Ascendant is truly behind all this and he learns of our suspicions, he may turn one of the Seven loose with orders to deal with the lot of us."

Alastair stopped rowing. He hadn't considered that. "That is truly sobering."

"As it should be. We are growing enemies faster than nits on a beggar."

As they approached the shore, Livingston tapped the pipe on the side of the boat and put it inside his pocket. "I appreciate your insights, Doctor. You are one of the few men I trust in this city."

Alastair's mouth fell slack. He didn't hear a lie. "I see. That is a surprise."

"It was to me, as well." They shared a muted laugh. "I will see what I can learn about the Ascendant. If I get too close, you'll hear of my death. I wanted you to know what I'm about so you can continue on if I am unable."

"You say that so calmly."

"We are all slated for the grave one day."

"I hope that day might be considerably in the future. For my part, I shall go hunting for Keats as best as I am able. Perhaps he can help us in some way."

The boat bumped on shore. Once the waterman had secured it, Livingston climbed out, followed shortly by the doctor. It felt good to be on solid earth again.

They parted a short distance from Traitor's Gate. "Good evening, Doctor," Livingston said, adjusting his top hat. "We will meet and compare notes as the need arises." He marched away, cape billowing behind him like a black sail.

*Providing we're still alive.*

27

2057 A.D.
*Time Protocol Board Complex*

Deposited into a nondescript room, Cynda wiped the beads of sweat off her forehead onto the sleeve of her dress, leaving a dark stain. This latest transfer had been the worst she'd ever endured. Whoever had run the chronsole didn't have the finesse of her buddy Ralph. The result was a case of world-class nausea and disorientation. Since her two escorts hadn't traveled with her, the chronsole jockey had probably done that on purpose, on the order of the higher-ups.

*Creeps.*

A few minutes later, the friendlier of the two bird dogs walked into the room and pulled over a chair. He appeared to be in fine shape.

"Tell the chronsole bozo they suck at transfers," she said, swallowing heavily to keep her stomach from anointing the floor.

"Didn't bother me." He was a bit younger, maybe twenty-five, with decent good looks. Pity he was learning how to be a jerk so soon.

She speared him with a glare.

"You'll have to talk to them, you know," he said.

"I'll talk to them when I'm ready," Cynda replied, returning her eyes to the polished floor.

"They're not likely to wait."

"Then they can go screw themselves."

He chuckled. "I've heard of you," he said. "You bend all the rules. When they told me to bring you in, I was jazzed. You don't get to meet a genuine celebrity that often."

After a very deep breath, Cynda cautiously raised her head. The world was the right color, but everything seemed to be a quarter-inch out of phase. "You're blowing smoke and it's not working."

The fellow looked genuinely surprised. "I'm not...honest. I'm a Rover with Time In Motion. All I've ever heard about was you and Defoe."

"I don't know why. I've not done anything that spectacular."

"Pulling a half-dozen Christian tourists out of a Roman arena right before the lions ate them isn't spectacular? I hear they wrote that one up as a miracle."

"The Christians did, not the Romans. They were sincerely pissed."

The guy spread his hands. "See? The rest of us haven't done stuff like that."

"The rest of you wouldn't have gotten into a crack like that in the first place." She thought for a moment and threw out some bait. "You know Frank Miller?"

He shook his head.

"I thought he worked at Time In Motion."

"Never met him, but there are a lot of new guys now."

"Why does the Time Protocol Board want me?"

"Something to do with Chris Stone." A slight pause. "I met him a couple of times when I used to work at ETC. Nice guy."

"Yeah, he was."

"Did you really bring him home against orders?"

"Yeah."

"Wow. I thought they were just making that one up."

"No." She waited a half-second. "What is this all about?"

The guy lowered his voice. "There are questions about Stone's death and what happened to that Mimes guy."

"I see." The truth was simple: she had Chris incinerated so he could come home and made sure Dalton Mimes returned to 2057 afraid of his own shadow.

"Of course, you didn't hear that from me," he added.

"Thanks. What's your name?"

A look of chagrin. "Johns Hopkins."

"Like the hospital?"

"Yeah. My mom had all her kids there. Loves the place."

"So why are you here?"

A boyish grin. "I just wanted to talk to a legend."

She couldn't help but feel flattered. "Well, Mr. Hopkins, let me give you a bit of advice. The big boys will work you to death. The only one who cares if you're alive at the end of a run is you. Remember that."

The guy thought for a moment and then nodded. "Thanks."

"No sweat. Now go tell my boss I'm in 2057 as per the regs, or

I'll start kicking up a fuss."

Hopkins sighed. "I don't think they're going to allow that. Your hearing's in an hour."

"The hell it is! I get thirty-six hours' rest before any official testimony. It's the law."

Hopkins' silence told her the regs were being ignored.

"Tell Morrisey I'm here, or I file an official protest."

"There's a no-contact order. I can't send that message. Sorry."

She groaned. "I hope you're taking notes, Hopkins. If they do this to me, they'll do it you someday."

The man's face grew grim. "I was just thinking the same thing."

To her extreme relief, Morrisey arrived in a barely controlled fury fifteen minutes before the hearing was scheduled to start. He'd not raised his voice one decibel, but he got the message across. Legal procedures would be followed, or there would be consequences.

Cynda made a mental note to buy Johns Hopkins a beer the next time she saw him. Somehow he'd managed to come through. She just hoped it wouldn't cost him his job. She was extricated from the room and handed over to her boss.

"Thanks," she said, and then barely missed throwing up on his tidy black shoes.

Once Cynda was inside Morrisey's compound, the lag-induced hallucinations kicked in for real, playing field hockey with her mind. The room was awash in watercolors, each with their own trajectory. Mr. Spider scaled the walls and parachuted from the ceiling at regular intervals, complete with eye goggles and a white Isadora Duncan scarf.

"Whee!" he shouted, sailing past her face and landing with a loud plop on the floor. A flurry of movement and he was up the wall again, ready for another launch.

"Whee!" Plop. Scurry.

"Miss Lassiter?" Morrisey inquired, his eyebrows furrowed in concern.

"Huh? Oh, sorry. Are there fluorescent dust devils swirling around here?"

He performed a tactful scan of the room. "None that I can see."

"Whee!" went the arachnid, narrowly missing her boss this time.

Morrisey leaned closer. "Perhaps you should go to bed."

"Alone?" she asked before she could stop herself.

He hesitated, clearly caught off-guard. "Yes, you're responsible for managing the time lag in your own fashion."

"Drat. You'd probably be fun." *Where the hell did that come from?*

"From what I've heard, I'm anything but."

Cynda blinked at the candid admission and then glowered. "They're lying."

The briefest of smiles. "One can only hope."

She finally crawled into the Thera-Bed to allow it to do its magic. It wasn't good at curing time lag, but it settled the nausea, tamed her headache and sent her to sleep. As she drifted off, she heard Mr. Spider scaling the wall in search of the perfect jump.

‡

Cynda sat in what was supposed to be a state-of-the-art ergo chair at the front of the hearing room. Victorian furniture was more comfortable. In her mind, the chair fit the room: a bleak sort of space that deserved an *Abandon Hope All Ye Who Enter Here* sign over the door. To counter her intense desire to fidget, she focused on Mr. Spider who was napping on the desktop in front of her. He was still wearing the scarf. At least the goggles and parachute were gone.

Ralph and her boss sat in the front row of the spectator's gallery. Morrisey's face was expressionless, as if transfixed in some meditation. Ralph winked to reassure her, but she knew him too well. He was frightened.

The sole judge, currently parked behind a desk, had a saggy sort of walrus face. The fact there was only one adjudicator wasn't a good omen. The more judges, the more conflict of opinion that might lead to an acquittal or a lighter sentence. If Walrus didn't like what he heard, she was toast.

The hearing began with a lengthy list of complaints against her. As far as Cynda could tell, they'd only left off the Kennedy assassination because she'd not been born yet. Noticeably missing was any mention of Harter Defoe and the attempted assassination in '88.

"Do you understand the nature of these proceedings?" the judge inquired.

"I do. Who filed the complaint?"

A pause, followed by scrolling through a holo document.

"Dr. Walter Samuelson."

*So much for gratitude.* She'd rescued the guy from a Victorian asylum only to have him file a complaint against her on behalf of his brother.

"No good deed goes unpunished," Mr. Spider observed.

"Is it true you have refused treatment for your Adrenalin Reactive Disorder?" Walrus began.

"Yes."

"Why was that?"

"I don't like drugs."

"Even if they would make you a calmer person?"

*Definitely.* "Yes."

Walrus typed a note into the document. "Please detail what you know of Mr. Stone's death and the aftermath."

"Aftermath?"

"How his remains were transferred to 2057."

Cynda pushed down her impatience, knowing she had to play the game.

"Mr. Stone was killed by Dalton Mimes the night I arrived in Whitechapel."

"For the record, Dalton Mimes is a pseudonym for author Geoffrey Samuelson, the complainant's brother." After a moment, he continued, "On what date did you arrive in Whitechapel?"

"25 September, 1888."

"A restricted time period?"

"At that point it was. TIC was making extra money by sending tourists into 'no go' zones."

"For the record, TIC is an acronym for Time Immersion Corporation, now closed due to bankruptcy."

*This one's going to be a pain in the ass.* "TIC did not authorize Mr. Stone's retrieval to 2057, so I devised another method of returning his remains to his family."

"You had the body cremated?"

She nodded, knowing the court VidCam would catch her response.

"Then you affected the transfer?"

Another nod. The less she said, the less likely he'd find some way to nail her.

"What was the cause of Mr. Stone's death?"

*Don't dare mention the autopsy.* "According to his killer, he was given an overdose of Chloral Hydrate and then dumped into the Thames to make it appear he committed suicide."

"Your Run Report states Mr. Mimes confessed to this act. Is it true you administered *two* doses of neural-blocker to subdue the tourist?"

*Uh-oh.* "Yes."

"Why would you do that?"

"To keep him from trying to cut my throat...again."

"You are referring to his alleged assault against you on 30 September, 1888."

"Alleged? I'd be happy to show you the scars if you wish."

A brusque shake of the head. "We have your medical records from TEM Enterprises. You suffered a..." more scrolling of the holographic record, "tension pneumothorax and a laceration to your throat."

"In other words, he damned near killed me."

A stern look. "Please refrain from profanity, Miss Lassiter."

"Only if you refrain from understatement."

In the gallery, Ralph's eyes widened in warning.

The judge returned to the screen. "Your Run Report indicates that Mr. Mimes acted as if he was willing to execute the transfer to 2057, but at the last moment, he assaulted you. Do you know why that was?"

"I believe he saw me as a threat to his plan to implicate an innocent man for the Ripper murders."

"Are you referring to a physician named Montrose?"

She nodded.

"Did Mr. Mimes give you any indication that he intended to become violent?"

"None whatsoever. One minute he's pushing to get back to '057, and the next he's buried a knife into my chest up to the handle. There was no warning."

"Is it possible your behavior triggered his act of violence?"

"No. He's a psychopath. They don't need a reason to kill you."

Walrus scrolled further down in the document.

"Explain why you felt compelled to contravene TIC's orders regarding Mr. Stone's remains."

"Chris deserved burial in *his* time, not some moldy grave in '88. Rovers always come home." *Always.*

"Now that you've had a chance to reconsider this action, would you have acted differently?"

"No."

"Did it not occur to you that TIC might have had information on the situation that you did not possess?"

"No. They were being cheap..." She squelched the next word on the tip of her tongue. "Chris had to come home. That's the bottom line."

"I see." More notes. From her position, she couldn't read a word of them, but she knew they weren't complimentary. Someone cleared their throat out in the audience.

"Did you transfer Mr. Mimes to 79 A.D. just prior to Vesuvius' eruption?"

Cynda shifted in her seat. This wasn't going the way she'd hoped. To keep her hands from jittering, she knitted the fingers together and parked them in her lap.

"Miss Lassiter?"

"Yes?"

"Why did you execute that transfer?"

"Mimes wasn't being forthcoming regarding Chris' interface."

"And the subsequent transfer to 1485?"

"I thought a glimpse of Torquemada might loosen his tongue."

"Did it?"

"Yes. He told me that Chris' interface was in the New High Street Bank."

"But it wasn't, was it?" She shook her head. "Earlier, you accused Mr. Mimes of torture, and yet it appears you employed the same technique."

"Protecting the time stream is paramount," Cynda said, parroting the first rule of all Time Rovers.

The judge's gaze hardened. "Subsequent to his arrival in 2057, Mr. Mimes experienced six different time periods, all quite emotionally devastating. Why did you do that to him?"

*Because he killed my lover and laughed about it. Because I didn't have the guts to cut his throat myself.*

"I was using a new time interface. I wasn't totally sure how to activate the forward function. I somehow set it to the multi-period hop setting."

"Are you saying it wasn't intentional?"

"My sole intent was to get the tourist to 2057 so he could stand trial for Mr. Stone's murder." *And give him a helluva ride along the way.*

"Are you aware that Mr. Mimes now suffers from delusional episodes secondary to the horrors he faced during that extended transfer?"

*Proof there is a God.* "I heard something about that."

"Do you have any remorse for your actions?"

A vivid image played in her mind: Chris quoting Shakespeare after they'd made love for what would be the last time. Then she saw him in his coffin, eyes closed forever. She remembered how cold he'd been when she touched him.

Tears began to form. She brushed them away, angry at showing weakness before this pinhead. "No remorse whatsoever."

"That will be all, then," Walrus replied.

Mr. Spider shook his head in dismay. "Now you're in for it."

✞

The judge cleared his throat and pitched his voice so everyone could hear him. "In regard to Case Number 2057 stroke 53-9

Lassiter, Jacynda A., on behalf of the Time Protocol Board, I render the following verdict."

He scrolled down the holo-document, which Cynda found odd. Why would the verdict already be in the records? It was usually appended after it was pronounced to allow for any last-minute changes or pleas.

She looked out at Ralph. He had his fingers crossed. Morrisey's stern expression told her he'd seen the document-scrolling as well.

*What are they doing?*

Walrus cleared his throat and announced, "Considering all counts and Miss Lassiter's continued avoidance of appropriate therapy for her Adrenalin Reactive Disorder, we order mandatory medical treatment. To ensure compliance, we insist upon six months' incarceration at a Minimum Security Facility. To compensate Mr. Geoffrey Samuelson, a.k.a. Dalton Mimes, for pain and suffering incurred during Miss Lassiter's interrogation, a fine of one hundred thousand Electronic Monetary Units will be levied. Further, we will recommend revocation of the defendant's Time Specialist license."

Surprised gasps burst forth from the back of the room. She heard people murmuring amongst themselves, voicing their disapproval.

"What kind of sentence is that?" someone called out.

Walrus ignored the protest, addressing Cynda. "Do you have anything to add before I close this hearing?"

She steeled herself. "Yes, I do. Mimes murdered a wonderful man, a Time Rover. What about *Chris'* pain and suffering? When does Mimes pay for *that* crime, and the fact that he nearly killed me *twice?*"

"All of that is secondary to your behavior in this matter."

"That's b.s. and you know it!"

A familiar voice cut through the chamber as Morrisey rose, eyes dark with anger. "TEM Enterprises appeals this egregious judgment."

"The appeal will be logged," Walrus replied.

Cynda already knew it would fail.

With a touch of the judge's hand, the holo-screen vanished into the tabletop, taking her career with it.

28

TEM *Enterprises*

After considerable legal wrangling, Cynda was released on bail and put under her boss' supervision. At present she was sitting on the floor in the corner of the room she'd been allocated in Morrisey's compound. Her chin was on her knees and Fred was enveloped in a fur-crushing embrace. They'd been played by pros. TPB wanted her out of the time stream, and her gut told it had something to do with Harter Defoe.

She heard the door whoosh open. It was Ralph.

"There *are* chairs in this room," he said, drawing near.

"I like the corner. It feels right. It's about the size of the cell I'll get."

He settled in on the floor next to her, drawing her into a tight hug. Old friends.

"The boss is pulling strings, but nothing's working. He's seething at the way you've been treated."

"I'm too tired to seethe," she said. "I'm just wondering how bad the medications will screw me up."

"I promise not to make fun of you if you drool," he joked.

She elbowed him, not too hard. "That's a rotten thing to say."

He chuckled and then grew sober in an instant. "There was a press conference at the asylum. Mimes is claiming he's been vindicated and is seeking release."

"That sonofabitch. I should have left him to roast in Pompeii."

Ralph gave her a long look. "Maybe it's a good thing you're going on the drugs."

She pulled away. "So what else is happening?"

"The union has filed a grievance on your behalf against the TPB. The other Rovers are coming unstuck at how you've been treated."

"That's nice to know."

Ralph hesitated before delivering his next news item. "Time In Motion just sent a Rover to '88 find Defoe. He came back via the *Dead Man Switch*, with a bullet in his heart."

"Who was it?"

"Some guy named Hopkins."

*Oh, no.* Cynda pulled herself upright. "Did he make it?"

"Yeah, barely. If the interface hadn't transferred him, he'd have been a goner. TPB is claiming Defoe did the deed."

She shook her head. "That's not his style."

"Unless he's gone off his rocker. Either way, they're going nuts trying to find him."

"I want to see Hopkins," she said, expecting an argument.

Instead, Ralph shrugged. "I'll talk to the boss."

‡

The trip to the hospital required a guard. He was TPB and announced the fact up front, along with a list of unpleasant things that would happen if she tried to *rabbit*, as he put it. Like she could go anywhere—they'd confiscated her interface. For once, Cynda listened to her better nature and didn't flip the guy off.

The fellow named for a hospital looked like hell, each breath labored. The Thera-Bed's status graph showed minimal blue: technology's hint that he should be drafting his will.

Cynda knew how this felt from the other side, and that only made it harder.

Hopkins didn't open his eyes when she touched his hand.

"Sorry, guy. Some people don't play fair. Get well, okay?" A nearly silent mumble passed his lips. She bent forward. "What?"

The mumble rose in volume. "Not...Defoe."

"Who then?"

"T...P...B."

Luckily, her escort wasn't in the room to hear this revelation–the price they paid for writing this guy off too soon. "Why would they try to kill you?"

"Found out...I work for Guv."

*Oh boy.* "Was it that jerk you were with in '88?" Hopkins nodded. "Don't worry, I'll sort out it, guy."

He pried open two bloodshot eyes and squeezed her hand. "Kick some...ass."

She winked, though she wasn't sure he could see her. "You got it. When we're you're better, the beer is on me."

"Deal."

She didn't bother to look startled when three black-suited men took their positions around her the moment she exited the room. Fortunately, Ramrod wasn't one of them.

"Guv or TPB?" she asked, spoiling for a fight.

"Guv," one of them replied.

"What happened to the TPB goon?"

"It was suggested that he go for some coffee."

"That's good. If you were TPB, I might be tempted to rack up an assault charge or two just to round out my record."

The man's eyes widened, but he held his position as they exited the building. The other spooks kept sweeping the scene around them, as if they expected trouble.

"The docs say Hopkins is doing better," she reported. The one agent nodded, as if he already knew. "He's a nice guy. He didn't deserve that." The agent nodded again. "Hopkins says TPB did it."

"We know." A momentary pause. "Senior Agent Klein wishes to speak with you."

Cynda threw up her hands. "Why not? My schedule's free at the moment."

✝

Another windowless room, another potentially uncomfortable chair. Behind the table was a senior Guv agent in his crisp black suit. She wondered if he had one for each day of the week.

"Why did you visit Mr. Hopkins?" the agent asked without looking up.

"Because he's a Rover and he got hurt on the job."

"How did you know about his injuries?"

"The Rover community is tight-knit, like you spooks. Word gets around."

A hint of a frown crossed his face.

Cynda chose a chair and parked herself in it, crossing her arms over her chest. "So you're Agent Klein?" she asked, since he'd not bothered to introduce himself.

"*Senior* Agent Klein," he replied, still not looking up from the paperwork.

"What's your game?"

His eyes rose to meet hers. "I see that TPB has ordered mandatory ARD therapy, six months incarceration and monetary payment to Mr. Mimes for pain and suffering. Oh, and revocation of your Time Immersion license."

"I can't pay that bastard if I can't work," she shot back.

"They don't care. They just want you out of the way." After more document-shuffling, he paused for effect, issuing a smirk that begged for a slap. "Then there are the federal charges."

Cynda's bravado evaporated. "What federal charges?"

"Oh, you hadn't heard about those? Let's see...five counts of a Class Four Felony involving the transportation of goods to Off-Gridders. Amazing how smuggling a few packets of tomato seeds can really rack up the jail time."

Cynda felt her advantage melt. "How long?" she asked.

"Ten point nine years."

"Community service?" she asked, knowing the question was absurd.

"Medium Security. Full sentence. After that, you're an Off-Gridder yourself with no visitation privileges."

Meaning she'd never see Ralph again.

"What do you want?"

The smirk grew. "Nothing. This isn't negotiable."

"The hell it isn't. TPB wouldn't have staged that ridiculous hearing if they didn't have a reason for wanting me out of circulation. That says I have value."

"And what value would that be?"

"TPB wants Defoe. I think you do, too. So what's the deal?"

The smirk vanished as Klein leaned closer across the table. "Bring him to '057, and we'll clear your record of all charges."

"Even the TPB ones?"

"We'll do what we can with those."

She gambled. "No way. Unless my slate's wiped clean and I keep my license, I don't find Defoe."

They stared at each other. "Deal."

*Holy crap.* "Why is he so damned important?"

Klein relaxed. "The Time Lag's finally got to him. He's gone rogue and tried to kill Hopkins. He needs to come home."

"You know that's b.s. Hopkins said a TPB agent shot him."

The corner of Klein's mouth twitched. "That's not your concern. Your worry should be the decade in prison."

"You don't even know if Defoe is still in '88. He could be long gone. I'm not fond of wild-goose chases when my neck is on the block."

A shiny object landed into the middle of the table with a decided thunk. It was an interface. The battered surface told her it was Chris'.

"Mr Stone was under contract with us while working at Time Immersion Corporation. His trip to 1888 made for a perfect opportunity to contact Defoe. As all his case notes are our property, we...intercepted his interface before TPB could access the files."

*Did Morrisey know what his nephew had been up to?* She sure as hell hadn't and they'd been sleeping together.

"You knew where Defoe was all the time?"

Agent Klein ignored the question. "Mr. Stone kept copious notes on his interface, unlike you."

*How do you know what's on mine?*

A few moments later, her dead lover's words were hovering in the open space between her and the Guv agent.

*9/20/1888 – I saw Defoe tonight, but lost him on the Strand. Just my luck.*

"Are you sure that wasn't the guy that's wandering around '88 giving away tokens for some promotion?"

Klein shook his head. "No. That stupid-ass stunt didn't start until last week. Stone spoke with the real Defoe."

"The interface registered his ESR Chip?" Cynda asked dubiously.

"Yes," Klein advanced the watch stem a notch, "though I suspect Defoe's removed the chip by this point."

*9/22/1888 – Spoke with Defoe and explained the situation. He agreed to consider our offer. Will meet tomorrow night. Hope this works. So much depends on it. Also closing in on missing tourist. Might be able to complete two jobs at once.*

Klein's voice softened. "Mr. Stone is killed the next day and never makes the meeting."

"What offer was he talking about?" Cynda asked.

"Not your concern." He shifted in his chair. "Our offer stands: find Defoe and your past is forgotten. Fail us, and we'll bury you in the prison system."

"You're not much for options, are you?"

Klein leaned forward, but the smug grin she'd been expecting wasn't there. "I'll even sweeten the pot. You find Defoe, and you're one step closer to the man who killed Chris Stone."

Her mouth dropped open. "It was Mimes. He admitted it."

"How very thoughtful of him." Klein rose from the table. "Good hunting, Miss Lassiter."

29

Keats' first night in Rotherhithe brought little sleep. Once he'd confirmed that the boarding house's bed, though lumpy, was clean and free of bugs and the creature in his room was a timid mouse, he collapsed, exhausted. Only an hour or so later, the telltale squeak of rusty bedsprings awoke him. It took him a bit to register just where he was. A few low moans punctuated the rhythmic squeaking and finally a loud shout. After that, blissful silence.

He rolled over and fell into a fitful sleep, only to have the noise return once more.

"Give it a rest, you lecherous sods!" he shouted, pounding on the wall behind his bed. He heard a hearty laugh and then it grew quiet.

Keats rose at dawn in a surly mood, unable to tolerate the bed any further. He resisted the urge to make an unholy racket and awaken the couple next door. Instead, he turned his mind to the task at hand.

He sat on the side of the bed, rested his elbows on his knees and tried to shift. It'd always been so easy, like donning a coat. He'd visualize the physical image in his mind and the change would occur. This time he began to tremble, and cold sweat sprouted on his forehead. Nausea rolled through him, making his stomach lurch.

"No..."

He ceased his efforts and the physical symptoms vanished. Exhausted, he lay back in the bed and stared at the water-stained ceiling.

Flaherty's blow to his head had ruined it all. "Damn you."

He heard the sound of voices. A door opened and closed, then the thump of boots on the stairway. Lying in bed feeling sorry for himself was not going to put things right. He needed to find a job with the other Irish dockworkers. A few careful questions might lead him to Flaherty's cache and his alibi.

After washing his face and realizing he had no linens to dry himself, he plodded down the stairs to the street, his hands dripping. The moment he stepped outside, he took a deep breath. It proved a mistake. The stench of Rotherhithe and the river invaded his lungs and he coughed deeply, making him clutch his chest.

He heard a sound and turned to find his landlady's sharp eyes watching him.

"Off to find work?" Mrs. O'Neill asked at a volume that would have leveled buildings. He nodded. "Worked at the docks, have ya?"

"Yes," he shouted back to compensate for her diminished hearing, "but it's been a long time."

"How long?"

"Ten years or so." Before he'd become a copper. He'd made it only a fortnight before calling it quits, not having the physical size to do the heavy labor. Then he'd done a stint with the railroad, working with explosives. Finally, he'd joined the police force, beginning his service as a constable at Arbour Square, in H Division. That had been his life ever since.

Now he'd come full circle.

"The call-on shelter is still on Redriffe Road," Mrs. O'Neill said, pointing southward away from the river.

"Thank you," he said. He tapped his cap instead of removing it, not keen to reveal the healing wound underneath.

He bought a meat pie from a vendor on the street, and some ginger beer to wash it down. It seemed to help. Then he set a course for Redriffe Road, keeping a weary eye out for anyone who looked familiar.

*As if I would recognize all the ones I've arrested.* Of course, they'd remember him. It was like wearing a sandwich board that said, "You know this one, lads. Have at 'im!" Anytime he saw a constable, he grew apprehensive. They seemed to be everywhere.

Was he being a fool? No doubt he was. But the fact remained that he was his own best advocate. Sitting in a cell awaiting trial would not solve his problems. Ramsey wouldn't give a damn about him and Fisher was under too much pressure to bend the rules much further. Viewed that way, he had little to lose by remaining on the streets.

Despite his early rising, there were easily a hundred men

252 | Jana G. Oliver

waiting at the call-on yard. He'd just arrived when there a shout
and the mass moved forward. Keats held back, not eager to risk
further injury in the crush. Some of the men were in fine health;
others were bent from years of work. Most had mouths to feed at
home. The hiring was quickly over, and Keats hadn't had a
chance. Disgruntled, he headed toward the nearest pub, hoping to
make contact with some of the other Irishmen. If luck were with
him, he might yet salvage something out of this miserable day.

‡

"You see that groove on the rib? That is indicative of a blade."
Reuben's authoritative tone didn't trouble Alastair; on the
contrary, he found his mentor's enthusiasm catching. Anything
that kept his mind off his problems was welcomed.
"Is there any way to ascertain what type of blade caused the mark?"
"Yes, it is possible if—"
One of the double doors opened, revealing a well-dressed figure.
Reuben looked up first. "This can't be good news," he muttered.
Raising his voice, he said, "Doctor Hanson. Welcome. Come in."
That pulled Alastair's attention away from the femur in his
hand. His former fiancé's father seemed older, less robust than the
last time he'd seen him.
Hanson remained in the doorway. "I have no desire to interrupt
your work, Doctors."
"You are not interrupting. Alastair and I were examining the
different sorts of marks one might find during a post-mortem.
How may we be of assistance?"
Once he had drawn close, Hanson took a deep breath. "I have spent
the morning with my daughter's fiancé and his father, the duke."
Alastair tensed, awaiting the dressing-down that would surely follow.
"I had heard disturbing rumors about Lord Patton's behavior,
and so I took my concerns to His Grace. To my surprise, the duke
reported the pair of you appeared on his doorstep, making the
claim that his son is afflicted with syphilis."
"No, that is not correct," Reuben replied. "We requested that he
have his son examined for the disease. We would not assume he
was afflicted without proper diagnosis."
"What was the basis for your concern?"
"When we performed the post-mortem on the woman murdered in
Mayfair, we found evidence of syphilitic infection. Lord Patton
appears to have been one of her regular bed partners, among others."

"How do you know that?" Hanson asked, his expression unreadable.

"The dead woman kept detailed records of her customers."

"Good heavens," Hanson murmured.

No longer able to hold his silence, Alastair pleaded, "Sir, if Lord Patton truly cares for Evelyn, he must submit to an examination, if for nothing more than to give you peace of mind."

Hanson fixed him with a troubled gaze. "I agree. I asked the duke to have his son examined by an impartial physician. He refused. When I pressed him on the matter, he grew angry. He claimed that you had threatened to reveal this information if you were not adequately...satisfied."

Reuben exploded. "If by satisfied he means we were attempting to bribe him, I shall see him in court, I swear it! I will not have my reputation ruined by such a perfidious lie."

Hanson shook his head. "I discounted his insinuation immediately. I know you to have a good reputation, Dr. Bishop." He turned to look at Alastair. "As for you, we may not have agreed upon much, but I know you to hold only the highest principles. In fact, it could be argued that even the gods would fall short of your expectations."

"I gather that is some sort a compliment," Alastair said coolly.

"It is."

"I appreciate your candor, sir," Reuben said. "This must be hard for you and your family."

"It has been a most unpleasant experience, I assure you. My wife and I spoke with Evelyn at length and she reassured us that the young man had not taken any liberties with her, though not for lack of trying." Hanson looked away, his face coloring with the barely subdued rage of a father.

"Thank God," Alastair said with a sigh of relief.

"Evelyn has decided to break off the engagement, though she knows it will cast her in an unfavorable light. We heartily support her decision. The truth will become known, you can rest assured, especially with regard to you gentlemen. I will see to that."

"If that is the case, then I shall not seek legal redress," Reuben said.

Hanson noticeably relaxed. "I had hoped that would be your response." He turned and moved toward the door with measured steps, only to stop abruptly and swivel back around.

"Dr. Montrose, if I had not meddled between you and my daughter, this disaster would not have occurred. I let my pride interfere with my daughter's happiness. That was a sincere error. I do hope you will accept my apology, Doctor."

Struggling to mask his astonishment, Alastair inclined his head. "Certainly, sir."

"I understand the duke has been instrumental in having you removed from your position at London Hospital. I have influence there. I would be willing to speak on your behalf."

"That is very kind, sir; however, I have taken an ardent interest in pathology as of late. I am now Dr. Bishop's assistant."

Hanson nodded his approval. "Excellent. I believe you will do very well."

"Thank you. Please send my regards to Evelyn."

A lengthy pause. "You are welcome to call at our house if you choose. I know she would appreciate seeing you again."

Hanson turned on his heels and was out the door before Alastair thought of a suitable response.

"Well, well, that was entertaining," Reuben said, his grin wider than his moustache. "I believe this is the first time I've ever heard of Hanson apologizing for anything."

Alastair could only nod, his mind in too much of a tumult.

‡

Keats eased himself into a corner settle at the Three Compasses, sipping his ale. He'd heard of this pub from his contacts in Whitechapel—it was as good a place to end the day as any. He'd made the rounds of the pubs, getting a feel for the area. It hadn't changed much.

From his vantage point, he surveyed the ebb and flow of filthy and cursing humanity in this corner of Rotherhithe. A pall of tobacco smoke hung in the air, along with the stench of unwashed bodies and stale beer. He wished now he had his pipe. He'd left it sitting on top of his diary in his study all those nights ago, never realizing he'd be a fugitive within a few hours.

Keats bought another pint, biding his time. This was a tricky business. He needed to blend in so that the other Irish dockworkers might trust him, yet not raise the interest of someone wanting to gain favors with the constabulary. He didn't expect to be acknowledged right off; that wasn't the game. If he were, then he'd lose his advantage.

He watched with jaded curiosity as a man appeared in the pub's doorway and pushed his way in. Keats tracked his movement to the bar, as did many of the other patrons.

*Plainclothes copper.*

The fellow had dressed down-market for the occasion, but his shoes were too presentable, his clothes not wrinkled or dirty enough, and he was trying too hard to be sociable. Keats kept his attention on his ale, hoping the fellow wouldn't attempt to talk to him. A short while later, the pub collectively heaved a sigh of relief when the copper finally shuffled outside, worse for wear on the gin, but light for whatever knowledge he'd been seeking.

"Rozzer," one of the patrons murmured to another.

"Bloody bastard," the other replied and spat in disgust. Keats nodded in agreement, as would be expected, and continued to sip his ale.

A voice rose above the din, immediately joined by others. An old Irish ballad filled the room, one that his mother used to croon to him when he was a small child. Keats found himself singing along, remembering happier times. When song ended, his eyes skipped over the pub again, taking inventory.

*What would my mother think of me now, spying on my fellow countrymen?* His copper's mind responded instantly. *Anarchists are anarchists, whether they're Irish or not.*

The answer didn't make him feel any less a Judas.

30

2057 A.D.

TEM Enterprises

Senior Guv Agent Klein was full of surprises. Cynda figured he'd stick her in a time pod and she'd be off to 1888 in a heartbeat. Instead, he handed over her time interface and had her escorted to TEM Enterprises with the caution that there would be someone watching her every move until she left 2057. Quite a departure from TPB's orders that she be stuffed in a cell and medicated.

Morrisey did not seem surprised when she'd appeared on his doorstep. "Come along, then," he said.

Cynda trailed substantially behind her boss as he wove his way through the complex. Despite her rest, the lag was still present. She figured they were headed to the botanical garden. He was known to prefer that location. Instead, after one brief stop to obtain some chocolate, he exited into the central courtyard.

A pagoda dominated the middle of the open-air space, surrounded on four sides by the main complex. The structure was cool—especially the multi-colored dragons perched atop its spiky peaks. It was the sand surrounding the building that gave her the willies. It always seemed to be on the move, though the handful of black boulders jutting from its white surface remained firmly in place.

Cynda shook her head to clear the vision. The sand continued to undulate in no discernable pattern. *It's just lag.*

Morrisey was already in the pagoda, in a Lotus position on the platform with his eyes closed. Cynda paced along the edge of the sand near where his shoes and socks were neatly deposited on the tile. Reaching him meant crossing the white sea.

*You did this on purpose.*

Muttering under her breath, she removed her own footwear. Right before she stepped onto the sand, she pulled out her new interface and stared at it. She'd bet a month's salary Agent Klein had futzed with it, installed some sort of sophisticated surveillance device. After dropping it into a shoe, she gingerly eased herself onto the sand. Each step created a ripple ahead of her, like waves on a still pond. Each footprint filled with sand the moment she raised her foot. Resisting the urge to run, she carefully edged forward across the expanse, waiting for the sand to open up and suck her downward.

If this was lag, it was beyond scary.

When she reached the solid wood floor of the pagoda, her heavy sigh caused Morrisey's eyes to open. She dragged herself up onto the platform and sat on the pillow next to him. It felt odd not to adjust a bustle.

Once situated, Cynda tracked an employee as he wound his way around the outer courtyard and then vanished inside one of the doors. There was a tap on her forearm. She found three candy bars near her right knee.

"Thanks." She opened one and took one bite, then another. When the bar was gone, she neatly folded the wrapper and set it beside her. To do otherwise felt sacrilegious here.

"Did they return your interface?" he asked.

"Yes." She pointed toward the edge of the sand. "I left it out there."

Morrisey nodded and picked up a brass bowl from near his pillow. As he ran a wooden mallet around the outer lip, a low vibration issued forth, rising in tone until a single note sang in the air. The sand was moving in a different pattern now, as if the sound was pushing it away.

*That's cool.*

Morrisey returned the bowl and mallet to his side. The sound gradually died away. "Now we may speak freely," he said.

"You sure about that?" she asked, gesturing to the open courtyard.

"I'd explain the mechanics involved, but I know you're not one for technical detail. Suffice it to say that once I've used the singing bowl and generated a particular tone for a certain length of time, we have complete privacy."

"You're kidding."

Her boss shook his head."

"What people see from the outside of the pagoda is not what is happening inside. That's why Harter and I conducted our business here, though he always complained about the lack of a comfortable chair."

A smile inched across her face. "He sounds like a kick."

"He was many things..."

"You're using the past tense."

He stared at the sand. "I didn't realize I was."

"Guv says he's still in '88 and that Chris was working for them. Did you know that?"

"I didn't know Harter was there, not until now. I'm not surprised, given his love of the time period."

"But you knew about Chris?"

"Yes, I was aware of my nephew's involvement with the Government. I cautioned him against it."

"Why didn't he tell me what he was doing?"

Morrisey adjusted his position on the pillow. "He knew your intense dislike of authority, and was concerned you would be angry at him."

"Damned right about that," she said. "It got him killed."

Morrisey frowned. "Why do you say that?"

"Klein said if I find Defoe, I'll be a step closer to the man who murdered Chris. He hinted it wasn't Mimes."

Morrisey's fingers collapsed into rigid fists. "What the hell are they playing at?" After three deep breaths, his hands unclasped. He rested them in his lap again, in classic Lotus position. If Cynda had not seen the rage within him at that moment, she'd never have believed him capable of such power. She made a mental note never to piss this guy off.

"It might just be Klein's way of messing with our minds. I have to find out either way," she said.

"I agree."

Cynda rubbed her face, exhausted. The smell of chocolate rose from her fingers. "I know I have killer lag, but 1888 feels...wrong."

Morrisey turned to study her with an intensity that unnerved her. "Wrong in what way?"

"I have no idea. It just doesn't feel the same. I've been there a few times before and this trip..."

A prolonged silence. "*When* did this sensation first occur?"

She pondered that. "The night I arrived."

"Let's set that aside for a moment and try an experiment. Close your eyes."

"What?"

"Just do it."

Cynda obeyed. As she tried to relax, she heard her own

irregular breathing against Morrisey's measured inhalations and exhalations. Around them came the faint rustling of the sand as it shifted, grain over grain.

*I gotta have more chocolate.*

"Open your eyes."

"And?" she asked, fumbling for another candy bar.

"How long did you have your eyes closed?"

"A minute, ten, no, eleven seconds."

Morrisey nodded. "Most people wouldn't have had any notion of how much time had elapsed."

"Apparently you did."

He pointed upward. "That's the only reason I knew you were correct."

Nestled amongst the pagoda's rafters was a peg clock. She'd not seen one in years. Thin strips of wood on three wires, one for the hours, minutes and seconds. The two sides of each peg were different colors. The number of similarly colored pegs situated upright told the time. The clock quietly flipped in a rhythmic pattern, as if triggered by some unseen hand.

"I use it to calculate how long I generate the tone with the singing bowl," he explained.

"Okay, so I can judge time without a watch. Whoopee. Great party trick."

Morrisey ignored her sarcasm. "What is the sand doing?"

Her eyes darted away in panic.

"The sand moves for you, doesn't it?"

Cynda swallowed the last of the candy bar, wishing she had a glass of water to ease the sudden dryness in her throat. "It's just a lag-induced delusion. It'll stop if I get enough rest."

"The sand moves for you." It wasn't a question this time.

"Yes," she confirmed in a harsh whisper.

"If an employee asks me about the sand, I know I have a time sensitive."

"A what?"

"A time sensitive—someone who interacts with the Fourth Dimension on a cellular level."

"Do a lot of them do that?" Cynda asked hopefully. Maybe she wasn't the only weird one.

"Only one, and he wasn't an employee. Harter could tell time to the exact second. It was very annoying. I could never acquire the skill, though I tried...repeatedly."

"You're jealous," she said before she thought. *Oh, that was swift.*

He quirked an eyebrow. "I guess I am. Harter wasn't much for software, but he can resonate with a time period like no one else

I've ever met. He knows when something isn't right and can pinpoint the flaw, then mend it."

"That's what Rovers do."

"No, not really. Most Rovers just transfer in and out of a time period, not paying much attention to it. You and Harter feel time in your bones. You know when something is fundamentally wrong."

"Wow. I just figured everyone felt that way." She cracked a smile. "Gee, Time Rover One and I have something in common."

"More than you might believe."

"Guv says if I don't find him, they'll put me in jail for the smuggling. I'll never be able to travel again." Then it dawned on her. Ralph had said that Morrisey had pulled serious strings on her behalf. "You were the one who forged that deal, weren't you?"

Morrisey nodded. "Having you track Harter is for the best. You won't kill him. Others might."

"They wouldn't do that," she protested.

"Think again."

"Who?"

"TPB, for whatever reason."

"What's my freedom costing you?"

Morrisey's expression changed to one of increased respect. He gestured, encompassing the buildings around them. "All of this is gone if you attempt to run off."

"TEM Enterprises? But you're...you're..."

"Doesn't matter who I am. TPB is consolidating their newfound power, which is making the Government more aggressive. All gloves are off. If you run, I lose my liberty as well. You're not the only one who's been funneling supplies to the Off-Gridders."

Her mouth fell open. "That's how you knew what I was doing with the tomato seeds. You..."

She leaned over and impulsively gave him a peck on the cheek before she could stop herself. A shy grin appeared on her boss' face, as if it was the first kiss he'd ever received. "You're a great guy, Morrisey."

"Or a very foolish one. History will judge my motives."

"Because of us, a lot of Off-Gridders didn't starve to death, my family included. The laws are stupid. Just because they want to live outside of society doesn't mean we shouldn't help them."

"Was it worth the ten-plus years of prison time?" he asked.

She didn't hesitate. "Yeah, it was."

If for nothing more than to piss off her brother, Blair, who'd always lorded it over her when they were growing up. She was the one who came to their family's rescue by supplying the seeds they could trade for food and other goods. Hopefully by now her dad had his medical practice up and running to generate income. Then they'd be okay. As usual, Blair hadn't risen to the challenge.

"History will see us as the good guys," she said.

"Depends on who writes the story."

Silence fell between them. The sand continued moving to its own rhythm.

"Thanks for the back story, by the way. Pinkerton's of all things," she said, shaking her head.

He shrugged. "I will provide you with a decoy interface," Morrisey said. "It is registered to another Rover and includes a valid ESR Chip, so it will appear as if he's making the journey, not you. I'll have it delivered to you in '88."

"I like it. Sounds devious."

"Communicate with Mr. Hamilton via your original interface to maintain the illusion that you are unaware of their scrutiny. Guv will monitor every communication. Should you find Harter, use the decoy to disappear."

"What?" she blurted. "You want us to go *walk about*? You'll lose everything!"

"It is necessary. You must be free to travel and mend. To do otherwise will allow history to shift in ways too hideous to contemplate."

"But you have..." She trailed off, suddenly understanding how it all worked.

"What?"

"Contemplated the hideous ways. That's what you do. Defoe might be able to fix things, but you're the one who sees the big picture. That's why you work so well together."

Another nod of respect. "You have seen to the heart of our arrangement. Someone is needed in the middle of the fray while the other stands at a distance, able to judge the battle."

"Battle?"

"I did not misspeak."

She reached for another candy bar and then changed her mind. More chocolate wouldn't help this mess.

Now was the time to ask all the deep questions. There was no guarantee her boss would continue to be so candid. "Tell me about the Virtuals."

He raised an eyebrow. "Virtuals are the rarest of Transitives. Do you know why?"

She shook her head.

"You are aware how a Transitive is created?" Cynda nodded,

eager to move along. "Once you've survived such a transformation, it is human nature to always want more. If you can change identities, what next?"

"Be able to balance my Vid-Net checking account," she quipped.

A wan smile. "Once a Transitive has mastered the ability to go *en mirage* as another person, some begin to probe the boundaries of that ability. A few choose the aesthetic route and emulate animal forms, like the Native American shamans. Some seek to embrace nature by taking on simpler forms, such as a tree or a rock. And then there are those who tend toward the darker forms."

"Werewolves, vampires and things that go bump in the night?" Cynda joked. When Morrisey didn't disagree, her sense of humor crawled away.

"Do you know what a Ninja is?" he quizzed.

Her mind conjured up a vintage martial arts movie she'd watched as a child. Her brother had caustically pointed out that Ninjas didn't really wear black. He'd always found a way to ruin things.

"They were Japanese assassins, weren't they?"

"Still are. There is always a need for espionage, sabotage or assassination. In our society, Virtuals fulfill that role."

"Why are they so rare?"

"Because to make the transition is to court agonizing death."

"If they're already a Transitive, what's the problem? Just a little more oomph and you've got it, right?"

"No. They have to undergo the *twice transformation*. The initial *Rite de la Morte*, the Death Rite, makes you Transitive. The *Rite Final* either makes you Virtual or kills you. The death is quite graphic."

"What are the odds of dying?"

"Ninety-six point eight percent, depending on their brain chemistry."

She whistled. "That's nasty. The ones who survive must feel like gods."

"Exactly. Have you encountered a Perceiver yet?"

"Yes." Alastair's handsome face passed through her mind. Strangely enough, she found herself missing his petulant lectures.

"Perceivers are equally scarce. They are often employed to determine if you are in the presence of someone *en mirage*. This is very important if you're conducting business or, for instance, marriage. In the Middle Ages they vetted the highborn newlyweds, so that paternity would be precisely as expected."

"I can only imagine what led to that."

"The history of the Transitives makes for interesting reading," Morrisey said, a faint smile on his face.

"You don't have to do anything special to become a Perceiver, do you?"

"That's correct."

"Makes sense. The one I know is very unhappy about being a shifter. I doubt he'd do anything more to enhance his curse, as he calls it."

"Is that Montrose?" She nodded. "Some of the most powerful Transitives are those who never wanted to be one in the first place."

"He knows what I do for a living."

She waited for the reproof, but it didn't come. Instead, Morrisey nodded approvingly. "Good. You need someone you can trust in that time period."

"I figured you'd be upset."

"I'm not pleased that someone is aware of your vocation, but the usual rules don't apply now. No one is following them anyway."

"When did Transitives first appear?" she asked.

"We're not sure, though there have been exhaustive studies. The current theory is that the ability came from the future."

"*Our* future?" she asked, taken aback.

"Yes."

"Why go back and meddle, then?"

"Some believe it occurred quite by accident. I don't think that's the case. If you are a threatened species, why not create more of your kind so that when the ultimate battle is enjoined, there are more of you to fight?"

The chocolate bar began to churn in her stomach. There was more here, she could feel it. "Did Defoe go into the future?"

"No, it came to him."

"He met a Future?"

"More than one, from what he told me. The news they brought was anything but comforting."

"But if they contacted him, that means they're trying to alter history. They can't do that."

"They can if they believe it's the only way to survive."

A shiver spiraled up Cynda's spine, despite the sunny warmth of the courtyard. "Just what the hell happens to us?"

Morrisey's dark eyes swung toward hers. "We do not listen to the better angels of our nature."

"Meaning?" she pushed.

"We self-destruct."

"The Transitives or the rest of us?"

"We assist each other in our mutual annihilations."

"How soon?"

"2062 is when the laws are changed to interdict Transitive behavior. By 2065, the resistance begins. In 2083..."

He was quiet for a time. She didn't push, sensing how hard this was. Finally he stirred.

"There is always an enemy awaiting for a moment of distraction, of weakness," he finally said. "Our petty internecine war provides that opportunity."

"What happens?" she persisted.

"Our conflicts are resolved for us."

"Fade to black?" she whispered.

"In all ways that matter."

31

*Monday, 22 October, 1888*
*Rotherhithe*

Keats rose two hours before dawn, bought himself a hearty meal and headed for the call-on shelter. There were only two other men present; from the looks of them, they'd spent the night there.

"Gents," Keats said, touching his cap in respect. A couple of nods came his way. Both fellows would likely be passed over for healthier specimens. Keats judged himself a more probable candidate, providing he could hide his chest injury. Pity Alastair wasn't close at hand. He could bind the rib tight to reduce the pain, though he would certainly give his friend an earful in the process.

He sat on the damp ground, leaned against a brick wall and closed his eyes. He dare not fall asleep, so he catalogued the sounds around him. The two men were talking quietly amongst themselves. One of them said his wife was sick. The other talked about his brother who was in Wandsworth Gaol for some crime.

A short time later, there were footsteps. He opened his eyes and pushed up his cap far enough to survey the figure as it approached. He guessed it was one of the foremen. The man studied him for a time and then headed in his direction.

"Good mornin'," the fellow called out.

"Good morning to you," Keats replied, rising to his feet.

"Can ya do a day's work?"

"I'll do my best."

"That's honest." He waved him forward. "We're loadin' rum today."

In a short time, the yard filled with eager men. He watched his new boss make his choices. Like the day before, the foreman walked past the ones who looked frail and chose the healthy specimens. Though sincerely pleased with the outcome, Keats' cautious nature took hold.

*Why go to so much trouble with me?*

Fretting would do him no good. He leaned against a wall, crossed his arms over his chest, trying to blend in. If he'd been made out as a copper, he'd know soon enough.

He'd not remained employed for very long, the heavy physical labor causing his broken rib to send shards of pain throughout his chest. He'd resigned rather than being fired.

After he gave his notice, curiosity got the best of him. "Why'd you hire me?"

The foreman shrugged. "Ya look like my younger brother. Figured ya needed a bit of help."

"That I do." *More than you can imagine.*

Keats knew he should find food, but he was too exhausted to go in search of anything. Once he'd reached the stairs to his room, he sat on the bottom step, placing his head in his hands to allow time for the ache in his side to diminish. A few minutes' rest and then he'd attempt the journey.

"Ya drunk?" He raised his head to find Mrs. O'Neill studying him with skeptical eyes. "No, yer not. So what happened?"

"I couldn't handle loading the rum. I broke a rib a while back."

"How'd ya break it?"

"Got worked over in an alley."

"Did ya give as good as ya got?"

He snorted. "I tried. I'm pretty good with my fists, but I'm not tall like some of them."

"Don't need to be tall. Just need to be fast. My husband was a little rooster of man, but ya'd not like to cross him."

Keats levered himself to his feet. "I need some sleep. I'll try to find some other work tomorrow."

She caught his arm. "I'll fix some food for ya. I'll not do this again, but I remember what it was like when my husband first worked on the docks. Damned near killed him," she said more quietly than usual.

He raised his voice so she could hear him. "I'll be pleased to pay for the—"

Mrs. O'Neill shook her head. "No need. Yer a good sort; I can see that. I want decent tenants, not drunken sods who tear up the rooms."

He moved so slowly that his landlady caught up with him on the stairs. She set the tray on his bed and positioned the chair so he could reach the food. "I sent one of the lads to get ya a pint."

He could have kissed her. "God bless you, Mrs. O'Neill. You are a very good woman."

A toothy grin. "Eat and get some rest. Then get a job. I'm not a soft touch."

He chuffed. "Not in the least."

He eased himself into the chair and flipped back the cloth cover to reveal cold mutton, golden cheese and bread. A feast. He'd just started on the lamb when there was another tap at the door. By the time he opened it, the lad was gone. A covered metal pail sat on the floor. Inside was an ample portion of ale.

Raising his eyes to the ceiling, he managed a weak smile.

"Angels watch over me."

✢

*2057 A.D.*

TEM *Enterprises*

It took most of the afternoon at a computer terminal for Cynda to do her research on the Father of Time Travel. Defoe had an extensive history. To her surprise, she'd found her security clearance had been upgraded a couple of levels, no doubt courtesy of Guv. She'd be sure to send Senior Agent Klein a thank-you note.

She'd quickly learned that Defoe was a throwback, a millennium man with Victorian tastes. Fluent in six languages, lover of classical music, fine wine, old scotch, expensive socks and excellent food, he was blessed with a roving eye and a load of chutzpah. Thanks to his distaste for following orders, he'd enflamed the Time Protocol Board's ire more than once.

"Sounds familiar," her personal hallucination observed from his location near a pile of thumb-sized nano-drives. He kept eyeing them. "You and Defoe could be twins in the personality department."

*He's a decade older than I am.*

"Minor difference." The arachnid nudged the nano-drive with a leg. "Are we going back to 1888 soon?" he asked hopefully.

*Yup.*

"Good. I'm peckish."

*Really? Missing the scones?*

A shake of the head. "Flies. You don't have any here. That's just so depressing."

*One person's hell is another's smorgasbord.*

✝

Monday, 22 October, 1888
Rotherhithe

After a long and deep sleep, Keats returned to the streets after dark, feeling much improved, though his chest still ached. The weariness that had dogged him since the injury seemed to be lifting at last. He'd only made it a block or so from the boarding house when a broken-down whore hailed him.

"Come on, luv, I'll do ya proper," she said and hiked her skirt a bit to display her calf.

"I don't think so," he replied, trying to ignore her. The smell of cheap gin enveloped him as she pushed herself up against him. Reflexively, he reached in his pocket and extracted a couple pence, pressing them into her hand. By the time he'd realized what he'd done, he couldn't take back the gesture. To do so would raise even more red flags. "Here, get some food."

She accepted the coins. "I don't take nothin' without earnin' it," she said, sizing him up.

"You can earn it by telling me where to find a good meal."

"Ya jokin' with me, luv?"

"No."

She thought for a moment and then pointed with a gnarled hand. "Mrs. Garner has a place, four streets over. It's a bit pricey, but it's good. I go there when I can."

"Thank you. That's all I need."

The dining room did have decent food and Mrs. Garner, a buxom young widow with an eye toward finding another husband, took an instant liking to him. She made sure he got enough to eat, piling on seconds the moment his plate was empty. He ate heartily, hoping to regain his strength. As he finished off the last of the mutton and started on the potatoes, he heard the scrape of a chair across from him.

Keats recognized the one of the dockworkers from the warehouse this morning.

"Food any good tonight?" the fellow asked.

Keats nodded. The dockworker waved his hand to get some attention from the widow. A plate full of mutton appeared. He paid Mrs. Garner and then set to work on the meal like he hadn't eaten in weeks.

Keats kept his attention on his own plate. When he heard a contented sigh, he said, "You eat here often?"

"Sometimes."

"Thanks for helping this morning. Couldn't have lasted as long as I did if you hadn't lifted those casks."

A rough shrug. "Feelin' better?"

Keats nodded. "I'll try to find lighter work tomorrow."

"Might be able to find some tonight, if yer game."

"Doing what?"

"Somethin' that earns money," was the swift reply. When Keats didn't respond right away, he added, "If yer not willin', say so."

"I just don't know who I'm dealing with," Keats said. "You could be a rozzer, setting me up."

A wide grin erupted. "Name's Moran, Clancy Moran." He shoved a hand across the table.

"Sean Murphy," Keats lied. They shook.

"Ya in or out?"

"In."

"Then come on with ya," Moran said, rising from his chair.

Keats trudged along with the Irishman, keeping an eye out for any coppers. When he spied one in the distance, he tugged his collar up higher to obscure his face.

Clancy caught the gesture. "In trouble with Johnny Law?"

"Who isn't?"

A hearty guffaw, followed by a slap on Keats' back. He winced as his rib flared up again.

"We're gonna be relocatin' some goods from one place to another," Moran explained.

"Relocating?"

A sidelong look. "We're being paid for our strong backs, but we don't see a thing, ya got it?"

"Got it."

"As long as the beat copper thinks his bribe is big enough, this'll go just fine."

"And if he doesn't?"

"Run like hell."

The moment Keats cleared the warehouse door, he scanned the faces of the five men inside. To his relief, none of them were familiar. Three of them looked like dockworkers and they gave Clancy a respectful nod in turn.

A man in a top hat glowered in their direction, and then returned to the conversation he'd been having. "I don't care about that," the toff growled. "Just get it done or I'll have your job."

The foreman dropped his gaze to his boots. "Right, sir."

Clancy leaned close and whispered near Keats' ear. "That's Effington, the warehouse owner. Right bastard. Mind yerself."

*Effington?* Keats repressed a grin. Fate was smiling on him tonight.

The gruff warehouse owner strode over to the double doors, gave the foreman another glare and then was gone. After an audible sigh of relief, the foreman pointed at the nearest man. "Go get the wagon. The rest of ya start movin' this lot toward the door." He gave Keats the once-over. "Yer too scrawny to do the liftin'. Keep an eye out for the rozzer. Ya see him, ya let us know. We'll take care of him."

Keats positioned himself across the street from the warehouse. The location offered a good vantage from which to observe the street in either direction. In time, the wagon drew up and the loading began. Usually there were jokes and conversation between the men as they worked. This lot kept dead silent. After each sack of sugar or cask of rum was placed on the wagon, the man who'd loaded it looked up and down the street as if expecting a horde of Blue Bottles to arrive at any moment.

Keats kept his ears trained for the telltale sound of measured boot steps on pavement. As time passed, he grew more nervous. What would he do if a copper came along? If they all ran, that was one thing. If they intended to harm the fellow, that wouldn't do. He'd have no choice but to risk discovery by siding with them against the outnumbered officer, even if the man wasn't on the level. That would surely lead to his arrest when reinforcements arrived.

"Come on, lads," he murmured. "It's not a damned Sunday picnic."

Clancy carried out a heavy sack of sugar and dropped into the back of the wagon like it was made of feathers. To Keats' relief, the foreman bolted the warehouse doors behind him.

While the wagon rolled away and then turned at the corner, the workers melted into the night. Clancy crossed over to where Keats stood in the shadows.

"That's it," he said, offering a handful of coins. "He paid ya three shillin's, the rest of us four each for the loadin'."

Keats took the money and dumped it in his pocket.

"Yer not countin' it?" Clancy asked, baffled.

Realizing his mistake, Keats bluffed, "If you're stealing from me, there's little I can do about it. From what I can see, you're not the kind to scrape with."

Clancy chuffed. "Come on, let's get a pint."

After the first pint was gone, they drank another and then wandered out of the pub, pleased with themselves. The evening had gone well. Clancy had proven to be a cagey bird when it came to conversation, but underneath his caution Keats sensed a Fenian. He'd made sure his own comments remained noncommittal, but pro-Irish. If he pressed too hard, Clancy would shun him in the future.

As they negotiated their way down St. Mary's Street near the church, Clancy gave him a puzzled look. "So how come ya talk so fancy?"

Keats had been anticipating that one and had his story ready. "Father was a schoolmaster and he made sure of it, with the lash."

"Ah, that'd be why."

*It's too much work otherwise.*

A block later, Keats asked, "How long have you been moving goods for Effington?"

"Over a year. He's short of brass, so he's takin' some off every load. He hides the goods in his other warehouses on both sides of the water." Clancy grew serious. "I meant what I said about him bein' a right bastard. Ya watch yourself around him, ya hear?"

*Time to up the ante.* "Is it true he's working with Flaherty?"

A sharp look from his companion. "How ya know of him?"

"Every Irishman knows about him. He's a legend."

A snort. "Or a butcher, dependin' on how ya look at it."

"I heard he killed some poor fellow and put him out in the Thames on one of those piers."

"Yeah. Johnny Ahearn. Flaherty cut him up like a dog. He's due to be taught a lesson."

Before Keats had a chance to exploit his companion's anger, he heard footsteps in their wake. He knew them as well as his own heartbeat. Taking a quick look behind him, he swore. It was a young constable, new to the job by the looks of him.

Keats turned back. "Rozzer," he said under his breath.

"He wants me," Clancy said.

"You sure?" Keats replied. Clancy chuckled in response.

The footsteps sped up and then a voice called, "You there, halt!"

"Ah, bugger," Keats muttered.

"See ya tomorrow, Sean."

"Good Lord willing, Clancy."

"Halt!" the constable shouted again, his footsteps drawing nearer.

The moment they reached the crossroads they broke in two directions, as if their moves had been choreographed. Clancy fled to the left as Keats hurried right on Albion Street toward the gas works. Repeated blasts of the two-tone police whistle split the air, but didn't prevent their escape.

## 32

*2057 A.D.*
*TEM Enterprises*

Suspecting that Keats' life was the most out of sync of those she'd encountered, Cynda accessed the sergeant's time line. There was no mention of a murder trial. Nicci Hallcox lived five more years before succumbing to syphilitic complications. In contrast, Jonathan Davis Keats lived to be a ripe seventy-seven years old, retiring to Bournemouth on a full police pension.

Following in his mentor's footsteps, he would attain the exalted position of chief inspector, working some of the most notorious crimes of the era. During it all, he'd had no time for a wife—not a surprise, given his distinguished career. Keats died of heart disease, sitting alone in his front parlor reading the evening paper, as was his habit. He'd been found by his housekeeper, peaceful in death.

For a brief time his name was in the newspapers again, belated homage given to the man who had caught the infamous Fenian Desmond Flaherty and saved a beloved London landmark from destruction.

Which was not the way things were going in the "new" 1888.

Cynda dropped a nano-drive into Morrisey's outstretched palm.

"I checked a couple timelines," she reported, shaking her head in dismay. "They're off the rails. I need your help with this."

He gave a curt nod and hiked away into the compound. She collected a couple more chocolate bars and retreated to her own room, her mood darkening with each footstep.

"He wants to see you," Morrisey's assistant announced from just inside the door to her room. Fulham looked as tired as she felt.

Cynda tried to wake up enough to be coherent. "Where is he?"

"His private office."

That cleared some of the cobwebs. From what she gathered, it was the rare employee who ever saw inside Morrisey's suite of rooms.

"I'll be there."

She plodded her way around the compound, encountering no one along the way. The lights switched on and off automatically as she passed, a mandatory energy-saving measure.

When she entered the suite, Morrisey beckoned her forward. He sat behind a glass desk that was overly clean by her standards. His office wasn't quite what she expected. It sat at the center of a cluster of rooms. Like other parts of the compound, this one had the requisite paintings on the wall, but these were all at the proper height. There were even chairs and Morrisey was seated in one. That surprised her. As she took a visual inventory, she noted a holo-portrait of a young woman with high cheekbones and beautiful Asian features on a nearby credenza.

"Therein lies a tale," Mr. Spider said, wandering across the piece of furniture to study the image closer.

Somewhere inside the suite, an antique clock tolled the hour. Two in the morning. By her math, her boss had been working on the 1888 problem for at least twelve hours straight.

*Where does he find his energy?*

"He doesn't time travel for a living," Mr. Spider replied before exhibiting his own yawn.

She matched it and then asked, "Well, boss? What did you find?"

Issuing a very long sigh, Morrisey looked up from the multi-colored electronic graphs hanging in the air in front of him. "To employ an old phrase, Miss Lassiter, things are going to hell in a handbasket."

Cynda sank into the closest chair. She was fully awake now. "How bad is it?"

"It's hard to tell from this end. The disconnect is nearly total. We see history progressing as it should, while 1888 is following an entirely new thread. Theoretically, this is not possible."

"Which tells you a lot about theories," Mr. Spider muttered.

"Instead of capturing Desmond Flaherty," Morrisey continued, "in all probability Sergeant Keats will be executed for Miss Hallcox's murder sometime on or before the fifth of November. Should that happen, Flaherty's plan will reach fruition undeterred and the Crystal Palace will become a pile of glass courtesy of the anarchist's explosive talents. The subsequent fallout leads to a new round of anti-Irish laws and will initiate a short-lived, but brutal, rebellion."

Cynda was speechless.

"Studying the sergeant's life as closely as possible from his memoirs, I have determined that his timeline diverged on the night of the twenty-seventh of September." His eyes moved to hers. "That was the night he was supposed to have arrested Desmond Flaherty on Dorset Street in what, according to his own words, was a completely insane maneuver given the dangerous location. Something prevented that arrest, generating the new time line."

"You," Mr. Spider prompted.

Her multi-legged conscience was correct. "I think I might be the reason. I was in Dorset Street that night looking for the missing tourist."

"What happened?"

"Keats rescued me from a couple of bad guys. If he'd stayed put in the pub, I bet he'd have seen Flaherty and arrested him."

Morrisey frowned, his fingers tap-dancing across the keyboard. The frown grew. "None of this makes sense, at least within the parameters of the Inter-Momentuary Thread Theory as postulated by..."

He went on and on in highly technical and gray-cell-numbing terms. The bottom line was that history wasn't behaving itself, and that she was responsible. Between that night in Dorset Street and her insistence that they talk to Nicci, Cynda had hijacked Keats' timeline.

"Miss Lassiter?"

"Hummm?" she said, coming out of her guilt-induced fog.

"I said that you must leave for 1888 immediately. Find Defoe. He'll help you get this back on track. The longer it continues, the harder it will be to mend, if it's still fixable at this point."

When she didn't answer, he pressed, "Do you understand, Miss Lassiter?"

Cynda rose and drifted to the door. It whooshed open immediately.

"Sure boss," she responded, supressing a bout of hysterical laughter. "How hard can that be?"

&#8225;

Cynda kept her expression stoic when Ralph wasn't behind the chronsole, though she was sure he was aware of her impending departure. She suspected his absence had something to do with the argument they'd had an hour or so earlier. He'd not wanted her to go back into the time stream. She had no choice, not with Keats' timeline so out of whack. Words had been exchanged, ones that had stung both parties. He'd accused of her of selling out Defoe to save her own skin and then stormed out of her room. She'd never had a chance to tell him how bad things really were, how she *had* to find Defoe to make it right.

To her surprise Senior Agent Klein was present, arms crossed over his chest. He sported a "don't give me a reason to destroy you" expression.

Morrisey hefted the battered Gladstone and handed it to her. Inside was Fred, Chris' portable shrine, a portable medical kit the Rovers called a Dinky Doc, and a mound of chocolate. To her dismay, she'd not been able to acquire a Neural-blocker, a handy little weapon if things went south. Guv had nixed that plan. She suspected she'd regret that.

Morrisey cleared his throat and whispered near her ear. "No matter what happens, don't come back. That's an order." He gave her arm a light squeeze. "Farewell, Jacynda," he murmured and then turned away.

It was the first time he'd ever used her given name.

Cynda entered the time pod, her emotions in a ferocious tangle. She'd not taken the opportunity to contact her family, worried that TPB might catch on that she was about to leave. Besides, it was probably best if her parents didn't know what was going on. Her brother would just blame her for the whole works. Blair was good at that.

She knelt to reduce the shock as the massive door swung shut and clicked into place, like it had so many times before. This time, the stakes were unfathomable.

As the transfer began, Cynda kept one goal embedded in her mind: *Jonathon Keats is not going to hang.*

A minute later, Morrisey's assistant hurried into the room. He shot Klein a nervous look and then whispered in his boss' ear.

"Tell them they're too late," Morrisey announced, his voice overlaid with gleeful malice.

"Sir?"

"Tell them Miss Lassiter is no longer available for their detention."

"Ah, um...yes, sir," Fulham replied, setting off to deliver the news at a less-than-enthusiastic pace.

"TBP?" Klein asked, eyes on the countdown timer as it worked its way back to 1888.

"Yes. They are here to escort Miss Lassiter to prison. I wonder why they waited so long."

Klein's attention remained riveted to the chronsole. "I heard they didn't have the proper clearances. Had to file their request with the Government...three times."

Morrisey's mouth curved into a pleased smile.

"Chron Transfer Complete," the computer announced.

"Thank God," he whispered.

"Did you tell her not to come back?" Klein asked.

Morrisey raised an eyebrow at the query.

Klein looked him straight in the eyes. "Because that's what I would have told her."

✢

*Monday, 22 October, 1888*

*Wapping*

Alastair tugged his collar upward as he loitered outside the Town of Ramsgate, a pub near Wapping Old Stairs. He'd visited a number of pubs in the last few nights, but had caught no glimpse of Keats anywhere. If his friend was able to go *en mirage* now, this was a waste of time. Even if the sergeant spied him, he might not give himself away. Despite Keats' and Livingston's impressions to the contrary, Perceivers had a limited range.

He had not gone *en mirage*, a step in a direction he was still unwilling to take. Instead, he'd opted for a set of worn clothes, muddy shoes and dirty hands. He lacked calluses, but there was only so much he could do.

Growing chilly, Alastair jammed his hands into his pockets. Jacynda was gone now. Instead of saying goodbye in person, she had sent him a note that had been oddly curt in its tone—almost dismissive.

By contrast, his mind slipped back to the cordial, lightly scented note he'd received from Evelyn just this morning, thanking him for his kind intervention on her behalf and inviting him to tea. He hadn't responded yet, although the notepaper was becoming worn from constant re-reading.

Did he want to wait for a woman who might never return? One who might be standing over his grave at this moment, trying to remember what he looked like? Alastair shivered at the thought.

A moment later, he felt a change come over him. He turned to watch an old beggar limping toward him, sticking out a palm.

"Tuppence, sir?" the old man asked, eyeing him from under a floppy hat.

Alastair obligingly pulled out the coins and handed them over.

Lowering his voice, he said, "So that's how you afford your fine clothes, is it?"

Beneath the illusion, Malachi Livingston issued a throaty chuckle. "Seen the sergeant tonight?"

"No, you?"

"No. How about the toff from Mayfair?"

"No sign of him."

Grumbling under his breath, the beggar rubbed his chin. "Last night he was in Rotherhithe. I keep hoping to learn where he's hiding his stolen goods and use that as leverage to find out what's really happening."

"You'd blackmail him?"

"For information only. I don't need his money. I make a good living as a beggar." He cracked a wry smile.

Despite his misgivings, Alastair was beginning to like Livingston. He scanned the streets once again. Nothing seemed out of the ordinary, other than the man in front of him.

"William tells me you've been treating him with great skill," his companion said. "I thank you for that."

Alastair nodded. "He's a resilient young man and the private nurse you hired was excellent. Not all of them are. She kept him well hydrated, and that made all the difference. By my estimates, he should be up in a week or so."

"Thank God. Any permanent damage?"

"None that I can see. Are the police going to charge his assailant?"

Livingston shook his head. "Someone higher up is preventing that. It's very frustrating. William warned me that would happen." He took a look around. "I have been working through Effington's guest list. I've found at least two judges who are on his payroll. I suspect his bribes extend into the lower classes, as well."

"Who are the judges?"

"Timsworthy and Dell."

"I'm not familiar with them."

"Hopefully, neither of us ever will be."

In the distance, Alastair spied a constable on his beat. "We've got company."

Livingston's voice mutated into that of the beggar once again. "Night to you, sir, and God bless ya," he said.

"Be careful," Alastair replied, though he had no idea why.

"No one pays a beggar no mind, sir."

"So you hope. If I can sense you, someone else can."

As Livingston limped off, Alastair headed away from the approaching officer, setting his course for the train station and his bed. He'd give Wapping one more night before heading across the river.

‡

1888 smelt like rank perfume in comparison to sterile 2057. Cynda took a deep breath and managed not to gag. Proof the Victorian Virus, as she called it, was busily replicating in her system, growing stronger with each trip. Thoughts of sticky toffee pudding made her mouth water. God help her, there were things she'd missed about this place.

A few seconds later, the time lag caught up with her, like delayed baggage. Street lamps flared purple. The noxious liquid in the gutters glowed like mercury. Lightning exploded around her in ridiculous colors, spiraling pinwheels into the misty air.

Cynda leaned against the wall and touched her forehead to the cool, sooty surface, taking deep breaths to curb the nausea. A moment later she was retching, though there was little in her stomach.

She dried her mouth with a handkerchief and tucked it away in her jacket pocket. A flock of sizzling arrows flew toward her like startled pigeons, careening off the walls and then bursting into flame.

This was Platinum Level Time Lag.

Cynda shifted the Gladstone between her hands, straightened her cap and continued on as if nothing were amiss. Each footstep seemed to sink two inches into the brick pavement. It felt odd not dragging pounds of skirt behind her, though the baggy pants, coat and slouch cap cleverly obscured the female beneath. If anything, she looked like an underfed clerk.

*Or the Ripper.* He was still out there, awaiting his final curtain call with a certain Irish girl in Miller's Court. *Providing he can find her with all the damned "tourists" underfoot.*

A few blocks later a figure stepped out in front of her, making her jerk to an abrupt halt. He was dressed like a postman.

"Miss...ah, Mister Lassiter?" he asked, clearly confused.

"Yes?" She placed a hand on top of her truncheon, just in case.

He rallied. "Delivery from Mr. Morrisey."

Cynda held out her hand and took the small package. She didn't bother to open it—it was the decoy interface.

She had no intention of using it, even if she found Defoe.

After the authorities dismantled T.E. Morrisey's company and his personal life, they'd just eventually hunt her down and drag her back to 2057, adding a few more decades to the sentence just to vent their displeasure. Some things weren't worth it unless it was a matter of life and death.

Cynda stashed the package deep in a pocket and continued toward Pratchett's Bookshop, which would become her new base of operations. The hotel was too high profile right now, though she'd miss the long, hot baths.

When she found a newspaper boy, she bought the latest edition. Keats was front-page news.

STEALTHY SERGEANT ELUDES POLICE
REWARD OFFERED FOR CAPTURE!
QUESTIONS ARISE IN WHITEHALL TORSO CASE

"You're still free," she whispered. The headlines could have easily announced his arrest. With such a severe time disconnect, there was no way to know.

By the time she made it to the bookshop, most of the more annoying lag symptoms had faded. The lightning was still there, but the flying arrows had flamed out.

*Not perfect, but better.*

Cynda came in the back way and cautiously unlocked the door. The room was untouched, her clothes just as she'd left them. In the morning, she'd inform Pratchett of her return and supply him another week's rent. She'd also have to let Alastair know she was back. Maybe he'd have some news of Keats.

After ten minutes of fussing with the kindling and the matches, she got a blaze going, but it produced little heat. Cautiously she added a bit of coal and applied the bellows with some success.

"No wonder they have maids."

A trip to the yard yielded water from the pitcher pump for the washbasin and an opportunity to free her hands of the coal dust. Once that task was completed, she dropped onto the bed, exhausted, staring at the frolicking lights the fire painted on the ceiling. Sleep did not come, another sign her string was unwinding. If things progressed on schedule, before long Endorphin Rebound would kick in, causing increasingly incapacitating hallucinations. Then you kissed your career goodbye.

"Not that I have one left, anyway." Not by the time she got done stiff-arming TPB.

Cynda swung her feet over the side of the bed. Her calf itched and she dug at the newly healed spot where her ESR Chip had once resided. Just below it was a bandage, the chip embedded in the linen. They'd learned that trick from Chris' killer. When the bandage was in place, she could be found. When it wasn't, she was indiscernible to a Rover's interface.

She ripped the bandage off and tossed it in the fire, letting the heat melt the chip. Now she could fly under the radar. She could still transfer home if needed using the decoy interface, but at least now she was harder to find. That would become very important once TPB learned she'd rabbited on them. She just hoped Morrisey could hold off the bad guys long enough for her to get some work done.

"Step One—ditch the chip." Defoe would have done the same once he realized someone was hunting for him, especially if he'd learned that Chris was dead.

"Step Two—disguise." She frowned. "Hard to maintain." It'd worked for her in the short term. For Defoe..."Step Two—go Transitive."

Although Morrisey had vehemently insisted his friend would not become a shifter, Cynda wasn't so sure. Her boss wasn't a Time Rover and didn't think like one. When cornered, a Rover did whatever it took to get the job done and stay alive to tell about it. If that involved becoming a shifter, that might be the best way to survive.

Her mind returned to the fellow in the alley, the one who'd saved her from Dalton Mimes' knife. He was definitely from her time and possessed a Rover's arrogance. And that was where her reasoning fell apart. The man who had saved her was a Virtual who'd appeared out of nowhere. According to Morrisey, only three out of every hundred shifters survived the right of passage to no-see-em. Time Rovers banked on good odds, and those didn't qualify.

"Too much risk. Defoe is not a fool."

*So who is the guy in the alley?*

After another prolonged scratch, she retrieved the newspaper and thumbed through the theater listings. Defoe was an enthusiast. She traced her fingers past advertisements for mezzotint engraving, a steam yacht for sale, an exhibition of brocades and silks, to the theater listings. Then she hit Gilbert and Sullivan at the Savoy Theater.

"Sounds promising," Mr. Spider agreed. He was parked on the edge of the paper near an advertisement for fly strips.

Digging in her pockets, she unearthed the two pocket watches. Cynda didn't like leaving one behind, but carrying both would be begging to lose one.

She hid her interface in a spare pair of socks and stuffed it the bottom of the Gladstone. Not very secure, but the best she could do under the circumstances. She grudgingly dropped the decoy pocket watch into a deep, hidden pocket. If she was lucky, she'd not have to use it.

As Cynda reassembled her male costume, ensuring her hair was tucked tight in the bun under her cap, the world did a three-quarter summersault. She sank on the bed, clamping a hand over her mouth until her senses righted themselves. An odd humming noise vibrated inside her skull.

"Give a spider some warning the next time, will you?" her delusion groused. That was just—"

"Just what?" she asked.

When he didn't answer, she opened her eyes. "Hello?"

No answer. Her personal delusion was gone.

Her gut told her that wasn't a good thing.

## 33

Cynda's plan had a flaw. The theaters disgorged hundreds of patrons at roughly the same time. Awash in jewels, furs and footmen, the posh folks loaded up in their swanky carriages and promptly created a sizeable traffic jam. Watching any one individual was nearly impossible.

"Bah," she muttered. She'd missed out on insomnia for this.

As she walked back toward the Strand, she noted a figure standing along the street eyeing the crowd. Frank Miller. He stuck out because he didn't know how not to. He pulled his interface from a pocket and checked it, no doubt hoping that her or Defoe's ESR Chip might give it a nudge. She tensed and then remembered she was invisible to that technology. With a decided frown, he dropped the watch in an outside pocket.

"What an idiot." No Rover kept an interface so easily accessible or flashed it on a street like that. It was just begging for some nimble-fingered thief to swipe it. As if on cue, Frank was bumped by a young woman. He immediately apologized, libido going into overdrive. Cynda watched in amusement as the lady adeptly lifted Frank's watch from his pocket. He didn't notice, attention firmly centered on her impressive cleavage.

*No wonder you're second-rate, buddy. Your brains are all south of your navel.*

Frank offered the lady a calling card, no doubt hoping to set up some late-night assignation. All against the rules, of course. The woman graciously took his card, pocketed it and set off alone. That should have rung alarm bells.

Ladies of good reputation did not travel on their own. A high-priced courtesan would have had him on her arm, not willing to let the punter wander off without parting with some of his brass after a quick romp.

That meant she was a tooler, as they were called. In this case, a very elegantly clad pickpocket. She probably made a handsome living trolling the theater district. The cops would be leery of shaking down a well-dressed young lady. It was a pleasure to watch a master at work.

Cynda caught up with her a short distance away. "Well, done, miss."

The woman turned, eyeing her suspiciously. "What do you mean, sir?"

"Lifted his watch beautifully. I am impressed."

A petulant frown. "You are entirely mistaken, sir." A pause and then, "Are you a copper?"

"No, and I'm not a mister, either."

The woman leaned forward and then smiled. "Good disguise. So what do you want?"

"That watch you just pinched."

"Why?"

"Because I'm going to give you five pounds. You can't get that at a pawn shop." If nothing more, Cynda was now an expert in how much used watches were worth.

"Fifteen," the pickpocket replied.

"Seven."

"Twelve."

"Nine and you answer a couple of questions."

The woman nodded, finalizing the deal. "What you want to know?"

Cynda gestured. "Watch?" The woman dove into a pocket and handed it over. Cynda shook her head. "The right one this time."

A mischievous shrug, and the correct watch appeared. Cynda delivered the money.

"Can't spend too long," the woman said, angling her head toward the crowded streets. "Losing money standing here."

"Have you ever seen a very distinguished gent about five ten, gray at the temples? He's got a swagger to him and a roving eye."

The woman rolled her eyes. "That's most of 'em, dear."

*Damn. What would make Defoe different than all the rest of them?* This pickpocket was a pro, and it would be the rare mark who noticed her at work. Defoe might. He'd been a Rover long enough. Maybe...

"Did someone who looked like that catch you lifting his watch?"

A knowing nod. "Just one. A nice looking fellow. Comes to the theater regular. I tried to nip something from him a few months ago, and he caught me straight out. He's a sharp one."

"What he'd do?"

"I figured he'd call a copper. Instead, he kissed my hand like a gentleman, told me to behave myself, and then asked me if I'd have a go with him."

*That'd be Defoe.* "Did you see him tonight?" The tooler shook her head. "Any idea where I can find him?"

"No. Why do you want him?"

"He owes me something."

"When you find him, just watch those hands of his," she said, laughing. "Good night to you." With that, she swept back toward the rich folk like a determined hawk after a clutch of baby chicks.

Cynda tucked away Frank's watch and chortled. She'd give it back to him eventually. Or not. One way or another, '057 would come for him and it would be a blot on his record.

"Be a jerk, pay the penalty."

Revenge could be so delicious.

✠

*Tuesday, 23 October, 1888*

Cynda's decoy pocket watch interrupted her insomnia. Bleary-eyed, she stared at the dial. It was only one and some change in the morning. She logged on.

*Have answer to your query.*

*Ralph?*

*Yes.*

Cynda winced. He was still pissed with her. Now was not the time to get into another argument. Maybe a little honey would make it easier.

*I appreciate your help on this.*

There was a hopeful pause. *This took a great deal of effort. The information was not on digital records.*

That was obvious. If it had been, she'd have found it before she left 2057.

*So what did you find?* she typed.

*Effington's household records show a Fiona Ryan, age 17, hired as a maid in June 1888. She left service without giving notice in early October same year.*

*Then what?*

*No further records for Fiona Ryan.*

*She couldn't have just disappeared.*

*She didn't.*

He was playing this out on purpose. Before she could growl at him across the link, the screen lit up.

*According to birth records, Desmond Flaherty had two children: a son, Ryan, who died in infancy, and a daughter, Fiona, born 1871.*

Cynda re-read the birth date and did the math.

"Which would make that Fiona seventeen, the age of Deidre's maid. Was it her?"

Ralph answered the question as if he'd heard it. *Fiona Flaherty concealed her last name, using her dead brother's given name instead.*

"Yes!" she said and then punched the air with a fist. "Smart girl." Few employers would want anything to do with an anarchist's daughter.

*How did she get the job at Effington's?* Cynda quizzed.

*No record of that. Next event is her death in 1901 from TB.*

*And in TEM's alternate time line?*

*She just vanishes. No further record.*

"Drat." *When did Flaherty steal the explosives?*

A slight pause. *End of September and first day of October.* There was a pause and then, *TPB knows you're gone. They filed an Article 43-B complaint against TEM.*

"A 43-B?" That portion of the Time Immersion Code dealt with transportation of dangerous objects or persons. Criminals fell under that section, not Rovers.

*Gets better. They've issued an arrest warrant for you and Defoe. Defoe's is an RFW.*

A Reasonable Force Warrant, which meant you were authorized to use whatever force it took to get the person to 2057, but nothing lethal. You'd expect that for Time Rover One.

Then it hit her. *And mine?*

*An Open Force Warrant. They don't care how you come back, Cyn.*

"An OFW!" That was unheard of. *Just like the Wild West. Wanted: Dead or Alive.*

*Sorry, Cyn. TEM says to watch your back.*

She erupted into nervous laughter. It was ridiculous. *Thanks, Ralph. You've given me something to work with.*

*Be careful, Cyn.* There was a hesitation, as if he was going to type something else and then, *Log Off.*

*Logged Off.*

It wasn't a complete rapprochement between them, but a start. It'd be a real bummer to go to one's grave knowing the only friends you had were a few Victorians, a stuffed animal and a blue delusion with too many legs.

A few minutes later, both Frank's watch and her old interface announced the news. *TPB warrants issued. Defoe–RFW. Lassiter–OFW.* There it was, for all the other Rovers to see.

"It's all posturing, Vid-Net hype," she said, trying to cheer herself up.

She was still their best bet to find Defoe. Killing her at this stage would be counterproductive. Or very prudent. It just depended on your point of view.

‡

"Good morning, Mr. S."

"Sir," Satyr replied, touching his hat in respect a moment before removing it. He was later than usual, and his superior had already tucked into breakfast.

After dabbing his mouth with a napkin, the Ascendant asked, "Are the explosives dispersed per my orders?"

Satyr transferred eggs to his plate and selected two pieces of lightly browned toast. "All is as you requested. As expected, Flaherty is agitating for his daughter's release now that his tasks are complete."

"Not yet. We have no leverage over him if she's no longer in our care, and I may have additional work for him. I gather she is in good health?"

"Yes. Unfortunately, I had to dispatch one of her guards last evening. He seemed to think that she was there for his personal amusement."

The Ascendant's face colored. "He did not harm her, did he?"

"No. I arrived before he had the chance. The other guard was holding him at bay."

"Be sure *that* man is rewarded. What did you do with the miscreant?"

"He's in the sewers." *Rat food.* Satyr smiled at the thought.

The Ascendant dropped his napkin on the table. "A certain party is pressing to have Effington arrested for assault."

Satyr's hand hovered over the bowl of sausages. "Who filed the complaint?"

"Mr. Livingston, of all people. Effington recently assaulted his amanuensis. Livingston was quite vexed by that, I gather. I have requested that the complaint be ignored. However, others have come forth recently with similar accusations. Effington's erratic behavior cannot continue unabated, especially in light of what just occurred with Miss Hallcox."

"Apparently, my warning didn't have the desired effect. Do you wish him to shuffle off this mortal coil?"

A grave nod. "The time has come. I have been overly patient with that thug. And should you find Miss Lassiter vulnerable at some point, please remove her as well. She has not located the failed assassin and hence, her value grows thin."

"Pity," Satyr said, putting his fork down. "I shall miss her. She has spirit."

The Ascendant frowned. "Spirit is appreciated in racehorses, not women. See to her."

"As you wish, sir." Satyr would indeed regret dispatching the Twig, as he called her. Well, at least he would ensure it was a unique kill. "How soon will you begin moving the explosives to their final locations?"

"In a few nights. I want them all dispersed by the fifth of the coming month."

Satyr chortled. *"Remember, remember, the fifth of November. The gunpowder, treason and plot."*

The Ascendant exhibited a rare smile. "I've always liked that rhyme. I wonder if they'll pen one for my efforts?"

*Only if you fail.*

✟

It was early in the morning, but that didn't make any difference at the Yard. It was always like a beehive. Constables and sergeants sat hunched over their desks, cups of tea within easy reach. Others toted files around like mindless drones.

"Don't expect a miracle," Reuben advised as they climbed the stairs to Fisher's office.

"Our findings should make some impact," Alastair protested, holding his medical bag in front of him so it would not bang into the wall.

"Not now—not after the jury has issued its verdict and the arrest warrant is in effect."

"God, I hoped I'd found a way to clear him."

They halted in front of the chief inspector's door. "No, my friend," Reuben replied. "What you've done is found a weakness in the Crown's case. As Keats' barrister, Lord Wescomb may be able to widen that gap when the time comes. It is our duty to let the Crown know they have a hole in the first place."

He rapped smartly and they entered the room.

Chief Inspector J.R. Fisher sat behind his desk, his expression unreadable. Tea steamed at his elbow. In a chair nearby, Inspector Hulme rolled a pencil between his fingers in agitation.

"Ah, there you are. Come in, Doctors," Fisher said, waving them forward. "Well, what is this about? You've had us on tenterhooks since we received your note early this morning."

Alastair took the lead. "We have devoted additional time to studying the marks on Miss Hallcox's neck."

Fisher leaned forward. "And?"

"We have determined the height of Miss Hallcox's killer," Alastair said.

"How is that possible?" Hulme demanded.

"Allow me to explain, Inspector."

"Well, then, get on with it."

Alastair bottled up his annoyance. He'd rehearsed this moment countless times. It had to be precise, or they'd dismiss it out of hand.

"Nicci Hallcox stood five feet, four and three-quarter inches in her bare feet," Alastair began, consulting his notes. "If her killer had been roughly the same height, the ligature mark would be nearly horizontal." Alastair deposited a piece of paper on Fisher's desk and pointed at it. "This is a diagram of the location of the mark as found post-mortem. Note the steep incline toward the cervical spine. That is indicative of a killer who is taller than the victim."

Fisher handed Hulme the paper. The inspector gave it a quick glance and then tossed on it the desk as if it were a week-old newspaper. "How can you be so sure?" he argued.

Reuben stepped in. "Dr. Montrose and I performed separate calculations and we both agree that the killer was at least five feet nine inches in height."

"You've wasted our time on this?" Hulme retorted. "Sergeant Keats has to be at least that tall. Metropolitan Police regulations require it."

"But he's not," Fisher said, a trace of a smile present underneath his moustache. "Sergeant Keats is considerably shorter. He had to receive special approval to become a constable. They only let him in because he could speak a foreign language."

"You're sure of that?" Hulme demanded.

Fisher eyed him coldly. "I pride myself on knowing my subordinates' departmental history, Inspector."

The junior inspector retreated. "I am sure you do, sir. Still, the butler insists it was him."

"Witnesses are mistaken on occasion."

"Yes, I know that," Hulme snapped. "Is it possible that Keats stood on a chair or a stool?"

Reuben huffed. "I think that unlikely, Inspector. The victim would hardly be inclined to allow her assailant time to prepare, would she?"

Hulme frowned. "This does not change my opinion on the matter. To be blunt, Dr. Montrose, your relationship with the accused puts your judgment into question."

"I will not lie to save my friend, Inspector. This is documented evidence. If you have issues with our findings, I am sure an exhumation—"

"That will not be necessary," Fisher interjected. "Is it possible to have these findings reviewed by another source to remove the question of impartiality?" He was looking at Reuben when he posed the question.

"We have already done so, Chief Inspector," Reuben reported. "We took the liberty of asking our colleagues at St. Mary's to review our findings. They concur. The evidence indicates that Sergeant Keats is not of sufficient height to have killed Miss Hallcox."

"Thank God," Fisher whispered, his shoulders sagging in relief.

Alastair turned to Hulme. "Surely this must alter the Crown's case," he insisted. "Cannot the arrest warrant be withdrawn?"

Hulme shook his head, collecting his hat and coat from the chair. "This is just conjecture, Doctors. The butler's testimony puts Sergeant Keats in Miss Hallcox's bedroom at the time of the murder, after a recent quarrel. *That* is the Crown's case. Now good day. I have other matters to attend to."

The moment the inspector was gone, Reuben let out a snort. "Either he's not a smart copper, or he's being blind on purpose."

Fisher pursed his lips, but did not reply. "How did you think to look for this discrepancy?" he asked.

"Ironically," Alastair explained, "it was Inspector Ramsey's disparaging comment that triggered my research. He called Keats a *garden gnome*, a remark that was clearly at odds with the angle of the ligature mark."

"Best not to tell Ramsey that," Fisher replied. "He'll not be pleased in the least."

Reuben chortled. "He's not the only one. My maid is now extremely leery of Dr. Montrose. She is just about Miss Hallcox's height and therefore had to endure a number of...experiments to help us reach our conclusion, though none of them as graphic as the victim had to suffer. I suspect that when my housekeeper learns of this, there will be repercussions."

Fisher locked his gaze onto Alastair. "It might be helpful if my sergeant were to learn of this development. Perhaps it might convince him that it is best to turn himself in."

Alastair gave a nod. "I'll see what I can do on that point, though it has proven considerably difficult to locate him."

"That does not surprise me. Ramsey has been employing his spare hours in hunt for my sergeant, without results. Keats is very good at what he does. I never thought that someday we might be on opposite sides of the law." Fisher rose and vigorously shook each of their hands in turn. "Excellent work, Doctors. You've given me hope where I thought none was possible."

Once they'd made it to the street, Reuben paused to put on his bowler. As Alastair did the same, he found his hands shaking.

"That was hard for you, wasn't it?" his companion asked.

"Very."

"Well, I think you handled it magnificently," Reuben replied. "You kept your ardor under control and presented the facts in a clear fashion. That's quite difficult under the circumstances. You'll need that kind of emotional discipline for the trial."

"Thank you," Alastair said, pleased. "Still, I had hoped it would make a difference."

"It only throws more doubt on that butler. Do ensure that Lord Wescomb gets a copy of these findings, will you?"

"I shall. Thank you, Reuben."His mentor hiked away, whistling a merry tune while swinging his cane.

Hefting his medical bag, Alastair headed in the opposite direction, toward the omnibus stop. He'd visit Livingston's assistant first, then a few of his other patients, including Mrs. Butler. Once he'd made his rounds, he'd continue his fruitless search for his best friend.

34

By dusk, Cynda's feet were sore. She'd worn her old boots to fit her working-girl outfit and her feet were protesting the decision. She'd been wandering through the side streets of Rotherhithe for hours in search of Keats. This was her seventh, no, eighth pub, and still no sign of him. He'd once remarked the best place to scout for Fenians was in the pubs. Eventually everyone needed a drink, he'd said. She hoped the same held true for wanted men.

During her hunt, Cynda had even shared a pint with the old sailor at the Spread Eagle and Crown. He caught her up on local gossip, none of which was very helpful. He did know most of the pubs, and she took mental notes when he listed them off at her request.

Light in the head from the pint, she set off for the Sun and Stars. According to the sailor, it was a watering hole preferred by the Irish. Maybe Keats would be there. Only a few steps away from the pub, a dry, whooshing sound filled her head, ebbing and flowing with each heartbeat. The walls of the nearby buildings bowed toward her and the horses' hooves on the bricks sounded like thunder.

Leaning against a lamp post for support, Cynda wolfed down two pieces of chocolate. Instead of abating, the sound grew worse. This wasn't good: she should have gotten over most of the time lag by now.

Cynda forced herself onward. In an effort to distract herself from her growing sense of panic, she mentally reviewed her plan. Tonight she would find Keats, explain the Fiona discovery and then go back to Pratchett's. Tomorrow, Ralph should be contacting her with a list of high-end courtesans and gambling houses in London. She'd work through those, one by one, until she found Defoe or until TPB caught up with her.

Up ahead, the pub was going full tilt, with brilliant yellow streams of light coursing through the front door. A man staggered out onto the road. A second later, he turned into a bat and flew off into the night.

*Geez.* Cynda groped in her pocket for more chocolate as the whooshing sound grew in intensity.

"Runnin' on empty," she said, pushing herself forward by sheer will.

‡

Keats and Clancy were on their second pint. They'd spent the afternoon unloading rope. Keats had been able to handle the work and it had earned them a few coins.

"You've been quiet today," Clancy observed after a sip of ale.

"Not much to say," Keats replied. That was a lie. The paper on the table in front of him said otherwise. At least there wasn't a picture of him this time, the only reason he'd bought the thing. There was rampant speculation as to his motive for killing Nicci Hallcox, all quite vulgar. What hurt more were the calls for Chief Inspector Fisher's resignation. His boss had become a lightning rod, drawing some of the vehement fire usually reserved for Police Commissioner Warren.

"Anythin' new?" Clancy asked, eyeing him closely.

Keats pulled himself back to the present. "A killing in the West End, more about the Parnell Commission and the Whitechapel killer."

"Caught the mad bastard, did they?"

"No. They're wondering why he's stopped killing. It's bothering them."

"And if he kept killin' they'd be happier?" Clancy asked. Keats shrugged. "That's a hangin' I look forward to. Even the doxies on this side of the river are afraid."

"They should be," Keats replied.

A woman slid into the booth next to him. "Not all of us, luv."

Before Keats could react, Jacynda pulled him close and kissed him hard on the lips. He hid his surprise, knowing others were watching. When the kiss ended, he nuzzled her ear and whispered, "Sean Murphy. Got it?" A slight nod returned. Then she draped herself over his shoulder like a cloak.

"Well, well, ya got a pretty one in your pocket, don't ya?" Clancy said.

"It's not his pocket I'm wantin'," she said, followed by a libidinous wink.

Clancy guffawed. "A tart one, too."

Keats delivered a mock glare at the newcomer. "What are you

doing here, girl? I thought I told you to stay in Whitechapel."

Jacynda shook her head. "Not safe over there. I got to wonderin' what ya was up to. Just had to prowl the pubs until I found ya."

"Hard to find work here," he admitted in all honesty.

"Did ya find any?"

"A bit. What about you?"

"Been sellin' flowers at the market," she replied.

He ran his hands down her shoulders and pulled her closer. Her eyes were unfocused and he could smell beer on her breath.

Clancy clapped a hand on his shoulder, making him jump. "Ya got a filly in heat, lad. Wouldn't want to disappoint her now, would ya? Go on, I'll see ya in the mornin'."

Keats gestured toward the door and guided his lady through the crowd. Right before they reached the exit, she jumped and swore. After shooting the offender a glower, Keats steered her onto the street.

Once out of the pub, Jacynda took his hand and squeezed it, leaning close. "You're damned hard to find, you know?" she whispered, and then stumbled. He slid an arm around her waist.

"You've been drinking, haven't you?" he asked.

Before she could answer, he heard footsteps behind them. As they continued along the street, the footsteps kept pace.

"Someone is following us," he said in the barest whisper. "Since you started this charade, you'll just have to go along with it. For both our sakes, you'd best act willing, or we could end up with our throats cut."

She gave a nod and then laughed brightly. "Ya always say that, Sean," she said, loud enough for their follower to hear. "Prove it, luv."

Emboldened, Keats pushed her up against the nearest wall, kissing her neck and running his hands up and down her sides. "Are you game for all night?" he said.

"I didn't drag my skirts all the way cross the river for a knee-trembler."

He leaned close and whispered, "Is he still there?"

She gave a faint nod. He slid a hand under her petticoat, grabbing a thigh, pressing himself into her. Keats felt his companion's mouth open in surprise and took the opportunity to extract a kiss, his body reacting to the closeness.

When they finally parted, her eyes were riveted on him. To his astonishment, she chortled and ground her hips into his. "Oh, you got what I need, luv."

*Good heavens, woman.* Clearing his throat, he ordered, "Come on, I got a room. If we wait much longer, I'll have you here and now."

Jacynda laughed again as he circled an arm around her waist and pulled her along. She babbled to him about her imaginary sister and how her older brother was in jail for stealing a loaf of bread. Precisely what their shadow would expect to hear.

When they arrived at the door to the boarding house, Mrs. O'Neill appeared in the hallway, judged the situation and elbowed him. "Got a smart-lookin' one there. She'll set ya to rights, that's for sure."

The moment the door to his room closed, Keats held up a hand for silence. He put an ear to the wood. There was no sound on the stairs. Once assured they were alone, he threw his hat and coat on the chair and rounded on Jacynda, dropping his voice to a forced whisper. "Why are you here? Don't you know how dangerous this is?"

"Everything's dangerous, *Sean.*"

She sank on the bed, removing her shawl and hat and placing them on top of his. Then she worked on her boots. First one, then the other hit the floor with a decided thump. Her raised skirts revealed shapely ankles and calves. Keats swallowed hard but didn't turn away from the sight.

"Why are you undressing?" he asked.

"I'm taking off my boots. That's not undressing."

"That is not an answer."

"My feet are sore. Besides, if I'm out of this room in less than a couple of hours, your bloodhound is going to know something's up—especially after that performance you put on in the street."

"I had no choice. If I'd treated you any other way, they'd know something was amiss."

"I know. You just surprised me, that's all." She dropped an envelope on the chair next to her hat. "More money. I'm not sure when I'll get back again."

"I didn't expect a social call," he groused.

She glowered. "This isn't one. The woman Flaherty is hunting is his daughter, Fiona. She used to work as a maid at Effington's. She went missing right after he stole those explosives."

Keats sank against the wall, irritation fading. "His daughter," he murmured, his thumb and forefinger smoothing his moustache in thought. "No wonder he's so upset." He looked up. "Perhaps she just ran away, afraid her name would be connected with his."

"No, she called herself Fiona Ryan, so no one would know the connection. Mrs. Effington said a strange man used to visit her husband, someone Hugo was afraid of. The way she described him, he sounded like a Transitive. Fiona went missing after one of his visits. I think there's more here than we're seeing."

He nodded. "I've felt that ever since Nicci's death. How did you find out about all this?"

Jacynda winked. "I have my sources." She removed a piece of paper from a pocket. "Here's a list of all of Effington's warehouses in Rotherhithe. Maybe that will help you."

He took it, amazed. "Thank you. That will be of immense help. I've made some progress on my own. I helped offload some of Effington's stolen goods the other evening."

"How'd you fall into that?"

"I got the job from Clancy Moran, the man I was sitting with at the pub. Clancy doesn't seem too keen about Flaherty. I might be able to use that to my advantage."

She beamed. "That's a good start."

"Well, since you found me, could you do me another favor?" He pulled an envelope out of his jacket and tossed it on the bed. "I made some notes for the chief inspector. I've addressed it to his home and it's already stamped. Would you post it to him? I would have done so myself, but I feared they could track me from the postmark."

"I'll mail it on the other side of the river."

"Good. He needs to know my side of the story and how my investigation is unfolding. That way if I am unable to complete it, he can. I want my innocence known, for my family's sake."

Jacynda tucked the envelope into a pocket. Then she yawned, barely covering her mouth in time. Extracting the truncheon from a pocket, she jammed it under the pillow and swung her feet up onto the bed, covering them with the heavy skirts. The bed squeaked, reminding Keats of the couple in the next room.

"Let's give it a few hours and then we can go check out the warehouses together," she advised.

"What?" Perhaps he'd misunderstood.

"You...me...warehouses," she repeated and yawned again.

"No. We'll wait a decent interval and then put you on the train to Whitechapel. I will investigate the warehouses on my own."

She stretched out in the bed. "I'm tired. Let me sleep for a bit and then we'll go." Rolling over on her side, she closed her eyes.

*Now what?* Unless he wanted to sit in the chair or sleep on the floor, he had no other choice but to join her. He debated for a time, watching her breathing even out and her limbs relax. With her in it, the bed looked very inviting.

Muttering under his breath about unfathomable women, he removed his jacket and his boots, and gingerly climbed in, fully aware of his bedmate's talent for koshing people on the head when annoyed. It proved a very narrow fit. He was acutely sensitive where their bodies touched.

"If Alastair ever hears of this, he'll tear me apart," he said.

"Then don't tell him," came the mumbled answer.

To his surprise, she rolled over and placed her head on his chest, nestling until she was comfortable. He curled an arm around her.

"You smell better than the last time we met," she observed.

"Visited the bath house. Couldn't stand myself."

"Definitely an improvement, *Sean*."

Keats allowed that this was rather nice. It'd been a considerable time since he'd had a woman in his bed and Jacynda's presence was arousing. If he was honest, it wasn't just desire. He was an outcast now, an exile. It touched his heart to have someone care enough to risk arrest just to help him, no matter how insane the gesture.

"Thank you," he said.

There was a muzzy "What?"

"Nothing. Go to sleep."

## 35

Keats woke later to the sounds of someone in the hall, the tramp of boots, the slam of a door. Without thinking, he nuzzled Jacynda's hair. It smelt nice, like sweet apples. He placed a delicate kiss on her forehead, followed by another. He'd not realized how he'd missed her. She moaned softly in response. Encouraged, he kissed her again. Her soft lips rose to meet his.

This kiss was not hurried, but savored. The next was deeper, more insistent, opening the door to other possibilities. He heard another moan escape as he nuzzled her ear and kissed her neck, lightly biting at the skin. They shouldn't be doing this, but God it felt good. His hand went to her shoulder, gripping it, pulling her closer. So very good.

Like a match thrown on dry tinder, the next kiss stirred the need within her. In the past she had toed the line, denied herself this comfort, this closeness with anyone who wasn't from her time. Not tonight.

As his mouth moved back to hers, his hand lightly caressed her breast. She didn't stop him, but ran her hand down his side, pulling him closer, feeling his desire tighten against her leg. It was a full statement of intent. As their caresses became more heated, he undid the first few buttons of her bodice and slid his fingers under the layer of fabric. They felt rough against her skin. He waited as if seeking permission, then stroked her breast as the kisses grew more urgent.

"I want you," he whispered.

"Yes," she murmured and reached for the top button of his trousers. The first one gave way with some difficulty, then the second. She slid her hand downward, and it was his turn to moan at her touch.

To ease her way, he shrugged off his braces, then kissed her again. Another button fell to her fingers.

"I swear, we'll never regret this," he whispered and lowered his mouth to her breast. Cynda arched into him, reveling in the sensation.

Without warning, the humming noise in her head began again. She tried to ignore it, focusing on the pleasure. The sound rose in pitch until it became unbearable, blocking out everything good.

"Jacynda?"

She turned her head. Chris was standing in the doorway. A gray sheet hung from his waist, river debris draped over his shoulders. He shook his head at her, as if disappointed. Then he faded from view.

"Jacynda?" Someone was shaking her shoulder. She pulled away, transfixed by the trickles of gray water seeping under the door. A claxon slashed the air. The trickle became a torrent, pushing against the wood with incredible force, bowing it inward.

"We have to go!" she cried, rolling off the bed. She landed hard on the wooden floor, bruising both knees. She heard the crash of crockery and the shouts of men as the floor arched upward at an unnatural angle.

"The ship's sinking! We have to go!" Cynda fumbled for the watch, but it fell from her shaking hands. She scrabbled after it, desperately grasping at the metal. She wound it, wound it again. Nothing happened. Someone touched her and she grabbed for the hand, gripping it tightly. Then the door burst inward, a deluge of water pushing toward them in an impenetrable gray wall.

*Oh, God!*

She awoke in stages. First the whole-body shivers ceased, then consciousness began seeping back in. She became aware of a cool cloth on her forehead. Keats sat near her, on the chair, his braces still hanging free, hair mussed. Concern poured from his eyes.

"Are you better?" he asked, leaning closer, brushing some hair aside.

"I think so." The sound in her head was gone and there was no water sloshing across the floor. It had all seemed so real.

He removed the cloth, wetted it in the basin and replaced it on her forehead. This had to have been hell for him. One minute they were headed toward blissful consummation, and the next she was on the floor, frantically trying to escape the overpowering delusions in her head.

"What happened to you? Was it some sort of...fit?" he asked.

Suddenly, it began clear: it was the high-intensity endorphin rise that had triggered the three-alarm hallucination. All those years of sex and chocolate had finally come full circle.

Endorphin Rebound. From this point on, massive surges of the biochemical in her system would trigger crippling time lag. That's what the whooshing sound had been all about. As long as she avoided excessive stress and the desire to bed a certain detective-sergeant, episodes like the one she'd just suffered shouldn't recur. Or at least, that's what they taught you in Rover school.

"Jacynda?" Keats pressed.

"It..." was the end of her career. It was over. If so much weren't riding on Defoe and the worried man next to her, now would be the time to give up and transfer to 2057 immediately. There wouldn't be much they could do for her, but at least she'd be safe.

"You wouldn't believe me."

"I am willing to try."

"I've...got some mental problems."

He sighed. "I noted that. Most women I've been with do not believe they are in the middle of a shipwreck." He adjusted the cloth. "What can I do to help?"

She shook her head.

"I've witnessed mental aberrations before, but not of such intensity. You honestly believed you were on a sinking ship."

*Tell him. Maybe this time he'll believe you.*

She looked him straight in the eyes. "My job did this to me."

Keats blinked. "I don't understand."

*Because you don't want to.* "I told you that I'm from the future. It's the truth."

He dismissed her words with a shake of his head. "Good heavens, Jacynda, that old jest again? Now, I could more understand your situation if it were some form of hysteria or—"

Cynda tuned him out. *Alastair believes me.* Of course, she'd had to reveal twenty-first century technology to drive the point home. *Let Keats think I'm nuts. It doesn't matter anymore.*

She swung her feet over the bed, barely catching the handkerchief before it fell away. "I need to go."

Keats was up in a flash. "Wait until morning. I'll escort you to the train. I don't want you to have one of these fits on the way back to Charing Cross."

"Help me with my boots, will you?" she pleaded.

Keats argued against it for the next minute or so, but when she refused to back down, he laced each boot and then helped her rise.

"One moment," he said, "allow me fix your bodice. You look like a harlot."

He got a smile for that.

"I'm so sorry," she said. "I really wanted..."

He nodded, focusing on the last button. Once it was complete, he delivered a chaste kiss on the cheek.

"Tell Alastair what's happening to you. Maybe he can help."

She nodded, if only to mollify him.

They parted at the train station. It proved very hard. There was no guarantee she'd ever see him again. Everything felt wrong between them now.

They hugged tightly.

"Keep yourself safe," she whispered.

"And you get well," he replied, his expression forlorn.

"You've got a deal. Then we'll do this right."

"I'll look forward to that," he whispered back, his voice cracking.

Jonathon Keats was many things, but he wasn't a good liar.

✝

Cynda's trip under the Thames proved to be a nightmare. Eyes jammed shut, she wedged herself into a corner near the side of the train carriage, feet up on the seat. The bizarre noise engulfed her again, along with the scream of grinding metal and those more human.

The reverberations in her pocket forced her back to the present. It was Frank's watch. She'd been carrying it as a backup, banking on the probability that he hadn't reported the interface's loss. Scrunching down so no one would see her, she performed the windings. The screen lit up in bright red flashing letters.

*Defoe in Wapping near warehouses. Execute RFW immediately.*

Cynda shook her head to ensure it wasn't her scrambled brains playing games with her. The message didn't change. She obscured it and hid the watch back under her clothes.

Then she grinned. Frank still hadn't let his bosses know his interface had been nicked or they'd have made sure it wasn't in the communications loop. The grin widened. If she could get there first, she could snag Defoe before anyone else.

36

Just off a train from Whitechapel, Alastair barely stifled a gasp as the woman with the red shawl exited the station in front of him. Jacynda's movements were disjointed, like a marionette with tangled strings. He'd known she was back in London—her note had arrived this afternoon and it had been much warmer in its tone than its predecessor. That had buoyed his spirits. What the note hadn't conveyed was the state of her health.

She veered toward a post box, pulled something from a pocket and dropped it in. Then she leaned against the box, her breathing ragged.

Alastair pushed his pace and caught up with her.

"Jacynda?"

She spun around, her hand diving underneath her shawl. "What are you doing here?" she snapped.

"I was looking for our...mutual friend."

Jacynda shook her head. "He's not here. He's—" Her eyes narrowed. "How do I know you're Alastair?"

Her caution was warranted. "The first time we met, you struck me because you thought I was a giant blue spider."

She shook her head. "Mildred would know that. She might have told someone."

"I asked you to marry me. You turned me down."

She shook her head again. "Not good enough."

Vexed by her paranoia, he stepped closer. "You learned *my* secret in a carriage from Colney Hatch. I learned *yours* at your lover's post-mortem. If that isn't enough for you—"

"All right." She turned away, eyeing the street warily. Then she turned back toward him, lowering her voice. "Our mutual friend is not on this side of the river."

"Then why are you here?"

"I'm hunting a Rover, someone very important."

"Is that why you left so abruptly?"

"Yeah. I didn't have a choice. They came for me."

With that she lurched away, leaving him to grumble under his breath as he tried to catch up. Once he succeeded, she stared at him as if she'd forgotten he was there.

"I don't need an escort."

"On the contrary, I think you do. You look ill."

"Not your problem."

"I think it is."

A wagon turned the corner and rolled by.

"How is our friend?" he asked.

She dropped her voice. "Pretty good. He's made some connections and hopes they will lead to Flaherty." She paused for moment as if struggling to recall something. "Oh...Fiona, the maid that Deidre mentioned? That's Flaherty's daughter. She went missing right after the explosives were stolen."

Alastair's mouth opened in surprise. "Does the chief inspector know this?"

"Not yet. I'm not looking forward to telling him. He thinks I work for Pinkerton's. It only complicates things."

"Are you a Pinkerton agent from—" He waved his hand to indicate the future.

"No!" she growled. "Don't be stupid."

Alastair was preparing a stinging rejoinder when a peculiar sensation slid over him. He caught sight of a dockworker walking along the other side of the street and then relaxed. "Ah, it's him."

"Who?"

"Wait for me." He took off before she had time to answer.

Cynda leaned against a fence, the humming sound in her head edging up in volume.

"No. Not now!" she said through gritted teeth. She fought it down, counting backward from twenty-five until it diminished. Across the street, the two men talked in earnest with the occasional look in her direction.

"Oh, the hell with this. I don't need a babysitter." The doc could catch up or be left behind.

As she passed others on the street, she examined their faces, for all the good it would do. If Defoe were a shifter, she could walk right by him and never know.

But Alastair would.

Swearing to herself, she slowed her pace so he could catch up with her. As she turned the corner, Alastair rejoined her.

"I asked you to wait!" he scolded.

"I got bored. Who was that, anyway?"

"Livingston. He's one of the members of..." his voice went very quiet, "the organization to which I belong."

"The Conclave?"

He grimaced. "Yes. Please keep your voice down."

"Wasn't he the reason your clinic was sacked?"

"No. That would be the others. Livingston is on the level. We're working together to figure out what's going on."

"How do you know that?" she demanded, walking faster. "He could be playing you for a sucker."

Alastair bristled. "On the contrary. He's the reason you're alive and so damned disagreeable right now."

She stopped cold. "What do you mean?"

"Your attitude, for one."

"No, what do you mean he's the reason I'm alive?"

"He told me what happened that night near the Paul's Head. He had to have been present to know those kinds of details." When she didn't react, he added, "Livingston prevented that man from cutting your throat." Cynda staggered, and he steadied her. "Careful!"

"What does he look like?"

"I've never seen his true form. He always hides himself."

"Why?" she persisted.

"He said if he didn't, it would invite 'repercussions of the fatal variety'."

She stunned the doctor by grabbing him and kissing him, hard.

"You're...you're...oh, you're great!" she said and kissed him again. "Come on, let's find this guy."

"Why?" he asked, clearly bewildered.

"Because I think he's the fellow I'm looking for!"

☦

Satyr descended from the hansom and took in his surroundings. The docklands were busy, as usual. At the shoreline, lightermen were ferrying in a load of wine. In the distance, he heard the chug of a steam launch on the Thames.

With a satisfied nod, he paid the driver.

"Evenin' sir," the jarvey said, touching his cap.

"Good evening to you."

Satyr set off at a leisurely pace, resisting the urge to whistle. Anticipation was everything. This was one kill he was going to relish. As he saw it, he was doing London a favor. Hugo Effington was a hideous bully, a monster of a man who believed his sheer bulk made him worthy of respect. His wife's scars bore testimony to a union of pain and domination. Few would miss the warehouse owner's vile attitude and fists.

A carriage was waiting in front of the warehouse. Satyr shook his head at that. He had expressly indicated that there was to be no one else present. No doubt the warehouse owner thought he'd be safer to ignore the order.

Well, that was easily solved. Satyr stepped into the shadows and changed form with ease. When he appeared at the side of the wagon in Effington's likeness, the teamster jerked to attention.

"Sir?"

He purposely kept his voice low. "Come back in an hour."

"Right, sir, as you wish," the teamster said and then flicked the reins.

Once the carriage was out of sight, Satyr took a cautious look around and then shifted into the form that Effington knew only as "Mr. S." It was unremarkable and not his favorite. But tonight, style would be found in the kill.

The warehouse was a pack rat's dream: stacks of exotic silks perched precariously on oak wine casks, sacks of sugar, barrels of aromatic spices, hogsheads of rum and bales of tobacco, all strewn about in no apparent order. This was Effington's bank vault, the place where he hid what he'd stolen from others.

Edging his way inside, Satyr noted a scraggly figure skulking around a bale of tobacco, dark eyes wide. It was one of the many dockland felines that lived on scraps and vermin. It slunk back under cover as he passed, eyeing him warily.

"You're smarter than most hunters," he whispered. "Not to worry; I'll have you a big rat soon enough."

At the sound of approaching boots, Satyr directed his gaze down an aisle crammed with goods. It was the hefty warehouse owner.

"What the hell is this about?" Effington demanded, a small notebook in hand. No doubt he'd been making a list of his spoils. "I've done everything you asked."

"Not everything. You still owe us answers."

Effington's face flushed. "I keep telling you, I don't know who he was," he retorted, halting near a bale of tobacco. He flipped the notebook shut and jammed it in a coat pocket so forcefully Satyr thought the fabric might tear.

"That is not helpful, Hugo."

Effington glowered at the use of his first name. He booted something at his feet. There was a sharp snarl and the cat shot away

The fingers on Satyr's right hand twitched in anticipation.

"Let the coppers sort out what happened that night," Effington said. "No business of mine. I've done what you asked. I don't want anything further to do with you or your superior, do you understand?"

"Why did you tell Nicci Hallcox where the explosives were hidden?"

Effington's face went white, confirming his guilt.

"As I thought."

Satyr's right hand flashed forward in a blur of movement. The blade neatly parted Effington's coat and slid through his vest and shirt. When the point reached its final destination, it slit the bottom of the heart, as intended.

The wounded man stumbled, grasping at his chest. "You...bastard."

"Not at all, Hugo. I'm quite legitimate. I'll be sure to help your wife choose her widow's weeds. After I spend the night making love to her, that is."

Effington crumpled to the ground in a groaning heap, blood pouring from his lacerated chest. His mouth moved, but nothing came forth.

"You deserved far worse." Satyr said, shaking his head in disappointment. He wiped the blood off the knife onto a large tobacco leaf and dropped the closed blade in a pocket.

"Lest you think otherwise, no one will mourn your passing, Hugo. I can lay odds on that." Something grazed Satyr's leg. He gazed fondly at the mangy feline. "Ah, there you are," he said and gestured at the newly-minted corpse. "It's all yours."

The next few minutes were full of debate. He wanted to torch the warehouse, giving Effington's corpse a glimpse of what awaited it in the afterlife. Something held him back.

"No, not this time." He shifted into nothingness and exited the building, leaving the double doors open. He'd very much wanted to bolt them shut and perplex the coppers when they tried to ascertain how the murderer had escaped. Nevertheless, sometimes simplicity was its own virtue. Effington's body needed to be found quickly. Others would understand the message.

He was partway down the street when he turned, as was his habit, to savor the moment by looking upon the location of his most recent kill. To his surprise, two figures were standing near the open warehouse. He recognized them instantly. The woman was petting the cat while the man scanned the street, as if somehow aware of Satyr's presence.

"You would be here, wouldn't you?" he said, shaking his head. "You just keep pressing your luck, Twig."

The Ascendant would not allow any further delay, at least when it came to this woman. Satyr moved into the shadows, his mind whirling with possibilities.

37

"Yuck. It's got blood on it," Cynda said, wiping her hands on her skirt.

"Probably something it killed," Alastair replied, searching the street. He appeared distracted.

"Sad little thing. I wish I had some decent food for it." As she rose, something just inside the warehouse caught her attention. She took a few steps forward, squinting in the dim light.

"Jacynda?"

The cat wandered inside and then turned, as if expecting her to follow.

Cynda blinked her eyes, but the scene didn't change. *Real or a delusion?* It had come down to that. There wasn't any humming in her head, so maybe her time lag symptoms had stabilized for the moment.

She edged further inside the warehouse, hand on her truncheon. It took some time for her eyes to adjust to the darkness. The overpowering scent of rum made her nose itch. A lantern sat on a wooden cask, illuminating what appeared to be a pair of boots protruding just beyond the wine barrel.

"Jacynda?" Alastair called.

"Shush!"

She moved at a snail's pace, listening for the slightest sound. Something brushed past her at floor level. It was the cat.

The boots gave way to a large body.

*Oh, great.* "I found where the blood came from," she called out.

Hugo Effington's alabaster face glowed like a full moon, his eyes staring heavenward, unblinking. A crimson stain dominated the front of his crisp, white shirt.

Alastair joined her. "Good God." He knelt, examining the corpse. "The weapon must have struck his heart," he observed, pointing to the slit in the fabric. "Death would have come very quickly."

"Would it take some skill to do that?" Cynda asked, turning in a slow arc, on her guard. There didn't appear to be anyone else present, at least none that she could see.

"Yes, or just sheer luck." Alastair dug through the man's pockets. "Doesn't appear to be a robbery. His watch is still attached to the fob. Perhaps I can find out who he is."

"Don't bother. It's Hugo Effington."

Her companion gasped, then rose, taking a cautious look around. "Do you think Flaherty did this?" he asked softly.

"If he blamed Effington for his daughter's disappearance, it's a real possibility." She sighed. "At least Deidre won't have to bother with the divorce."

"I'll look around," the doctor said and then cut down one of the rows of tobacco.

The cat rubbed up against her again with a throaty purr. "Pity you can't talk. I bet you saw it all."

When Alastair finally reappeared, he shook his head. "No knife, no sign of the assailant, on any level."

That was great news. Just because you couldn't see someone didn't mean they weren't there. Having Alastair around was very useful.

"If you are sure you'll be safe, I'll find a constable," he said.

"I'll be fine here."

Cynda positioned herself by the open doors, drawing in the river air to erase the smell of blood from her nose. She didn't intend on hanging around, though that's not what she'd told Alastair. He'd handle the police without her, and Defoe needed finding.

Impatient, Cynda watched as the doctor ducked down an alley toward the main street.

"Good." As she turned to leave, something lightly brushed her cheek, like a feather.

"Hello, Twig," a voice said near her ear.

The next contact was a heavy blow to the back of her skull.

‡

Cynda woke to searing pain. She gingerly rose to a sitting position, hand firmly clasped on the back of her neck. She was seeing at least two of everything. She closed her eyes for a bit longer. She'd left her Dinky Doc at Pratchett's. *Dumb.*

Once her vision cleared, she noted the lantern was gone from its place on the cask. Yet there was still light in the building, a dancing sort that rose and fell. Her eyes started to water and she coughed, making the pain in her head increase tenfold. The cat shot past her and out the door as a distinct popping noise issued from the rear of the warehouse.

*Fire.*

Using a tobacco bale as leverage, she rose unsteadily to her feet.

Grasping Effington's feet, she tried to drag him toward the open door, but he was just too heavy. At least Alastair had managed to examine him.

"Jacynda?"

It was Alastair's voice. He was standing near the open doors.

*Good timing!* "Help me get Effington out of here!" she called.

The doctor didn't move.

"Come on, help me! He's heavy."

The laugh that filtered back wasn't anything Alastair Montrose could have produced.

She stared. "Who the hell are you?"

"A genuine admirer, so you have my sincere apologies up front. You should have remained unconscious, you silly woman."

With that, he bowed and vanished.

Cynda rushed the doors, but they swung shut in her face, caroming her back into the warehouse. Then she heard the outer bar falling into place, followed by the metallic clinks of heavy chain.

"No!" She threw her scant weight against the doors with no effect. Hammering on the hard wood, she screamed, "Let me out!"

The only answer was the popping fire as it grew, bright and greedy, seeking more fuel. She pounded again, shouting louder.

A hissing noise grew behind her, like a dozen frightened cats, causing her to turn. Carried by a rolling wave of rum, molten fire spread across the warehouse floor. In its wake, it ignited silk, crates, and tobacco, birthing a thundercloud of deadly fumes and smoke.

"Which one is it, sir?" the constable asked, stomping along next to Alastair.

The doctor hesitated, then frowned, eyes darting from building to building along the row. "That's odd, the doors were open." He lit upon the one with the green hinges. "That one there," he said, pointing.

The constable walked a few paces forward. "Oy, that looks like smoke!"

A fraction of a second later, a concussion blew one of the half-moon windows outward, showering the ground with splintered glass.

"Fire! Fire!" the copper bellowed, blasting his whistle. A returning cry came from somewhere nearby, followed by another shrill whistle.

Alastair broke into a run. When he reached the entrance, he thought he could hear muffled shouts from inside, along with frantic blows against the wooden doors.

"Jacynda?" he shouted, pulling on the bar. The pounding grew more agitated. Alastair jerked hard against the metal, but the massive lock held. He cursed and tried another assault. A dockworker appeared at his side, crowbar in hand and they tried to force the bar, but with little result.

"Pull harder!" he ordered. A billow of acrid black smoke drove his helper back, but he refused to retreat, hands cramping around the crowbar.

Inside, Cynda rammed herself into the heavy door, driving splinters into her shoulder. At the sound of a dull explosion, she turned and watched in horror as a rum cask cartwheeled into the air. Incandescent liquor rained downward like flaming tentacles. Eyes streaming tears and with lungs near to bursting, she fought with her petticoat, stripping it off with shaking hands. Flinging it over her head, she used it as a tent to shield her from the burning debris.

Turning her back to the blistering heat, she fumbled to retrieve her interface. The moment she opened it, she knew it was Frank's. It didn't matter. A quick hop, that's all she needed. A few minutes into the future, a few hundred feet. That's all it would take. With her ESR Chip removed, if she died, the *Dead Man Switch* wouldn't kick in and send her body to the future.

"Come on, come on," she said, repeating the windings when the first set didn't start the transfer process. To her relief, a countdown clock appeared in the ash-laden air above the watch.

Working on instinct, she wound the watch chain around her wrist, clipping it so it wouldn't fall free if she fainted. Bending low to the ground near the doors, sucking in air, a prayer tumbled out of her lips.

"Please God, not this way." Keats would hang and Morrisey would lose everything. Her family would never have a body to bury. "Please!"

The remaining rum casks rocketed upward in a cacophonous explosion that blew out the windows and transformed the double doors into deadly missiles. A talon of flame clawed its way outward, a fire beast in search of another victim.

38

Cynda flailed upward, choking on the water sucked deep into her lungs. When she finally broke the surface, she cascaded into a coughing spasm, bringing up Thames effluent.

As she struggled to regain her senses, it became clear that Frank hadn't set his interface properly. Rovers never transferred into water: reflexes were too inhibited, the mind not fully focused on survival. It was an invitation to drown. If her leap had taken any longer, she'd be drifting to the bottom of the river right now.

*The man's a moron.*

A spasm of intense shivering made her teeth chatter and muscles knot. Cynda rolled over, floating to buy time. Broken barrels and rotting fish bumped against her. Her eyes burned. Blinking them did nothing to improve her vision.

Ensuring she still had the interface in her hand, she began to swim toward the dock. Fortunately, the watch was waterproof. She wasn't. The shivering intensified beyond that of just a transfer, making the diagnosis plain: hypothermia.

*Keep swimming. You'll make it.*

She thought someone was calling to her. That couldn't be right. Another shout. Cynda ignored it. When she finally reached the dock, she inched her way, hand over hand, along the worn timbers until she found a ladder.

*I want to sleep...*

Maybe she'd just stay in the water for a while, float around and take a nap. Just a little nap. Not too long.

"Get up here!"

The rude command shocked her awake.

"Come on, climb!"

Cynda made it halfway when her strength gave out. Right

before she let go, someone grasped a wrist and yanked her upward. She landed in a coughing, sodden heap at the feet of a dockworker. Shaking the water off the watch, she pried the chain from her wrist and stuck it in a pocket.

When she caught her breath, she stared upward at her rescuer. He looked hazy, as if her eyeballs were coated with oil. He was dressed like a dockworker, one that looked familiar.

"I can't believe you did that," he said, shaking his head. "How amateur."

She recognized the voice; it was the man from the alley, the one who'd saved her from Mimes. *Was it Defoe?*

He glowered and tapped a worn boot in displeasure. "I just can't believe you did that. Every newbie knows to set the non-water landing parameter."

*Frank didn't.* "Not...my watch," she said.

"No excuse. If I hadn't been here, you'd be fish food. I can't believe it."

"I was too busy...being burned to death...to worry about the small stuff."

"It is a helluva fire, I'll give you that. How'd it start?"

"Someone tried to kill me." She looked up into his face and gambled. "A Virtual."

His jaw tightened. "Come on, let's get out of here."

As he levered her upward, water flowed off her like a rainstorm. Her boots squished and the hat was gone, her hair hanging in wet tendrils.

A quick check confirmed she'd lost her truncheon. That she regretted. She dug frantically through her pockets—the decoy interface was still there.

*Thank God.*

Cynda turned toward the brilliant glow a few streets away. "Alastair..."

"Come on!" her rescuer urged, tugging on an arm. "We can't stay out in the open."

"Alastair needs to know I'm out of there."

"Not right now. It's too dangerous to stand around."

She ignored him and sank back to the ground, raising her feet to allow water to pour out of the boots. While they drained, she angled her foggy eyes upward again. Her rescuer was swiveling around like a mongoose on the watch for a cobra

"How did you know I was going to be here?" she asked.

"I didn't. I heard the splashing. Now come on, will you?"

She gave in and followed him.

‡

Alastair sat on the back of a wagon, pressing a wet cloth to his face in an effort to dull the stinging sensation. He gingerly touched his moustache. It was singed, as were his clothes. None of that mattered. If he'd been standing in front of the doors when they disintegrated, more than his garments would have been crisped.

He shuddered at the thought.

Since the explosion, there'd been no sign of Jacynda inside the furnace. He didn't want to think about it. She'd escaped. She always did.

He watched as firemen and dockworkers scrabbled over broken bricks and twisted timbers to pump water onto the blaze. Other men emptied adjacent buildings as the flames spread.

His attention was drawn to a pair of bystanders a few feet away.

"Right nasty one this time," one fellow remarked before spitting on the ground with gusto. "I wonder how it started."

"Rats. They start fires all the time," his compatriot replied, nonchalantly sipping on a ginger beer as if they were watching the Lord Mayor's Day procession.

"That's a load and you know it," the first one said. "Rats don't do that."

"How do you know?" the second asked.

"You never find any charred ones inside. They always get out."

"That don't mean they don't start the fires in the first place."

Alastair rose and walked away, not wanting to hear about charred rodents or anything else. It would be hours before they beat down the flames. There was only one way to know if Jacynda was in there. He'd have to pick through the rubble for her remains.

‡

"Quite a fire, isn't it?" Satyr asked, *en mirage* as a young clerk. He looked expectantly at the constable next to him, awaiting a reply.

"Sure is."

"Anyone in there?" Satyr nudged.

"A dead body is what I heard. Some gent."

"No one else?"

The constable gave him a strange look. "I should hope not."

"How true."

Finding no amusement from that quarter, Satyr turned his back on the conflagration and continued his trek through the warehouse district. He'd secure a hansom eventually. Besides, the evening was cool and currently scented with burning tobacco. Not entirely unpleasant.

He stopped and looked back the way he'd come. Why was Dr. Montrose still here? It was plain that the Twig was dead. No one survived an inferno like that.

"And yet, she outlived tangling with those work horses pulling the beer wagon," he muttered.

Jacynda Lassiter was the sort who would fight until the very end.

Abruptly, Satyr cut toward the heart of the docklands. His assassin's instinct told him his job wasn't complete.

## 39

"This way," Cynda's escort ordered, hauling her by the arm. When she faltered, he gave her a disgruntled look and then sighed. "You can barely walk."

He angled her into a doorway, then slipped a hand into his coat and retrieved a Vespa box. With a flip, it became a Dinky Doc.

That she understood. "All right, go for it." A minor pressure against her neck. More mumbling, then more pressure. She immediately felt warmer, her lungs more capable of taking in air. Her vision cleared.

"My God, you're carrying a load of time lag. What stage are you?"

There was no reason to lie. "End Stage."

"You're in Rebound? Why the hell didn't you stop before that?" he demanded, more upset than she'd expect.

"No choice."

"Nonsense. You always have a choice." He did another reading and tut-tutted. "Well, I can't do anything for that, but at least you won't die from all the garbage in your lungs. I still can't believe you—"

Momentarily buoyed by the treatment, she swung around. "Give it a rest, will you? I'm alive. That's all that counts."

A reluctant grin appeared underneath the grubby moustache. "You're right."

"Thanks, by the way."

The grin turned smug. "Three times over."

She stuck out her hand, trusting her instincts. "Pleased to meet you, Mr. Defoe."

He ignored her gesture. "I have no idea who you're talking about."

*Yeah, right.* "Why don't you just admit it and we'll move on?"

"Nothing to admit."

She didn't intend to let this charade go any further. There was only one way to get this guy to blow his cover, and that was by breaking his concentration. Unfortunately it would involve pain, for both of them. Her rescuer averted his eyes as he tucked away the Vespa box. That was all she needed.

"Sorry," she said, the moment before her fist struck the side of his jaw with great force. If she were wrong, this was going to be very hard to explain.

The man staggered back. His hand came away from his mouth, smeared with blood. "Dammit woman, what the hell are you—"

The illusion gave way to a face she knew as well as her own: Harter Defoe, Time Rover One. She smiled in triumph.

The moment the change was complete, he swore under his breath. "I think I should have let you drown."

"No fun that way," she said, still rubbing her knuckles. "We've got some major problems, you and I. TPB has issued a warrant for both of us."

Defoe raised a solitary eyebrow and then effortlessly shifted back to the dockworker persona. "Ah, that's better. Is this about Chris' death?" he asked, dabbing at his mouth with a handkerchief.

"No, it's bigger than him now. We've got a severe time disconnect in the works. TPB doesn't want either of us in '88 for some reason."

"I've felt something was wrong, but couldn't quite get my mind around it."

"That makes two of us."

He studied her intently. "Let's go somewhere and compare notes. It's not safe here. You may have led the hounds to me."

"No way; my chip is out."

"So is mine. There are other ways to track a Rover."

Cynda shook her head. "Not this one."

"Don't be too cocky."

She grinned at being chided by the greatest of them all.

"Why are you in Wapping?"

He frowned, apparently not used to such direct questions. "I have a particular interest in Hugo Effington."

"Well, you can scratch him off your interesting people list. Someone just put a knife in his heart. He's currently in the warehouse being cremated with a side order of rum and tobacco."

Defoe glowered. "Dammit all to hell. Will nothing go right?"

"Nope, not from my experience." The question she'd been waiting to ask popped into her mind. "Did you try to assassinate someone at Effington's dinner party?"

"No."

"Whoever did it looked just like you."

Defoe eyed her uneasily. "Then it had to be someone from *our* time."

"Or someone who saw you on the street and decided to mimic you."

He shook his head. "I've been *en mirage* since shortly after I arrived."

"Even when Chris found you?"

A nod. "I still had my ESR Chip in place. It was a foolish oversight. It was a bit of a shock for the boy, but he dealt with it."

*Which meant Chris knew about the shifters.* That made sense, given his uncle was one of them.

"What does Theo say about all this?" Defoe asked.

"Who the hell is Theo?"

"Morrisey," he replied with a grin.

*No wonder he uses his initials.* Cynda sniggered, triggering another coughing fit. "He thinks—"

"Lassiter!" a voice rang out. It was Ramrod. Neither of her interfaces registered his presence.

*Had the TPB goon heard their conversation?*

The moment she turned toward him, he waved her forward. "Come here, Lassiter. We don't want to involve the locals," he called.

*He doesn't know it's Defoe.* A wave of relief washed over her.

"Guv?" Defoe asked quietly.

"TPB," she whispered back. "He's already tried to kill one Rover."

Her companion swore under his breath. "Just move slowly to allow me time to change. I'll come back. You understand?"

"Um...hum."

"So who's this, then?" he asked, loud enough for Ramrod to hear.

"The old man," she said. "He always finds me."

Defoe waved his hands in surrender. "I don't want no trouble. Good day to ya, sir," he said, tapping his cap and slinking off.

Cynda took deliberately slow steps, hoping to deflect his attention away from her retreating companion.

*How did he find me?*

She'd half-expected an answer from her personal delusion. There was none. He'd gone quiet just about the time the humming began in her head.

"Come on, move it!" Ramrod ordered.

She voiced the question. "So how'd you find me?"

"Miller's watch. We tracked it to the pickpocket. She told us all about you. It was easy to set you up with the false message about Defoe," Ramrod boasted.

She stopped about ten feet away. "There you go," she said, tossing the telltale interface at him. "Tell Frank he's an idiot, will you?"

The watch skidded to a halt at Ramrod's feet.

"That's a nice start," he said. A pistol emerged from his pocket. As with his clothes, it was time period appropriate.

"That's pretty primitive," she observed. "You've got better choices than that."

"Not if I want to inflict pain."

"Like you did to Hopkins?"

The gun sank lower. "Let's get you focused. I'll start with a knee. Those are really painful." He cocked the trigger. "Where is Defoe?"

Cynda's mouth went dry. "That's a bit over the top, don't you think?"

"Not for you. I can bring you home in pieces and no one will care."

The blow struck so hard Ramrod careened off the nearest wall. As he bounced like a human basketball, the pistol in his hand discharged. Cynda was moving before he hit the ground. She wrestled away the firearm and delivered a satisfying thump on his skull with the butt end of the weapon. He fell slack.

"That was for Hopkins."

A few moments later, Ramrod's comatose body was on his way to 2057, courtesy of Frank's interface. Pity she wouldn't be around to hear him explain that twist to his bosses.

"Score one for the good guys!" she crowed.

"Not...quite." A waver in the air became Defoe, his hand grasping his chest as blood oozed around the fingers. He sank to his knees with a deep moan. "Too cocky, by far."

Cynda was at his side in an instant. The small bullet hole in his shirt sprouted a red halo. "Come on, we have to get out of here. Someone will have heard the shot. I'll get you some help."

It took incredible effort to pull him to his feet, much more than he'd needed to move her a few minutes before. A half block away, knowing they'd not get much further, she pushed on a gate. It swung open with a rusty, dry creak. The yard was deserted and it reeked of something dead.

Once inside, Defoe sank to the ground and leaned heavily against an unpainted fence. The handkerchief pressed to his chest was bright crimson.

"I had hoped it would be...minor." He groaned as she unbuttoned his waistcoat, revealing the extent of the bloodstain. He pressed harder on the handkerchief, not realizing the thin linen was inadequate to staunch the flood. The wound was near the breastbone. It was only a shade smaller than the one that had killed Effington.

Cynda dug through his pockets, unearthing male detritus:

opera tickets, a comb, money, pipe and tobacco. She found the Dinky Doc and pressed it against the side of his neck. The readings were catastrophic: acute shock, pulmonary congestion, internal bleeding. The list continued, but she didn't bother with it.

She let the device do what it thought best and then dropped it back in his pocket. The humming sound began in her head again. She fought it down, desperate to stay in the moment.

Then she found his watch. He murmured something.

"What?"

"Not an...interface."

Indignant, she snapped it shut and dropped it into the closest pocket. "Where is it?" she demanded.

"I don't...carry it. They can track them."

*So I noticed.* "Every newbie knows to carry their interface."

A half-smile. "Got me...there."

His breathing grew labored. She knew how it felt: every breath closer to the last, the cold panic creeping into his bones, the rasping sound of death sharpening his scythe. He'd saved her life repeatedly. It was time to return the favor, whether he wanted it or not.

Cynda began the winding procedure on the decoy interface. Morrisey would just have to figure out how to hide Defoe once he got to 2057, providing he survived the transfer. The other Rovers would think she'd turned him in just to save her own ass, but she didn't care. He had to live.

The wounded Rover saw her movements. "No..."

"Here equals dead. There, you have a chance."

The humming in her head ramped up like a revving motor.

*Stop it, stop it, stop it!*

Hands shaking, she set the watch and looped the chain around his wrist, clicking it in place so he couldn't shake it loose. Then she folded his fingers around it.

She leaned close, the humming sound making it hard to hear anything. "Stay alive, okay?"

Defoe coughed violently, spraying her with blood droplets.

"You must know...the Ascendant. I think—"

A moment later, the holographic blur encompassed him and he was gone. The humming was so loud now that she couldn't bear it.

Her mind conjured up the lion, muzzle stained with blood. It arced across the open arena and leapt upon the fleeing man. He screamed in high-pitched terror as it raked its claws across his back, shredding flesh. She could hear the crunch of bones, the muted death shriek. The coliseum erupted in a roar of ecstacy.

Cynda slowly came to her senses, slumped against the fence.

Her hands were coated with dried blood. Pulling a handkerchief out of a pocket, she mechanically went about the business of cleaning her hands. As she scrubbed on each finger, the fog began to clear.

In the course of her time in Victorian England, she'd lost a lover, been thrown under a wagon, knifed in the chest, hit on the head, barbequed and damned-near drowned. Despite all that, she'd still managed to find the greatest of all Time Rovers.

Then she'd sold him out.

40

On auto-pilot, Cynda doggedly trudged toward the fire. It made an easy beacon. The humming sound in her head was growing again. The emotional turmoil of Defoe's shooting had taken its toll. She shivered as her clothes dried in the chilly air. In front of her, a pillar of fire ignited in the middle of the street, swirling like a cyclone. Not caring if it was real or not, she let it pass right over her, welcoming the searing heat, then the steady pull of the funnel's updraft on her clothes. Then it was gone. Another delusion. She kept walking toward the distant glow, fixated on her goal.

"You were wrong, Morrisey," she muttered. Defoe was a Transitive and a Virtual to boot. Probably the only time in Theo's life he'd made a mistake. It'd been a big one.

Was Defoe still alive? God, she hoped so. He was too cool to die. Once they realized he was in 2057, TPB would probably stick him in a cell somewhere to guard their "national treasure" while history melted down like a chocolate bar left on hot pavement.

*Like me.* She was melting. She could feel it. Her vision had no definition, the air surrounding her seemed heavy, like right before a rain. She'd known a Rover who gotten this far out on the limb. He went into Endorphin Rebound and then killed himself. Tossed himself in front of a Grav Rail train. It made the front pages of the Vid-Net News for three days. *Like I will.*

An absurd giggle escaped. "Yo, Mr. Spider! I could use some help here," she called.

No reply.

"Nobody home." She shook her head. That sucked.

Right foot, left foot. Right foot, left foot. As long as she kept moving, she'd find the doctor. He'd know what to do. He always helped her.

Smoke drifted toward her and Cynda stopped for a moment to

catch her breath. The smell triggered memories of fires past. 1666. San Francisco after the earthquake. Dresden. And now that warehouse. She'd never drink rum again.

She was on her knees sobbing when the time slips ended. Someone called her name. Raising her eyes revealed a pair of boots. A man knelt in front of her. He looked familiar.

The fellow chuckled. "You are very hard to kill, Miss Lassiter."

That was when she recognized the face of the man at Effington's party. The one who wore too much macassar oil. "You're Deidre's lover?"

He nodded. "Among other things."

"Who are you...really?"

He gave a resigned nod. "You've earned that, at least. Some call me Drogo."

Her heart skipped a beat. The last time she'd seen that name, it'd been on a piece of waterlogged paper in the pocket of her dead lover.

Cynda tried to straighten up, but the blinding headache stopped her. She had no will left to fight. She only wanted the truth. "You killed Chris Stone?"

He ignored her. "I am also called Satyr. No doubt you will remember me from Nicci's party, though not in this form."

The lusty mythological being who had been Queen Victoria's partner.

"Were you the target at Effington's party?"

"I was. Thank you for your assistance that night. It was very grand of you. Have you discovered the assassin's identity?"

"No."

"Pity. Neither have I," he said. "Quite an elusive soul."

"Did you kill Effington?"

He smiled broadly. "Certainly, and Nicci, too. I've been very busy as of late."

"You framed Keats," she hissed.

"Purely an accident. I regret that. Well, maybe not that much."

"Why did you kill Nicci?"

"She was a threat."

"To whom?"

He evaded her question again. "You present me with a dilemma, Miss Lassiter. You are supposed to be dead. I locked you in a burning warehouse and lo, here you are. You passed my test yet again. How does that happen?" he asked, genuinely curious.

"Yet again?" she repeated, trying to wrap her fragmented mind around this bizarre man.

"The first time would have been perfect if you'd behaved

yourself and fallen under the beer wagon as intended. I almost forgot myself and applauded when I realized you were still alive."

"Why did you try to kill me?"

"Because I was ordered to do so."

"By whom?"

"My superior, of course." A knife appeared in his hand without any apparent effort. It seemed to glow, like something an archangel might carry.

He twisted the blade for a moment and then shook his head. "This is not right for you, I think. You've earned a gentler death, of sorts."

The weapon vanished and was replaced by a silver tube, maybe five inches in length.

"Do you know what this is?" he asked smiling cheerfully.

She shook her head, now barely able to keep her eyes open. The throb in the back of her skull was supplanting nearly everything else.

"This is a remarkable weapon. I've never felt the need to use it until now. It will not kill you, at least not physically. It's far more subtle. It destroys that which makes you unique." The smile grew. "Far more humane than a blade to the chest."

"I don't understand," she said, gritting her teeth against the pain.

"You will. Or actually, you won't. That's the problem with this method. It leaves so little untouched."

Before she could ask another question, he placed the cold tube against her left temple. Her feeble attempts to stop him were easily thwarted.

"I thank you for this merry chase," he whispered in her ear. "It's been a long time since someone has provided this much of a challenge. Farewell, Twig. Enjoy the twilight."

A fiery brand of molten heat bored inward above her left ear, racing along her neural synapses like heat lightning across a darkened sky. Suddenly, her eyes began blinking without her command. She opened her mouth to scream, but couldn't remember how.

✝

Keats wandered aimlessly about Rotherhithe, despondent since putting Jacynda on the train. The expression of heart-stopping panic on her face still haunted his thoughts. At that instant, she truly believed what was happening to her was real: the hallmark of incapacitating mental disease. Her claims to be from the future were just too extraordinary for words. Yet she'd willingly cast

324 | Jana G. Oliver

herself into the fray, fighting off the Fenians to save him only a few weeks ago. He remembered how she'd held him and cried that night in the carriage after he'd taken injury.

"Dear God," he whispered, shaking his head mournfully. As if his troubles weren't numerous enough, his heart had been captivated by a madwoman.

As he passed the Spread Eagle and Crown, he noted a knot of people clustered on Church Stairs. Strolling closer, he found what had caught their attention.

"Which dock is on fire?" he asked the fellow next to him.

"Not a dock. Some of the warehouses," the man said. "God help us if it spreads."

Keats broke away from the crowd and headed along the Thames. He passed a constable, but the copper was too distracted by the fire to notice him. Not keen to return to the boarding house and his lonely bed, he kept on until he found a set of empty stairs that led to the river. He sat a few steps down from the top, elbows on knees, watching the fiery glow across the water.

"What a bloody mess," he said.

"Amen to that."

He turned at the voice. Clancy Moran was standing at the head of the stairs. Without waiting for an invitation, he took a seat next to Keats.

"Why are you following me?" Keats asked

"Keepin' ya alive."

Keats tensed. "Who wants me dead?"

After a wary look around, Clancy replied, "Just about everyone, as far I can tell. Flaherty wants yer nads, and the coppers want yer neck for the noose."

*Oh, God.* There was no point in lying. "When did you know?"

"The moment I met ya. Ya nicked my nephew a few years back. I remember ya from the trial."

Keats felt an odd sense of relief. "What was his name?"

"Patrick MacArthur."

Keats riffled through his Arbour Square memories. "He stole a joint of beef from a butcher."

Clancy eyed him. "Ya remember all that?"

Keats nodded. "Not a bad lad. Just hungry. I didn't want to arrest him, but the merchant insisted."

"Pat said ya gave money to his wife so she wouldn't go hungry while he was in the clink."

Keats shrugged.

"I heard ya were fair to Ahearn's widow, too. Why'd ya do that, now?" Clancy looked genuinely puzzled. "Why d'ya care about a few dirty Irishmen?"

"Because the law has no heart, and sometimes the judge doesn't, either. Your nephew was just trying to feed his family. If he'd had a chance at a good job, he wouldn't have been on the wrong side of the law."

The irony struck home.

Laughing bitterly, Keats gestured around him. "That's a load, isn't it? Look at me! One moment I'm headed toward a brilliant career and comfortable retirement, and the next I'm bound for the rope."

"God loves to play silly buggers with us," Clancy observed.

"Odd sense of humor, that's all I can say."

"Who fitted ya up, then?"

Keats looked over at him. "How do you know I didn't kill that woman?"

"Not yer way."

Keats nodded. "I have no notion who did this to me, but somehow it's all tied up with Flaherty and those damned explosives."

Clancy extracted his pipe and lit it. "Why d'ya think that?"

"The Hallcox woman said she had information on where Flaherty was hiding."

"Think he killed her?"

"No. Do you know anything about Flaherty's daughter?"

Clancy shook his head. "He was a quiet one. Never said much. We didn't see eye to eye."

"His daughter's a part of this. And Effington, too."

Clancy worked the pipe for a time, the smoke curling in Keats' direction. The fugitive inhaled deeply.

"I'll make a deal with ya," Clancy said and then looked over his shoulder once more. "I'll help ya catch Flaherty."

Keats felt his heart leap. "In return for what?"

"Yer reward money. I hear it's up to fifty pounds now."

"Seventy-five," Keats said. "Not quite as high as the Ripper, but I'm gaining on him."

Clancy laughed. "So what do ya say to that, *Sean?*"

Keats reflected for a moment. "Why are you doing this? Flaherty's one of your own."

Clancy shot a puff of smoke out of his mouth. "Johnny Ahearn was a friend of mine. He shouldn't have died that way."

"And the money?"

"I want to start over in Canada, buy a pub."

"Why not in London?"

"If I stay here, I'll be in jail or the grave within a year."

Keats stuck out his hand. "You get the right to turn me over to the coppers when the time comes. You'll even get Flaherty's money if you do it right."

Clancy's hand hovered in the air. "Don't want Flaherty's reward. That'd be blood money."

"And mine won't be?" Keats asked, confused.

"Nah, yer a filthy rozzer." Clancy grinned.

Keats guffawed. "That I am."

They shook on it.

"Come on, let's get ya home. It's not safe out here."

As they rose, Keats confided, "My mother was Irish."

Clancy shot him a startled look, and then a nod of understanding. "That's why ya won't give up."

**41**

*Wednesday, 24 October, 1888*

The constables were leery of making a decision, especially when there might be a dead body involved, so Alastair was told to stay put until their superior arrived. It was a wasted command. He had no intention of leaving the site until he knew of Jacynda's fate.

Effington's carriage and driver arrived shortly thereafter, adding credence to Alastair's claim that the warehouse owner had been inside the building before the blaze began. He just didn't bother to mention Jacynda's part in all this. He'd face that issue if she was found in the wreckage.

The next arrival was a sergeant, a tall man with a bushy moustache. He wasted no time. "You sure this Effington fellow was dead?"

"Yes, I'm a doctor. I know such things," Alastair replied dryly.

The man's face tightened. "I remember your name. You were in the newspapers about that set-to with the Fenians. What are you doing down here?"

It was tempting to say he'd been on a medical call, but Alastair didn't have his bag with him and they'd demand to know the name of the patient. He opted for the truth. "I'm looking for my friend, Sergeant Keats. I had hoped I could locate him."

"For what purpose, sir?"

"To encourage him to turn himself over to the authorities."

One side of the sergeant's moustache rose, as if in a smirk. "I see. So why were you so desperate to open those doors once the place was on fire?"

"It's hard to solve a murder if you don't have a body."

"Any other reason?"

Alastair couldn't remember what he'd yelled while he fought

the doors. Had he cried out Jacynda's name? Maybe the constable had heard him and reported it.

"I thought I heard someone calling from inside."

"Who?"

"I am not sure," Alastair lied.

"Alastair?"

He turned to see Reuben Bishop walking toward him at a brisk pace.

"Good morning, Reuben."

"I got your note. The constable was most adamant that I come at once."

"Who are you, sir?" the sergeant demanded.

"Doctor Reuben Bishop. Dr. Montrose is my colleague."

"You vouch for him, then?" the sergeant queried.

"Absolutely."

The sergeant gave a shrug and let them be.

Reuben scrutinized the dying fire. "Good Lord, what happened here?"

Alastair told him the tale, minus Jacynda's involvement.

"Why are you still here, then?" Reuben inquired. "The local coroner can handle it from here."

"I need to ensure the corpse inside the building is that of a large male. I'll explain later," Alastair said quietly.

Reuben frowned, but thankfully he held his next question.

It was nearing dawn when a constable beckoned them forward. Steeling himself, Alastair moved forward gingerly over the uneven ground, through charred bits of wood, shattered bricks and broken glass.

"What a tangle," Reuben said, nearly losing his balance when a board snapped under his boot.

They found the corpse half an hour later, entombed under a mound of broken bricks. Alastair knelt next to it, swallowing repeatedly to cope with the stench of burnt flesh. The victim did not lie in peaceful repose, the heat having contracted the leg and arm muscles. Most of the flesh was gone, leaving a leering and charred skull. Pushing aside his emotions, the doctor studied the remains with as much professional detachment as he could muster.

The rib cage and the skull appeared too large to be Jacynda's, but he had to be sure. Using a piece of wood, he delicately shifted the burnt clothing. He thought one piece was the remnant of a waistcoat.

Reuben bent forward and pointed. "Long leg bones. Heavy pelvic girdle. Most likely male," he reported. It tallied with

Alastair's findings. He kept the sigh of relief to himself.

More shifting of clothing disgorged a pocket watch, which fell into the soot. Alastair retrieved it. It was still warm. He brushed the grime off with his thumb. The back was engraved.

"*With all my love, Deidre,*" he read. "It's Effington's."

The sergeant in charge peered over at the corpse. "A bit cooked, isn't he?"

Reuben rose, clearly displeased by the man's cavalier attitude. "Is the coroner on his way?" he asked. A nod returned. "Did you find anything else of interest?"

"Not yet. Could be anything in here," the man replied.

Alastair's heart sank. Jacynda's slight figure could easily be obscured under the wreckage. "No," he whispered. She'd been at the front of the building, near the doors. They would have had to trip over her corpse to get inside.

Once they were settled in a hansom bound for Whitechapel, Reuben coughed heartily to clear his throat and then wiped his mouth with a handkerchief. After tucking it away, he turned toward Alastair.

"So, tell me, who were you *really* looking for in that building?"

‡

She awoke to a feeling of pressure on her ankle. Someone was tugging on her left foot, trying to take off her boot. Forcing her eyes open, she found herself in semi-darkness.

"Oy, she's awake," a voice croaked.

She retaliated with a kick. There was a cry and the sound of someone shuffling away.

Edging herself into an upright position, her hand immediately went to the spot above her left temple. It was raw, like someone had pressed a hot iron against it. When she touched it, it sparked a bolt of lightning behind her eyes, making her moan in agony. Cradling her head, she rocked back and forth until the pain subsided.

The voice spoke again. "Those are fine boots. I'll get 'em yet."

*Boots?* She blinked, and then rubbed her eyes. She was clad in a drab dress, dark blue or navy, she couldn't tell. It had patches and smelled bad.

Another tug on her foot. She kicked harder this time, resulting in a curse and a hurried retreat.

"Leave me alone."

The others fell to whispering. She thought there were two of them. In the distance, a song laced its way through the stones. A howl pierced the air. Whispers meandered through her mind, asking questions she couldn't answer.

*Who are you? Why are you here?*

She didn't even know where *here* was.

The voices reached a crescendo. They sounded familiar, like she'd heard them before, been *here* before.

Stark panic seized her, feeding the desire to flee. She dug in her pockets, but came up empty. What was she looking for? No idea. She clawed her way to her feet, wavering until her balance righted. Working along the stone wall, she came to a wooden door. Pounding on it brought no response. Sliding down to the floor, she leaned her head against the cracked wood, feeling slivers wedge themselves into her forehead. The pain felt good; so far, it was the only thing in this place she could understand.

"Where?" she asked. "Where?"

The croaking voice wheezed a cough. "I'll tell ya for the boots."

"Oh, leave the lamb alone," a softer voice said.

"Don't ya tell her—"

"Yer in Bedlam, dearie. We all comes 'ere in the end."

"Bedlam?" She had no idea what the woman meant.

"The asylum, luv."

*Asylum?*

Touching the raw spot on her temple shot off more streaks of fire through her head, making her cry out. The face of a man came to her. He had a brittle laugh that sounded like wind across the moors, and hair that glistened in the night. She grasped her chest. An alley, nearly dead. Another man, one who had wept as she left him behind.

Someone had taken it all away. Callously ripped her mind apart like a sheet of thin paper.

Hand over hand, she crawled to the corner and sank onto the damp straw. Tears cascaded down her cheeks, stinging the small cuts on her face.

She would get out of this place. She would find who did this. She would make him reveal her name.

Right before she killed him.

## About the Author

Jana Oliver admits a fascination with all things mysterious, usually laced with a touch of the supernatural. An eclectic person who has traveled the world, she loves to pour over old maps and dusty tomes, rummaging in history's closet for plot lines. When not writing, she enjoys Irish music, Cornish fudge and good whiskey.

Jana lives in Atlanta, Georgia with her husband and two cats: Midnight and OddsBobkin.

Visit her website at: www.janaoliver.com

Photograph by Jennifer Berry,
Studio 16

# Madman's Dance

Time Rovers ~ book 3

# Jana G. Oliver

## Coming Fall 2008

AN EXCERPT FROM:

# MADMAN'S DANCE
# TIME ROVERS ~ BOOK 3
# FALL 2008

This day began like all the others: the grate of the bolt on the cell door, followed by the sound of metal bowls sliding across the stone floor, carelessly tossed inside by one of the attendants. She ignored the food. It held no interest. The others would eat it.

She closed her eyes and returned to the wasteland of her mind. Little snippets of memories floated by, erratic clouds pushed by a light wind. None of them made sense. A man's face. He kept saying a word she couldn't understand. Another face, warm and smiling. The smell of sheep. Something blue.

Her head still throbbed, though the place near her temple was less sore now. She'd hoped that as the pain dulled, her memories would reassemble themselves. Wishful thinking. Asking her cellmates did little. One of them didn't know her name. The other demanded her boots in payment for any answer.

She'd never been brave enough to ask any of the attendants. Most of them frightened her. If she admitted to them she didn't know who she was, they'd never set her free.

If she could just remember. That would be a beginning. Once she knew her name, she could start to reconstruct the other missing pieces. There were so many of them.

What she discovered so far was of little comfort. The solid stone walls around her belonged to a mental asylum. The name, Bedlam, was apt: tormented shrieks rent the air at all hours. All mad people here, one of her cellmates had said.

She didn't feel crazy.

"Little miss?" a voice called.

She opened her eyes. One of the attendants, the nice older one, stood inside the door, his hands full of empty bowls.

"Did you eat?"

She shook her head.

He sighed. "You got someone to see you, missy."

A woman entered the cell, glanced quickly at the two other occupants, then halted in front of her. She knelt and peeled back the light veil she was wearing. Her hair was dark brown, her eyes hazel. "My God," she whispered. She hesitated and then asked. "Do you know how you got here?"

"No."

"Do you know who you are?"

"I, ah..." She shook her head. "Do you know?"

The woman leaned closer and whispered, "Yes."

A thrill of hope rushed through her, even as she worked to tamp it down. "I won't give up my boots," she declared, fearing some trick.

"No, you keep them. You'll need them." She leaned even closer and whispered, "You are Jacynda Lassiter."

*Jacynda?* "Why don't I know that?"

"You've been hurt. Now repeat the name to me."

She couldn't. She'd forgotten it already. Tears threatened to flow.

"Jacynda Lassiter. Now you say it."

She did. The next time she tried, it was gone.

"I know it's hard." The woman rummaged through a pocket until she retrieved a piece of paper. She tore a small section off and handed it to her. "Can you read it?"

She studied the finely printed letters and sounded it out. "Ja...cynda Lass...iter."

"That's it," the woman said, smiling encouragingly.

She pointed to another word. "What's this one?"

"Cynda. Your friends call you that. Now keep this paper safe. Repeat the names over and over until you know them without looking at it. You must eat and—" a pause and the voice lowered, "find a way out."

"I don't know how."

"If you stay here, you will die. Do you understand?"

She nodded. "Can't I go with you?"

"No. You have to find your own way out. Eat and survive. It's very important for all of us, Jacynda Lassiter."

The woman lowered the veil, stood and then knocked on the door. It swung open, courtesy of the attendant. A moment later, the door bolted behind the visitor.

She looked at the paper and sounded out the letters. "Jacynda Lass...Lassiter."

The kind lady had given her a name. It might not be her real one, but she'd claim it anyway. She knew no other.

Dragon
Moon

# DON'T MISS THESE EXCITING TITLES BROUGHT TO YOU BY DRAGON MOON PRESS, EDGE SCIENCE FICTION AND FANTASY AND TESSERACTS!

Claus Effect by David Nickle & Karl Schroeder, The
(pb) ISBN-13: 978-1-895836-34-9
Claus Effect by David Nickle & Karl Schroeder, The
(hb) ISBN-13: 978-1-895836-35-6
Complete Guide to Writing Fantasy, The Volume 1:
Alchemy with Words, edited by Darin Park and Tom
Dullemond (tp)
ISBN-13: 978-1-896944-09-8
Complete Guide to Writing Fantasy, The Volume 2:
Opus Magus, edited by Tee Morris and Valerie
Griswold-Ford (tp)
ISBN-13: 978-1-896944-15-9
Complete Guide to Writing Fantasy Volume 3: The
Author's Grimoire, edited by Valerie Griswold-Ford &
Lai Zhao (tp)
ISBN-13: 978-1-896944-38-8
Complete Guide to Writing Science Fiction Volume 1:
First Contact, edited by Dave A. Law & Darin Park
(tp) ISBN-13: 978-1-896944-39-5
Courtesan Prince, The, Lynda Williams (tp)
ISBN-13: 978-1-894063-28-9
‡
Dark Earth Dreams, Candas Dorsey & Roger Deegan
(comes with a CD) ISBN-13: 978-1-895836-05-9
Darkling Band, The, Jason Henderson (tp)
ISBN-13: 978-1-896944-36-4
Darkness of the God, Amber Hayward (tp)
ISBN-13: 978-1-894063-44-9
Darwin's Paradox, Nina Munteanu (tp)
ISBN-13: 978-1-896944-68-5
Daughter of Dragons, Kathleen Nelson (tp)
ISBN-13: 978-1-896944-00-5
Distant Signals, Andrew Weiner (tp)
ISBN-13: 978-0-88878-284-7
Dominion, J. Y. T. Kennedy (tp)
ISBN-13: 978-1-896944-28-9

Dragon Reborn, The  Kathleen H. Nelson (tp)
    ISBN-13: 978-1-896944-05-0
Dragon's Fire, Wizard's Flame,  Michael R. Mennenga
    (tp) ISBN-13: 978-1-896944-13-5
Dreams of an Unseen Planet,  Teresa Plowright (tp)
    ISBN-13: 978-0-88878-282-3
Dreams of the Sea,  Élisabeth Vonarburg (tp)
    ISBN-13: 978-1-895836-96-7
Dreams of the Sea,  Élisabeth Vonarburg (hb)
    ISBN-13: 978-1-895836-98-1

‡

EarthCore,  Scott Sigler (tp)
    ISBN-13: 978-1-896944-32-6
Eclipse,  K. A. Bedford (tp)
    ISBN-13: 978-1-894063-30-2
Even The Stones,  Marie Jakober (tp)
    ISBN-13: 978-1-894063-18-0

‡

Fires of the Kindred,  Robin Skelton (tp)
    ISBN-13: 978-0-88878-271-7
Forbidden Cargo,  Rebecca Rowe (tp)
    ISBN-13: 978-1-894063-16-6

‡

Game of Perfection, A,  Élisabeth Vonarburg (tp)
    ISBN-13: 978-1-894063-32-6
Green Music,  Ursula Pflug (tp)
    ISBN-13: 978-1-895836-75-2
Green Music,  Ursula Pflug (hb)
    ISBN-13: 978-1-895836-77-6
Gryphon Highlord, The,  Connie Ward (tp)
    ISBN-13: 978-1-896944-38-8

‡

Healer, The,  Amber Hayward (tp)
    ISBN-13: 978-1-895836-89-9
Healer, The,  Amber Hayward (hb)
    ISBN-13: 978-1-895836-91-2
Human Thing, The,  Kathleen H. Nelson (hb)
    ISBN-13: 978-1-896944-03-6
Hydrogen Steel,  K. A. Bedford (tp)
    ISBN-13: 978-1-894063-20-3

‡

i-ROBOT Poetry,  Jason Christie (tp)
    ISBN-13: 978-1-894063-24-1

‡

Jackal Bird,  Michael Barley (pb)
    ISBN-13: 978-1-895836-07-3
Jackal Bird,  Michael Barley (hb)
    ISBN-13: 978-1-895836-11-0

‡

Keaen,  Till Noever (tp) ISBN-13: 978-1-894063-08-1
Keeper's Child,  Leslie Davis (tp)
    ISBN-13: 978-1-894063-01-2

‡

Land/Space, edited  Candas Jane Dorsey and Judy
McCrosky (tp) ISBN-13: 978-1-895836-90-5
Land/Space, edited  Candas Jane Dorsey and Judy
McCrosky (hb) ISBN-13: 978-1-895836-92-9
Legacy of Morevi,  Tee Morris (tp)
    ISBN-13: 978-1-896944-29-6
Legends of the Serai,  J.C. Hall (tp)
    ISBN-13: 978-1-896944-04-3
Longevity Thesis,  Jennifer Tahn (tp)
    ISBN-13: 978-1-896944-37-1

Lyskarion: The Song of the Wind,  J.A. Cullum (tp)
    ISBN-13: 978-1-894063-02-9

‡

Machine Sex and Other stories,  Candas Jane Dorsey
    (tp) ISBN-13: 978-0-88878-278-6
Maërlande Chronicles, The,  Élisabeth Vonarburg (pb)
    ISBN-13: 978-0-88878-294-6
Magister's Mask, The,  Deby Fredericks (tp)
    ISBN-13: 978-1-896944-16-6
Moonfall,  Heather Spears (pb)
    ISBN-13: 978-0-88878-306-6
Morevi: The Chronicles of Rafe and Askana,  Lisa Lee
& Tee Morris (tp) ISBN-13: 978-1-896944-07-4

‡

Not Your Father's Horseman,  Valorie Griswold-Ford
    (tp) ISBN-13: 978-1-896944-27-2

‡

On Spec: The First Five Years, edited  On Spec (pb)
    ISBN-13: 978-1-895836-08-0
On Spec: The First Five Years, edited  On Spec (hb)
    ISBN-13: 978-1-895836-12-7
Operation: Immortal Servitude,  Tony Ruggerio (tp)
    ISBN-13: 978-1-896944-56-2
Orbital Burn,  K. A. Bedford (tp)
    ISBN-13: 978-1-894063-10-4
Orbital Burn,  K. A. Bedford (hb)
    ISBN-13: 978-1-894063-12-8

‡

Pallahaxi Tide,  Michael Coney (pb)
    ISBN-13: 978-0-88878-293-9
Passion Play,  Sean Stewart (pb)
    ISBN-13: 978-0-88878-314-1

Tesseracts Ten, edited  Robert Charles Wilson and Edo van Belkom (tp) ISBN-13: 978-1-894063-36-4

Tesseracts Eleven, edited  Cory Doctorow and Holly Phillips (tp) ISBN-13: 978-1-894063-03-6

Tesseracts Q, edited  Élisabeth Vonarburg & Jane Brierley (pb) ISBN-13: 978-1-895836-21-9

Tesseracts Q, edited  Élisabeth Vonarburg & Jane Brierley (hb) ISBN-13: 978-1-895836-22-6

Throne Price, Lynda Williams and Alison Sinclair (tp) ISBN-13: 978-1-894063-06-7

Too Many Princes, Deby Fredricks (tp) ISBN-13: 978-1-896944-36-4

Twilight of the Fifth Sun,  David Sakmyster (tp) ISBN-13: 978-1-896944-01-02

‡

Virtual Evil, Jana Oliver (tp) ISBN-13: 978-1-896944-76-0

EDGE

Dragon
Moon

Made in United States
Orlando, FL
15 August 2022

20918469R20225